ABOUT THE AUTHOR

David Tolfree is a retired chartered physicist with fifty years' experience in nuclear research and consultancy in technology exploitation. Currently he is an Executive Vice President of the Micro and Nanotechnology Commercialisation and Education Foundation, an international body. He has over 150 publications including articles in journals, books, newspapers and conference proceedings, and co-authored the books, 'Commercialising Micro-Nanotechnology Products' and 'Roadmapping Emergent Technologies'. The Millennium Conspiracy is his first novel.

David Tolfree

THE MILLENNIUM CONSPIRACY

To Carolyn & Steve

Best wishes

David Tolfree

29.12.11

Matador
Troubador Publishing Ltd
9 Priory Business Park
Kibworth Beauchamp
Leicester LE8 0RX, UK
Tel: (+44) 116 279 2299
Email: books@troubador.co.uk
Web: www.troubador.co.uk/matador

ISBN 9781780881256

A CIP catalogue record for this book is available from the British Library

Matador is an imprint of Troubador Publishing Ltd

Printed and bound in the UK by TJI Digital, Padstow, Cornwall

For all the unknown men and women who work undercover and risk their lives to protect our democratic way of life.

ACKNOWLEDGEMENTS

I owe a debt of gratitude to countless individuals who unknowingly gave me the knowledge and inspiration to write this novel. Some are scientific and business associates with whom I worked during my career as a physicist and business consultant. Some are friends in politics who gave me an insight into the workings of Government. Some are family and friends who had to endure my talking about writing the book over many years.

My very special thanks go to my friends, Clive Davenport, Richard Leach and Christine Pearson, for their endurance in reading the manuscript and making constructive and useful suggestions to text and content.

I am indebted to my wife, Valerie, for her expertise and fortitude in proof-reading and correcting the manuscript, also for her sufferance during the extended period of writing the book. Without her support and patience I would not have completed it.

AUTHOR'S NOTE

This is a work of fiction and, except in the case of historical fact, any resemblance to actual persons, living or dead, is purely coincidental. Characters, organisations, situations and philosophies are either the product of the author's imagination or, if real, have been used fictitiously without any intent to describe or portray their actual conduct.

We often take for granted the undercover work done by those whose job it is to protect us and our democratic way of life. Today we face continuing threats by people and organisations that are bent on change by destructive methods. Sometimes, in the public interest, information has to be withheld to ensure that those who threaten us are discovered and brought to justice.

In this story fictional characters are placed in historical events to give it a sense of realism. The threat of nuclear conflict was a dominant feature of the foreign policies of Governments during the cold war period of the twentieth century. Now in the twenty-first century, the exciting advances in science and technology pose new opportunities and challenges but also dangers from those who seek to use them for economic and political self-interest.

CONTENT

CAST OF CHARACTERS

UK-London

Paul Cane	Investigative journalist
Jeremy Simms	Estate agent
John Henning	MI5 agent
Henry Fellows	Nuclear physicist
(Malcolm Walker)	
David Simons	Nuclear physicist
Ruth Goodman	Henry Fellows' niece
Gladys Cook	Post Mistress, Bisley
Fred Palmer	Church Warden, Bisley
Abu Zadre	Al-Qaeda terrorist
Kamel Neghal	Al-Qaeda terrorist
Rupert Arnold	Head of Anti-Terrorist Branch Metropolitan Police
John Nicholas	Superintendent, Metropolitan Police Special Branch
Sir George Day	Valerie's father
Margaret Day	Valerie's step mother
Flo	Valerie's aunt
Henry	Apartment block security guard
Sir John Cane	Paul's father
Sam Woods	Susan Woods' father
Colin Bradley	BA Executive

UK-Fort Halborn

Brian Smith	Halborn electronics engineer
Dr Philip Snow	Halborn Director
Dr Bill Jones	Halborn Division Head
Dr Ray Spicer	Halborn physicist

Dr Susan Woods	Halborn computer expert
Maud Simpson	PA to Snow and Fellows
Dr Mike Durant	Halborn physicist
Dr Jeff Adams	Halborn physicist
Dr Scott Roberts	Halborn physicist
Dr Terry Gibson	Halborn physicist
Dr Rob Turner	Halborn physicist
Dr Richard Jenson	Halborn explosives expert
Dr Charlie Barton	Halborn explosives expert
Jack Sillar	Halborn engineer
John Waters	Halborn police inspector
Dave Nugent	Army liaison officer
Robin Ellis	Halborn trial's officer
Tom Briggs	Laboratory assistant
Mrs Johnson	Fellows' housekeeper at Halborn
Tim Rowley	Halborn Security Chief
Dr Paul Fields	Government Advisor/ New Order Cabal member
Anna Fischer	New Order Cell member
Alan O'Leary	New Order Cell member
Robert Mueller	Halborn computer expert/ New Order Cell member
Bob Fuller	Superintendent, Metropolitan Police Special Branch
Richard Adams	Detective Inspector, Metropolitan Police Special Branch
Charles Rigby-Smith	Personal Director, Atomic Energy Authority
Sir Donald Fielding	Director of Intelligence-Ministry of Defence
Martin May	Senior official, Cabinet Office
Adrian Custodio	Lord Globe
Christine Hunter	Diane Hunter's daughter

Washington – Tucson – Martha's Vineyard – New York

Valerie Day	Paul Cane's girlfriend

Robert Carville	Paul's friend and agent
Victor Adams	US Vice President
Alan Sherman	Senator Republican Party Presidential Candidate
Prof Stanley Rheiner (David Simons)	Professor, University of Arizona, Tucson
Richard Houseman	CEO, American Gulf Oil Company
Bill Lopez,	Head of the US Office of Foreign Affairs
Chloe Rogers	FBI agent, Valerie's protector
Buck Jones	Major, US Special Forces
Robert Shaw	Commander, USS Kansas
Mark Hamdene	Lieutenant, USS Kansas
John Howard	Captain, US Army explosives expert
George Bradley	Admiral, US Navy
Alicia Garcia	Head of Intelligence National Security Agency
Mark Brooks	Assistant Director CIA
Gary Stevens	Assistant Director FBI
Sean 'Curly' O'Brien	C5, CIA contractor
Alan Garbo	New Order's assassin
Elena Tolstoy	Old Russian woman
Carol Johnson	Valerie's neighbour in Martha's Vineyard
Ben Carter	FBI agent (Martha's Vineyard)
James King	Robert's friend in Washington
Rebecca King	Valerie's friend in Washington
Agent Mallory	FBI agent
Farah Bell	Al-Qaeda terrorist cell leader
Olga Petrovitch	(Re-Anna Kolzak) Cabal's assassin
Mohammed Khan	Al-Qaeda terrorist cell member
Ahmed Fazi	Al- Qaeda terrorist cell member
Vladimir Koslov	Al-Qaeda terrorist cell member

Germany

Dr Colin Niedermeyer	Expert cryptologist
Anna Bacher	Niedermeyer's fiancée
Ludwig Menzies	Director of Freiburg Engineering

New Order Cabal

Jean Dupius	(Fox) Leader (France)
Jonas Gould	(Eaglestar) US
Heinz Kluge	(Wolfman) Germany
Takaki Tobata	(Serow) Japan
Boris Sudakov	(Bear) Russia
Diane Hunter	(Lionheart) UK
Daman Khan	(Tiger), India
Leon Seperkov	Sudakov's Assistant

Task Force Codes

Falcon	Danger warning
Merlin	Act immediately-use telephone.
Peregrine	Wait for further instructions
Whirlwind	Codename for the millennium bomb threat

PART 1
THE DISCOVERY

PROLOGUE

November 1998

The old man sat back in the well-worn black leather armchair and switched on the table light to read a book. It had been a particularly cold November day. Old Cotswold cottages lacked the amenities of double-glazing and central heating systems unless they had been modernised. A crackling log fire added warmth and gave off a therapeutic scent, but there was still a chill in the room. After many years the occupant had adapted to the lack of comforts offered by more modern dwellings to be found in the towns. He enjoyed the safe seclusion which the cottage gave him.

Dr Henry Fellows was a retired physicist in his early eighties but still retained an athletic posture. At Cambridge he had won many medals for sport. Back-pain and walking difficulties were offset by an active brain which enabled him to continue taking an interest in world events. He was highly intelligent and had recently completed his memoires – a written account of his life's work which he knew could never be published. An event that had led to the deaths of some of his colleagues and friends had troubled him all his life. He owed it to them to leave a written record. The dark secrets he possessed could not be taken to the grave; one day someone might want to act on the information and the truth would then be known. At the very least it would allow some gaps in the history of the last fifty years to be filled. Official historians sometimes distort history, either purposely or through a lack of access to information that has been locked away in Government files, often wrongly classified as secret or top secret to cover up mistakes and bad decisions made by politicians and generals. One day, when they are released, some of the history of the twentieth century may have to be re-written.

Henry Fellows was one of two people still alive who had been members of the British team who participated in the Manhattan Atomic Bomb Project during the Second World War. He had witnessed the detonation of the first atomic bomb on 16 July 1945 at Alamogordo in the desert of New Mexico. Like many others, including Robert Oppenheimer, who led the project, he was not proud of the legacy of death, destruction and fear it had brought upon the world. But, as a scientist, he believed the realisation of atomic energy was one of the most outstanding scientific and technological developments of the twentieth century. Its controlled use eventually resulted in an efficient clean source of energy, now used by many countries. Unfortunately, since the war, it was the creation of the atomic bomb, rather than the beneficial use of atomic energy, that had turned the public mind against it.

Countries who were the victors of the Second World War, namely The United States of America, the Soviet Union and Britain, vigorously pursued nuclear research programmes with weapons development as their primary objectives. These fuelled the Cold War which, for over four decades, produced political insecurity and instilled fear in millions of people. Paradoxically the atom bomb provided security for those nations who possessed it but perceived as a threat by others. It had preserved an uneasy peace and prevented any major war since 1945.

After the short Suez War and oil crisis that followed, an urgent need for an alternative source of energy that did not rely on oil stimulated the development of nuclear power reactors. These were also necessary for the production of weapons grade uranium and plutonium so the technology required became highly developed.

At the end of the Second World War, suspicious of Britain's ability to keep secrets from the Soviet Union and uncertainty about the security of Europe, the US Government decided not to share its atomic weapons' secrets with Britain, even though British scientists contributed to the Manhattan Project. In 1947, Prime Minister Atlee and his cabinet therefore gave the go-ahead for a British independent atomic weapons programme. Henry Fellows was appointed to be the Chief Scientist and Deputy Director of

Britain's first top secret atomic weapons research establishment at Halborn. He was later promoted to Director after the mysterious death of the first Director in 1959.

As a young man at the University of Cambridge, Henry Fellows had been one of the founding members of The International Brotherhood of Scientists. It was originally inspired by a group of German Jewish scientists who were contemporaries of Einstein. They fled to Britain from Nazi Germany in the late 1930s. David Simons, the original founder of The Brotherhood, became a friend and colleague of Fellows. Together they recruited other like-minded scientists. They wanted to prevent a recurrence of the disastrous situation that was enveloping Europe at the time from reaching over to Britain. Most of the able atomic scientists left Germany after the Nazis came to power so depriving them of the capability of developing an atomic bomb. The Brotherhood became a secret organization dedicated to preventing dictators like Hitler from using scientific discoveries for evil purposes. In 1938 it was financed by a wealthy English benefactor and became a Foundation. A charter was drawn up which required its members to take a secret oath of allegiance and seek advisory positions in Governments and Industry in their respective countries so they could exert a positive influence on policy decisions.

After the War broke out on 3 September 1939, David Simons went to the US and later, together with Henry Fellows and Paul Fields, another British physicist, joined the Manhattan Project at Los Alamos. At the site of the detonation of the first atomic bomb they were to make a discovery that would affect their lives.

After the war, The Brotherhood Foundation became successful in many of its objectives. Its membership grew in the US and Europe. Unfortunately, power corrupts and some members, driven by self-interest and profit, joined a breakaway group known as The New Order. Fellows and Simons were aware that under the umbrella of their Foundation this group flourished. The Group had a strict code of secrecy so nobody knew the names of its members or associations. It distorted the original aims of The Brotherhood Foundation in the same way that extremists and fundamentalists do with religions. The purpose of The New Order was to infiltrate governments and powerful multi-national companies to exert influence and eventually take control. Like the Italian Mafia and secret bodies, it used threats, intimidation and even murder to achieve its aims. Unfortunately, some of the original members who formed The Brotherhood Foundation, became attracted to The New Order by the promise of riches and power.

It was an incident perpetrated by the agents of The New Order at the Halborn Research Establishment in 1959, resulting in the deaths of four scientific colleagues, that had the most devastating effect on Fellows. Important devices and secret documents were stolen, threatening the success of Blue Star, Britain's Hydrogen Bomb project. Fellows felt responsible since he was really The New Order's target. After discovering Fellows was a member of The Brotherhood, the Government gave him an ultimatum, be prosecuted for breaching the Official Secrets Act or let them arrange his fake death and retirement under a new identity. He reluctantly agreed to the latter but vowed to hunt down those members of The New Order who were responsible for the Halborn incident and the deaths of his colleagues.

The Government publicly announced Fellows' death due to a car accident. His new identity listed him officially as Michael Walker, a retired bank manager. He was given the money to buy a cottage at Bisley, a small village tucked away in the Cotswolds. This gave him a refuge that offered life anonymity. Very few people knew where he lived; a precaution necessary for his survival, but one day he knew his enemies would find him and it would be the end.

Henry Fellows, alias Michael Walker, saw the newspapers were full of a new crisis brewing in the Middle East. Iraq had just failed to agree to let the UN weapons' inspectors to continue their work. They were being withdrawn and a bitter exchange between the United Nations and US took place. It was a recipe for another Gulf War. Fellows believed that Saddam Hussein had, or was trying to acquire, an atomic bomb. It troubled his mind when he thought of the consequences of a nuclear war in the Middle East. He knew about the devastating effects of atomic bombs.

As he watched the flames engulf the wood in the grate, Henry Fellows thought of the only two women in his life. Dr Susan Woods, a brilliant mathematician, whom he had brought over from America to work on the Blue Star Project. She had become his close friend and confidante and was one of the four victims of the fire at Halborn.

Ruth Goodman was his only living relative. He was very fond of her. She was the only daughter of his niece, who died with her husband in a tragic car accident when Ruth was twelve. Since that time, Henry had supported Ruth, paid for her boarding school education and helped her gain a place to study classics at his old college in Cambridge. She was an intelligent girl and wanted to be a teacher after she graduated.

During Ruth's visit in the summer, Fellows had told her about his life's work. Until then she had known very little about the old man. He told her about The Brotherhood Foundation, his wartime experiences working on the Manhattan Project, the incident at Halborn in 1959, and why he was forced by the Government to resign and assume a new identity.

Fellows told Ruth she was to be the sole beneficiary of his will. On his death she would inherit all his possessions, including the cottage, his diaries and papers relating to his work. He told her the papers were in a bank deposit box for safe keeping and gave her a key for it. Among the papers there was a coded list of names of people who had been members of The Brotherhood and others who were now members of a Cabal that controlled The New Order. He believed The New Order was now the most powerful secret organisation in the world and was, in some way, with the Al-Qaeda terrorist group, planning something big.

Fellows told her that on his death she was to immediately send all his papers to David Simons who lived in Tucson, Arizona, under the name of Professor Stanley Rheiner and who would know what to do. His address was in the files. He omitted to tell her that handwritten copies of some of the documents were also hidden in the attic space of the cottage. She respected his need for secrecy so did not ask any searching questions.

The fire was burning itself out and it was late. Fellows was getting tired so, easing himself out of the chair, he checked the locks on the doors and windows, drew the thick curtains and went upstairs to bed. He normally liked to write in his diary or read before going to sleep but there was little to write about these days. He finished reading the last chapter of his book and switched off the bedside light, not hearing the click of a key turning in the door downstairs. With an image of Ruth, and particularly her loving smile in his mind, he drifted into a shallow sleep.

The stranger slipped into the darkened room. Opening the door with the key had been easy. It was the kind of key professionals used to open any door. First, a visit to the fuse box located in a kitchen cupboard. Once the power was cut, the work could be carried out quickly. The intruder's eyes narrowed as she saw a dim light and sensed movement in the bedroom. But then the light went out and all was quiet. Concerned that the element of surprise had been lost, she faded into the shadows of the room.

Professional killers had an instinctive advantage over an unsuspecting prey. There was to be no violence, no struggle or physical signs of unnatural death, that was in the contract. A fee of three hundred thousand pounds bought that level of commitment. It was more than was usual for a relatively unknown person. Assassinations of Presidents, Prime Ministers, Chief Executives and well-known entertainers did command more than a million, but retired bank managers were not normally in that league. She didn't know who Michael Walker really was, or the value of the knowledge he possessed. It was not her concern. In addition to the killing, she was tasked to locate and destroy certain documents the victim possessed.

Fellows was awakened by what he thought were the muffled sound of footsteps and a door opening. For an old man, his hearing was still quite acute. It was usually quiet on a winter's night in that part of the country so even the slightest unusual sound was discernable. Still half-dazed, he sat up in bed and stared into the darkness. He always left the bedroom door slightly open to allow fresh air to circulate; it also helped to alleviate a fear of claustrophobia. Suddenly he went cold; he sensed that someone was in the house. Burglars were rare in the countryside but the police were always giving out warnings as there had been cases recently in the area. Fumbling for the bedside light, he pressed the switch but nothing happened, there was only darkness. He felt his pulse racing out of control and his heart beating as though it would burst. Adrenaline was filling his veins but fear immobilised his body. He could see and hear nothing but felt that someone was nearby.

Opening the door wide, he crept down the stairs into the living room; the dying embers of the fire were still visible. He went to a desk on the far side of the room where he remembered a torch was stowed in a drawer. Pulling it open, he fumbled for it. Then, just as he was about to withdraw the torch he felt a searing pain in the back of his head. It felt like a hot needle had been plunged into his brain. For a moment everything went white, as though he was being blinded by an intense light. Turning swiftly around, his sight returned for a split second to see a towering black figure looming over him. The dim light just caught its outline then everything started to fade. He levered himself to his feet and staggered towards the door. He had a sinking feeling that he was leaving the world, going somewhere else. He could just make out an outline of the room, his head was spinning and everything was going fuzzy. He tried to move but every muscle seemed to seize up. He collapsed onto the floor, no longer being able to support himself. The soft light faded away as the life drained from his body. The mark of the hypodermic was barely visible in the hair at the base of the neck.

The intruder checked that nothing had been disturbed. She summoned all her strength to drag the body upstairs and placed it on the bed. The victim was supposed to have been asleep when the lethal drug was administered to avoid any signs of a struggle but she had misjudged the situation. The death would look like a heart attack; a hybrid of the drug succinylcholine injected into the body would not be traced. Fifty years of development had perfected one of the best murder weapons ever devised. She methodically removed any signs that someone had entered the room, no finger prints, no DNA for forensics. Since there was no motive and the death would look natural, there would be no reason for an investigation. She thoroughly searched the cottage for the papers without finding them. Only letters to a Ruth Goodman were found stashed away in an old desk. She took the letters, checked all the rooms and left the cottage, failing to notice in the dark, the concealed hatch leading to the attic.

She hoped her masters would be pleased with the night's work. But she had not found the papers, the job was not complete. If she lied about them who would know? There was her professional pride, she had never failed. They always paid into her Swiss bank account within a day of receiving the telephone call. The line was highly secure and the coded message was stored until read then it would automatically self-destruct. It was impossible to trace and left no evidence. She had no contact with a person – only a recorded voice. On this occasion she would not make the telephone call until she had paid a visit to Ruth Goodman. The call could only be made when the contract was complete. But they would know when the death was reported. She would be expected to call before that time. It was possible, just possible, that Ruth Goodman had the documents. That would need to be confirmed before taking any action.

Olga Petrovitch, or R2 as she was known, had become a very rich woman, her KGB training had paid off. Her new employers were honourable people. They gave her total anonymity and guaranteed protection because she was the best. She did not care about the clients who were the designated targets so long as the payments were made. Her bosses had never let her down; she knew the penalty if she failed. It was the thirteenth contract, but she wasn't superstitious. As she left the cottage and walked along the path, an uncomfortable feeling came over her. She hadn't experienced it before. Was it an ill omen?

The man whose body had been vaporised at the Trinity site in the Alamogordo Desert in New Mexico in 1945 had now been revenged. He was the dead father that she never knew. But she did not know the connection between the man she had just killed and the event that had taken place fifty-three years before. The rain had stopped and a clear night sky displayed a full moon as the black BMW slipped quietly away from the cottage and drove towards the M4 motorway.

CHAPTER 1

Kuwait
October 1999

The direction which our lives take is more often determined by chance events than by plans. Looking back it all started with the early morning phone call. It woke me up when I didn't want to be woken up. Its incessant ring tone abruptly ended my rather pleasant dream. I was half asleep when I switched on the bedside light and reached out for the phone. For many years the telephone had been part of my toolkit. It was often my sole companion, my personal friend, my connection to the outside world, so calls couldn't be ignored. Early morning calls I don't like. They often bring bad news. Callers living in other time zones across the world are usually oblivious to such inconveniences.

The last two weeks of my life had been mine, not organised by a diary of meetings, travel schedules or other people's agendas. I returned from Kuwait a month back after a gruelling experience and spent the first two weeks writing a report for my American client. I did offer to fly to New York to present the material to him but since he didn't respond I was glad to continue with my recuperation. My agent, Robert Carville, had already received the money for the work I did in Kuwait so I assumed that was it. The cheque, less Robert's exorbitantly high commission, would be in the post. Robert had served me well so I didn't mind. He acted as a buffer to people who wanted me to carry out crazy assignments. Over the years we had become good friends and I was one of his best clients.

Since my return from Kuwait I had suffered headaches and bouts of depression. My doctor told me I had been close to a mental breakdown, probably caused by the unfortunate events that took place at the end of my visit to Kuwait. Fortunately, HM Government had rescued me from a possible long sentence in that country's terrible jails. Governments only do such things when they need something in return so I knew there would be a payback. At the time, the relief of being free and able to return home numbed my thoughts to what that might be. The arrest by the Kuwait police was justified as a huge mistake and although I received no official apology, being back in England was enough, so I decided not to pursue it further.

My doctor recommended a long holiday. A temporary escape from the real world to recharge my batteries. Before taking a holiday, I thought a good night out at one of London's best night clubs, followed by sex with a beautiful woman, preferably of Anglo-Saxon origin, would initiate my road to recovery. It had been my weakness for beautiful women and my sexual indulgence in Muslim Kuwait that had contributed to my being arrested and thrown into jail; although I later discovered it was a set-up and the woman picked the wrong room. I believed that my journalistic success in Kuwait, recognised by the large fee paid by my client, allowed for some carnal pleasures. It was a fitting reward for the risks I had taken. Unfortunately, alcohol numbs the brain and memory becomes the first casualty. I remembered the food and drink and an attractive blonde escort leading me to my room but what followed was a little hazy. My empty wallet provided evidence of the fulfilment of the night's objectives. Pity I didn't remember it all. I seemed to be developing a habit of sleeping with beautiful women only to find they had abandoned me by the next morning.

'Paul, it's Robert. I'm in New York. Sorry to call you at this early hour but I have some bad news. Abdel Salam has been killed in some sort of car accident in Kuwait City. It's not clear what happened but I think he was murdered. Thought you had better know before its made public, you will appreciate the implications.' Before I could say anything, I heard that click which meant someone had just tapped into the call. Robert must have heard it too. 'I will call you again later,' he said, and rung off. I knew at that moment my chances of a vacation were greatly diminished.

The assignment in Kuwait had been won by my esteemed agent and friend, Robert Carville, against serious competition. As a freelance investigative journalist, I had worked on previous assignments in Israel and Iraq during the Gulf War and gained a reputation for on-the-spot reporting. The war had been over for two years but problems in the Gulf area still remained. Rumours of another war and the increased activity of extremist terrorist groups were worrying many Governments and oil companies. It was pushing up the cost of crude oil, with dire consequences for nations like ours that relied on Middle East supplies. Some people said that the Iraq war was about oil. That was partly true, but the rise of dictators like Saddam Hussein and fundamental Islamism were more serious underlying issues. The Iraq army was the largest in the Middle East and Hussein's insatiable desire for power and unrelenting rejection of the UN's resolutions after his invasion of Kuwait on 2 August 1990 had made the Gulf War, known as Desert Storm, inevitable. In addition, the Islamic faith was being subverted by extremists who wanted to establish a new global totalitarianism. They were becoming active in many countries with significant Muslim populations.

Robert had been approached at a business meeting in New York by Richard Houseman, the new CEO of the American Gulf Oil Company. He wanted someone with knowledge of the Gulf region to give an independent assessment of the region's political stability and economic viability. His concern was to protect the company's billion dollar investments in the region. My name came up in a conversation with Houseman who had read my articles in the Global Economist, a monthly international journal to which I was a regular contributor. I did a series of reports on the Middle East, warning about the growing threat of terrorism. An increasing number of well-funded groups from different religious factions were becoming active against the West. It seems they were filling the political vacuum left after the ending of the Cold War. This time, after the occupation of Afghanistan, the Russians were now the enemy. It was ironic that our old Cold War enemy, who we criticised for invading Afghanistan, was now being targeted by Muslim fundamentalists in their country.

Robert called me to say Houseman's proposal would be a great opportunity to make a lot of money. I think he meant for himself, with agent's fees at twenty per cent. If I agreed, he would arrange for a contract to be signed and then set things up. It meant, of course, I had to do all the work. For me, money was not the first priority but raising my profile with a large multi-billion corporate in the US was an opportunity not to be missed. There were risks but anything worth doing has risks. I didn't know then how great they would be. If I had, I would have walked away.

I agreed to sign a contract for a fee of two hundred thousand dollars plus expenses, payable two weeks after delivery of the study report on Kuwait and the Gulf region. It seemed like a lot of money but for a large multi-national oil company it was small change. Anyway it was the going-rate for such market intelligence. Robert would use one of his contacts in Kuwait to set up a series of one-to-one interviews with prominent Arab businessmen from the region. The schedule was tight and there were penalty clauses in the contract. Failing to meet delivery dates would cost me a lot of money. Normally I didn't like such clauses but the risks seemed minimal. I also had to sign a confidentiality agreement giving exclusive rights to the contractor for all the information acquired. It seemed strange the oil company required the information so urgently.

There was extreme competition in the region for new business contracts. Companies were offering incentives to the many sheikhs who controlled the money. Kuwait and the Emirate states of Dubai and Abu Dhabi were embarked on rigorous infrastructural development. Oil, the black gold of the Gulf, was the currency. Those with foresight saw investment in infrastructure as an imperative safeguard for the future if the demand for oil was reduced when alternative sources of energy were developed. The Gulf region has the largest oil reserves in the world but political, ecological and economic issues make future sustainability of supply and demand filled with uncertainty.

Abdel Salam was a well-respected journalist and contributor to the news network, Al Jazeera. Robert and I had met him on a number of occasions at conferences. Educated at Oxford and with a Harvard MBA, he was one of the new breed of journalists on which the region now depended for effective contact with the outside world. He became our colleague and friend; he was the eyes and ears of the Gulf but this high profile also made him enemies.

It was now October 1999 and much of Kuwait City had been rebuilt since the devastating occupation of the Iraqis who had ransacked it eight years previous. Most of the 600 oil fields set on fire by the retreating Iraqi military had been made operational, thanks to expert American fire-fighters. The continued development of the State and the region depended on further inward investment and political stability.

My thoughts turned to Abdel and his family. If he had been murdered, I felt partly responsible, having involved him in our study activities. I was greatly concerned about why he was killed and by whom. He knew the risks of helping us and was probably being watched by his enemies. It was believed the Iraqis and Iranians had spy rings in the country. Abdel had found a lot of prominent business people for me to interview. It had been a difficult job to overcome their natural suspicions but they were still grateful to us for liberating their country so were willing to help.

I tape-recorded the interviews and copied them onto a disk using my laptop computer. My laptop had, like my mobile phone, become my indispensible travelling companion. It was one of a series of new portable machines that were now becoming available. They were scarce and expensive in the UK so I had to get Robert to buy one in the US. It was made by Hewlett Packard and contained some special software. I wanted an IBM computer but the company had concentrated on larger machines, having failed to foresee the massive market for portable computers.

The revolution in information technology enables journalists to upload reports with photographs and video clips to their main offices immediately they had been acquired. With access to a satellite dish quality material can be transmitted instantly. A good example was bringing the Gulf War into people's living rooms as it happened. Unfortunately it became like a soap opera, whetting appetites for the next bulletin or instalment, making the horrors of death and destruction look like a video game being played out in the safety and comfort of the home. I watched live as the first volley of cruise missiles plummeted from the dark sky onto their unsuspecting targets in Baghdad, lighting up the surrounding landscape with their massive explosive warheads. At first it was surreal but when it became a nightly event then reality kicked-in. Hundreds, maybe thousands, of innocent people were being killed, not knowing why and defenceless to do anything about it.

I showered, dressed, switched on my computer and went on-line. While the hard disc was whining away, I partially opened the window blinds to look outside. My flat was on the fourth-floor of an apartment block in the fashionable Knightsbridge district of London with a panoramic view of Hyde Park and the Serpentine. Directly below, the view of a well-maintained paved courtyard was always the same. Many of my neighbours were politicians, senior company executives and high-level civil servants who wanted a degree of seclusion and didn't want to mix socially. The security system made it almost impossible to gain unauthorised entry into the building. CCTV cameras monitoring every walkway were viewed by a guard who sat inside the building on a twenty-four hour watch. People could be seen entering or leaving the building.

My father, Sir John Cane, a wealthy banker and commodities dealer, died with my mother in a tragic car accident on the M4 eight years previously. I was the sole heir to their estate which included the flat in Knightsbridge. Fortunately, my inheritance provided me with sufficient income to live in style in London. My social and business lives were kept separate. Many of my friends were suspicious of my wealth and thought I received income from drug dealing or some other criminal activity. Close friends knew my circumstances so didn't need to concern themselves with such questions. I had many girlfriends as any unmarried thirty-year old would have, but too many of them had marriage in their sights.

When I detected that point had been reached we parted company since I valued my bachelor state. So far all my relationships had been platonic. I had yet to fall in love with the ideal woman. I wasn't sure how I would know but my friends informed me that I would when she appeared in my life. My assignments usually took me overseas so I could not devote the time and dedication necessary to make a lasting relationship work. At present, like many men, I enjoyed the hunt rather than the conquest. But I knew one day I would become the hunted.

I was destined to work in my father's company after graduation but, to his disappointment, I studied history and languages, primarily because they were my best A-level subjects. Travelling extensively with my father to Egypt and Israel during school holidays helped to develop my language skills and a knowledge of the Middle East. Perhaps I had inherited a certain gene from a distant Jewish relative on my mother's side of the family. Writing and solving mysteries were my real passions so I became interested in investigative journalism. Sherlock Holmes was my favourite detective. I became the editor of my college newspaper and took part in all university debates. In my finals, to the surprise of my tutor and friends who believed my drinking, gambling and womanizing would finish me, I did gain an upper-second BA degree in history.

After graduating I worked for a local newspaper to gain practical experience but, a disagreement with the editor, made me decide to set up my own office as a freelance journalist and rely on work from my friends and acquaintances in the newspaper business. Somewhat reluctantly, my father did support me, so, unlike many other aspiring journalists, I did have the benefit of a private income.

At first, I had to be content with rather mundane commissions. The lucky break came early when, through a chance meeting in London, I met up with my old university acquaintance named Robert Carville. He had established a successful agency in the US for journalists and consultants in Middle Eastern affairs with offices in Washington and New York. The deteriorating situation between Israel and its hostile neighbours, and the threatening posture posed by Iraq, was of great concern to many American and British oil companies with investments in the region. Both before and after the Gulf War, a demand existed for experts with knowledge of the area who could speak the language and were willing to go there to acquire local knowledge. Governments and their embassies were not forthcoming with information about what was going on in the region owing to the sensitive political situation and the vested interests of the major powers. The war and the escalating price of oil had political and economic repercussions throughout the world.

I had friends and contacts in Israel so I did some reporting for a number of prominent newspapers and TV channels during the Gulf War. Robert obtained some contracts for me from American newspapers and journals, including the prestigious New York Times. I actually went to Iraq at the end of the fighting to report on the aftermath. The devastation and death everywhere left a lasting impression on me. Now, many years after the Gulf War, new players were emerging in the region and instability was again threatened.

Only a small number of people knew my address and my telephone number was ex-directory. The new innovations in communications technology were making it increasingly difficult to remain anonymous. Most of my work was confidential to clients and success depended on keeping their trust and information secure. The encryption software on my computer helped to ward-off hackers. It had been given to me illegally by a retired CIA operative whom I once did a favour for in Iraq. But I think it originated from MI5 in Britain.

I switched on my computer to re-check some data files and then went on-line. There were no important emails. Robert rarely used emails, he preferred the telephone. He was one of a band of people who, although clever enough to understand it, resisted new technology and preferred to use traditional methods. I think it goes deeper, some people prefer to talk than to write. In his profession that was a more valuable asset.

My computing was interrupted by an international telephone call. I anxiously picked up the receiver thinking it was Robert, only to hear a woman's voice.

'It's Atiya, Abdel's wife.'

She sounded distressed.

'I wanted to tell you that Abdel was killed today. It was a car accident but no one was to blame.'

She repeated it several times as though someone was telling her to say it. She didn't sound like a wife in grief. I thought I could hear a muffled noise in the background. In view of my friendship with Abdel her message was brief and not very friendly. Before ringing off she told me the funeral would take place that day in private with only family attending. It was a Muslim tradition to have the funeral very soon after death.

I wondered why she kept insisting it was an accident and why the call was so short. She was unlikely to know that Robert had already told me about Abdel's death. It was clear she was not alone when making the call. Something strange was going on. I needed to speak to Robert again to get more information.

I returned to my computer and continued to check the Kuwait files. Somewhere amongst them might be a clue to Abdel's death. I had concerns about the security of the files when my computer was left in the hotel room in Kuwait City after my arrest. My tapes were in a secure place. I had re-checked my data files on the hard disc and the website when at the airport in Kuwait. My sense of relief was short-lived when after further checks I discovered someone may have accessed the files. Only the CIA or MI5 could break the encryption code. In New York it was still very early in the morning but I decided to call Robert anyway on his cell phone* but he didn't answer so I left him a message to call me back.

Light was breaking through a rather cloudy dawn and reminding me it was only seven o'clock in the morning. Making myself a black coffee and some toast, I started to think back on the events that had taken place in Kuwait a few weeks previously.

---

* The term cell phone is generally used by Americans instead of the term mobile phone.

Kuwait – one month previously

It was an evening in late September when Robert called me to say he was flying to London and could I meet him to discuss the prospects of a new assignment in Kuwait. I had just completed writing a series of articles for a journal so needed some work. My girlfriend and I had just split up. She found a pop star more exciting than a journalist. It wasn't a serious relationship, more physical than anything else, so the parting was mutual. I was, therefore, ready for a new challenge and, with nothing planned, Robert's offer was timed perfectly.

We met at Heathrow's Holiday Inn for dinner since Robert was flying out to Kuwait the following day. He told me the assignment was for The American Gulf Oil Company but warned me of the dangers. I didn't want to be exposed to danger and wasn't desperate for money but did need the challenge and a new experience. Robert's business depended on attracting Fortune 100 companies who paid out millions of dollars for market intelligence. He looked at me with surprise when I displayed an eagerness to do the job, even before discussing money.

'OK' he said, 'I will need you in Kuwait in a few days and you must sign a confidentiality agreement as part of the contract. You will need a short-term entry visa and must go through some security checks.'

He paused, frowned at me, and added,

'That won't be a problem will it?'

'No,' I said.

He didn't know about my small skirmishes with the law over driving offences. I knew these would not prevent me from obtaining a visa. I signed the appropriate papers and drove back to my flat in Knightsbridge looking forward to my new challenge. Robert told me that all the travel, hotel and arrangements for interviewing would be made. He would expect to meet me with his contact, Abdel Salam in Kuwait, at the Marriott Kuwait City Hotel located in the city just 12 km from the airport

A few days later I flew to Kuwait and took a taxi to the hotel.

Robert, who was also staying at the hotel, met me in the lobby with Abdel Salam, a Kuwaiti journalist and a friend of Sheikh Jaber, the Crown Prince and leader of Kuwait. I checked into my room which, to my delight, was a suite. My client had done me proud. There was a knock on the door. Robert and Abdel came to brief me on the arrangements for the interviews.

Abdel had obtained approval from his Government to invite a number of prominent businessmen for me to interview privately. Some had connections to Government ministers and the royal family. Unfortunately that placed a political element to the project that our client would be unhappy about but without support from the Prince it would impossible to operate in the country.

We were worried about the interviews being bugged so to foil that possibility, I suggested we changed the booked interview room prior to the start of the interviews.

Abdel said, 'I will check with the hotel if a late change of room is possible'. Robert looking worried replied,

'If the Government had bugged the room the hotel would know and will not let us change the room. We shouldn't alert them by asking. Let's find an empty room or use this suite.'

Abdel agreed and said, 'I will make some discreet enquiries but first I want to give you an outline of events since the war.' We sat down and he continued,

'Although Saddam's army was defeated and pushed out of Kuwait, the UN's coalition force failed to pursue the Iraqi army to Bagdad since it was not included in their mandate. President Bush had been under pressure from his military commanders for the force to go to Baghdad and depose Saddam Hussein but he wasn't willing to go beyond the UN mandate. If he had done so then international support for the coalition would have broken up. Many people in America were convinced this showed weakness and gave Iraq the freedom to continue with its aggressive tactics towards its neighbours and be a continuing source of trouble in the region. The Iraqi army had been weakened but not destroyed and there was a consensus at the time they were developing weapons of mass destruction. Sooner or later it was believed there would be another war. This fact was producing a state of unrest which was being exploited by terrorist groups who see the British and Americans as enemies. Be on your guard as I cannot guarantee your safety from such groups while you are here. I know most of those who have agreed to be interviewed this week but it would be wise not to leave the hotel during this period.'

Robert's worried look had not diminished as he listened to Abdel. I also was beginning to wonder what we had got ourselves into. Abdel told me I was free to ask any questions but reminded me of the sensitivities that still existed between the Muslim community and the West. No individuals would be named and confidentiality in the information they provided had to be guaranteed. Apparently, approval for my visa had been granted by the Government on the condition I was doing market research for potential investors. It was a convenient cover. If the truth had been known I wouldn't have been granted one. I had already perceived the risk I was taking.

The interviews were to start the next day in a private room. Abdel offered to take us for a drive around the city to see how much had been achieved since the war destruction. I noticed on three separate occasions a car following us but on arriving back at the hotel, it had disappeared. Since he lived in the city with his wife and son, Abdel left us at the hotel. Robert and I proceeded to the bar for a last drink before retiring to our rooms.

I noticed an attractive Asian girl sitting alone at a table in the corner of the bar, looking at me. I judged her date had not turned up as she looked dejected. I should have realised it was unusual for such a girl to be unaccompanied in a hotel bar in a Muslim country. Robert observing my interest said,

'Be careful, even in a hotel you know the rules here. I've had a long day and will see you at seven o'clock in the morning for breakfast.'

I nodded and continued to look at the long black-haired beauty in the mirror conveniently located above the bar in front of me. Since I had my back to her, I thought my gaze would go unnoticed but she could also see my face in the mirror. I detected a movement in her lips which could have been mistaken for the wishful beginnings of a smile.

My mild flirtation was interrupted by a waiter speaking to me in a broken accent, 'Mr Paul Cane, a telephone call for you. Please go to reception.'

I hurried to the desk clerk, who said he would put the call through to another phone in a more private corner of the lobby. It was Robert calling from his room to say that he had received a call from the British Embassy wanting a list of the people we were going to interview as Al-Qaeda suspects were known to be in the country. It was unusual for the Embassy to be working so late. I guessed it was really the secret service making the request. It had all the hallmarks of MI6 or the CIA. He reminded me to be very careful to whom I spoke and not to drink too much. I think he was really afraid I might have other things on my mind. He was right, I did. I went back to the bar to finish my double gin and tonic but my beauty had gone. The barman looked at me and with a smile raised his arms in an expression of – better luck next time.

I took the lift to the sixth floor and walked along a corridor. It was uncannily quiet, like I was the only resident. The thick-piled patterned red carpet exuded a sweet scent; it was like walking through a bed of flowers. I came to my room, slotted in the keypad and pushed open the door to my luxury suite. The room was in darkness except for a shaft of artificial light coming through a narrow gap in the curtains. For a reason I cannot recall, I didn't immediately put the keypad in the light switch to bring on the lights, which is the normal arrangement in hotel rooms. Instead I went over to the window and pulled back the curtains to look at the city lights which lit up the clear cloudless night sky. Looking out to the city, I thought how frightening it must have been for the residents when Saddam's tanks rolled into the city streets and the army started pillaging buildings. They occupied the State for seven months until the American-led coalition ousted them.

As I turned towards the light switch I caught a smell of perfume, it was similar but different to the smell of the carpet. A muffled sound emanated from the king-size bed. I diverted my gaze to see before me, bathed in silver light from the window, the girl from the bar, sitting naked on my bed, except for a sheet pulled over her breasts. She just stared at me and smiled. I was too dumbfounded to speak. I walked over to touch her but like a wild cat she recoiled into the bed releasing the sheet to expose her large well-rounded breasts.

Was this my client's welcoming gift? It was not unknown for wealthy sheikhs to be given such gifts. For them, young blonde girls were usually provided. Approaching the bed I looked at her more intensely and realised she was of mixed race. Guessing that she could not speak English, and without saying a word, as words seemed inappropriate, I clumsily undressed and jumped into bed beside her. She turned, looked at me with her large brown eyes, threw her arms around me and placed her mouth onto mine. She kissed me hard, fiercely, almost angrily. I had been kissed by many women but never experienced a kiss like that before. It instantly aroused me. After the kiss, which left me breathless, and with surprising strength she rolled over and sat astride me. What followed was beyond description. Her shapely body gyrated erotically like a tango dancer in the ghostly silver light that permeated the room. After what seemed like hours but was probably a lot less, of continuous love-making, I became exhausted and had to pull her off. She then rolled over and putting her hand on my chest tucked her head into my neck. Her body was soft and warm. I wondered if I was dead and had gone to heaven. Maybe the Muslim faith was right about death after all. We still had not spoken when I must have drifted into blissful sleep.

Everyone dreams before they awake. Mine was running to catch a train but just missing it and then running along the track to catch up. I woke up hot and sweaty. It took time for my memory to remind me of the night before. I felt for the girl but she was not there. I began to wonder if it had been real or just a fanciful dream but the scent still filled the room. My clothes were spread out in an untidy heap on the floor where I had left them. My first reaction was to call Robert but after his polite warnings, he might not be too pleased.

It looked like I had been set up and was a fool not to have realised it. But by whom and for what purpose? I took a shower, dressed and went down for breakfast. On the way down I decided not to say anything about the girl, still wondering who she was and how she had gained entry to my room. Robert was already seated reading a newspaper while munching some toast. He looked up and greeted me with a grunt. For some people early mornings are not the best times of day. This applied to us. We did not speak for some time so I was able to hide my embarrassment.

After some coffee and a bowl of corn flakes, I asked Robert if everything was OK. He looked at me scornfully saying.

'Those buggers at the Embassy are trying to stop us interviewing business people. I told Abdel about their requests but he refused to send them the confidential list. They called to warn me about possible consequences.'

'But all the invitations have gone out and been accepted.' I replied.

Robert said, 'I called Abdel and asked him to sort it out with the Prince who has absolute power in Kuwait. The Embassy cannot stop us without causing a diplomatic row which they will not want to do, but they will be watching us like hawks. I'm afraid we are going to make some enemies. We are expecting our first guest at ten o'clock so you had better check out the room for bugs and any hidden cameras.'

I collected my computer, tape-recorder and notes on the invited guests provided by Abdel and went to the room on the first floor that had been booked for the interviews. My first thought was to change the room to avoid the possible problems raised by Robert. No one would know about the room change except me so that would be the best security. I was, however, curious enough to find out if any surveillance devices had been secretly installed. After looking in all the obvious places I found nothing. It temporarily allayed my concerns but without all the specialised detection equipment made it difficult to be certain. I suggested to Robert that we still change the room. He agreed and booked one on the fourth floor.

As expected, Abdel called to say everything had been cleared with the Embassy and we could go ahead. The Ministry of Information refused to give the names of our guests to the British and American Embassies since the project was a private matter involving only Kuwaiti citizens. The Kuwaitis were still greatly indebted to America and Britain for liberating their country so they were unlikely to make serious political issue out of it.

Abdel warned me to observe tradition and not expect too much, preferably to use the basic technique of conversation for fact finding rather than asking questions. Letting the interviewees express their concerns through their own values and culture. No names were to be used. Candidates were known by numbers.

My first candidate was a tall well-dressed Oxford-educated man dressed in the traditional Arab long-sleeved white cotton Dishdasha. On his head was a Gutra with a black band holding it in place known as an Ogal. He displayed his wealth by the numerous rings and other jewels that decked his body and attire. He seemed to be well-briefed on what was required and did not object to being tape-recorded. When he knew I could speak some Arabic and observed my interest and understanding of the Arab world, we immediately had a rapport so he was very forthcoming and provided a lot of valuable information.

He gave me a brief history of his family and then talked about the need for foreign investment. As expected, he expressed his bitter opposition to the fundamentalists who were undermining his country. He told me about the ancient rivalries that existed between the six Arab tribes, particularly Sunni and Shai Muslims. Kuwait and the rest of Saudi Arabia was predominately Shia and although they were numerous in Southern Iraq, Saddam Hussein's Sunni Muslims controlled the country. All Arabs opposed the Jews and the occupation of Palestine in the State of Israel. The American support and protection for Israel was alone the underlying problem which fuelled the Middle East dispute with the West. But the need to sell oil, and the riches it brought to the desert kingdoms that possessed it, helped to neutralise this anger. After an hour of talking I had already gained a lot of valuable information and an insight into the concerns of the local Arabs.

Three days of interviewing other people similar to my first candidate enabled me to acquire enough information for my report. In fact, the information I collected was beyond my expectations. The business community was keen to attract inward investment, particularly from America. But there was real concern about continued threats from Iraq and Iran and a number of terrorist groups that wanted Jihad with the West. It was the names they gave me which provided some valued intelligence. Little did I know then how one of those names would determine the direction my life in the coming months and lead to an event that would threaten our very existence.

On the final day I was satisfied I had enough information for my client. Abdel departed for his home in the city and Robert had some business calls to make. We agreed to meet up for lunch before checking out of the hotel to fly home later in the day.

Feeling satisfied with a job well-done, I decided to order a taxi and do some sightseeing around the city on my own. Abdel had warned me about going out alone but I thought I would be safe within the confines of a taxi; that proved to be a big mistake. As my taxi pulled up in front of the hotel, I noticed a well-dressed girl getting into a large grey Lexus, parked just in front of us. She turned towards me as I opened the taxi's door so I caught a fleeting glance of her. It was the girl who had been in my bed on the previous night. The Lexus sped away and I was not sure if she saw me. A worried feeling came over me. My colleagues knew nothing about my first night's experience so I had to face the consequences alone. If I had been set up, the big question was why and by whom? I was lost in thought when the driver asked me where I wanted to go.

' Just a drive to the city,' I said.

We had only travelled a few miles when the taxi was stopped by a police car. Two armed policemen approached and asked me for my identification, so I gave them my passport. They asked me to accompany them to their car.

I asked, 'What is wrong?'

The larger of the two said, 'We are doing a routine check and need to ask you a few questions.'

They indicated they did not want the taxi driver to hear. I thought it a little strange but with some reluctance agreed to leave the taxi. As I approached the police car I felt a hand on my shoulder. The tall one then pushed me into their car which then drove swiftly away to the dismay of the taxi driver who had not been paid.

Protesting did little good. They pretended not to understand. I was taken to a police station and locked in a room. My requests for an interpreter and an explanation were ignored. I didn't tell them I knew some Arabic as I wanted to learn what it was all about. The room had no air-conditioning and I was left alone for what seemed like an eternity. Finally the door was opened by a well-dressed man who asked me to follow him to an interview room. Two armed policemen followed. I was being treated like a criminal for what was obviously a mistake. Two other burly guards, not in uniform, came into the room. My heart started to thump in my chest. I was pushed down onto a chair placed in front of a bare table. Fortunately, I did speak some Arabic so I decided to ask politely why I had been arrested. Taken aback by my request in their own language, without speaking, the tall man in the suit took some photographs from a drawer in the table. He threw them down in front of me. It was then the bombshell exploded, my worst nightmare came to reality. My first night of ecstasy had come back to haunt me. I looked at the photos in denial but they unmistakably were me and the girl having sex in the hotel bedroom. I remembered the room was in darkness so the pictures were taken with an infra-red sensitive camera. It just proved that the people had set me up who were professionals. My worst fears were now confirmed.

I asked what crime I had committed. The suited man looked angrily at me and growled. 'The girl was only sixteen. It was illegal to have sex with her and possess drugs. We found drugs in your room this morning. You realise that offence carries the death penalty. We need to know who provided you with the girl and the drugs.'

He looked menacingly at me, almost threatening to beat me to get the truth. I had heard about the way suspects were treated in Arab police stations. Torture was commonplace and people admitted to crimes they did not commit just to prevent further torture. My British passport seemed to mean nothing to my accuser. I decided that attack was better than pleading my innocence. After all they had the photographs. I looked straight into the man's eyes and shouted,

'You must know that I was set up. The girl was in my room before I arrived. I did not possess any drugs.'

It became obvious that I was not believed so I asked to make a phone call but it was refused. This was Kuwait where my human rights meant nothing to these people. They believed I was a criminal so treated me like one. Nobody knew I was here except my captors and I was not sure if they were even the police.

I continued with my attack and demanded to see a high-level official and saying that I was in the country at the direct invitation of the Prince. I gave them Abdel's telephone number to call. That statement seemed to worry the suited man who immediately left the room. The two guards smiled at each other and came over to me making threatening gestures. I went to get up but was knocked down and handcuffed to the chair. They uttered some words in Arabic that I recognised to be rapist and drug taker. I was about to be hit by one of them when the suited man returned. The guards spoke to him saying that I had tried to escape and had to be restrained.

I asked him if he had called the number. He did not respond so now I was overcome with real fear. These people were not police, or if they were, on whose orders were they acting on? I asked for a glass of water. The suited man told one of the guards to fetch water. The handcuffs were removed and I was given a glass of water.

The attitude of the suited man then changed. He apologised for the rough treatment and said I would be looked after if I signed a statement admitting to my crimes. I refused and restated that I wanted to make the phone call. The suited man threw up his hands and told the guards to take me to the jail. I was dragged protesting down some stone steps and literally thrown into a small dark prison cell with nothing but a wooden bench and straw on the floor. It reminded me of one of the dungeons in a thirteenth-century castle. At least they left me my clothes but took away my cell phone. I felt like I was living a nightmare and hopefully would soon wake up.

Time loses its meaning in solitary confinement so I do not recall exactly how long I was in the dungeon. My despair turned into hope when I realised that Robert would be searching for me as we had agreed to meet for lunch. But since I had no telephone he would not be able to locate me. I could hear distant voices that sounded like someone speaking on a telephone. Soon after the door opened with a loud clang and the suited man and two guards appeared, unlocked the door, and took me up the stone steps to a well-furnished room much smarter than the last one. I heard car doors bang and shouting, followed by the door being burst open by Robert and Abdel and another well-dressed Arab. The suited man now looking very demure left the room.

'Robert, how glad I am to see you both.' I yelled. My nightmare had ended. The white clad Arab was not introduced but shook my hand and apologised for the misunderstanding, stating that there would be an enquiry. My telephone, passport and other possessions were returned. I got into Abdel's car which took off back to the hotel.

I learned that the taxi had returned to the hotel to report what had happened to me because he had not been paid and was also suspicious about the police who had stopped him and arrested me. The desk clerk immediately informed Robert who contacted Abdel. Phone calls were made to various people including the Prince and the British Ambassador himself. This started a chain reaction, resulting eventually in my release. But why was I stopped and on whose orders was the question not answered? Robert was more concerned about my safety and the interview tapes. At least the people who arrested me were police. They did not explain the reason for my being stopped and arrested but it had come from a high level source. I began to wonder what I had got myself involved in. Was I the bait for some wider conspiracy? The girl in my room was the key. Robert and Abdel did not know about her so I decided, at least for the time being, not to say anything.

I went to my room and discovered that everything was in place. The tapes were still in the secret zipped pocket of my case and the laptop had the encrypted files. If anyone had been in my room they did not leave any evidence of their presence, but I still had my suspicions. The whole experience placed me in a state of shock.

My first instinct was to find out about the girl. I made some enquiries at the desk and although it wasn't hotel policy to give details of guests, they did confirm that no woman of her description had stayed at the hotel. It confirmed my suspicions that she must have had inside help to gain access to my room. I did not want to draw further attention to myself so decided not to ask further questions. Someone had obviously been observing me from the time when I first arrived at the hotel.

Robert told me to quickly pack and leave with him for the airport. My flight to London was later than his to Washington but it seemed the airport might be a safer place to be. I was really glad to leave Kuwait. At the airport we went into the business suite and took a private room. I told Robert about the girl and the reason given for my arrest. He looked at me with a smile and said,

'I know all about it and yes it was a set-up.' Jokingly, he continued,

'Someone knew your weakness for pretty girls. You know it caused quite a stir and went right back to London via the Ambassador. You can thank the British Government for getting you out of jail. After you went missing, I contacted Abdel who was not surprised. He made some phone calls. An hour later a car arrived and we set off to the police station.' Robert noticed my amazed look.

'But why did it happen? Who set it up? I want some answers,' I retorted.

'You won't get answers for now. I think there is something big going on and unfortunately it's got mixed up with our work. I don't know anymore but you were mistaken for someone else. The girl went to the wrong room,' he replied. I was slightly relieved but wondered how Robert knew so much.

'Who told you all this?' I asked.

'Abdel, he made some high level enquiries.'

Robert's mood changed.

'Look, I know it's been an ordeal for you but let us focus on the work for our client. He is paying us well and I do not want any of this getting back to him. Can I suggest you tell no one, at least until we get paid. Are the tapes safe and did you get all the information you wanted?' he asked.

'Yes I did. But that's what worries me,' I replied. He looked concerned.

'I was given the names of people and organisations that could be real trouble. When I get back I will carry out some checks but Houseman's concerns about the region are well-founded. I may have recorded intelligence that I shouldn't have – and it goes beyond the Middle East.' Robert went quiet into one of his thoughtful moods.

'Knowing it would get back to the Americans, do you think the people who were giving this were using you?' he asked.

'It's difficult to know but two of them did look worried and asked me to keep what I was told confidential. Have you ever heard of groups called The Brotherhood Foundation or The New Order?' I asked.

Robert thought for a moment and said, 'No.'

A call went out for Robert's flight.

'I will call you in a few weeks when the report is finished. Let me know if you have any problems,' he said. We then parted company. I began reflecting on what he'd said about the girl. It didn't make sense. If I was the wrong victim, then who was being set-up and for what reason? It seemed like something out of a Robert Ludlum novel. Honey traps were well-known methods used by spy agencies to blackmail people into working for them. Was this really intended for me, I wondered?

It was at least an hour before my flight would be called so I booted up my laptop and called up my Kuwait files. I was surprised how much data I had collected from the interviews on the new political situation developing within the various Muslim factions in the countries of the Middle East. There was an unrepentant hatred directed towards Israel, America and Britain. One of the businessmen I interviewed mentioned some names that stayed in my memory. He spoke about a wealthy group of Saudis who had recently visited the country seeking information about investment opportunities in America but they also wanted to know about American installations. They referred to their leader as Osama bin Laden and their organization as Al-Qaeda.

Bin Laden was a Saudi millionaire and seen by the CIA as a more significant threat than many of the other fundamentalist Muslims because he had the wealth and means to make things happen. Al-Qaeda was thought to be responsible for a number of bombing outrages against American embassies. The interviewee, who mentioned the name, anxiously asked me not put it in my report. I went on-line but the connection in the airport suite was slow. Eventually I linked into the Internet and checked on Bin Laden and his connection to Al-Qaeda.

Al-Qaeda had its origins in recruiting foreign Mujahedeen for the war against the Soviets in Afghanistan. It was founded by Abdullah Yusuf Azzam, a Palestinian Sunni Islamic scholar and member of the Muslim Brotherhood. Bin Laden became a major financier of the Mujahedeen, spending his own money and using his connections with the Saudi royal family and the petro-billionaires of the Gulf in order to win public support for the war and raise more funds. At the time it was an aid to American foreign policy directed toward removing the Soviet communists from Afghanistan so the CIA paid little attention to his activities.

Even more surprising was the name given by a Kuwaiti Professor, who was the last person I interviewed. We were talking about financing academic and scientific collaboration across the Islamic world. He cited Bin Laden and a European group but no name of the group was given. They apparently had funded a number of universities in countries like Dubai and Abu Dhabi but very little else came up except a quote from a website he told me to look up about *building a better democratic world through cultural and political exchanges.*

The West's worst nightmare scenario was that one day a terrorist organisation would possess a nuclear bomb and threaten to use it. The fear that rogue countries like Iraq or Iran might be developing an atomic bomb underlined the tension in the Middle East. Weapons inspectors were trying to get into Iraq to verify that the country was not building so-called weapons of mass-destruction but Saddam Hussein was doing everything to make that difficult. Generally such countries could be contained because if they attacked any country with such weapons, they would face complete annihilation by those that possessed them. Terrorists, however, hide behind a religious or political belief and are not necessarily based or aligned with any particular country or state. Taking swift retaliatory action would become difficult unless it could be proved they were supported by a particular country. This is what makes terrorist groups like Al-Qaeda so dangerous. They were like the many-headed hydra of Greek mythology. Remove one head and it was replaced with two more; the difference being the hydra had a lair but terrorists can exist anywhere.

I closed my computer when my flight was called. It was only when I went through the lounge suite that I noticed a tall, smartly dressed Arab man reading a copy of the Financial Times. He watched me cross the room but averted his gaze as I passed. A bad feeling came over me as I walked out of the room. My inner fears were heightened when I next saw him on the plane sitting a few rows back in Business Class.

I suppressed my inclination to confront the man as I only had an unfounded paranoia he was following me. I ordered a large gin and tonic and tried to put the events of the last week out of my mind, consoling myself with the latest airline magazine. Ironically, it advertised a beach holiday displaying bikini clad bronzed-tanned women. My thoughts went back to my experience of the first night. At least whoever was responsible for that night gave me something to remember.

Looking out of the window and seeing the White Cliffs of

Dover passing thousands of feet below and knowing that home was not far away was a reassuring sight. That same comforting feeling must be experienced by many returning home from Europe. The sun was low in the clear western sky. It produced a silver sea lapping on the shore and a cloth of gold over England's green and pleasant land. Whenever I see that sight, I am reminded of Shakespeare's immortal lines from Richard II.

'This precious stone set in the silver sea,
Which serves it in the office of a wall
Or as a moat defensive to a house'

Wherever we travel to, our inner spirit always longs for home. It's where we ultimately want to be.

As I collected my luggage I didn't see the tall Arab go through passport control. I held back but he didn't re-appear. It was only later, when boarding a taxi, I saw him with two other men getting into a black Jaguar. He had gone through the VIP channel and been met. This confirmed by suspicions that he worked for one of the security services.

I was glad to be back in my London apartment after my harrowing experiences in Kuwait. The next day I called Robert and told him about my suspicions. He told me to forget about everything and to write the report which the client wanted within the week, reminding me of the penalty clause in our contract. I agreed and got to work on analysing the interviews. After doing this it became obvious I was in possession of information that would be of great value to intelligence agencies. If that was known it would explain why I was under surveillance. My dilemma was how much to put in my client's report. I was asked not to record names but was being paid to give a realistic assessment of the situation in the Gulf. I decided to highlight the concerns given to me about the growth in terrorist activity but leave out names, except those of the organisations since they could be found on the Internet.

Robert called me daily. He seemed to be worried I would not deliver the report within the agreed timescale and invoke the penalty clause. At the end of the week I had completed the work and couriered it to Houseman in Washington. To Robert's relief a cheque was deposited in his bank account a few days later. Houseman's PA just sent a note acknowledging its acceptance. Robert had failed to speak to our client who had apparently left the country and was not immediately contactable.

London two weeks later

Robert had not responded to my early morning call so I decided to leave the apartment and get some fresh air. I went for a walk in St James's Park along the path which runs by Duck Island in the direction of Horse Guards Parade. I often took that route rather than walking across the road to Hyde Park and around the Serpentine since it was more interesting. Stopping to sit down on a bench facing the lake, with its twenty-three species of water birds, most of which seemed to be swimming on the lake, I caught a glimpse of a bearded man walking past. The weeping willow trees cast an almost perfect reflection in the still waters, only occasionally disturbed by a duck paddling. It was one of my favourite quiet places in the middle of London, just less than a half-a-mile away from Downing Street and Westminster.

Suddenly the man stopped, turned and walked cautiously back towards me.

'Excuse me for asking but is your name Paul Cane?'

Before I had time to reply, he said, in an Oxford accent, 'Do you remember me?' I looked and for a moment didn't recognise him.

'John Henning, Bridge Club, Christie College,' he replied, stretching out his hand. Then I saw through the beard and remembered who he was and shook his hand.

'Yes, I remember you now. How are you?' I asked.

'I'm fine,' he replied.

I asked him what he did after leaving Oxford.

'I joined the Civil Service and am now a Senior Executive

Officer working over there in the Office of Statistics, I always liked figures.'

He quickly turned the conversation back to me.

'See you're a successful journalist. I read your articles in the Global Economist. Damned good they were too. You seemed to have a good knowledge of the Middle East.

Have you been there lately?' he said, pausing for a reply.

Sensing he already knew the answer, I said, 'No, not lately.'

'Getting to be a dangerous place. Can't believe anything they tell us about what's going on there. It's a haven for bloody terrorists. We ought to round them all up and put them in jail.'

Realising by my body language that I did not wish to get involved in a prolonged conversation, he looked at me hard and uttered,

'Well it was good to see you again old chap after all these years – take care, I must get back to the office, have to look at oil prices and stuff like that.'

That last remark had an intended potency. He then walked swiftly away in the opposite direction towards the Mall. Yes, I did know him from my Oxford days but it was a strange coincidence he should see me now. Even stranger that working so close to where I lived, I had never seen him before, particularly as I frequently walked in the park.

The man was a good actor but I was not fooled by the performance. He had been told to make contact. Whatever the reason, it looked like MI5 or one of the Government security services had marked my card. It ruined my day in the park so I returned to the privacy of my apartment feeling even more depressed.

Using the Internet I started to research something that had worried me since the first time Robert had told me about the Gulf Oil Company's need for information about the Middle East. Being a large corporate they must have had many operatives in the region who could have supplied the information they sought. Why were they willing to pay an independent outsider a large sum of money for a report? That was the big question. I was now convinced that I had been set up in Kuwait. The story about a mistaken identity just did not add up. My greatest worry now was Abdel's death and the fact that I was under surveillance by various security services. It had all the hallmarks of MI6 and CIA involvement. But why me?

I switched on the TV to see the news. The flash headline was, *'Terrorist bomb destroys hotel in Kuwait – many feared dead.'* The reporter went on to say that no group had claimed responsibility but the hotel in the centre of the city was used by foreign reporters and businessmen. It had only just happened so information was still confused. It was the hotel we had stayed at. Was this the 'big event' Robert had hinted at in Kuwait? How did he know that something was going to happen? My thoughts were interrupted by the phone ringing. I picked it up to hear Robert's voice say, 'Did you hear the news from Kuwait? It may explain everything that happened to you. I'm glad we got out when we did.'

'I think I'm still being watched,' I replied. Maybe they think I have the names of people who could be the terrorists. I did not put them in the report.

With an anxiety in his voice, Robert said, 'Can you come to Washington? We need to talk to Houseman. I think he might know more than he is telling us.'

I explained that I needed some rest and wanted to get away from everything for a while.

'Anyway it's something we shouldn't get involved in,' I said.

'We may be already involved if the names of the people or organisations we have on the tapes are members of the terrorist organisations that bombed the hotel and murdered Abdel,' Robert replied.

'But we have no proof of that, unless you think the Government or security agencies believe we have such information,' I answered.

'That's exactly what I think. Have you stored the tapes and files in a safe place?'

'Yes I have – I hope no one is listening to this call. You remember what happened earlier.'

'I'm using a pay phone so it should be safe,' Robert said confidently.

Not wishing to say no, I suggested to Robert that he find Houseman and talk to him first. Then, if necessary I would fly to Washington.

He was obviously disappointed at my caution but agreed to call me if the situation changed. It was now approaching midday. I tried to get myself back into London life. Time to call up some old friends. Before I went to Kuwait I had asked Jeremy Simms, an old university friend who ran an estate agency in Oxford that specialised in country houses, to find me the proverbial cottage-in-the-country, a retreat from the hustle and bustle of London. I cannot deny that London holds all the attractions for a wealthy bachelor. It has the best clubs, best theatres, hosts all the banks and corporate offices and businesses, has the largest airport and the hub for rail and road travel. It's a great place to work. But at weekends the city empties, giving way to outsiders on weekend sightseeing breaks who clog up the transport system. For those who do not have a circle of friends who actually live in the city, it can be a lonely place.

At heart I am a country boy. I enjoy the natural environment and the peace and quiet it offers. After graduating from Oxford I lived and worked for a number of years in Banbury, a small town on the edge of the Cotswolds. Working on the local newspaper, I made many friends and became part of the local community. Places and happy memories often go together. I once met a girl at a hotel near Stow-on-the-Wold who I later discovered was from a well-known aristocratic family who owned one of the largest manor houses in the area. We had a short fling but I loved the village and the surrounding countryside.

It seemed like a good time to find out if any property had come on the market. I dialled Simms Estates.

'Hi Jeremy, it's Paul Cane, have you had any luck with finding me that ideal cottage?'

'Good to hear from you Paul. Glad you're back in London. As a matter of fact a property is just about to come on the market that might suit you. It's in the Cotswolds, in a village called Bisley in Gloucestershire, just four miles from Stroud. The village is a gem, with three churches, two old pubs, a post office and general store.'

I said, 'Sounds interesting, but can you tell more about the property?' sensing a sale, he replied in a very upbeat voice.

'Yes, it only came onto the market last week, although the owner has been trying to sell it for a few months. It's priced at about two hundred and twenty thousand pounds which is quite low for that part of the country. It does, however, need updating and some money spent on it. It's a two-hundred-year-old stone building with two bedrooms, a wood-burning stove and flagstone floors, named Stones End.'

He went on to say, 'The property is owned by a Ruth Goodman who inherited it from her uncle, Malcolm Walker, who died late last year. I can't leave Oxford this week but if you want to take a look at it, I can arrange for someone local to let you have the key. It can be obtained at the village Post Office by contacting a Gladys Cook, who runs it and the local store. When it's closed you can find her in the Bear Inn, near the village centre.'

Jeremy paused and said, 'Do you want to see it?'

'It sounds just what I'm looking for and I do need to get away from London this weekend. Sunday would be a good day,' I replied.

'The Post Office is closed but I will tell Gladys you will meet her in the Bear Inn around midday, if that's OK?'

'Fine, please arrange it,' I replied.

Suddenly I felt good again and already with my visit to the Cotswolds planned for the next day, my mind went away from the events taking place in Kuwait and elsewhere.

CHAPTER 2

Stones End, Bisley
14 November 1999

It was a typical English late Autumn morning. The drive from London along the M4 had been without delays. It was Sunday and too early for the usual day trippers. I left the motorway and took the road to Swindon and Stroud. As my grey Mercedes sped along the narrow country lanes edged with trees, the sun was trying to break through the clouds. Holding the road effortlessly, the car negotiated the sharp bends; it was a confirmation of German automobile engineering. The woman's voice on the satellite navigator was telling me where to go. Navigators were expensive and difficult to acquire since they were not generally available to buy. I was one of a selected number of Mercedes customers who were asked to trial test the instrument. My destination was about ten miles ahead on the road from Stroud in the village of Bisley close to the heart of the Cotswolds. I set the postcode for the Bear Inn, in the centre of the village.

A crossroad loomed ahead forcing me to brake the car to a sharp halt. My quiet, powerful V8 engine always meant I drove too fast. The absence of traffic gave me a false sense of security. The road widened as it approached the village, winding through a mixture of modern and old stone cottages. The Bear Inn protruded into a road junction looking like a trap to catch any unaware motorist. There did not appear to be an entrance to the car park at the rear of the building so I had to be content to park on the narrow road outside. I locked the car and walked to the front of the Inn to be confronted by an overhanging portico supported by Jacobean pillars. The entrance was through a narrow door fitted into the stone framework.

It was too early for lunch and there were few people at the bar. I looked around for Gladys Cook but could not see a woman resembling Jeremy's description. All eyes were turned on me as I surveyed the scene. This time of the year unexpected strangers would always invoke a degree of curiosity. A portly barman broke off a conversation with a group standing at the bar and sauntered towards me. I ordered a beer and some beef sandwiches and asked the barman if he knew a Gladys Cook.

Looking at me suspiciously he said, 'Yes, I know her well, she's the local post woman and comes here for her Sunday drink. She should be here any time.'

I sat down on a well-worn wooden seat in a quiet corner of the bar, close to a seventeenth century Queen Anne's pattern fireplace. The room had low wooden beams that probably dated back to Elizabethan times. Local eyes were still searching for an explanation of why a stranger would be in their sacred inn so early on a Sunday morning. Before I could start on my sandwiches, an elderly grey-haired lady, probably in her late sixties or early seventies, came in. Since I was very conspicuous, she immediately spotted me and came over to introduce herself. We shook hands and I offered to buy her a drink and some food which she gladly accepted. I ordered a pint of Guinness which the barman knew was her usual lunchtime drink. We engaged in some introductory small talk, after which I decided to tap into Gladys's local knowledge to find out more about the cottage and its history, and the village. I had already discovered from the Internet that a number of celebrities and well-known public figures lived in and around the village. These included the well-known author, Jilly Cooper.

Bisley was first mentioned in the Domesday Book and a Saxon charter was granted to it in AD896. Throughout the local area, the hills are littered with burial barrows and there is evidence of Roman occupation near the village. Like many Cotswold villages and towns, in earlier times the village became wealthy through the trading of wool and cloth. The cottage, known as 'Stones End', derived its name from a stone in the garden which was believed to mark an ancient burial site. Previous owners had tried to make it a listed building but had failed through lack of historical verification.

I asked Gladys about Malcolm Walker, the previous occupant. She admitted that neither she nor anyone else in the village knew much about him. He was thought to be a retired banker but, since his post was never delivered to the village Post Office, she didn't know of his connections to the outside world. She thought he collected and sent mail from a private box in Stroud or Gloucester. He clearly went to a lot of trouble to protect his anonymity.

Gladys continued to say, 'Mr Walker had lived in the cottage for about forty-eight years but was rarely seen in the village. There was no telephone in the cottage so he clearly wanted seclusion. I think he was a bachelor but he did get occasional visits from a young lady.' Gladys did remember a man with a foreign accent once stopping at the Post Office and asking directions to the cottage, but that was last year.

'Did he have any visitors just before he died?' I asked.

Gladys replied, 'I can't be certain but a stranger was seen in the Bear Inn a week before but I don't know if he went to the cottage, but then many people stop here on their way across the valley to Stroud or Gloucester. We are on the Cotswold's tourist route.'

'Do you know who found Mr Walker's body?' I asked.

'He was found by Fred Palmer, our Church Warden who lives near the church.'

She paused to sip her drink, and then continued. 'Fred was walking his dog along the lane near the cottage, when it started to get restless, howled and then ran towards it. Dogs sense death, particularly sheep dogs. Fred went to investigate and found the door of the cottage partially open so he called out for Walker. On getting no reply, he went inside and found Walker dead on the floor of the bedroom. It's all recorded in a statement to the police who were called soon after.'

'I thought there was no telephone in the cottage?' I said.

'No, there wasn't so Fred had to use a phone box in the village. The nearest police station is in Stroud. I assumed he had died of a heart attack but no one told me, so I can't be certain. The police from Stroud carried out an investigation in the cottage but strangely no post-mortem was reported in the newspaper. The only relative that could be traced was a young niece who lived in Cambridge. I assumed she arranged the funeral, but it was not conducted locally. I only know that much because when it was arranged for the house to be sold, the girl, whose name was Ruth Goodman, came to the Post Office shop to tell me Simms Estates, the sales agents, wanted a local person for any prospective buyer to contact for the key.'

It seemed a bit strange that Walker's body was taken away so suddenly without anything being mentioned in the local paper or the police making enquires. Before continuing, Gladys paused to finish off the Guinness.

'And that's all I can tell you about Mr Walker. I do hope you will buy the cottage, we need a nice young man like you in the village.'

I thanked her for the information and asked directions to the cottage. I was about to walk away when she said,

'You will need the key to the cottage and these notes.'

'Thanks,' I replied.

I was surprised to see the key looked relatively new and it fitted a Yale lock. I put the notes in my pocket. Gladys told me the cottage was only about half-a-mile away from the centre of the village and just within its boundary. It was located at the end of a gravel path, well-hidden from the road by woods. I inserted the postcode for the cottage into the navigator.

'*In two hundred yards take the next exit left,*' said the lusty woman's voice from the dashboard. There was only one exit so I didn't have to judge the distance. Following the road to the top of a hill, the car rounded a sharp bend. On either side of the tree-lined road was well-cultivated farmland with shoots of corn just visible. I drove past a concealed gravel path which disappeared into the woods.

'*You have reached your destination,*' said the voice repeatedly.

I braked hard, reversed and pulled over to stop off the road on a grass verge. Nearby, faint tyre tracks were visible in the soft mud ahead of me. They looked like they had been made recently by a truck or four-wheeled drive vehicle. Jeremy had told me I was the first person to ask to view the cottage since it had only just been advertised for sale. I locked the car and walked along the footpath which led to a clearing in the woods.

My first glimpse of the cottage was the appearance of outhouses. A dilapidated greenhouse with the roof damaged through weather and time came into view. Holes in the roof offered a stark contrast next to the unbroken panes that were just catching rays of sunlight through the misty haze. A large stone-sided barn, supported by wooden struts, so old that they bowed under the weight of the stone, was almost shrouded by overgrown saplings.

The buildings were almost buried by overgrown vegetation. The unkempt garden, which in better times looked as though it had been well-cared for, was now back in nature's possession. Suddenly, a two-storey cottage came into view. The square-cut yellowish grey stonework of the cottage gave it a strong long-lasting but warm appearance. I approached the building from the side. There were unevenly worn steps leading down from the garden to the door. Broken flowerpots, left or perhaps forgotten, were scattered about the garden. At the top of the steps a stone archway with a slated roof supported by timbers protected a solid wooden door to the cottage. Windows on either side had mullions, supporting a stone lintel. Wrought iron had been worked in the building of the casements which dated the cottage from the early nineteenth century.

I took the key from my pocket to open the door. The lock operated with a sharp click but the door required a forceful push to open it. I stepped inside to be greeted by stale, cold air. A shiver ran through my body as I entered; it was like opening a tomb, going back in time. Buildings that have been locked up for some time exude a smell characteristic of the materials from which they are constructed. This one was no exception. It was an unpleasant, sickly musty odour. A deathly stillness pervaded, broken only by the faint movement of air through the open door and the drone of insects visiting plants outside.

Natural shafts of light from small but effective leaded windows produced shadows in corners of the room and reflected diffusely from the white-washed walls. The living room was deceivingly large. It had a strong timber floor leading to a traditional Cotswold stone fireplace. Well-seasoned oak wood shelves were inset at each side, obviously used by the previous occupant for storing books. Most of the furniture had been removed; I wondered who had taken it, remembering Gladys's comments.

I decided to look at the notes Gladys had given me. It was clear the two-storey cottage had been vacant for about a year. The owner, Ruth Goodman, had inherited the property on the death of her uncle, Mr Malcolm Walker. The note did not state the cause of death but I remembered what Gladys had told me. Being short of money and a student at Cambridge, the new owner wished to sell the property quickly and was apparently prepared to accept a below-market price. Further details could be obtained from the sales agency.

I was looking for peace and seclusion. Some work was required but the cottage basically had what I needed. The large living-room dominated the ground floor; a small but compact kitchen separated what could have been a dining room. Two bedrooms and a bathroom surrounded a small landing upstairs. I noticed a small trap-door in the ceiling above the landing. Being tucked away in the corner, it was easily missed unless the light from a narrow window shone onto it. The sun was just in the right place to illuminate that landing. Intrigued by what might be in the loft space, I decided to look so went back to the car for a flashlight. I found an old rickety stepladder in the shed at the bottom of the garden which enabled me to reach up to the trap door. The loft-space was a good place to see the condition of the roof beams, always important in older property.

After some difficulty, I opened the trap door in the ceiling and was showered with the inevitable dust and cobwebs, although not as many as might have been expected. Wooden eaves were just visible as they descended down to the roof beams. Apart from some old wooden planks and newspapers there was little else to be seen. I was about to close the door when a scuffling sound followed by a whine disturbed the quietness, it came from the corner of the roof space. I shone the torch in the direction of the sound and just missed what looked to be a squirrel. It must have had its nest somewhere in the roof space.

The light illuminated what looked like an old leather suitcase. I squeezed into the space and pulled it towards the opening. It was very heavy and covered in dust. After some difficulty I brought the case down and placed it on the floor. The lock on the case was damaged so the lid opened easily. Inside were handwritten documents, some books, and diaries. I could hardly suppress my excitement at such a find. But what were they? They had clearly belonged to a previous owner of the cottage. But what caught my attention were the faded words *Top Secret* stamped across some of the documents.

On closer examination I found them to be photocopies of classified papers dating back over forty years. It was a treasure trove for any journalist, but what were the implications of illegally possessing such documents? Were they copies? What was the connection to Malcolm Walker? It was the diaries and handwritten notes that aroused my interest. They looked like the draft of a person's memoires. On looking through them quickly, I made a discovery that shook me. The diaries clearly showed that Malcolm Walker was actually a Dr Henry Fellows, a high ranking scientist who had been a member of the British team on the Manhattan Atomic Bomb Project of the Second World War and later a Chief Scientist in the British Nuclear Weapons Programme at an establishment called Fort Halborn. For some reason he had changed his name at the time of purchasing the cottage. It was the name 'Fellows' that made by heart pound. In my Internet search for names I had been given by the Kuwait Professor, a Dr Henry Fellows came up. He was the founder of The International Brotherhood Foundation, which later appeared to have had some tentative links to Al-Qaeda.

My heartbeat was still racing, either from excitement or apprehension. Thinking about the coincidence and the one-in-a-million chance of the name Fellows appearing a second time just prolonged my condition. Why had Fellows changed his name? What was he doing living here in this remote Cotswold village when he was reported dead about forty years ago? The mystery deepened and now I was becoming inextricably linked to it. I felt like fate had taken over my life. Was my destiny planned by some unknown entity? I was not religious and believed one had some measure of control over what happened in life. Now I began to doubt my own beliefs. I had to find out more about this man and his life.

The contents of the case made me temporarily forget about the cottage. I could only think about what was in the papers and diaries. I felt like a trespasser looking into someone's personal life. Whatever these papers contained, some of it was state property. Why had they been deliberately hidden? If so, there had to be a reason. I needed to find out. I was an investigative journalist. That justification, however, did not obscure my feeling of guilt, and an uncomfortable feeling that someone might find out I possessed state secret papers. Many questions went through my mind. Should I report my findings to the police? Should I tell Jeremy? Should I contact the owner, Ruth Goodman? Should I tell Robert? When faced with such decisions I have always followed my instinct; it was to investigate further. Once again, what was meant to be a weekend break to find a quiet place of refuge was becoming a new assignment. Like it or not, I was now involved. There was no escape.

I reassured myself that the probable historical value of the documents justified their removal. Stimulated by my recent experience in the Middle East, I wondered if I was being set up again. Had someone already visited the cottage seeking these documents? I was reminded of the old maxim – don't trust anyone.

Inadvertently, I placed the case on the floor near the south-facing window so I could see the contents more clearly. Shafts of sunlight intermittently blocked by passing clouds were finding their way into the room through the small leaded windows. At the instant I opened the battered suitcase; a ray of sunlight illuminated it. Was it a warning? I remembered the Greek myth of Pandora's Box, and I had opened it.

The sunlight now lit up the cottage and changed the atmosphere from one of sadness to one of joy. It was as though a message was being sent from above. The fireball responsible for this light radiates continuously; it was the bringer of all life on earth, everything living owed its existence to the energy being released by countless trillions of hydrogen atoms being fused into helium atoms at temperatures of hundreds of millions of degrees. The sun is a continuous nuclear chain reaction producing a furnace of heat energy on which all life depends. Man had learned how to generate and release these energy liberating processes but has yet to learn how to control them. The possibilities of unlimited sources of energy are within reach. Unfortunately we have only succeeded so far in producing the thermonuclear bomb which hovers over mankind like the *Sword of Damocles*.

Even though the sun produced a warm glow to the room, I began to feel cold and shivered. I could sense evil in the room. Something dreadful had happened here. The room had an aura which I hadn't noticed before. Whatever it was, the sun had triggered it. Perhaps it was the thought of breaking the law. The Official Secrets Act was quite clear about the consequences of possessing classified documents. My earlier brief encounter with the security services was still uppermost in my mind and added to my apprehension, but it might be something else.

I looked out of the rear window and noticed for the first time the magnificent panoramic view across the valley. It was a typical English country scene. The landscape was bathed in a golden sunlight. Stone cottages nestled in the hills like they were painted in by an artist. This was an enchanting place, but now tainted by a mystery surrounding its deceased occupant.

I placed the suitcase on the back seat of my car, resisting the temptation to read more of the papers. Returning to the cottage to lock the door, I noticed that one of the windows was partially open. It ought to have been closed from the inside. On closer examination, it looked as though it had been recently forced open. Had someone else been to the cottage? That would explain the tyre tracks, but why? Could they have been looking for the papers that

I had discovered, or was it something else? The mystery deepened. My investigative instincts were activated. I closed the window. Looking down at the floor, I noticed a small piece of tissue paper with a light red stain on it. I instinctively placed it in my pocket. After taking a last look around, I locked the front door and walked to the car. It was getting late so I decided to return to London.

During the drive back to London through the Wiltshire countryside and the M4 motorway, my thoughts were on the papers. I then remembered I still had the key to the cottage that I had agreed to return to Gladys at the Post Office. The excitement of my discoveries had completely blocked my memory. I would call her in the morning. It was almost dark when I arrived at the underground garage of my apartment block in Knightsbridge. I inserted a special security card into the machine to gain entry. Some of the tenants of the prestigious apartments were senior civil servants and police officers. Their identities had to be protected so the very best security system had been installed. Realising their nearness only added to my fears about what I possessed.

The first thing I noticed on entering the apartment was the light flashing on my phone. There were two calls. One was from security, informing me that a letter had been delivered by hand to me. I went down to the foyer and collected the letter from Henry, the security guard. It had no postmark but my address written clearly on it. I took it back to the apartment and opened it. Written on the single sheet of paper was a single telephone number that I didn't recognise. Out of curiosity I dialled the number. A woman's toneless voice said, '*Your life is in great danger* short pause *Watch your back.*' It was obviously recorded. When receiving a threatening call it becomes compulsive to listen to it again. I redialled the number but the message had been removed. It must have been a self-destruct phone message which made the call even more intriguing. Somebody had gone to a lot of trouble using the latest technology to get the message to me. But why? I phoned Robert who had made the other call only minutes before I returned to the apartment. He answered immediately.

'Glad you called; things have developed here in the US. The

White House Press Office has invited us and other international journalists to a conference on the Middle East in Washington next Thursday, 18 November. You must have impressed someone high up in the Administration.' He paused, so I wondered what was coming next.

'I couldn't locate Houseman. He seems to have disappeared and his PA wouldn't say when he will return. I get the feeling that he doesn't want to speak to us. Anyway I have booked you on a Concorde flight to Washington on Wednesday, assuming you can come over.'

Putting on my angry voice I said, 'You should have asked me first before you made the arrangements. Remember I'm supposed to be recuperating after the Kuwaiti ordeal. I have just received a death warning on the telephone. It must be associated with my visit to Kuwait. I'm beginning to wish I had not accepted the assignment.'

There was a long silence. I deliberately omitted telling him about Henry Fellows and the find at Stones End. He probably perceived my lack of enthusiasm and annoyance and said, 'Sorry you feel that way but as your agent I thought it would be a great opportunity for you. We can't put the clock back. If you're in danger wouldn't it be better to have the Government and FBI protecting you.'

'OK, but there are things we need to talk about. I will come to Washington and thanks for the Concorde seat. I have never flown on a supersonic jet before.'

He continued, 'The short flight will remove the jet lag and after your problems in Kuwait it was the least I could do. You can collect the tickets at the airport. I will meet you at Dulles airport on Wednesday, take care.'

I looked over at the old case full of documents which lay on the floor beside my desk. My physical body longed for sleep but curiosity got the better of me so I looked through a few more papers in the treasure chest that had by chance fallen into my possession. After pouring myself a Napoleon brandy to revive my senses I began to reflect on the day. It had started with a search for a peaceful haven to get away from it all. It had ended with being in possession of what could be the greatest story of the century and finished with being invited by the White House to attend a conference on what looked like a Middle East crisis in the making. I thought it strange to be selected by the White House Press Office when I had no past close association with it. I did know some Washington journalists during the Iraq war but that hardly qualified me for such an invitation. It had to be related to my Kuwait visit. There was much to do. First, I had to see if there was anything in the Fellows' papers that could shed some light on what was happening in the Middle East. There had to be some connection to the current crisis. I still had a feeling of uneasiness about the papers. There were questions to be answered. Who was Henry Fellows? Why did he change his name and live in seclusion? Why did he possess top secret material going back over forty years? Were they revealing some dark secrets of murder, corruption and espionage? I instinctively knew the answers were buried somewhere in papers. With the benefit of hindsight and knowing what lay ahead, I would have thrown the papers in the bin and refused to go to Washington.

Before opening the case I switched on the computer to check my emails. The last one contained the same warning message as on the telephone. The sender had both my email and postal address. I began to wonder if my watchers, whoever they were, knew about Fellows. They certainly knew how to find me and access my computer. I created a new encrypted file to enter key bits of information obtained from the Fellows' papers. This would enable me to keep a safe and secure record. It was going to be a long night. I wanted to find out as much as I could before the meeting in Washington.

The papers were carefully filed by date as though they were being prepared to be used as evidence in a court. There were documents extending back to 1934 totalling about three hundred pages. Most related to Fellows' professional and personal life. They essentially constituted his memoires. It was tempting to work back from his death since I wanted to know about his life, so it would be necessary to start at the beginning. Realising it would take a lot of time, I quickly scanned through what he wrote in the year before his death. Fellows had a visit from his niece Ruth Goodman. Had he told Ruth about the papers? I found a handwritten scribbled note attached to the last paper. It was like a last will, stating that in the event of his death the papers, which were deposited in a bank safe, should be given personally to Dr David Simons. It gave no further details except saying that Simons would know what to do. It assumed that whoever possessed the papers knew the identity and whereabouts of Simons. No doubt that was revealed somewhere in the papers. It meant that what I possessed were copies of the original papers. Some of the writing was poor and hardly discernable. Scientists, like medical doctors, are known to be poor writers. They think ahead and often miss out words.

The more I read, the more I was intrigued with Henry Fellows' life. But what I read was enough to make it urgent to talk to Ruth Goodman and find out more about her uncle. It was obvious that she must have acquired the original memoires. I would call her in the morning using the pretext of being a prospective buyer of the cottage. Jeremy would have told her my name and my interest in viewing it. I wondered how much she knew about her uncle's work and the secrets he had so carefully hidden away. Some people would kill for the material that I possessed. If that was the reason why Fellows had died then it raised very worrying questions. Was he murdered, or did he die of natural causes?

There was something bugging me about the find. Clearly Fellows had taken great care in safely placing his papers in a bank depository but why stash away copies in an old case in the loft of his house, not exactly the most secure place, knowing that one day they would be found? There was something illogical about doing that, especially for a physicist.

It took me an hour to write notes on the computer. I used the password 'Trinity' to protect the computer files; it seemed appropriate. After placing the papers in my safe and activating the security system, I retired for the night. As I undressed, the stained tissue paper I had picked up from the cottage dropped out of my trouser pocket. Not appreciating its relevance at the time and for reasons unknown, I placed it in the bedside table drawer rather than the bin; perhaps because it had on it what looked like a blood stain. I was desperately tired. Oblivion was all I craved for, but I had a problem getting to sleep owing to the adrenaline still flowing in my veins after the day's events. Eventually I slipped into a deep sleep.

At eight o'clock the next morning I was again awoken by the bedside telephone. The metallic tone vibrated my eyeballs and I felt my stomach follow in unison. It was the voice again warning me of my impending doom. Before I could say anything the caller rang off. I checked the number but none appeared. Instinctively, I switched on my computer and, as expected, the same message was in my email box. Fortunately the call was not on my mobile – so at least the mystery caller did not have that number. I showered, cooked myself a hearty breakfast, relieving my over-stocked fridge of bacon and eggs. I had learned a long time ago that starting the day with a full stomach meant lunch can be missed without any detrimental affects to the daily diet, particularly when the day ahead could be full of uncertainties. My brain had already mapped out the agenda for the day. I would read more of Fellows' papers and scan the most interesting parts into my laptop. I would then track down Ruth Goodman. She was a student at Cambridge so that should be easy. I knew the university very well. In my Oxbridge days, competition between the universities meant frequent exchanges in sporting events and scholarly endeavours. My first action was to call Jeremy about the cottage and find Ruth's telephone number. Then I would disconnect the phone to avoid interruptions and more threatening calls. If it were not for my current predicament, I would have contacted the police, but that would require explanations too difficult to contemplate.

I dialled Simms Estates. 'Hi Jeremy, its Paul. I viewed the cottage yesterday and it has potential. I need a few days to think about it. Meanwhile can you let me have Ruth Goodman's telephone number as there are few things I would like to know?' There was a pregnant pause. I realised too late I had opened myself up to an obvious question.

'What do you need to know? I have all the background information on the property.'

'I just wanted to know what her uncle had told her about living in the area,' I replied. It seemed like a weak answer. Jeremy told me that she did not have a personal number and I would have to go through the university exchange.

He then said belatedly, 'I forgot to tell you there is only a hundred years lease left on the property which is why the price is so low.'

'Who are the owners?' I asked.

'A trust company here in London.' I perceived Jeremy was not as friendly as usual and was holding something back. Agents do not like potential buyers talking to their clients, fearing side deals. He may have received a call from Gladys telling him about my questions. I thanked him for the opportunity to see the cottage and told him I would post back the key and call him in a few weeks. Before disconnecting the phone, I called Gladys to apologise for not returning the key. She understood and said that she had a spare one anyway. I asked her if anyone else had been to the cottage in the last few weeks. She replied, 'Not to my knowledge. I have the only keys, although Ruth might have one.' I thanked her and rang off. I disconnected my main telephone but kept my mobile switched on, then set about reading the Fellows' papers.

PART 2
THE HISTORY

CHAPTER 3

The Brotherhood Foundation
1933-39

Now the rain had stopped, David Simons stepped out from his one-bed roomed flat in Barter Street, a short distance from the British Museum in Bloomsbury, on a cold grey morning. It was Thursday, 14 September, 1933. The streets were wet and slippery from the rain that had fallen all night. As he crossed the street and walked along Kingsway towards the Strand, thoughts stirred within him about the future, his future, the future of the world. His thoughts were inspired by a book he had recently read by H. G. Wells called, *The Shape of Things to Come*. Published in 1931, it portrayed with simple clarity, Wells' dream of the future.

Born German Jews, the Simons family foresaw the dangers that lay ahead with the rising power of Nazism. German defeat in the First World War resulted in rage, unemployment and disenchantment with the 1919 Treaty of Versailles. It was fertile ground for the nationalism and the rise of the Nazi Party. Jews were being blamed for the economic decline of the country and were in the firing line for persecution. David Simons had gained his PhD in physics on atomic structure at the University of Berlin in 1930 against this rising threat. He was an intelligent young man with an analytical mind but was also a thoughtful and caring person.

When Adolf Hitler was appointed Chancellor of Germany on 30 January, 1933 after the Reichstag fire, the persecution of the Jews started. Later in 1935, the Nazis passed new laws at Nuremberg depriving Jews of their rights to citizenship. In spite of this, David's parents did not want to leave Berlin but decided that their son should do so. They arranged for him to travel to London via the channel port of Calais in France. Being fearful for their lives in Germany, it had been hard for him to leave but the prospect of a teaching job at Imperial College in London was too good an opportunity to miss. An old family friend was a lecturer at the university and arranged for David to have a temporary appointment as a Research Assistant. Money was transferred to a London bank from Berlin since academic pay was very low. About the same time, thousands of German Jewish scientists and scholars lost their jobs and were emigrating to America and England bringing with them ideas and knowledge which would later prove invaluable to their host's nations. The British Government placed limits on immigration, admitting only those with skills or academic qualifications required at the time. It was the start of a mass exodus from Europe to America. Britain still valued freedom and protected democratic institutions but the Nazis in England were also becoming active. The speeches of Oswald Mosley, the English Nazi and leader of the British Union Party, in the East End of London and the antics of his followers, resulted in street riots. They frightened the Jewish community.

David Simons had a day off from the university and decided to attend a lecture being given at Kings College, in the Strand, on the new X-ray physics. The lecture was being given by Dr Leo Szilard,* a Hungarian Jewish physicist who had also left Germany in fear of persecution. Later, David discovered Szilard had known H. G. Wells and, like he, was a great admirer of his books so they shared a common interest. As he approached the university a small crowd was gathered outside. There were many other foreign students at the university. Szilard's lecture stimulated much interest and evoked many questions from the audience about where recent developments in nuclear physics would lead.

Szilard was a powerful character with a profound sense of destiny. He spoke at length about the destiny of the world and the need for scientists to have more influence over events currently dominated entirely by politicians and political systems. The events

* *The character David Simons is fictitious but Leo Szilard was a major player in the development of the atomic bomb and its political aftermath.*

that were taking place in Europe were clearly uppermost in his mind. He had a profound effect on the students attending the talk. After the lecture they invited Szilard for tea. They quizzed him about his ideas of a new world in which science and scientists would play a more dominant role.

Szilard told the students a true scientist must be above politics, have a free mind and seek knowledge for the benefit of humanity. Knowledge gives power, but with it comes responsibility. Scientists must not allow knowledge to be limited to the few, it must be universal. Scientists must take the consequences of their actions.

He went on to tell them about his ideas for a 'Republic of Science'. Something he had taken from H. G. Wells' book, The Open Conspiracy. Wells had foreseen a society in which scientists, industrialists and financiers colluded to establish a world order. Szilard and Wells had met in 1929 and discussed many of the themes expressed in the latter's books.

He had already started to think about such a New World Order whilst at the University of Berlin with contemporaries such as Einstein, Wigner, Max Plank and Max Von Laue. The students were spellbound by Szilard's words. They were said with a forceful conviction. He left them that day with new ideas and visions which were to have a profound effect on the lives of some of them. The students agreed to meet again in about a month's time to discuss further how they might form a society. As he walked back to his flat, David Simons pondered on whether a group of students, however well-intentioned, could ever succeed in the political climate now developing in Europe.

Two months later the group of students did meet and together with others who had not attended Szilard's talk, formed a society. They named it 'The Brotherhood Society of Scientists.' David had made many friends and was excited at being one of the founders of this new Brotherhood. In the following year, the Brotherhood Society recruited a wealthy graduate named John Cecil who generously donated to it the sum of £2000 on the condition a constitution for the new Society was established. There would be an elected Council and a President. It was to be organized like other professional societies that existed in London at the time. Cecil wanted assurance it would remain non-political. The Council would review the qualifications and aspirations of people who wanted to become members. An annual membership fee would be charged. John was thought to be a distant relative of Robert Cecil, the late nineteenth century Prime Minister, Lord Salisbury, who had also been the Chancellor of the University of Oxford.

The twelve founding members of The Brotherhood agreed to accept Cecil's terms and elected him to be their first President. David, one of the twelve, had originally asked Leo Szilard to be the President since it was his talk that gave students the idea of forming the Society. Szilard fully supported the ideals and aims of the new Society, but did not want to belong to anything that might hinder his chances of emigrating to America and later becoming an American citizen.

The Brotherhood became known as *Der Bund* among its many German members who became a significant driving force behind it. The Constitution proposed to bring together scientists with a common scientific purpose whose ultimate aim would be to exert a strong positive influence on society and democratically elected governments.

Members would be encouraged to acquire influential positions in public and private institutions and when possible in government. There was a predictable opposition from all the learned societies and established institutions who saw The Brotherhood Society as a threat since it had adopted many of the ideals and aims that were already embodied in their own institutions. The difference was The Brotherhood was to be open to international members and was inclusive of scientists from all disciplines. At the time there was no such international organization dedicated to bringing like-minded scientists together. People who possessed knowledge and the understanding of how it could be used to develop a new technological world had to possess the power to use it. In the late 1930s it was a lofty idea when the threat of a Second World War loomed on the horizon.

In the years that followed to 1939, the membership of The Brotherhood increased to forty scientists, mainly from English universities, although a small number were from continental Europe, mainly Germany. The worsening situation in Europe made communication between countries increasingly difficult. In early 1939, David Simons replaced John Cecil and became the President.

The 1930s were an important decade for science. New fundamental discoveries were made about the basic structure of matter. Theories of the possibilities of the release of immense energy from the very heart of atoms were being pursued experimentally. Chadwick's discovery of the neutron in 1932 marked the beginning of the understanding of how the atomic nucleus was structured. It was uncharged and, therefore, once released from the nucleus could be used to probe the nucleus of atoms. David Simons took an interest in the exciting work being carried out in nuclear physics, particularly Chadwick's work. New ideas were discussed about how it might be possible for the neutron to be used to break up the nucleus and release other neutrons thus starting a chain reaction. Each break-up would release energy in excess of that of the bombarding neutron. He was becoming increasingly aware of where such possibilities would lead if the theories could be proved to be true. But he would have to wait until 1938 when Fermi discovered induced radioactivity by neutrons which led to the proposition that a chain reaction resulting from splitting the atom could produce enormous quantities of energy.

In September 1938, Henry Fellows, a star pupil at Wellington, the famous public school, went up to Cambridge having won a scholarship. He was one of a number of brilliant young men who were at Cambridge at the time. Born into a military family, he was expected to follow the traditional army career but he excelled in physics and chemistry and was destined to make his mark on history in a different connection.

Henry was six feet tall, with an athletic physique and took most of the school prizes for sport, unlike most of the other science students who preferred more sedentary ways to spend their time. He was, however, a brilliant scholar and won prizes for mathematics and philosophy. After writing a thesis about new sources of nuclear energy, he was noticed by Dr Robert Schiller, a Senior Fellow and distinguished theoretical physicist who had been working on the transuranic elements. He became Henry's mentor and close friend. Long into the night, they discussed the threat to Europe of Nazi Germany. Military power depended upon the application of technology to make weapons for war. The Cambridge scientists formed a society like The Brotherhood Foundation but they were more of a debating society motivated by political idealism than a scientific group. They believed it was time to replace the irrationalism and insanity of war with rationalism and reason – the true path of science.

Schiller told Fellows that a professor from Cambridge visiting London a few months earlier had been approached by a David Simons, at a Vice Chancellor's dinner, about the Cambridge scientists joining their new society known as The Brotherhood Society of Scientists. They wanted to be strong enough to exert influence on the Government to only use scientific knowledge for the betterment of society and humanity. It had a small but distinguished membership and was gaining strength.

Schiller said, 'It seems this society may have much in common with our own. Can I suggest that you write to this chap Simons and arrange a meeting?' Two weeks later, Simons drafted a reply to Fellows' letter suggesting they met as soon as possible to discuss the matter, preferably in London.

Dark war clouds were gathering over continental Europe but on the day of the meeting, the sun was shining in a cloudless blue sky over the River Thames. The date was 3 September, 1939. The Houses of Parliament were in deep session due to the failure of Germany to respond to the ultimatum given by the Prime Minister, Neville Chamberlain. Time was running out, war looked inevitable. The two scientists met at Westminster Bridge and walked along the river embankment. They instantly took a liking to each other and discussed at length their respective societies. It became clear there was a close synergy in their aims. They agreed that a single society would be more effective. The two men had minor differences of opinion on how secret it should or could be. Fellows was worried about the Brotherhood Society being used by the wrong people for the wrong purposes. Secret societies were always viewed with suspicion, the Freemasons were an example.

Simons said, 'The Brotherhood Society is different since it is based on reality and truth and not ancient myths.' Fellows replied, 'Yes, that's true, but the aims are similar, influencing those with power, placing members in positions of power and having an exclusive membership. But like the Masons, we must declare our aims to be for the good of humanity, otherwise people may view us with suspicion. We will only succeed if the names of our members are kept secret. In that sense we have to operate like the Masons. We need to make sure that our governing council operates like an inner sanctum with the power to vet new members and ensure that The Brotherhood Society is not infiltrated by people with their own selfish agendas.'

The two men agreed to take a proposal to amalgamate their societies back to their members. It would require a change to the constitution. They agreed the need to change the name to 'The Brotherhood Foundation.' They also realised that an increased membership would make secrecy difficult to maintain. The real power would reside with members of the Council or Inner Sanctum. They would be given aliases to protect their identity. Only the members of this would know each other. This secrecy was not what they wanted but was necessary as a protective safeguard against those who might wish to infiltrate it for the wrong reasons.

The two men mused over the new science and the developments that were going to change the world. It had been an eventful year. The Nobel Prize laureate, Albert Einstein, had escaped from Germany to America after the Nazis had seized his property. Two German Chemists, Otto Hahn and Fritz Straussman, split the uranium atom, thus demonstrating fission was possible. The gate had been opened to a new future. Scientists now had an awesome responsibility, from which they could not abdicate. They possessed the knowledge, but lacked the power to make decisions on how it should be used. It was a timely driving force for the formation of the new Brotherhood Foundation.

Fellows and Simons walked back to Westminster Bridge just as a barge loaded with a heavy cargo concealed by a dark covering was passing under it. It had probably been downloaded from one of the many ships in the East India docks. They looked up at the large buildings clustered around them and thought how vulnerable large cities like London were to air attack. Workmen were already constructing makeshift shelters as though expecting one. Whilst walking up towards Charing Cross station they heard a newsboy shouting, '*War Declared, read all about it*'.

They looked gravely at each other. What they had come to London to discuss now seemed to pale into insignificance, but future events would show their new Foundation would have a significant role to play. At that moment as they looked at each other in silence, a solitary Spitfire roared overhead, just skimming the top of Big Ben.

It was 11.15 am on 3 September, 1939. Shortly after, Prime Minister Neville Chamberlain went on the radio to announce to the British people that they were at war with Germany.

Fellows said to Simons, 'I must return to Cambridge, there will be much to do now that we are in a state of war'. He knew he would be called into military service. Being a German Jew, David Simons was uncertain about his fate. He had been considering emigrating to America to join his many friends and colleagues but that was now going to be very difficult. He would write to Leo Szilard, who was at Columbia University working on uranium fission and also an advisor to the American Government. Perhaps he would be able to find him a job. England had been Simons' home for six years but it was no longer a safe haven. If Hitler successfully invaded and conquered Britain, then all Jews would suffer the same fate as their brethren in the other European countries that had fallen to the Nazis. He was fearful of the fate of his family in Berlin since he had received no letters from them for over a year.

David Simons called a meeting of members of The Brotherhood and invited Henry Fellows to be present with three other Cambridge scientists. Its purpose was to discuss the new proposals for changes to the Constitution for the setting up of 'The Brotherhood Foundation'. All existing members would automatically be transferred to the new body. Their names and details would be kept confidential. Simons updated those present with the latest scientific developments taking place in uranium fission. The possibility of being able to make a sustainable chain reaction and, therefore, a massive explosive bomb, an atom bomb, looked increasing likely. Thirteen of the sixteen members assembled in a locked room at Kings College to discuss the future of their new Foundation. The three who were not present had already left to work in America. The proposals put forward by Simons and Fellows were accepted and a new constitution was agreed for the Foundation. Simons would stay as President and Fellows would be the Vice President. The original thirteen members would form the secret Inner Sanctum of the Foundation. It would acquire funds to support its work. This would be done through the creation of a commercial arm to be known as Science International which would be the public, non-secret part of the Foundation. It would derive income from sponsors, conferences and meetings. The impending war now made it imperative for scientists to work together to defeat the German threat of world domination. The prospect of developing a super bomb was fast becoming a reality since most of the physics was understood. It was imperative Nazi Germany was stopped from developing such a bomb.

Britain was under threat of invasion and did not have the physical resources to develop an atomic bomb. The Inner Sanctum agreed that if the Americans decided to undertake such a task then The Foundation should strive to have its members involved. But first, America would need a reason to be brought into the war.

They had to wait until 7 December, 1941 for the attack on Pearl Harbour on the Hawaiian Island of Oahu for this to happen. Before then, London would be bombed and almost devastated. The decision made by a number of British nuclear scientists to go to America, some of which were Foundation members, was, in hindsight, a wise one.

On Christmas Eve 1939, a letter arrived from Szilard inviting David Simons to work with him on a new project being planned in Chicago, but he would need to find his own way to America. He immediately wrote to Henry telling him about the job offer.

Henry Fellows had submitted his thesis to the university but was expecting to be called to military service, particularly in view of his family connections. Robert Schiller was very impressed with Fellows' work and wrote to the Prime Minister about arranging for him to be exempt and continue with his research on uranium separation. Churchill had been briefed about the atomic bomb work and decided he needed his own personal secret advisory committee. Schiller and Fellows were invited to join the committee, which gave them the opportunity to influence events. The Brotherhood had made its first significant step. Henry was pleased to receive David's letter asking for a meeting of the Inner Sanctum of The Brotherhood. He would have some good news for them.

On 2 August, 1940, Szilard[1] went to see Einstein about the war in Europe and persuaded him to write to President Roosevelt about the dangers facing the world if Germany developed an atom bomb. The President's rather indifferent reply caused concern, but at least the matter had been brought to his attention. The American scientific community knew what was going on in Germany so took steps to speed up their own nuclear research programme.

Over thirty German scientists were in British universities. Many were being lured to America by attractive job offers in research. Intelligence sources indicated the Germans were embarked on an atomic weapons development programme. The atomic scientists knew the country still had both the scientific and material resources to make a bomb. But did the Nazis have the understanding to support it? Germany had a well-established chemical industry and access to natural uranium from the Belgium Congo, but research on how to extract the required uranium 235 from the natural ore was urgently needed.

An official liaison between the American National Defence Research Council and the British government started in the winter of 1941 with the visit of James Conant to London. He had been an outspoken opponent of American isolationism since the start of the European war so Churchill was pleased to meet him on the first visit. It had been the Prime Minister's constant annoyance that his friend Roosevelt had been unable to convince the American people to join the war. There was a significant German community and others who had no stomach for another European war. America enjoyed its degree of isolation.

During his visit, Conant was granted an honorary degree at Cambridge. Fellows and Shiller had the opportunity to meet him and discuss the feasibility of making a uranium bomb, without saying too much about the success of British researchers on uranium separation techniques. They said nothing about their work on Churchill's secret advisory committee. Conant's visit was political rather than technical, but the man had a good grasp of the physics and chemistry problems associated with uranium purification and tried hard to extract information from the scientists. Thus two members of the Brotherhood succeeded in making contact with a key person in the American government, particularly as Conant promised to send one of his aides to help set up a joint working party.

The British Committee, known as MAUD[2] (Military Application of Uranium Disintegration) submitted its report to Roosevelt. Shortly after, a recommendation was made that Britain should collaborate with America on the urgent development of an atomic bomb. Roosevelt made the decision to build an atomic bomb on 9 October, 1941. The Manhattan Project[3] was initiated. It would be for a four-year development programme. Eight British scientists, including Henry Fellows and three other members of The Brotherhood, were invited to join the Manhattan team. David Simons, who was already working in America, also joined the team. This was the chance the members had been waiting for, the possession of unique knowledge which would give them power.

CHAPTER 4

New Mexico July-August 1945
The Manhattan Project

Now I am become death, the destroyer of worlds
Robert Oppenheimer

The bright blue sky changed to a deep ultra-violet colour as the sun started to set below the horizon over the Jornada del Muerto desert on the evening of 15 July, 1945. Cool air slowly replaced the oppressive heat of the desert, which during the day had resulted in temperatures in excess of one hundred degrees Fahrenheit. The army jeep bumped over the dirt road now lit up by the sinking sun. Behind it the Oscuro Mountains cast a shadow that stretched almost to the forward test site. Henry Fellows wrestled with the wheel trying to avoid the soft patches in the track produced by an unexpected rainstorm earlier in the day. David Simons, sitting uncomfortably next to him, scanned the horizon, while Paul Fields on the back seat gripped the leather strap securing the test instruments. Three miles ahead was the steel tower which carried Fat Man, the code name for the atomic bomb that was nicknamed 'The Gadget'. If successful, its similarly named twin would be dropped on Japan if the country failed to unconditionally surrender.

The 'Bomb' was the final outcome of the Manhattan Project which started in November, 1942; the culmination of three years' work involving the world's best physicists. Thousands of people in different parts of America had participated in the project without knowing exactly what they were building. The physicist Dr Robert Oppenheimer (Oppie) and General Leslie Groves were jointly responsible for it. The latter was technically in command as it was classified as a military project but all the scientific decisions were taken by Oppie and his team of thirteen scientists based at Los Alamos. They, and a number of Groves' senior military personnel, were the only ones who knew everything about the ultimate purpose of the work. For security reasons, everyone else only had knowledge relevant to their jobs on a need-to-know basis. Even other scientists closely associated with the development of the bomb were unaware of all its scientific and military implications.

Ahead was a prefabricated steel tower over 100 feet high. Its four legs were anchored by 20 feet of concrete into the hard desert sand. The top was braced to hold an electrically driven heavy-duty winch used to lift the bomb. A number of observation stations, constructed to house instruments, were located at what was considered to be a safe survival distance from the tower. These included reinforced concrete bunkers with thick bullet-proof glass built to house cameras and other observational equipment.

A shiver ran through Fellows as he thought about what had been achieved. There was no turning back. Soon all the calculations, all the theories, all the arguments would be put to the test. Deep down he had a feeling of unease, like a trench soldier who knew his time had come to go over the top. Unknown territory lay ahead. History was about to be created which would irreversibly change the world.

Henry Fellows and David Simons had come a long way since their meeting in London in 1939. Their Brotherhood Foundation had become a serious organisation. It had endured the war years and been strengthened by increased membership from many leading American and British scientists. Four members worked on the Manhattan Project at great risk to themselves since they had not declared their membership of what could be considered a secret organisation. The FBI probably knew of its existence but did not see it as a threat, but because members' names were kept secret they would have contravened their status to work at Los Alamos.

A rainstorm over New Mexico was predicted to pass near to the test site. It caused the team some concern but Oppie was advised by the meteorologist that the weather conditions would be right at dawn on the 16 July. On that date the count-down was started and Zero was set for 0530. The site, Ground Zero, was evacuated and final checks for detonation started by the firing team, headed by the test Director Kenneth Bainbridge;* a Harvard experimental physicist; he was responsible for setting up the Trinity site and the desert laboratory. During his short stay in England he had recruited a number of good British physicists to work on the Manhattan Project, among whom were William Penny and James Chadwick.

Just before sunset the firing team was informed that a fault had been found in one of the firing circuits. A call was made to base camp for Fellows, Simons and Fields who had been involved in setting up equipment at the site, to drive to Ground Zero, find and correct the fault. They had less than four hours to complete the task before the count-down clock would be started. The fault had been traced to equipment located in a forward instrumentation bunker that housed the firing circuits. It was located about five hundred yards from the tower. The firing sequence required unlocking master switches in forward bunkers. Bainbridge's job in the control centre bunker would then be to throw the final switch to initiate detonation.

Further tests had shown up a faulty electrical connection in a cable that would carry the firing commands to the detonators on the bomb. This was so serious that Oppie ordered an immediate investigation; otherwise the test would have to be postponed. He and Groves were under strong political pressure to test the bomb as soon as possible. Delays meant security could be breached and the whole project placed in jeopardy. This problem added to the high degree of apprehension already felt by all members of the team.

Events had taken place during the last few months which showed that someone was out to sabotage the bomb test. Groves had suspected there were possibly spies and saboteurs in the Los

*Bainbridge was actually a real Harvard Physicist and the Trinity site Director.

Alamos Camp. Such suspicions were heightened when during the assembly of the bomb two weeks previously, a young electrical engineer named Peter Petrovitch disappeared. Security officers searched in vain to find him. He possessed invaluable knowledge and fears that he might have been kidnapped were raised. Before Petrovitch's disappearance, the firing codes for the test had been stolen. Groves immediately placed everybody on a total security alert. Nobody was allowed to leave the site or go anywhere alone. A checking in and out procedure was established. A new set of codes had to be formulated which put a short delay in the test programme but it did confirm that a saboteur was in the camp.

Petrovitch, a graduate of Moscow University, was a Russian émigré engineer who had fled to America before the war because of his anti-communist views. He defected while attending a conference in London, and was smuggled by ship to New York. After a lengthy investigation he was granted political asylum. The Government arranged a job for him as technician at the University of Chicago. Spotted by Fermi, he was later recruited to work on his team building the famous Chicago reactor pile. He proved to be a very able engineer and took a masters degree in electrical engineering. Fermi arranged for him to work on the team at Los Alamos. Because of Petrovitch's Russian origins, Groves had placed a special watch on him. There was nothing in his record or past activities which connected him with espionage or any illegal activity.

The date for the test of the bomb had already been delayed through bad weather. Political pressures were increasing. War casualties were mounting. An invasion of Japan was considered too costly an option since thousands of lives would be lost. It was imperative that the test went ahead as soon as weather conditions permitted. Too much depended on it; nothing less than the ending of the War. The President had been informed about the possible security problem but ordered Groves to proceed.

As time Zero approached, Fellows was reminded that a successful detonation was the ultimate test. There would be no second chance. For a moment in time, just a blip, it would be the most dangerous place on earth, a milestone in human history.

As Fellows drove up to the covered observation bunker nothing moved, except the shimmering heat waves rising from the hot desert. The temporary bunker assumed a ghostly aura of its own. Alone in the desert almost in the shadow of the tower it stood like a sentinel, the last outpost of civilisation. He parked the jeep close to the bunker. The three men gathered their test instruments and went inside, failing to see the tracks on the path leading to the tower.

The hundreds of cables connecting instruments and detonation lines were buried in the sand for protection against the high temperature of the desert. Extensive checks had been carried out at each stage of the assembly and installation of the bomb on the tower, so something had happened within the last twenty-four hours which caused the problem. Oppenheimer had insisted that only certain scientists and military experts were to be allowed near the bomb during the final crucial stages.

First, Fellows checked the cables to the detonators fitted to the explosive charges around the bomb. His worst fears were realised when he discovered a short circuit in one of the cables linking the firing circuits to the detonators. Fellows radioed the findings to control at base camp. He detected a concern when the firing officer wanted to suspend count-down, and inform Oppenheimer who said he would get back to them. The waiting seemed interminable. Outside the temperature was still in the seventies. The sand re-radiated the heat from the day. Ducts constructed deep in the sand to route the cables to the tower provided essential protection from the heat. Mattresses laid at the tower base as a precautionary measure in case the bomb fell, gave the scene a strange appearance.

Fields was standing outside looking in wonderment at the tower and its awesome load when he noticed something on the track leading to it. Alongside the many vehicle tyre marks were a number of human footprints. It was one set which seemed out of place; isolated from the rest and surrounded by deep furrows in the sand that led to one of the cable ducts. Fields had one of those unexplainable feelings that something was not quite right. He shouted to Fellows and Simons,

'Do you see anything unusual out there, about twenty yards along the track?' Both men adjusted their eyes to the fading light.

'Yes, there's an object sticking out of the sand. I only saw the footprints at first, but now I see it,' said Fellows.

Simons also saw the object which looked like a branch of a tree. They secured the hand-radio in the truck and walked to the site of the object. Fellows stopped suddenly as they approached the object, and shouted, 'My God, it's a leg.'

All three looked at it in amazement.

'David, get a shovel from the hut,' ordered Fellows.

Fortunately, shovels had been left in the hut in anticipation of them being needed for an emergency situation. They pulled the body out of the sand and discovered the damaged cables underneath it. The head was badly beaten but it was Petrovitch. He had either fallen or been placed in the cable duct over the cables. The three men looked at each other in shocked silence. Their worst fears were realised.

Simons fetched the radio from the jeep and was about to contact base when Fellows stopped him abruptly.

'We must think this out before we talk to control.'

'What do you mean think it out?' snapped Simons.

'Henry, a murder has been committed, we must report it,' shouted Fields, who further examined the body lying in the sand.

'I think he's been dead for many hours. He must have been put here after the team completed the main assembly of the bomb on the tower,' said Fellows.

'Then someone on the team must have been responsible, but why? And how did he get here?' asked Simons.

'Maybe he was killed yesterday and brought here after everyone had left the site,' said Fields.

'But why, for what reason would someone bring him here at such great risk and then damage the cables, knowing he would be found?' asked Fellows.

'Perhaps he was meant to be found,' suggested Fields.

'For that to have happened more than one person had to be involved,' said Fellows.

They knew that Oppenheimer would be in conference with the others about the cable problems and would soon be calling them. Little time was left to decide what to do. Fellows and Simons had suspected some members of their Brotherhood might be working for the enemy. There were an increasing number of scientists who had openly expressed doubts about the ethical validity of the atomic bomb and the secrecy that surrounded it. Others were worried about destroying the world. Some believed that the scientific discoveries and technology should be made universally known; it was part of the scientific ethos. But the Manhattan Project was born out of the need to win the war and was strictly under the control of the military and the Government. Einstein and other eminent scientists had tried in vain to stop the US Government from developing the atomic bomb.

Paul Fields was not a member of The Brotherhood. He had worked hard with the team but had concerns about the morality of what was being done. The question that faced Fellows and Simons was, could he be trusted with their secret? They had little choice now but to confide in him. They knew the risk but a quick decision had to be made.

'Paul' shouted Simons. 'We need to talk.'

The three men returned to the bunker. Fellows spoke first.

'We are going to tell you something which might, I say might, because we do not know yet, have a connection to the murder. Four of the scientific team belong to a secret organisation founded by David and me, known as The Brotherhood Foundation. It was established back in England in 1939 as a secret society by a group of English and German scientists. Its aim was to ensure that politicians and governments can never have complete power to use the inventions and developments of science for evil purposes. It was the Nazi take-over of Germany and the subsequent Second World War which made us decide to start the society. We named it The Brotherhood Foundation.

The bomb sitting on top of that tower is the most powerful thing ever created by scientists; they must have the power to influence future governments on its use. With that comes responsibility. Therefore to ensure our aims are not usurped, the names of members of our Foundation must be kept secret.'

Fields listened intently while Fellows continued to tell him how the worldwide network was set up and about their plans after the war. He emphasised they were not motivated by political ambition and did not intend to challenge the authority of democratically elected governments, but they were deeply concerned about the knowledge of how to make the bomb falling into the hands of Fascists or Communists who would use it to threaten the peace of the world. The Brotherhood had pledged itself to preventing that from happening. The events of the last few months and now the murder convinced them that a spy ring was operating inside Los Alamos and information was being leaked out. Fields looked at both men and said, 'Count me in. How do I become a member of your Foundation?'

'For now just swear to secrecy, but I warn you that members who break our code are expelled and dealt with severely,' Simons said.

Without going into further details, Fields agreed to abide by the rules and swore an oath of allegiance. They could now talk about what to do with Petrovitch's body. It was obvious that someone or people close to the project knew about the murder. Did they want it discovered to delay the test? Did they want it covered up since there would be no trace after the test? These questions weighed heavily on their minds. If they reported the murder then Oppie would have no choice but to postpone the test. Things could then go very wrong, the weather, the equipment, further sabotage. Washington would send in the FBI, the whole thing would be in a state of chaos, but if they repaired the cable and said nothing, only the murderer would know.

They agreed in the interests of the project not to report their discovery or ever reveal it to anyone but to keep it a secret for all time. They would always be thought of as conspirators in murder if anyone found out, knowing, of course, that someone back at base camp would know the truth. Fellows proposed the body be given a proper burial. Fields volunteered to dig a grave. The heat of the explosion would vaporise everything anyway. All the sand close by would be turned to glass and no possible trace would be found, perhaps a fitting tomb. Sharing the responsibility they all lifted the body into the shallow grave. Just as the last shovel of sand was put into the grave a message came over the radio from the control room telling them to proceed with the cable repairs and return as soon as possible.

Oppenheimer had consulted Bohr and Fermi or Baker and Farmer, as they were called. Code names were used to conceal their true identity from the media as both men were Nobel Prize winners and, therefore, famous names. He telephoned Groves and his close confidante Robert Serber, who were busy organising the viewing arrangements on Compania Hill, 20 miles northwest of the tower. People from Los Alamos were already arriving there to witness the great event. It was agreed the count-down be continued. Oppie told Serber to increase security since the project was in its final hours. He was the only person whom Oppie trusted. The two men had been close friends before the war. Serber had written the Los Alamos Primer, which had become a sort of manual for the scientists working on the project. He commanded respect from everyone on the team and would become a key person in the American atomic weapons programme after the Trinity test.

Robert Oppenheimer's eyes betrayed tiredness. He was the mastermind of the Manhattan Project with the intellect and political will to succeed. But he now felt the awesome responsibility of what lay before him. The failure of equipment at this late stage had always been a worry. There was no turning back, the bomb had to work. He was driven more by the scientific challenge than the military implications of the project. Watching the crew raising the bomb to the platform on the tower had added to the tension. Chain smoking and meditating poetry gave Oppie some relief. He had read the Bhagavad-Gita, an extensive work discovered while at Harvard. At Berkeley he had learned Sanskrit from the scholar Arthur Ryder. It gave him a greater understanding of the original text, a copy of which he kept on his book shelf.

Oppenheimer thought deeply about what he was about to do. The world would be changed forever, mankind would make one of those giant leaps forward when theory would be tested and verified. What would be done with it? He knew the creators, the scientists would not be the controllers; the power would be passed on. That worried him greatly, but without the money and necessity to end the war, the project would still be on the blackboard. Huge advances had been made in communication, medicine and aircraft design as a result of the war.

He reflected on what could be done after the war to provide the same impetus for science and technology. Was it always necessary to have wars to make such investments? Scientists must have a greater influence on events. Politics and science must have a meeting place. He did not know then about the secret Brotherhood Foundation and the members of his team who were part of it. Without realising it he had identified with the Foundation's aims.

The weather forecast given by the meteorologist reported light winds and clear skies over the test site. The favourable weather report confirmed the decision to detonate the bomb on at 0530. It was Monday the 16 July, a day to remember.

It took the three men over three hours to replace the broken cables and test out the equipment. It was close to midnight before they returned to Control to be greeted by an anxious firing director. The command centre was directly connected by telephone to Base Camp which was ten miles from the Ground Zero. Simons and Fields uncomfortably set about checking instruments with the knowledge that one or more of their colleagues, perhaps someone close to them at the control centre was a murderer and a traitor, but now it was time to focus and concentrate on their task.

It was a dark clear night; the air was still and cold in the desert. Suntan lotion was passed around. It was a strange sight to see the world's most distinguished scientists putting on suntan lotion at night. They put on dark glasses so they could look straight at the tower.

The count-down was relayed to Base Camp by loudspeaker.

The speaker in the control room warned everybody not to look directly at the flash but to turn away and lie down to avoid the shock wave. It was obvious that nobody on the hill was going to take any notice and miss seeing an historic moment and the results of years of work. At 0525 a green Very rocket went up and burst brightly in the sky. It signalled the start, also heard by the sound of a siren at Base Camp. Some observers were in shallow trenches near the Camp, located ten miles from the tower; they included the men who had installed the detonators. If nothing happened at Zero it could be their fault; they would be blamed. Their nerves were at breaking point; two sat down and looked at the earth. The others turned their backs and started to pray.

The tension became unbearable as the time approached. At 45 seconds to Zero the automatic timer took over. At 30 seconds, four red lights flashed on the control panel. The voltmeter needle flipped from left to right to register the full charging of the firing circuit. The timer was counting down five …four…three…two… one. The needle fell to zero and the firing circuit closed. The high voltage capacitors discharged and fired the detonators. simultaneously igniting the explosive shells packed around the nuclear sphere of material. Would the bomb detonate and release the immense energy predicted?

Henry Fellows and David Simons stood together in the control centre as the seconds ticked away towards zero. All they had planned for, their dreams and aspirations hung on the rate of flow of electric currents into a detonator. Their lives flashed before them like a fast-moving film. The books they had read, the many lectures attended, endless late night discussions about Einstein's theories, the origins of the universe and the very meaning of life. They were about to unlock the secrets of the Universe, release the energy of the atom. It was like seeing God's work. Was it forbidden territory? Man was about to enter a new unknown world.

Fellows felt a sense of guilt, a sense of betrayal about what he and the others had done for their own purposes. The evidence would soon be removed beyond recall, just fragments of glass in the desert. But it would not be removed from his conscience. His body was filled with mixed emotions as the loudspeaker on the wall blurted out the seconds to zero.

Suddenly the whole sky lit up, the flash, brighter than a thousand suns, lasted only two seconds. Then it diminished silently and an enormous ball of fire grew and grew, it went yellow, scarlet then green. It looked menacing but beautiful. A new thing was born, a new understanding, a new control for man over nature. There was an uncanny silence followed by a loud bang as the sound and shock waves hit the observers. No one on Earth had ever seen anything like it before. It was an awesome sight. The complex energy exchange processes were over in seconds. The actual fission multiplying process generates the energy in microseconds. The resulting fireball reached temperatures of tens of millions of degrees before it hit the ground thus vaporising everything in its path.

Gasps emanated from the people on the Hill. Some removed their dark glasses to see the dying remnants of the fireball, just as the shock wave, weakened by travelling through twenty miles of air, reminded everybody of the force of the explosion. Groves and Oppenheimer breathed a sigh of relief. All the planning, the work, the anxiety had paid off. The two billion dollar Manhattan Project which had taken just under three years to complete had been successful. Much further work would now be needed but the first milestone had been passed. The concept and theories had been proved. It was a triumph for physics and America but for many observers emotions were mixed. For a few seconds the darkness of night was replaced by the light of day. Now a dark shadow hung over the site at Zero. Everything had disappeared. All that remained was some twisted fragments of the tower and a variety of unrecognisable debris. The bomb blast had an estimated explosive power equivalent to 21 kilotons of TNT, four times what the scientists had calculated.

Oppenheimer recalled a line from the Hindu scripture, the Bhagavad-Gita: 'Now I am become Death, the destroyer of worlds.'

He was observed at Base Camp to have changed, visibly shaken by the awesome sight of the detonation of the bomb. People were saying the successful test meant the war was now virtually over.

But the Japanese had yet to be convinced. The plans to ship the bombs to the Pacific were well in hand.

It took some time for the men at Base Camp to fully comprehend what they had witnessed. The two second flash of light followed by an eight second ball of fire seemed to last forever to those watching in the trench.

A number of scientists on Campania Hill looked directly at the explosion with no eye protection. Afterwards they were blinded for about thirty seconds. At Los Alamos, while Groves and Oppenheimer were preparing their report to Stimson for the Potsdam Conference, an army sergeant and two scientists were secretly planning their next move. That night they met Klaus Fuchs, who, unknown to them, had been passing information to the Russians from the commencement of the project. He was not a member of the Foundation but the unsuspected master spy, the one sought but as yet to be caught by Grove's security police.

Back at Los Alamos Fellows found out that enough uranium and plutonium had been refined to make four bombs, although officially there was only enough for two to be constructed in addition to the test bomb just detonated. Two bombs had been engineered to be dropped from B29 bombers onto targets in Japan. They were of totally different designs and known as Little Boy[2] and Fat Boy. It was the Fat Boy design that was tested at Trinity because of the more sophisticated plutonium implosion design.

Fellows and Simons met privately with Paul Fields at Los Alamos to discuss the situation and how their Foundation would react to the news that an informant and a murderer could be one their members. The most devastating news came when they discovered that design information had leaked out of Los Alamos to Stalin, even before Hiroshima. Simons had suspected for some time one of its members was using the Foundation as a cover for their own clandestine activity. Huge profits were being made by arms manufacturers out of the war. They would pay tempting sums of money to acquire information about the bomb that could be sold or used to gain lucrative contracts in the future. It was clear the arms industry was about to get a massive boost.

Now the war was about to end it was time for the six remaining members of the Inner Sanctum to meet and plan for the future. A date was set to meet in New York at the end of the year. Simons and Fellows did not know that a third bomb of the Fat Boy design had been assembled to use against Japan should the surrender not take place after Nagasaki.

Los Alamos was still a wartime army post and under military security but a more relaxed atmosphere existed and the civilians were allowed more freedom of movement. The scientists wanted it to become a national nuclear physics research laboratory devoted to nuclear weapons; a desire that was later to be fulfilled by the Government.

Oppenheimer and most of his colleagues took up research and teaching posts at American universities. After a time he and the others reflected on what they had done. It had ended the war, but the cost was high. The final death toll from the Hiroshima bomb amounted to over 200,000 people. But even this was small in comparison to the millions of deaths on both sides during the war.

Edward Teller, being passionate about building a hydrogen bomb, stayed on at Los Alamos after the war. The British members of the team returned to university and Government posts in their own country which was going through post-war political turmoil. Britain had a massive rebuilding job but was basically bankrupt. It was forced to take a massive loan from the United States that placed it politically in a weak position.

A large lorry arrived at the Sunnyvale base with armed guards. Papers were handed over and the bomb was loaded. Lt. General Halifax, who was an army chief at Los Alamos, called the commander at Sunnyvale instructing him not to send the bomb to Tinian. He gasped when told it had already been loaded and returned to Los Alamos.

'Who ordered that?' shouted Halifax.

'You did,' was the reply, 'I have a signed copy of the order here,' replied a very frightened army major.

'I gave no such order, how long ago did this happen?'

'Three hours,' came the reply.

'Find the bomb – give it top priority,' shouted the General in an angry tone of voice.

Halifax ordered an extensive search for the vehicle and the men involved but no sign of it was found. It had just vanished. Border road blocks were set up and all airports and train stations secured. The people manning these were not told what they were looking for as only a small number of people knew of the existence of the third bomb. If the Trinity bomb is included it was actually the fourth bomb. Halifax decided to put a security clamp on the disappearance of the bomb and to compile a list of all personnel who knew about it. There was to be a cover-up to avoid the inevitable consequences to those responsible. He decided not to tell Groves, who was in Washington with Oppenheimer and the President. He hoped that nobody would worry about it for now with all the publicity being given to the ending of the war with Japan but there would be huge political fall-out when the truth became known. Halifax had already prepared his escape plans. But a week later a body found in a burnt out car in the desert was identified as General Halifax, US Army.

A phone call was made from a call box in Albuquerque to a private number in Washington. The caller said, 'Package delivered and safely stored.'

CHAPTER 5

Fort Halborn
1958-59

New Recruits

As the train pulled out of the station, Brian Smith sat back in his seat and opened the newspaper he had hastily bought at the station bookshop. The third class compartment was empty. Late afternoon trains from Paddington to Swindon were little used but in a few hours they would be uncomfortably overcrowded with London commuters. He had travelled from Portsmouth to London by train a few days before to collect some papers from the Air Ministry. Smith glanced at the headlines. The Egyptians had just closed the Suez Canal and a crisis was in the making, but his mind was elsewhere. He was thinking about what the new job would require of him.

Success in the Civil Service Commission examination was followed by a gruelling ninety minute interview board. Little information was given about the job except that it would be a post as a Scientific Officer in the newly-formed United Kingdom Atomic Energy Authority. The work would be highly secret and in the interests of national security he would be required to sign the Official Secrets Act. As a flight sergeant in the RAF, Smith's duties had involved the development of a new radar system which impressed the interviewers. It apparently compensated for his lack of scientific qualifications which the post required. Normally an honours degree was necessary but this was waived if the candidate had exceptional experience directly related to the job. He was placed in an experimental post which required more practical knowledge than theoretical ability. The system assumed that all scientists had been to university or were from universities. But unfortunately many of the best academics lacked practical experience or had left-wing political tendencies. The Cold War tended to make the Civil Service look for recruits with the opposite political leanings.

Smith had left school at sixteen, having passed five O-levels, to work as a clerical assistant for Portsmouth City Council. He was a radio enthusiast and as a member of the Amateur Radio Society he had a licence to transmit and receive. It was that experience and knowledge of radio which made him decide to sign up for five years in the RAF instead of doing National Service, which was compulsory in 1951. After basic training, Smith was sent to work as a radar technician at the RAF communications headquarters in London. He spent the last three years of service working on a secret project involving a new radar guidance system for use in the new V-bombers. He quickly rose to a senior non-commissioned rank of Flight Sergeant. Before leaving the RAF, he wanted a technical job, so during the last few months of service, he applied for a vacancy advertised by the United Kingdom Atomic Energy Authority. They were desperate for experienced personnel for their new establishments.

When the official buff-coloured envelope dropped through the letterbox of his flat in Portsmouth, Brian knew it was the result of the interview. Nervously ripping it open, he saw the words on the first line *'Your application has been successful,'* it was all that mattered. He had secured a job that he hoped would enable him to continue working in the electronics field since designing electronic circuits had also become his hobby. Now he wouldn't have to return to the boring Council job, although it had been left open for him. He did, however, have a more personal reason for wanting to leave Portsmouth.

The Berkshire countryside became more discernible as the train slowed in order to stop at Reading. Like many others, the station was dirty and in need of modernisation. Since the war the Government had neglected the railway system. Priority was being given to the motorway building programme as car manufacture was a growth industry. Smith glanced out of the carriage window and noticed a young man with ginger hair, holding a battered suitcase, searching for a space in the carriage. He glanced at the compartment in which Smith was sitting and opened the door.

'Is this seat free?' he asked, casually looking at Smith as he went to sit on the seat opposite.

'Yes, but it's a non-smoking carriage,' Smith said.

'Good, can't stand cigarettes myself, I once tried a pipe whilst at university, seemed like the done thing, but didn't like it. By the way, the name's Bob Turner' he said, 'I'm Brian Smith, are you going on holiday?'

Turner swiftly replied 'No, I'm starting a new job at a research establishment somewhere near Swindon, not sure exactly what they do there, but they seemed to be in desperate need of scientists and engineers, so maybe I will get to practise my physics.' Smith was glad to know someone who was going to the same place.

Showing his sense of relief, he said, 'Well what a coincidence, that's where I'm going. Glad to know you. Sounds like we have both been kept in the dark. I must confess I don't know what I am letting myself in for.' Turner turned to him and said, 'Me too, but it's a challenge.'

During the thirty minutes the train took to reach Swindon, the two men exchanged backgrounds and became friends. They discovered their job interviews had taken place on the same day but being at the beginning and end of the day they missed each other.

Turner said, 'We're lucky, only four of the twelve people interviewed were offered posts.' The ages and backgrounds of the two men were different but they had similar views on most of the important issues of the day. Turner had a PhD in nuclear physics and was very excited about continuing his research in plasma physics. He admitted he was not very practical but liked theory. They were both concerned about the dangers of the Cold War and the threatening behaviour of the Russians. Both believed that Britain should have its own nuclear deterrent.

The train arrived on time at Swindon. An old-style coach was parked outside the station to take them and the fourteen other new recruits, of which two were women, to an address each had written on their official buff-coloured acceptance forms. After a rather uncomfortable journey, the coach eventually arrived at what looked like a depressing Second World War army camp that had been converted into a holding hostel. It was located about twelve miles south of Swindon, near the village of Halborn. The name of the Government atomic research establishment where they were destined to go was called Fort Halborn. The coach was met by an official-looking elderly woman who directed the passengers to a reception building, behind which were rows of wooden huts. After scrupulously checking the name on each person's acceptance form against a list, she gave them keys to their rooms and told them dinner would be served in Hut 6, which was behind the administration building and easy to find. Smith and Turner were not impressed with the service or accommodation but after the long journey were too tired to complain. The two men agreed to meet for dinner at six o'clock.

The dining room was, as the old lady had said, easy to find. Smith opened the door and entered the room. Looking around and recognising some of the people who were on the coach, he went and sat on a vacant chair at the table where Turner was already seated with a number of the other new entrants. Everybody introduced themselves and exchanged dissatisfaction with the food and catering facilities. Apparently the same conversation took place each month with new recruits. The hostel was run like an army camp because that's what it had originally been. A tall thin-faced man, sitting at the end of the table stood up and introduced himself as Rodney Crane.

'But you can call me Roddy, I have been here for two weeks and it doesn't get any better. You will not be moved for at least three weeks.'

Then he went on to say, 'The Atomic Energy Authority wants to keep everybody together for security reasons, that's why they are building a special apartment block near to the Halborn Establishment.'

With a wry smile, Roddy said, 'Tomorrow you will all be lectured on security by the Establishment's security officer, retired Brigadier Rowley (Old Rowley). He's an old fart but you had better take him seriously. He will tell you in a threatening voice that you are all subject to the Official Secrets Act and anybody considered a security risk will be dismissed. Something big is going on and certain people may be put onto top secret projects. I work in the Procurement Office, a sort of equipment supplier to the Establishment, so we get to know what's coming in. At present we are on standby for a large delivery.' He paused, then blushed realising that he was saying too much and stopped talking.

Sitting opposite Smith were two men. Mike Durant, a first-class honours physics graduate from Oxford and Jeff Adams, an electronics engineer from the University of Southampton. Durant was a quiet but obviously intelligent man, who seemed to be more of a listener rather than a talker while Adams was the opposite. The latter was outgoing, liked to joke and spoke freely on almost any subject. They seemed to have befriended one another having also met on the journey to the hostel. Next to Turner was the only woman at the table. Her name was Susan Woods, a brilliant mathematician from Manchester University, who had just returned after two years working at Livermore in California. She had worked in a group associated with the American H-bomb project but had not been concerned directly with it. The Atomic Authority required her specialist knowledge and experience so persuaded her to return to Britain. Uncharacteristically attractive for a mathematician, she was in her late twenties, had a round impish face, a fair complexion and a lively personality. Badly fitting clothes showed she lacked dress sense but disguised a well-proportioned figure.

Smith had particularly noticed Susan on first entering the room. Turner was sitting next to her and started up a conversation. He had a girlfriend back in Reading but enjoyed flirting. Women scientists are a rare species. It is, therefore, usual for them to receive a lot of attention in what was in the 1950s predominantly a man's profession. There were only two in the room of about forty men.

The other was a ginger-haired older woman, dressed like a man so she went unnoticed.

While in the RAF, Brian Smith had been engaged for two years to a Portsmouth girl. On returning home unexpectedly one evening, he had found her in bed with another man. There was a violent scene which left him emotionally devastated and her with a black eye. That experience fashioned his current attitude towards women whom he now saw as sex objects. Being tall, dark and good looking, he had no difficulty in attracting women.

Turner left the table to get the coffee and Smith seized the opportunity to sit next to Susan. They made eye contact and he introduced himself. Smith suddenly felt a physical desire for her. She sensed it and looked away embarrassed. He quickly brought back her attention.

'You remind me of my first girlfriend' he said, attempting to start up a conversation.

'Really, was she a mathematician too?' she replied with a wry smile.

'Is that what you are'? Smith asked, with a hint of surprise in his tone of voice.

At that moment Turner returned with the coffee, but seeing Smith's obvious interest in Susan, placed the coffee on the table and went away to talk to the others. Smith and Susan spent the rest of the evening together talking about their lives and jobs. Long after everybody had left they were still talking. Smith's usual technique was to seduce a woman and take her to bed the same night but Susan was different. He wanted to but it had been a long day and the uncertainty of what lay ahead still caused him some anxiety which was not conducive to good love-making. Anyway they were both tired and only just met. He hoped there would be many other opportunities as they said goodnight and retired to their respective rooms.

The next day a bus took the group on what seemed like an endless journey to Fort Halborn through the Wiltshire countryside. As it approached the entrance, Smith estimated the Establishment was near to the edge of Salisbury Plain. Well-hidden by trees, and built on what looked like an old wartime RAF aerodrome, it was divided by what was left of the old runway.

The Establishment bore no likeness to a Fort, although it was named Fort Halborn, a subterfuge for what was really an Atomic Weapons Research Establishment. It sounded like a name that would be given to an old army base in the American Wild West. Surrounded by ten feet high wire fencing, barbed outward at the top, it bore more of a resemblance to a prison camp.

Newly constructed rather ordinary looking buildings could be seen on either side of the wide road. They looked like offices and perhaps housed laboratories. Large grass-covered mounds were dotted about like overgrown mole hills with heavily reinforced concrete entrances. Smith had seen such objects before; they were storage bunkers for explosives, with four feet thick concrete walls. Heavily guarded construction work on an underground bunker was still in progress at the far end of the site.

Smith sat next to Susan on the bus but said very little during the journey. She was reflecting on the importance of the work that she was about to undertake. Although mildly attracted to Smith she was not ready for a relationship. Unlike the other recruits, she knew more about her new job; her briefing in America had been thorough so knew what was at stake. The people who had interviewed her did not identify themselves. It was all done in a mysterious way; almost as though she had been pre-selected for the job. She was offered a good salary and career incentives to accept the job but had to first sign the Official Secret Act. Unknown to her interviewers, she already knew Henry Fellows, Halborn's Chief Scientist and Deputy Director. Her father, Professor Sam Woods, had been a Government Scientific Advisor before his untimely death. Woods had been a close friend of Fellows and an early post-war member of the Inner Sanctum of The Brotherhood Foundation. Fellows had taken a fatherly interest in Susan almost to the extent of falling in love with her but their age difference prevented it from developing. Susan had been recruited specifically as a software expert to solve a serious design problem associated with the shaping of the explosive shock waves essential to ensure the efficient detonation of the H-bomb. To solve the problem massive computation beyond the capabilities of many existing computers was required. It had contributed to the failure of the first American H-bomb in 1951 and delayed the design of the second, although it was eventually successfully detonated at Eniwetok in the Pacific in 1952.

The actual placements of the new recruits was kept from them until they had passed through the security briefing. This was given by Brigadier Tim Rowley. Halborn was built on a wartime military base and although run by a civilian authority it was organised and operated like a military camp. Some of the key staff members were ex-service personnel. Armed police guarded the gate and scrutinised everyone who entered. They were all hand-picked, experienced and well-disciplined men; most had served in the military police.

Before being allocated their stations, the new entrants were taken to what was termed the interrogation room. There, old Rowley lectured them on their security obligations and reminded them of the Official Secrets Act they had all signed which bound them for life. He told them even minor misdemeanours would attract disciplinary action. What that actually meant was not defined. Left-wing political activists and newspaper reporters were constantly trying to approach and subvert staff. The Cold War had produced international tensions and a state of national hysteria about atomic weapons.

It was known that the Soviet Union was developing a so-called Super-Bomb. It was a dangerous and seemingly unstoppable escalation of the arms race. The media knew that Halborn was planning to hold bomb trials in the Pacific and were eager to find out more about what was being tested. The 'Ban-the-Bomb' campaign driven by left-wing elements in the Labour Party was gaining ground. In 1957 it became established officially as The Campaign for Nuclear Disarmament (CND). It had well-known politicians, actors and writers listed as its members. Recently, many thousands of its members had marched from London to Fort Halborn to protest against the Establishment's work. Fellows and

Rowley knew the country's enemies were using the CND to further their aims. They were worried that some of the more active elements would attempt to break into the Establishment. The armed police were instructed to defend themselves if threatened and secure property.

After the talk, the new entrants had to wait for their escorts to take them to their work locations. Smith and Turner found out they were assigned to building X10, in the middle of the site. The two men had become close friends over the last few days and were pleased they would be working together. The escort introduced himself as Dr Terry Gibson. They followed him along a number of passages with doors on either side that opened to laboratories. Loud cracking noises from electrical discharges emanated from one of the laboratories. White-coated people could be seen peering down into the faces of cathode ray tube oscilloscopes.

'What is going on in that lab?' asked Turner.

'You will find out in good time, some questions should not be asked,' said Gibson, walking quickly to the laboratory at the end of the corridor. As they approached it, they were met by a thin-faced young man. Gibson introduced him as Dr Bill Jones, the Head of the Electronics Systems, known as ES. He shook their hands and greeted them with a friendly smile.

'Good to meet you, gentlemen, let's go to my office and talk, then you can meet the rest of the staff'.

They went into a small and sparsely furnished office situated within a large electronics laboratory in which three people were working around a large metal chamber festooned with looms of cables; some were connected to recording oscilloscopes. The two men noticed their files on Jones' desk and some scribbled notes on his pad. He welcomed them to his group, sympathising with them about the hostel accommodation which he had himself endured. With a smile, he said, 'They only do it to single people, so it's a real incentive to get married, but it won't be for long as I'm told the new apartment block will be ready in a few weeks.'

He went on to say, 'The work of the department is classified to highest level of security – Top Secret Atomic. Security measures are in place to restrict what staff can do, who they can talk to and where they can could go without a pass. You will always work with another member of staff for both safety and security reasons. I am now going to tell you what we are doing but it must not be divulged to anyone outside this laboratory. The information is strictly classified, and I can only tell you on a need-to-know basis.' His facial expression changed to a man who was burdened with a heavy responsibility.

He started by relating some history of the development of the atomic bomb since 1945. After a pause to accept coffee from a white-coated laboratory assistant, he continued, 'The success of the Manhattan Project resulted from the joint efforts of American and British Scientists. One of those who played a key role in Oppenheimer's team was Dr Henry Fellows, our Deputy Director. The Director is a Dr Philip Snow who reports to the Board of the Atomic Energy Authority and has a direct line to the Prime Minister's Office. He is thought to be related to the well-known writer C P Snow, but that's unconfirmed.

After the war, British scientists were denied access to vital information acquired from the Trinity test of the first atomic bomb. Fellows and his British colleagues who were members of the Manhattan Project were surprised at that decision. Apparently the informal understanding that Churchill made with Roosevelt during the war was not recognised by Truman, who considered Britain a security risk. Leaks of classified information to the Russians made by the spy Klaus Fuchs during the war were blamed but it was believed there were other more political reasons. The US wanted to maintain monopoly of bomb designs. It is doubtful if the Russians could have been prevented from developing their own bomb anyway but the whole business sadly damaged relations with the US.

The Americans were providing loans for the re-building of Europe so the post-war Atlee Labour Government decided not to press the matter. The Cabinet agreed that Britain would build her own atomic bomb – the so-called independent nuclear deterrent. Atlee initiated a limited programme of research and development. It was soon realised that the level of funding made available was totally inadequate. As the country was virtually bankrupt after the war it could not afford the large sums required. However, the Government found money for the bomb programme from sources that were never disclosed and only known to a few people. The British public were kept completely in the dark about the new programme under the cloak of the Official Secrets Act, which were specially strengthened to prevent political intervention. Only certain members of the Cabinet are privy to our secret programme.' Jones paused to take a breath. Smith and Turner looked at each other. 'Yes, gentlemen, both of you will know more than most of the British Cabinet,' said Jones.

'Does the Queen know?' asked Smith.

'A good question, to which I have no answer,' Jones replied.

Jones continued to tell them that the British programme had made significant advances based on the bomb tests carried out in South Australia.

He said 'It was known that the Russians and Americans were working on a Super H-bomb. To achieve the millions of degrees required to initiate the fusion reaction requires an atomic bomb as a sort of primer. The fusion process liberates more neutrons to enhance the fission process so the H-bomb was really a super fission bomb with a much higher explosive yield. Last year scientists at Imperial College in London made a discovery which could put us in the lead and enable a revolutionary new weapon system to be made. We brought the scientists who did the work into the Establishment. It is the responsibility of my group to exploit their results and produce a prototype bomb to test within a year.' Smith's attention was temporarily distracted by a loud bang.

Noticing his anxiety, Jones said, 'Don't worry it's Ashworth carrying discharge chamber tests in the end lab.'

Jones continued with his discourse.

'Although it's almost an impossible mission, Fellows has been given virtually unlimited funds to achieve it. If anyone can do it then he can. The deadline, set by the Prime Minister, is that a British H-bomb be successfully field tested by the end of this year.

Since the Soviet test of an H-bomb last year, he has been under extreme political pressure to succeed. Britain has an opportunity to remain a world power and protect itself from any Soviet attack. The Soviets have been making threats undermining the peace and security of Europe and the West. It seems to be up to us to redress the balance of power. So you see the importance of our work.' Jones paused to find some papers on his desk but continued to talk.

'You and the others have been selected to work on this project because of your specialist experience, skills and ability. I must warn you the work is dangerous, we are at the limits of knowledge and you will be working with unpredictable explosive materials.' He stopped to hand the men some technical reports on experiments that had recently been carried out. He told them they had to be returned to the safe before the end of the day and suggested they commit the relevant conclusions to memory. Smith was introduced to Dr Ray Spicer under whose supervision he would work. Turner was assigned to a three-man team headed by Dr Scott Roberts.

Susan Woods was taken to the Theoretical Physics Division which had just been equipped with the latest and most powerful IBM computer. She was to join a small group developing mathematical models for explosive shock waves. It was essential to understand the behaviour of materials that were transformed from solids to gases in microseconds by intense pressure waves. A highly intelligent woman, she quickly realised the immensity of the task she was being asked to undertake but felt an excitement from the challenge it brought. Smith had not entered her thoughts until she realised they had a lunch date but she did not even know where he was stationed.

Henry Fellows met with Brigadier Tim Rowley. They discussed the latest intake and decided that the staffing levels were now sufficient for the weapons programme. Fellows was concerned about security and wanted the new accommodation block completed as soon as possible so the key people working on his project could be put there and observed. Checks would be made on their movements and their visitors. Rowley expressed concerns about two of the new entrants; Dr Susan Woods, whom he thought knew too much and Dr Stephan Mueller. Fellows kept the knowledge he had about Susan Woods to himself. Rowley did not know everything. Fellows brushed off the remark by saying her experience at Livermore was essential to the project.

Rowley told Fellows that Dr Stephan Mueller, who had worked at the University of Chicago, had been a student of Fermi after the war. His expertise in computer modelling of neutron diffusion using Monte Carlo methods would be invaluable to the project. Rowley did not possess all his security files although the investigators had given him high-level clearance. Fellows was concerned about Mueller's appointment since he didn't know much about him and hadn't been consulted He told Rowley to do a further security check on Mueller without him being aware of it.

When Rowley left the room, Henry Fellows locked the door and told his PA whom he shared with the Director that he wasn't to be disturbed. He poured himself a brandy and took a locked box file from the safe in the wall and sat back in the large comfortable black leather chair behind his desk. In the file was his diary. He made the following entry against the date. *The team is now complete. Project Blue Star can proceed. Still have concerns about security and spies in the camp. Must contact David Simons.*

David had stayed on in the US after the war to become a member of Oppenheimer's General Advisory Committee to the US Atomic Energy Commission and also worked with him at Princeton after the problems he experienced with the MacArthur Communist witch hunt.

In the late 1940s The Brotherhood Foundation had been re-established and new members recruited. The atom bomb had made possible the realisation of some of the objectives it had set itself back in 1939. Now the devastating potential of the H-bomb brought those prospects of even greater power but with it awesome responsibilities. The Cold War was now a threat to world peace made worse by the weapons of mass destruction that existed.

Henry Fellows and David Simons had re-taken over control of The Brotherhood Foundation but others with different motives had infiltrated it. Two Inner Sanctum members had been murdered in

America and death threats made against three others. It was thought to be the work of the Mafia or a breakaway group known as The New Order. Many secret societies existed but few had the power base possessed by The Brotherhood Foundation so it naturally became the focus of attention amongst the criminal fraternity. The CIA and MI5 were aware of its existence and knew the identity of some members but not those of the Inner Sanctum. They didn't see it as a threat to national security. Some Inner Sanctum members held senior Government positions in their respective countries.

Fellows was responsible for the British H-bomb project known by the code name, Blue Star. History was repeating itself. Being a key member of Oppenheimer's team at Trinity, he was now involved in something which would again change the course of history. But a new threat was looming. The left-wing CND movement had popularised a growing 'Ban-the-Bomb' campaign. Newspapers inspired by public anxiety about nuclear weapons, were prepared to break the law to gain access to secrets. Three newspaper reporters were already serving short jail sentences for breaking into the Establishment; one had been injured after jumping out of a helicopter onto the roof of a test bunker. It was believed he had an accomplice who was not caught.

A Daily Express reporter had surreptitiously mixed with scientists in the bar in the apartment block to find out about their work. Fortunately his identity had been discovered so a group of scientists decided to feed him false information, knowing that next day it would appear in the newspaper. That was exactly what happened to the unsuspecting reporter and to the amusement of the scientists.

The publicity and attention being given to the Establishment and the H-bomb project worried Fellows. It was putting pressure on the Government, the scientists and engineers, and making security a major problem at a time when the success of the project need concentrated effort on solving serious technical problems. Fellows knew from his contacts in Government that the Prime Minister was getting very concerned about the security situation. Two civil servants from the Foreign Office and been caught spying for the Russians. MI5 knew there were more. But who were they? And where were they? Agents were believed to be working at Halborn in spite of intense security screening.

Smith, Turner and the others went to lunch together at the site restaurant located about ten minutes' walk from the laboratories. They found most of their colleagues rather dull and boring because being so absorbed in their work they had little else to talk about. None of them were married. It appeared there had been a deliberate policy to recruit bachelors who didn't have the baggage of family life. Smith thought there might be a more sinister reason. The work involved handling the most deadly materials known, uranium and plutonium. Over sixty percent of the personnel who had worked at Los Alamos on the Manhattan Project had died from cancer. It was true much had been learnt about the dangers of radiation and poisonous materials and their handling but now they were combined with the most powerful explosives ever devised. The two together were a cocktail even the devil would have had difficulty devising. The more Smith thought about it the more he wondered why he had sought such a job.

Turner noticed that Bill Jones did not join them for lunch. He was seen scurrying off in the direction of the Director's office. Spicer was chewing on his pipe and was about to speak when Scott Roberts said, 'The Welshman's going for his briefing.'

'Arse licking more likely', said another voice from behind.

It came from a squeaky voice with a cockney tone owned by a dapper little man who had crept up behind them. Turner had seen him in the laboratory.

'Don't believe we've been introduced, my name's Tom Briggs, I look after the labs, what you might call, the odd job man.'

'Pleased to meet you,' said Turner.

At last he thought, someone with a sense of humour. The others had walked on ahead. 'What did he mean about Jones arse licking?' Turner asked.

'Well he wants promotion. There could be a vacancy for a Director of Research. It's rumoured Fellows will be commuting to the States and wants someone to look after things while he is away.

Seems as though he doesn't trust Snow because he's too close to the Government. The Chairman put him here to watch over Fellows. There's a lot going on we don't know about. The whole bloody place is full of spies and Government agents. It gives me the creeps when you think we've enough bloody explosive here to blow up all of England,' said Roberts.

The others turned their heads back and beckoned Turner, Roberts and Briggs to follow as they were about to go into the restaurant. Like Smith, Turner started thinking about the job he had just let himself in for, was it what he really wanted?

They queued up for their dinners. Like at the hostel, dinner was partly self-service, canteen style but the choice was good. The dining room was vast. It seated about a thousand people. Turner was last in-line and observed there was a protocol. Groups tended to sit together. Mixing was not encouraged, security reigned supreme. You didn't sit with those you didn't work with or didn't know. It was not the social climate he had experienced at university; in fact, quite the opposite. The whole place was devoid of any social atmosphere. He also noticed there were very few women. Those that were scattered among the groups didn't sit together. But then they were a special breed. Not the types you find gossiping over the garden wall or at the corner shop.

Smith looked around to find Susan and was just feeling disappointed when she walked through the door. He tried to catch her eye but she was too far away. A warm feeling came over him, replacing the disillusionment he had been feeling since Jones' talk. Turner also saw her and knew what Smith was thinking. The two men had become close during their short acquaintance and seemed to be able to read each other's thoughts. Deep down, he also felt attracted to Susan but had a girlfriend whom he loved and to whom he had vowed to be faithful. Susan Woods was a girl you wanted to know, perhaps to conquer but not to fall in love with. She was no blue stocking. Being a brilliant mathematician put her in a class above most men. To some it would be a turn-off but to others a challenge. Something like seducing a nun – biting the forbidden fruit – he was sure a psychiatrist would have the answer.

Susan sat down with members of her group on a table near the window. Smith had been less observant about the hidden protocol and made straight for the table. She saw him coming towards her and greeted him with a welcoming smile. There was no room to sit and from the curious stares he was receiving from her colleagues, he decided this was not the place to talk.

'Where are you working?' he enquired.

'Not sure I'm allowed to tell you but it's in the computer building by the fence. I can't talk now but let's meet for dinner tonight at the hostel.'

She scribbled her telephone number on a scrap of note paper and handed it to him. A rather sinister looking man with bushy eyebrows and wearing a dark grey suit which stood out from the others, stared at him menacingly. Smith didn't linger and returned to his group to sit down to a cold dinner, but it had been worth it. Seeing her again made him forget about the job. It made him feel like a teenager again just about to go on his first date. He looked at his wristwatch; it was one-thirty, only just over four hours to go before he'd see her again. Turner had observed Smith's flirting but was more concerned with the onlookers. Hundreds of people had seen that it was more than a casual friendship. Notes were being taken, events recorded for the files. A security paranoia pervaded the place. There were too many watchers; even watchers were being watched by someone. But the Cold War was at its height. The whole world lived in fear.

Around the table the group discussed a range of topics, either connected with science or politics. There were fears about the dangers posed by the US air bases that were springing up all over Britain. One was close to Halborn which made it a prime target for the Soviets. They were just about to leave the table when there was a deafening bang followed by a dull thud. It sounded like a thunder clap. The ground shook momentarily and cups fell on the floor. The sound of sirens filled the air. Black smoke could be seen rising on the far side of the site. The scientists looked at each other. What they had all dreaded had finally happened, an explosion in a bunker.

After the penetrating noise of sirens, an uncanny silence hung over the Establishment. People were stunned. Nobody wanted to talk about the explosion. Only a few people had knowledge of what had happened as there was a security clamp-down. It had happened in one of the most sensitive areas of the site where explosive material was being transported for preparation in bomb trials. No official announcement had been made by the end of the afternoon but it was generally assumed that due to the magnitude of the explosion many people must have been killed.

Smith looked at his watch, it was four o'clock. Staff were told to finish work and leave the Establishment. Like the others, Smith was concerned about the explosion but his thoughts were more of a selfish nature, meeting Susan for dinner. She had not been on the bus which had left early to take its passengers back to *la maison*, as the hostel was affectionately known.

He wondered how she would travel, but there were men with cars who would only be too glad to give her a lift. He felt jealous; that was a bad sign. It had brought him trouble before. He realised his sexual ardour taking control. Last time that happened it led to a disaster so he must take a grip of himself. Deep down he still missed his ex-fiancée. He had been let down badly but still felt love for her rather than hate. Pride had stopped him from forgiving her, but that was the past. He must look to the future. Susan had agreed to meet him at six o'clock in the restaurant, but he decided that he would knock on her door beforehand.

Turner and the others had found out from contacts who worked in Area E, where tests with explosives were carried out, that three men had been killed when transferring a ton of the latest high explosive, one of the most powerful explosives known, from a low loader into one of the storage bunkers. Except for one shoe no recognisable remnants of their bodies were found. Only small fragments of metal from the loader were discovered embedded in the grass mound covering the bunker.

The most stringent safety precautions were always taken when transferring such material, which was the most powerful and dangerous ever devised. Under certain conditions the explosive could flip into a state of instability. It would probably never be known what really happened.

Immediately after the incident, the Director, Dr Philip Snow, consulted with Fellows and Rowley, to ask if they suspected sabotage and could offer any explanation as to why the explosion occurred. He knew there would have to be a full enquiry but due to the highly classified nature of the work it would be held in absolute secrecy. A statement to the staff would have to be made and the Prime Minister's office informed. There were procedures and channels of command for such incidents. The ground rules had been laid down at the start of the programme.

Unknown to Snow and Rowley, Fellows had his own private worries. Simons' news from the US about the infiltration of The Brotherhood by members of The New Order and the murder of five of its members was disturbing. He believed that British members were being targeted. Someone was talking. Paul Fields now held a high level advisory position in the Government. Others were in similar positions in the US. But their lives were now in danger.

Fellows decided to send an encrypted message to David in Washington telling him about the incident at Halborn. Rowley, being head of security, was no fool. During the war he had worked at Bletchley Park and been responsible for many secret code-breaking operations. He and Fellows had a good working relationship but they didn't trust each other. Fellows knew that Rowley had files on all staff. He was busy chasing people whom he believed were homosexuals and vulnerable to blackmail.

Rowley was suspicious of Susan Woods whom Fellows had brought into the project. That particularly worried Fellows because she was a member of his Brotherhood Foundation, and being the only woman on the team was very visual. Her apparent attraction to the new recruit Smith had been reported to him. It was for that reason that Fellows asked to see her at five o'clock, after working hours. To conceal the real reason for seeing her, the meeting was logged to talk about the new computer.

Fellows had used his contacts in the US to help recruit her back because of the work she had been doing at Livermore since it had some connection to Teller's H-bomb development programme. After Oppenheimer's troubles, Teller had become known as the father of the H-bomb and replaced his former mentor as the Government Nuclear Advisor. He had delivered to the Government the most powerful and devastating weapon ever devised. Most thought that a fusion weapon was impossible. By using a simple but ingenious idea, originally developed from a Russian technique, Teller had succeeded in making a fusion device which was successfully tested in the Pacific. But the cost was enormous and the device could not be made into a reliable operational weapon. It was a political weapon rather than one that the military could use. In short, it was not an engineered bomb but a cumbersome device.

The scientists at Halborn were on the edge of making a breakthrough, something the American scientists were also striving for, a method which guaranteed reliable detonation and a high energy yield. If successful, it would put Britain in the forefront and give the Government a political advantage over America and the Russians. After the spy scandals and the damaging Middle East crisis, the Prime Minster and the Government desperately needed such a boost.

Britain's special relationship with America, so carefully fostered by Churchill and Roosevelt during the war, experienced a set-back after the war, when Truman refused to share atomic secrets. A successful test would give Britain the respect and status she deserved and help to strengthen the alliance against Communism which now threatened the world.

At the time, Teller and the US Government still took a negative attitude towards Britain when it came to sharing nuclear secrets. It was a relic from the post-war period when Fuchs gave the Soviets information about the Trinity bomb. Britain was considered to be a spy-ridden country leaking secrets to the Communists. But Fellows knew he had the full support of the British Prime Minister and his own Foundation's Inner Sanctum. Many scientists in America were concerned about the amount of influence Teller had on the US Government.

The full details of Blue Star were only known by a small group of scientists at Halborn. Fellows knew that CIA and KGB agents as well as the enemies of The Brotherhood Foundation were targeting Halborn to gain access to secrets. No price was too high for those willing to pay. And there were many willing to pay highly; it gave Fellows sleepless nights.

After the meeting with the Director and Rowley, at which a statement to the staff about the explosion was agreed, Fellows returned to his office. All staff had been told to go home so his secretary was not at her desk. An uncanny silence pervaded the building.

Fellows had just started to prepare a message to David Simons when there was soft knock on the door.

'Come in,' he said, momentarily forgetting he had arranged a meeting with Susan Woods. She walked nervously into the room. Fellows got up from his chair and gave her a kiss on the check.

'I'm glad to see you again, Susan, and sorry that your early days here have been so eventful. Please sit down. Speaking as a member of our Foundation and not as the Deputy Director, I want to talk to you about the dangerous situation now developing for Project Blue Star. We know that New Order members possibly working with, or for, the Russian KGB are trying to infiltrate the Establishment to gain secrets on Blue Star.'

Seeing the worried look on Susan's face he paused for a moment. Then went on to say, 'David Simons in Washington has sent me a message to say people may have already infiltrated Halborn. Whoever they are, it's likely they will be on a specific mission to disrupt Blue Star, steal secrets, or sabotage the project. They desperately need to know if Blue Star will work so are more likely to strike after our tests are complete. If they can't wait then your computer simulations might be enough for them. It's vital these people are identified and removed. I fear we may be in their direct firing line.'

He added, 'Incidentally, Rowley also has suspicions about spies in the Establishment. He even thinks you are one; so be careful.'

'Was the explosion an accident or sabotage?' she asked.

'We don't know yet, but the Director has asked me to chair an immediate enquiry.'

Fellows began to feel uncomfortable as he tried to find the right way to approach the subject of male friendships.

'Susan your work is vital to the success of Blue Star. It demands total commitment. The added dangers of coping with our enemies means that no one can be trusted. You must be very careful about any relationships with other members of staff. Unfortunately, at the present time your life is not private, you are being watched, both by us and by our enemies. You are an attractive woman. Love affairs inevitably bring problems. They produce a conflict of confidentiality, something which you must avoid. The lives of millions of people in the world may depend on what we do in the coming months. If the Communists, international spies, or members of The New Order succeed in gaining the secrets of Blue Star then no country in the world will be safe from threat.'

Realising her friendship with Smith had been noticed, she decided to raise it.

'I understand what you say, Henry. Let me assure you that my acquaintance with Brian Smith, of which I'm sure you are aware, is nothing more than a platonic friendship.'

Fellows responded by saying. 'Thanks for being frank, but you should know he has a reputation for womanising and being unstable. He beat up his ex-fiancée for being unfaithful. We had some reservations about employing him but his specialised experience in electronics gained from radar and radio control in the RAF is essential to the project. He worked on communications systems now used in the V-bombers. These planes are scheduled to be used to drop our test weapons in the forthcoming Pacific trials. Smith has a limited security rating, although he will be working on top secret projects. Susan admitted that she was attracted to him but would keep things under control.

'Remain friends and be careful not to make Smith suspicious, we need him to work on the project and not be distracted,' said Fellows. Susan raised the problem of the new computer.

She stressed, 'I cannot develop and test the software for the detonation system unless I have priority access to the new computer.

'I will make sure that is arranged,' Fellows said.

Susan stood up and gave Henry a warming hug. He was still very fond of her, more than she knew.

'I will keep you informed about events. Please only contact me in an official capacity through my PA, even I am subject to scrutiny. Rowley probably has an interesting file on me.'

As she was about to leave, Susan suddenly realised that she had missed the bus and had no way of returning to the hostel. It was nearly six o'clock, the time when she had agreed to meet Brian Smith.

'Henry, I have missed the bus back to the hostel.'

He picked up the telephone, 'Fellows here, could you send my car immediately to pick up Dr Woods and take her to the hostel please.'

'Thank you,' she said.

The black Jaguar was observed arriving at the hostel at six forty-five by someone who, in the future, she needed to fear. There was a note on her door from Smith who had been there at five forty-five. She would now have to give him an explanation as to why she was late. Five minutes later there was a knock on the door, it was Smith. In a voice that hid the embarrassment of his remark, he said, 'I was worried about you so I thought I would call before dinner.'

She told him that something important had come up at the office relating to work so she had to stay behind. A site car had brought her back. He seemed to accept the explanation.

'Can you give me ten minutes to change, I will meet you in the restaurant,' she said in a dismissive tone of voice.

'Ok, I will save you a seat at the table.'

The restaurant was full. People whom Smith had met on the previous night were all seated at the same table. It seemed as though it was claimed territory for the new recruits. As could be expected, the topic of conversation was centred on the big event of the day. A lot of information was being disseminated about the explosion. Apparently four men had been killed, one more than was previously thought. Their identities were not being revealed. All the people working in the area were sent home to obscure any missing staff members. It was generally thought to have been an accident. Nobody raised the spectre of sabotage. Smith noticed a stranger, sitting next to Turner.

'Brian, this is Stephan Mueller, he arrived a few days ago but is staying at a hotel in town, but has come to meet his fellow new starters.'

Mueller stared at Smith with deep penetrating eyes like he was trying to pass a message. His thick dark hair, weather-beaten complexion and well-tailored suit gave him a professional appearance in total contrast to the others, who looked exactly like scientists were supposed to look.

'Nice to meet you, Brian. Rob has been telling me how you met on the train.'

He spoke with an air of confidence.

'I came to Halborn by car. Picked it up second-hand in Lewisham. The thought of being down here in the country without a car was unbearable. I had one in Chicago. You can't work in America without a car, the distances are too large. Glad to give a lift some time.'

Smith took an instant dislike to him. He was cocky and seemed to be putting on an act.

Turner said, 'Stephan is lucky, his girlfriend lives in Swindon.'

'Does she? I guess we won't be seeing much of him at the hostel then,' Smith said, with a sarcastic tone of voice.

Sensing it in Smith's remark, Mueller replied, 'It's not exactly a place you would book in advance is it?'

Smith turned to talk to the others when Susan walked up to the table. She was dressed in black trousers and a close-fitting sweater which accentuated her curves beyond anything Smith had seen before. It started to arouse his passions. Out of politeness, Smith reluctantly introduced her to Mueller.

Mueller was tall, so looked down on most people he met. It gave him an air of superiority. Smith immediately sensed his liking for women and a possible competitor for Susan. Sensing Smith's jealousy, Susan was quick to reply.

'You must let us meet your girlfriend sometime, there's a shortage of women here. What is her name?'

He hesitated before answering. 'Beth Anderson.'

Susan detected something in the tone of his voice which indicated he was not telling the whole truth. She avoided his dark staring eyes. They betrayed something sinister. The man was not to be trusted. She turned to talk to Smith.

Susan said, 'Come, Brian, let's get some food.'

Leaving the others, they walked to the food hatch. 'Mueller is a strange chap,' she whispered.

'Yes he is, apparently he worked in Chicago,' replied Smith.

Alarm bells immediately began to ring in Susan's head. That, coupled to his strange demeanour, raised her suspicions; she must be on her guard. They collected their food, a large helping of cottage pie, peas and potatoes and a dessert of rhubarb and custard was not exactly straight out of the Savoy Grill but it was well-cooked and plentiful. A small table became free in the corner of the room so they made for it.

They talked about the day's events and exchanged concerns about their new jobs. Susan was growing to like Brian Smith and was flattered by his charm and obvious infatuation with her. But she wanted to find out more about him after recalling what Fellows had told her about an hour ago. She decided to let him talk about himself. At first he was reluctant to do that but after she opened up about her own experiences when a student in Manchester, he did tell her about his unfaithful fiancée but not about beating her up.

'Would you like a coffee?' he asked, looking around the room and noticing again that all eyes were on them.

'No thank you, but let's have one back in my room,' she replied.

Smith could feel a sexual passion building up within his body. Was this an invitation?

He noticed that Turner, Mueller and the others on the table were also watching. She was an attractive woman and had no competition so it was not surprising they all took an interest in what she was doing and with whom she was interested.

Smith closed the door of her room. It was larger than his own and was dominated by the single bed. They looked at each other in silence, each knowing what they felt. They did not speak.

Smith kissed her, pulling her body next to his so that she could feel him. He could sense her own excitement as she twisted against him. But she was pulling away, catching her breath.

'No', she whispered softly, moving further away from him.

He forcefully grabbed her arm, but when he saw her angry eyes, he took his hand away and instead gently stroked her face. She relaxed, feeling less threatened. Smith had made love to many women, some responded to angry passion, others to gentleness. He seized his chance and said, 'I want to make love to you.' It was the direct approach which often worked.

'I know you do,' she said quietly.

She looked at him with a look of intimacy. 'But not now, not here.'

She buried her face in his chest.

'Brian, please understand I have things on my mind. I cannot have a love affair.'

It wasn't easy; she felt a need for him. It had been a long time since she had made love. People were beginning to think she was a lesbian or a blue stocking dedicated to science, not interested in men. Nothing was further from the truth.

She remembered the disastrous affair with a married man while a student in Manchester. It had made her wary, cautious and unbelieving of men. She kept thinking about what Fellows had told her. There was a job to do, an important and dangerous job, one that would affect the lives of millions of people. He had placed on her an awesome responsibility. She must not become involved, at least at the present time.

Driven by the urgency of fulfilling his physical need, Smith felt disappointed and frustrated. Was she playing games with him or were there things he didn't know? Perhaps there was another man. He knew he had to be patient.

'Forgive me for coming on so strong. I thought you wanted to...'

Before he could say anymore, she placed her hand over his mouth saying, 'It's not your fault Brian, it's mine. There is something you need to know. I have been given a very special assignment in this project. It needs my full commitment. Anybody who associates with me could be in danger. I am being watched. Our brief contact in the restaurant was noticed. Being here with me may be placing you in danger.'

Smith became curious. 'How do you know all this, has Rowley been talking to you?'

'Yes.'

She wanted to conceal her relationship with Fellows so decided it was best to lie.

'But I have the top security clearance' he said, with an anger in his voice.

'You know what they're like, there's a lot happening at the moment, with the trials imminent and all this spy stuff everybody is pre-occupied with, so don't read anything more into it. You know that I can't tell you about my job, but the success of the project may depend on the results of my work. Brian, I am very fond of you, please understand. I need more time. After all we have only known each other for a few days. Please be patient.'

Squeezing her hand, he said, 'OK but I want to protect you, please be careful.'

He leaned forward, took her in his arms and kissed her. She opened her mouth to him, taking his tongue into it. They explored each other for a long time. Things were beginning to get out of control when the telephone rang.

'Hello, this is Susan Woods speaking,' she said.

There was obviously someone on the line but nobody answered. 'Who is there?' she asked.

'Strange, must be a wrong number,' she said, looking back at Smith, thinking perhaps the call had stopped them from going too far, but a call so late, in view of the day's events, worried her.

Believing that she had succeeded in temporarily satisfying Smith, a sense of relief came over her. Brian I'm tired now so can we say goodnight. I will see you tomorrow.' He realised that he had gone as far as he could so kissed her again gently on the cheek and closed the door.

She climbed into bed and disconnected the telephone. She knew the call was a warning, a message to say we are here waiting for you. For the first time fear began to take hold. What had she let herself become involved in? This wasn't what she had come to Halborn to do. She fell into an uneasy sleep.

During the months that followed the new recruits settled into their jobs. Various relationships developed, both inside and outside of the Establishment. Susan and Brian Smith become more than close friends. She did eventually succumb to his advances. Everybody moved to the new apartment block where the accommodation was four star compared with the hostel. It had a bar and a club atmosphere soon developed. This was exactly what the Atomic Energy Authority wanted so as to reduce the number of people developing friendships outside the confines of the Establishment. It did, however, encourage more outside visitors. This resulted in a number of security breaches. Those involved were instantly dismissed. It was a ruthless procedure. Some people just did not arrive for work and were never seen again. What fate had befallen them was not revealed to their colleagues. Ex-employees were bound by the Official Secrets Act so were not permitted to make public any information relating to their work at the Establishment. Those who had broken the law went to jail but no press coverage was allowed so no one except their close families knew about it.

There was no doubt that human rights had been sacrificed for national security. In the mid-1950s, the Cold War was at its height and the threat of a Third World War in which nuclear bombs would be used made it necessary for strict measures to be enforced on those involved in national security matters. This was generally accepted by people so although concerns were expressed, most just got on with their jobs.

As the Deputy Director, Fellows was privileged to have one of the two blue security telephones on his desk. They were both linked directly to the Prime Minister's Office. That office had a red telephone link to the President in the White House. The routing of the lines was Top Secret; it had to be. In an emergency the fate of nations depended on it. If war started, the four minute warning would at least make it possible for one telephone call to be made. The line was regularly tested by persons whose identities were unknown. This was to ensure its total security and operational status. Fellows never understood why the Establishment had two such phones or why his office had one of them. He didn't ask for it, but for reasons of security he was empowered to take control should the Director become incapacitated, but he believed that there were other reasons.

The blue telephone symbolized the fragile peace of the free world. Therefore, when it rang, Fellows' heart jumped a beat. It had never rung before. Only a few people knew the code numbers to enable it. A few seconds passed before he gathered enough courage to pick it up.

An unfamiliar high pitched voice, it could have been a female, said, '*Remember Petrovitch.*'

Fellows knew that his enemies had arrived. The voice was obviously recorded but how could the line have been accessed? They were showing their hand, but why now? He felt sick; his nervous system became highly charged. Temporary panic came over him.

Quickly recovering his mental faculties, he started to think. He suddenly realised that the other blue telephone in Snow's office would have also rang as they were linked to the same line. He rushed down the corridor to see the Director's office door open. Inside, Snow was sitting at his desk dictating a letter to his secretary, the elderly but efficient Miss Maud Simpson.

'Hello Henry, is it urgent? I need to finish these letters to catch the post, can we talk later?' he said in a friendly but authoritative tone.

'Yes, it can wait,' said Fellows.

Fellows returned to his office still not knowing if Snow had received the call. It left him with an uncomfortable feeling. There was something that Snow had said which worried him even more. There was no post to catch. All official mail from the Director went from the Establishment by special courier.

Only two other people in addition to those responsible for the murder knew about Petrovitch, the dead man they had found in the desert at the Trinity site all those years ago. It confirmed something that Fellows had always believed, that the guilty people were among those who had betrayed them at Los Alamos in 1945.

He must warn David Simons and Paul Fields. First, he would send a coded telex to David relating what had happened since his friend would be in bed. He was also worried about Susan now the enemy had showed themselves. He telephoned Susan and asked her to meet him for lunch outside the Establishment in a less conspicuous place.

Fellows knew that he and Snow had to attend a briefing with senior Government officials and War office personnel about Project Blue Star in a few days. The test programme was behind schedule and the security problems were adding to concerns about meeting the deadlines for the overseas trials in the Pacific. Everything depended on the trials being a success. The stakes were high for the Government, the Prime Minster and the whole team at Halborn.

The desk phone rang, it was Maud Simpson,

'Dr Snow can see you now,' she said in her usual authoritative tone. Fellows had already decided on the cover story, but he needed to know what Snow was hiding, did he receive the telephone call? What did he know?

'Come in,' Snow said. Fellows opened the door of his spacious office.

'Can I get you a drink?' Fellows declined the offer and decided to move Snow's attention to the matter that concerned them both.

'I want to talk about Blue Star and the security problem. We must bring the field trials forward and test the new initiation system. Many technical questions need to be answered before we can proceed with production of the bomb for the overseas trials. The Russians are employing their best spies and the Americans want to know if it will work before signing a collaboration agreement.' Fellows deliberately provoked Snow to observe his reaction, particularly with regard to the personnel issue.

He observed Snow's hesitation and uncomfortable demeanour before he looked up and replied, 'I agree, Henry. We must make some short cuts and bring the test programme forward. I will call a meeting of the Senior Superintendents, perhaps you could chair it. We shall then be able to answer any tricky questions put to use by the Government. It's important to get inside their heads and anticipate their questions before the meeting. The PM's under pressure to release more information to Parliament. I am going to tell you something that has a top secret classification. MI5 believe that a Soviet Agent or informer exists in the Government, maybe in the Cabinet Office. They also think agents are on this site. I have already alerted Rowley and asked him to do another security check on everybody.'

He paused and stared at Fellows before saying, 'Even us, dear boy.'

Fellows had never heard him use that phrase before. Snow was not married and had often been seen socially in the company of younger men. He wondered how Snow would respond to the Head Office memo about staff working on classified projects publicly declaring themselves if they were homosexuals because of the risks of being blackmailed. Rowley would delight in having his Director admit to being one. They clearly didn't like each other so his departure would not be missed. Recent Soviet and American spy cases had identified sexual blackmail as a weapon. It had been used effectively to recruit a number of British spies. Some civil servants had already been caught and jailed.

Snow had given little away. The fact that he had not mentioned the phone call could be interpreted three ways, either he knew that Fellows had taken the call and therefore was implicated in it by saying nothing, or he knew about it and was testing Fellows, or he knew nothing. But the two telephones were supposed to be connected together, unless some knowledgeable person had changed that situation.

Fellows had to find out the truth before he spoke to Susan. He had two courses of action. To check with Maud, who should have heard the Director's phone ring, or to ask security to look at the telephone connections. Either would raise suspicions but he decided on the latter since the dutiful secretary Miss Simpson would likely tell her boss.

'Inspector Waters, this is Dr Fellows. Could you arrange for a routine check to be carried out on the blue telephone connection? Please observe the usual security and report only to me as soon as you have done the check.'

John Waters, a career policeman, was trained to obey orders without question so Fellows knew nobody else would find out.

The phone rang; Fellows closed the office door and pressed the security button.

He said, 'Waters here, your blue telephone is operationally connected and has been tested satisfactory. No external calls have been made within the last twenty-four hours.' Fellows thanked him. The mystery deepened. The call must have been made from within the Establishment which was supposed to be impossible. If someone had tampered with the line it might explain why Snow's phone had not rung. Unless Snow was involved in some way; that thought left him cold.

Susan was worried. The latest computer calculations were showing that the implosion wavefronts would not guarantee criticality at the right time for maximum weapon yield. It confirmed the need to have experimental results to enable optimisation of the design of the explosive shells. She wondered why Fellows wanted to talk to her privately. He was taking a great risk doing so as they could be seen by someone from the Establishment. They were to meet in a pub located in a village three miles outside of Halborn. It was rarely visited by other members of staff and anyway Fellows had a private room at the rear.

The pub was close to a small stream and well-camouflaged by trees and shrubs. Susan had borrowed a colleague's car which she parked on a grass verge behind the building, keeping it away from the only other one, a Riley Pathfinder which she identified as belonging to Henry Fellows. She opened the door of the pub and walked into back room. Fellows was sitting at a wooden table close to the window in the back room. He looked worried and thoughtful. She knew what he was going to say to her. Susan was ten years younger than Fellows, but was mildly attracted to him but both had never married. Susan was classically a stereotype female scientist but inside the veneer hid a sexual woman. Fellows had never shown any romantic interest in her, which made him a challenge. A plate of ham, cheese and tomato sandwiches and a pot of coffee were laid out on the table. He started by saying 'Susan we have some serious problems facing us. I now know there are definitely enemy agents operating in Halborn. They know about us, the Foundation and the incident at Trinity. I believe our lives are in danger.'

She wasn't surprised. 'Do you have any suspects?'

'No, but Rowley is looking into the backgrounds of some of the new recruits. My guess is that one or more of our enemies may have linked up with someone already on the team.'

'Does David Simons know what is happening?' she said rather anxiously.

'Yes, I sent a coded message to him and am waiting for a reply.'

Susan told Fellows about her calculations and that unless she had results from field trials it was impossible to design a system for the bomb that would produce a high yield. It was also known that the Russians and Americans had not succeeded in perfecting such a system. The agents from both countries had a vested interest in being the first to be able to do so. There were international criminal groups who would sell such secrets to the highest bidder. Driven by profit and not ideology they were the more dangerous enemies; The New Order was one such group.

Fellows told Susan about the call on the blue telephone and his suspicions of Snow. She instantly interrupted, 'You know that he is a homosexual? It's been hushed up but he was seen by a female cleaner with a young Cambridge graduate.'

'Why wasn't I told about this?' Fellows said trying to suppress his anger.

Susan replied, 'I was only told yesterday by Brian Smith. Apparently when caught, Snow pretended they had been working late on some report, but unknown to them she had been cleaning in the room next door and overheard everything. Being curious she decided to go into the room. When she told her boss about what she had seen, he strongly advised her to keep it to herself otherwise face charges for breach of security. The poor woman was so upset that she told her boyfriend, a technician who works in Brian's section. He was so concerned that he told Brian who thought that I should know.' Outwardly showing anger Fellows said,

'The man's a fool and has left himself wide open to blackmail. Rowley must be informed. I will contact Paul Fields, one of our members close to the Government and find out what he knows about the situation here. Nothing must interfere with the trials. You must be very careful not to be alone in the Establishment. My guess is that they want the trials to succeed so that the results have a real value. It is then that they will strike.'

Before leaving, Susan turned towards Fellows and said, 'Supposing they wanted to prevent the trials from taking place so depriving us of the knowledge, would that not place us in immediate danger?'

Fellows instantly responded, 'That's a possibility but I believe we are dealing with criminals, not spies. They can sell such secrets to our enemies for vast sums of money.' She wasn't convinced. They parted company and returned separately to the Establishment.

Brian Smith and Ray Spicer had just completed a series of experiments with a new initiator to improve the efficiency of the fission process in the bomb. This would increase the yield by allowing more fissile material to be used before the plutonium core was destroyed. The breakthrough was in the electronic timing device they developed which also involved a new design for an explosive delay line. Laboratory tests were very encouraging but a full-scale field test was now necessary.

Jones had been through the results and decided to classify them. Ironically this meant that Smith and Spicer were refused access to their own work, but that was the system. They were not supposed to keep notes but most scientists did. Anyway they carried most of the essential details in their heads.

The chief laboratory technician, Tom Briggs, had worked on the apparatus with Smith and Spicer and although he did not understand the technical details appreciated the importance of the data. Excitement was tempered with anxiety as the new results would now have to be converted into a practical design and tested. The new innovation could not be incorporated into the bombs designed for the Pacific trials until field tests had been successfully completed. It was impossible to delay the latter as arrangements couldn't be changed. Therefore, a crash testing programme would be required. A top level decision would now have to be made.

After looking at Smith and Spicer's results Jones became very excited. An ambitious man, he decided to take them personally to Fellows. He was breaking the normal protocol of discussing them with his immediate boss first but he knew it would place him and his Department in a favourable light with the Deputy Director. Blue Star was already late. The Prime Minister and the Government needed a positive result to increase their negotiating power with the Americans. This development could put the project back on track.

Fellows immediately called Susan with the good news. It was just what she needed to help her calculations. If the results of the tests were positive then she could programme them into her design for the new H-bomb tests in the Pacific. A meeting of all the Division Heads was called and a crash test programme set up to be carried out at the army range on Salisbury Plain. It would be necessary to use the newly developed high explosives for the final bomb tests. The nuclear cores would be simulated with similarly dense materials machined into hemispheres.

Susan had a meeting with Jones, Smith and Spicer to review the new developments. They were also joined by Charlie Barton, Richard Jenson and three technicians and an engineer from the division responsible for monitoring explosive shock waves. That team would have to provide new designs for the tampers and a method for measuring the shock waves. The problem the team faced was to transmit all the data before the whole assembly was destroyed. An explosives expert, Captain Dave Nugent, was also seconded to the team. He was stationed at the army unit on Salisbury Plain and was to oversee the arrangements for the trial and provide the army liaison. Civilian staff were given temporary ranks when working under military supervision. This was done to avoid liabilities in the event of accidents and to ensure that military commanders were given due respect. Jones became Major Jones, Smith became Captain Smith. It also enabled them to use the officer's mess on the camp.

The team had only a month to be ready for the tests at Salisbury. Smith was pleased to be working officially with Susan although most of their colleagues knew they were seeing each other outside of work. Brian Smith was a happy man. He had found a girlfriend and was successful in his work. It was Spicer's knowledge of nuclear materials that contributed to the breakthrough but Smith's skills in designing electronic circuits for the delay lines that made it a practical reality. Jones enjoyed the kudos it gave his team and was the first to realise the potential of what had been achieved.

Rowley, although not on distribution lists for anything related to the research programme, did get a copy of the minutes of Fellows' meeting with the Division Heads. He called up Fellows and asked for an urgent meeting in his own office, refusing to say what it was about over the telephone so Fellows went immediately.

Without saying anything, a sober looking Head of Security passed over to Fellows a file, marked *Highly Confidential*. It made alarming reading. Rowley's people, or Gestapo, as they were called by staff, had unearthed Snow's private life. There were photographs, statements and a host of incriminating evidence in the file.

'How long have you had this?' asked Fellows.

'We did have some unreliable gossip some time ago but no firm evidence until now. It was the memo from Head Office that I sent around that made someone with a guilty conscience and fearing the consequences of being found out so risking their job, to come forward,' he replied.

'This could not have come at a worse time for the Government or indeed the Atomic Energy Authority since it was them who appointed Snow. The man's an utter fool to believe he would not be found out. Has anyone else seen this material?' asked Fellows.

'No, but I am duty bound to bring in the police and inform the Chairman of the Authority,' said Rowley.

'I agree you have no option, but I am puzzled why this has only just come to our attention now; at a time when a crisis is looming for us and the Government.'

Rowley was a very perceptive man and understood the meaning of the statement.

'This could have been set up by people who want to discredit us and the Government. We need to check out the people who gave the statements before we bring in the police. Homosexuality is illegal but if spying is involved it's a much more serious offence. We need to know if Snow was being blackmailed. He does have access to all our top secret information. This puts Blue Star at risk.' Rowley hadn't thought that far ahead.

Fellows wondered why he had not heard from Paul Fields on the matter as he should by now be back from America. Fields was scheduled to meet David Simons who would have alerted him to the problems at Halborn.

Fellows asked Rowley to defer doing anything for twenty-four hours to give him time to find out if Snow had leaked any secrets. Snow's secretary, Maud Simpson, might have known something. She was very loyal but would soon come forward if threatened with prosecution for not helping an investigation. Knowing how intimidating Rowley could be to people, Fellows suggested that he spoke to her first. Rowley was unhappy about not contacting the police fearing it might reflect back on him in any future investigation. He asked Fellows for a signed note to cover the request. Being an ex-service policeman, he knew the importance of covering his back. Fellows also did not want any written evidence that could be used later, so declined.

Both men agreed that before releasing the file to the police further evidence needed to be gathered in the interests of national security. This seemed to satisfy Rowley, at least for the present time. But he would continue to discreetly investigate Snow's contacts and the files of the new recruits. He was still worried about the late-comer Mueller.

Fellows left the room. Before returning to his office he first went to the Personnel Officer for Simpson's file. Maud Simpson was a woman in her late fifties, never been married, totally efficient and work dedicated. In her career she had worked for many senior civil servants and knew the system well. She was a stereotype civil service administrator and did everything by the book. He rang Maud and asked her to his office. Fortunately, Snow had left for the day so she was not busy.

Fellows took a relaxed approach and asked Maud how she liked her work. She saw all the important documents and probably knew more than anyone else on the site. He asked tactfully if she understood the memo from head office about homosexuality and had she seen anything that aroused her suspicions concerning the memo. She paused before answering. Fellows detected a slight sign of embarrassment in her face, before she replied, 'No.'

He pressed the matter. 'Are you sure?' he said.

'I am not making an accusation but Dr Snow does seem to have a lot of young male friends. They call him sometimes, although he tells them to use his private telephone.'

'Are the calls made within the Establishment?' asked Fellows.

'Yes,' she replied.

'Can you tell me who made them from the numbers used?'

'No. because they use a general number from a phone in the restaurant,' she replied.

He could sense her suspicions about Snow so decided to tell her about the evidence Rowley had uncovered. It might make her more forthcoming about other people Snow might have had relationships with within the last year.

She was not unduly shocked by the news and actually showed a sign of relief. Her own suspicions had been proved true. Fellows told her to think carefully about who else Snow could have been communicating with off-site.

'Sometimes he would take documents home but I have a record

of them and they were always returned. He told me he needed to work at home sometimes on papers as there was never enough time during the day.

'Can I see the list of those he took out?' asked Fellows.

She went back to her office and returned with a log book. Over a period of about a year, Snow had taken out most of the documents related to Blue Star, some of which were so recent that they had not even been classified. It was difficult to understand what he was doing with them. Being the Director, he had certain privileges but they did not extend to removing classified documents off-site.

Maud said she did tell him that strictly speaking he shouldn't take them home. She didn't report it to records as she had no reason to and didn't want to lose her job as his trusted PA. Fellows copied the list and thanked Maud. He told her that she must say nothing to anybody about what she had learned and she might be interviewed later by the police. Fellows asked where Snow was at the present time.

'He told me he was going home to rest after a bad headache,' she said.

She left the room. It was four o'clock in the afternoon so Fellows called Paul Fields. His PA answered.

'Is Paul available?' Fellows asked.

'Yes, I will put you through,' she said.

'My apologies, Henry, for not returning your call but I've just got back from Washington to a pile of urgent business on my desk. The Cabinet is getting worked up about the spy business. There are meetings going on all the time with MI5 chiefs. Rumours abound about who could be trusted or not trusted. The situation is chaotic.' Fields stopped to take a breather.

Fellows seized his chance to say, 'We have a crisis here. I do not want to talk over the telephone. Can you come over here to meet with me? It concerns Blue Star and the Foundation.'

'You've picked a bad time for a meeting. I cannot get away at present. Let me call you tomorrow and see what can be done. Sorry but I must go.'

Fields rung off, leaving Fellows worried even more about what to do next. He had only agreed a twenty-four hour time slot before Rowley brought in the police. Fellows called David Simons. He answered immediately on his secure line.

'How much do you know about the crisis we have here at Halborn?'

Simons said he knew about the Government's problems but nothing about Halborn. Paul Fields had recently briefed him. Fellows told him about Snow, threats to himself and other members of The Brotherhood and the possibility of soviet agents being on site to gain secrets about Blue Star. He did not tell Simons about the latest research results. The telephone was supposed to be very secure but after the incident with the blue phone, Fellows had lost confidence in the system. He was reminded by a notice placed on every telephone at Halborn – *speech on the telephone is never secret.* People unintentionally gave small snippets of information away to their friends when speaking that identifies who and where they were, sometimes even the work they were doing. People at the GCHQ Cheltenham could listen to conversations on Russian phones so equally they and others could break into any telecommunications systems. Fellows knew that David Simons had a voice encryption system provided by the FBI but Blue Star was a critical stage and no one, not even his trusted friend, needed to know about it.

Simons said, 'Be on your guard Henry. It looks like our old enemies from The New Order could be involved. It's likely the Soviets could be paying them to do their dirty work. It would be politically safer for them to use a secret organisation whose people are not known by MI5 or MI6. I need to ring off as the safe call-time has been exceeded. Please keep me informed about developments. I will try and find out from my informant what's going on and let you know. Good luck.'

Next day Fellows received an early morning telephone call from Rowley asking him to come immediately. At the office Rowley was accompanied by two policemen. He wasted no time in telling Fellows, 'Snow is dead. He did not answer the door when his driver went to collect him for work this morning. The police were called and broke into the house. They found him dead in bed. Apparently he had a heart attack in the night. There will have to be a post-mortem and an investigation.'

Fellows replied, 'Could we talk in private?'

Rowley asked the policemen to wait outside.

Fellows continued, 'You appreciate what this means. With Snow dead of natural causes there is no need to for us to reveal our prior knowledge of his homosexuality. The Chairman of the Authority and the Government can put a clamp on any investigation.'

Rowley responded with a shaking of his head. 'The police are already involved so it's out of our hands. Let's see what the post mortem reveals. They will want to know about Snow's recent activities.'

Fellows said, 'We can get the Home Office to intervene if necessary but this will need to go to the Prime Minister. It isn't going to be our decision.'

Rowley just put up his hands and said nothing. Fellows called Paul Fields. His secretary answered and put him through.

'Unpleasant business. I heard it from the Secretary of State this morning,' he said.

'The Home Office will be putting a clamp on this case. No press releases or statements yet until the Cabinet has discussed the consequences. You will take over as Acting Director. We must proceed with the Blue Star Programme. The Chairman will be contacting you after the Cabinet meeting this morning. Henry, don't worry this could be an advantage for you but it also puts you on the front line.'

'Seems like Snow's death was very convenient to all concerned,' remarked Fellows.

That remark produced a long silence.

Fields said. 'I have to go to a meeting. I'll talk to you later.'

Fellows told Maud Simpson about Snow. At first she showed some emotion but then seemed to accept that her boss would not be returning. Since Fellows was now the Director, Maud was now his PA. He informed her of the new arrangements. She agreed with a smile.

Fellows called Susan and told her the news. He detected her concern about Snow's untimely death. Like her, he wondered if it was natural. There were serious security questions to be answered. Was he being blackmailed? Who was the informer to MI5? Who were his sexual partners? Was The New Order involved? Was Snow a security risk? Fellows was still worried about the blue phone issue and the telephone threats that he and Susan had received.

Brian Smith and Ray Spicer were working with other colleagues to produce a device to test on Salisbury Plain. Jones and the trials director planned for simulated weapon testing to take place within two months. Susan would need the results for Blue Star programming so that the new test weapons could be ready in time for the Pacific trials.

Now Fellows was Director, the burden to make Blue Star a success fell on his shoulders. He thought back to 1939 and 1945 when he, David Simons and other members of The Brotherhood Foundation planned to have members in high level positions so they could make a positive difference. They had made good progress towards achieving their aims but along the path a new enemy had evolved from its own membership. The New Order had become the dark side of The Foundation. It was thought its leaders were among some of the wealthiest people in the world who had control of large multi-national companies and could have influence on the policies of Governments. They had stolen The Brotherhood's forte and been even more successful in concealing their identities. But the time was approaching when a showdown was imminent. Fellows believed The New Order was after the biggest prize – the knowledge of how to make and maybe acquire the most powerful weapon of mass destruction ever devised. The Blue Star H-bomb project was that prize. The new compact initiator system would be easy to sell to countries such as America and the Soviet Union who already possessed the H-bomb but others would follow. Then the world would become an even more dangerous place.

Fellows decided there was an urgent need for the members of The Brotherhood's Inner Sanctum to meet to discuss the crisis. More than ever before their combined influence would be required to combat their enemies. Since the six remaining members were in America, Britain, Germany, Canada, France and Singapore this would only be possible through a secure telephone link. David Simons could set it up. He knew that David had an informer who had access to one of the members of The New Order's Cabal. Unlike The New Order, The Brotherhood did not have any of its members in the security services after the spy problems at Trinity.

A situation existed where two clandestine organizations were at war with each other. Their joint resources, including intelligence gathering, matched those of national security agencies. Fellows knew a dangerous game was being enacted.

Brian Smith was now more openly able to see Susan Woods and used every opportunity to do so. He had fallen in love with her but, although she was very fond of him, she held back her affections. Their work precluded too much socialising but they used the weekends to go out together. Susan felt uncomfortable with Brian's possessiveness. He was a jealous man who tried to prevent her becoming too friendly with other men. It was this trait that had caused problems with his previous girlfriend. Using her need to concentrate on work, she did her best to pull away from him. But he was so persistent that she decided to talk to Henry.

Fellows alerted Jones to the situation since Smith's history of instability could affect his work, and at this critical time, the project. There had already been a minor accident in the laboratory when Smith had carelessly detonated an explosive charge without using the standard safety precautions resulting in some equipment being damaged when a small fire broke out. Fortunately, it was quickly extinguished by his colleagues who were working nearby. He was given a few days' rest, after working too many long hours but it did show a potential problem.

A station order was issued immediately to inform staff working on classified projects not to become involved with female staff similarly engaged. It was not possible to reinforce this officially but it did serve as a warning. It infuriated Smith who knew why Fellows had initiated it. He complained to Jones who said he understood his feelings but everyone was under pressure and the work must take priority, making the point about the accident. Under normal circumstances, Smith would have been transferred to non-classified work but he was now an essential part of the Blue Star team. Ray Spicer was asked to keep an eye on Smith and report anything that concerned him. They had an uncomfortable relationship, partly due to their different personalities and also because Smith was jealous of Spicer's friendship with Susan. Jones put another electronics engineer to work alongside Smith as back-up should any problems arise. Susan's computer group also provided her with two other staff members. One was Stefan Mueller, who would help with the analysis of the results from the Salisbury trials.

Two months later the new device was assembled and installed in a dummy bomb. It was then transported from Halborn to the test site on Salisbury Plain. The bomb was set up in a two metre deep pit in the ground. The team set up the firing circuits and measuring equipment in a bunker located about 100 metres away. It was protected by a 10 metre high earth mound. Susan stayed behind at Halborn to await the results but Mueller went with the team as an observer.

The next day the wind was in the right direction so the range officer gave permission for the detonation to take place at eleven o'clock in the morning. There was a flurry of activity in the bunker while equipment and circuits were tested. Fellows and some of his senior staff arrived at ten o'clock. He knew the Prime Minister's office awaited his call when the test was completed. It was that important. Unfortunately, with everybody watching the final preparations, a cry went up from the firing officer to stop the count-down. An open circuit signal in one of the firing cables was detected. This was connected to the high explosives packed around the dummy sphere simulating the plutonium core of a real bomb. It would have to be disconnected and replaced. This meant powering down all the systems and a five-hour delay before a new count-down could be started. For safety reasons it was decided to postpone the test until the following day. Fellows made the appropriate calls and returned to Halborn but planned to come back the following day.

Smith and Riley and two Army engineers volunteered to go to the pit and replace the cable. They did so because they wanted to make sure their device was not damaged and disconnected. It took two hours to carry out the replacement, knowing that the explosive charge could become unstable at any time. Smith was perspiring; his hands trembled as he removed the device. Noticing his condition, Riley took charge and made him return to the bunker. They discovered the broken cable had been gnawed through by a rat. It was a well-known problem in the firing range. The fields were rat infested. The creatures often mistook the polythene insulation in cables for food, probably cheese. Many had been found electrocuted alongside the evening meals. These rats seemed to be immune to conventional poison so the army sent out shooting parties but they didn't diminish the population.

Fellows called Susan to tell her about the problems at the site. He had already called Jones about Smith's condition and suggested he was sent back for reasons of health and safety. Riley refused to work on explosives with Smith so Jones had to take some action. There was something worrying Smith. He was clearly disturbed. Nobody knew he had received a letter from an unknown sender saying that Susan was having an affair with Fellows. The letter said they were lovers. After Smith confronted her with the letter she had to admit she did have a special relationship with Fellows but they were not having an affair and were not lovers. She told him someone was trying to break them up.

Smith refused to believe her, lost control and went into a rage. It gave her the chance to tell him that their close relationship was over and she now just wanted to be friends on a professional basis. He stormed out, swearing and saying that she would be sorry for her actions. This had taken place just a day before the Salisbury trial so it explained Smith's mood. When told about Smith's condition, Fellows ordered him to return to Halborn.

The trial did take place the next day and was witnessed by

Fellows and the Blue Star team. The initial results were positive. It would take a few days to analyse all the data. Much of it had to be acquired from scanning negative films from cameras fitted to the oscilloscopes. These displayed the electrical pulses from detectors and sensors placed around the dummy bomb. The team were so confident of success that Fellows called the Prime Minister personally on the blue telephone to tell him that, subject to confirmation, Blue Star would work. He could only imagine how that news would go down in Cabinet. The Government's nuclear bomb programme was being strongly criticised by the Opposition who were gaining popularity in the country. More importantly, the Government wanted success to bring about a collaborative agreement with the Americans. Britain could not afford to continue with an extensive independent nuclear programme.

The data was sent to Susan, who used it to re-construct her computer programmes for Blue Star. Jones and Riley and the team engineers had to carry out more laboratory tests on the new materials used to find ways of integrating them into the initiation systems for the bomb. Smith did not arrive for work. It was assumed he was taking sick leave but officially he did not apply for any. Charlie Barton and Smith often drank together in the evenings at the bar in the club house located just outside Halborn. Having returned from the successful Salisbury trials, Charlie decided it would be good to celebrate. He hadn't seen Smith on the final day and was only told later why he had been sent home. They had become good friends over the last six months and confided in each other about their personal problems.

Charlie knocked on the door of Smith's apartment. There was no reply. Smith had not been seen for a few days, even though his car was in the garage. The block manager was called since he had a master key that would open any door. The two men went inside to be confronted with a sight that made them gasp. Smith was hanging from the ceiling by a strong electrical cord tied tightly around his neck. A chair which he had obviously been standing on had fallen over and was directly below his feet. The police were called and the building sealed off. Awakened by the sounds of policemen stomping about raised the curiosity of other residents of the block. Smith had been dead for some time. No suicide note or any other evidence pertaining to Smith's state of mind was found. Fellows was immediately informed. He told Susan and Rowley. Susan was horrified and felt responsible for the way she had treated him. She didn't appreciate the depth of his feelings for her. Having been rejected by his former fiancée, her rejection was probably the last straw for Smith.

Fellows was now worried that another death coming so soon after Snow meant an enquiry would be carried out. It was the worst time for that to happen. The team now had the test results it needed to make a bomb which would be technically superior to the American and Russian weapons. Much work still had to be done before the Pacific trials so team morale was going to be a significant factor.

Fellows called Paul Fields on the secure line and expressed his concern about the two mystery deaths. Fields was worried that it might be the work of their enemies. Was someone trying to stop the trials and demoralize the team? Fellows had the same response from David Simons. It was increasingly looking like their old enemies, The New Order, had people at Halborn.

Fellows asked Rowley if his security checks had been completed and sought his opinion about Smith's apparent suicide. Rowley told him that Smith's door had not been locked but there was evidence of another person having been in the room. A partial fingerprint had been found on the cord that was attached to Smith's neck. His body also contained traces of a sleeping drug and alcohol. Rowley asked the police to investigate Smith's life, friends and relationships. He did know about Susan but it was the person who sent the note who had to be found. Smith was a loner and had few friends. He did spend most of his time working and took his job seriously but suffered from bouts of depression. His work with Spicer in Jones' Division was essential to the project's success. But the knowledge he possessed would be invaluable to enemies.

Fellows thought back to Trinity when they had found a murdered colleague just before the test. The culprit was never identified. Spicer, Jones and Susan were given special police protection and their movements outside of Halborn restricted. Susan was given a computer terminal in Jones' laboratory. Stefan Mueller was assigned to help her. This enabled them to access the new IBM machine, installed specifically for work on Blue Star. Other scientists and engineers, such as Charlie Barton, Richard Jenson, Jack Sillars and Captain Dave Nugent associated with the project were also briefed on security and placed under observation. Most didn't like it but, because of the recent events, accepted the need. Nugent, being an army secondee, had extra security. Army intelligence worked closely with Rowley and the Atomic Authority police since they provided test facilities and escorts when equipment was moved to their sites.

The trials group, headed by Dr Robin Ellis, a hearty Scotsman, met with Fellows and the team to set a date for the first of the Pacific Island tests. It was agreed it would be in one month. Most of the equipment had already been shipped and the air force and army personnel were already camped on the island. The bomb would be dropped from a Valiant bomber and detonated at 1000 feet, twenty miles from the Island. The Blue Star team would provide the final firing codes. These were kept locked away in a secret safe in the WES building. Only Fellows and Jones knew its location and key code. Enough design data now existed but Jones wanted more laboratory tests. Scientists were never satisfied with their data.

Paul Fields called Fellows to tell him the Prime Minister had asked the Home Secretary to put a clamp on any investigation or inquest on Smith in the interest of national security. But internal enquiries would proceed and MI5 would be involved.

A Daily Express newspaper reporter was apprehended by the police for writing an article about an incident at Halborn causing the death of a leading scientist. It was thought to have come from someone who lived in the same block as Smith but the source was not revealed. The Atomic Energy Authority had to put out an official statement about one of the scientists dying from a heart attack to allay further reports. Fortunately, Smith had no relatives or next of kin so his death was easily hushed-up. It added further to the tension and pressure already placed on the Blue Star team. Fellows believed the danger was already inside. The people involved had to be found before another disaster took place. He had an ominous feeling there was more to come. As the trials date came closer the enemies would become more desperate.

CHAPTER 6

Death in the Afternoon

It was late in the afternoon and Fellows had just completed his secret progress report on Blue Star and asked Maud to arrange for it to be sent by courier to the Prime Minster in London when he heard the fire sirens. Immediately the emergency telephone rang. It was the fire officer. There was an explosion and fire in the WES building. A security cordon was placed around it and men with breathing apparatus entered. Fellows rushed downstairs where a car was waiting to take him to the scene. Rowley, the Fire Chief and other senior staff members were already positioned behind a safety barrier across the road from the building. Flames were piercing through the black smoke which now enveloped the roof. As Fellows arrived, firemen were bringing people out. They were coughing and choking. Some had burnt clothes while others were clearly in shock.

A message came back that the fire was still raging where it had started and firemen could not get near enough to rescue people trapped in one part of the building. Fellows' heart nearly stopped when he discovered it was Jones' laboratories. He knew that in the laboratory was a safe containing the new initiators and other vital information on Blue Star. Fortunately it was fireproof. But his concern now was for the Blue Star staff. Instinctively he rushed forward to see a woman being brought out on a stretcher who looked like Susan. At first, her blackened face and badly burnt body obscured her features. She had an oxygen mask over her face and was clearly badly injured. They loaded her into an ambulance, which then sped away. Two more bodies were brought out but this time in body bags. On enquiring, Fellows found out they were Jones and Spicer. There followed at least seven more who were badly injured, including Tom Briggs, the laboratory technician.

Fellows immediately called Paul Fields and the Prime Minister to tell them about the disaster that had just taken place. Rowley pulled Fellows aside and told him that a man had been seen by the police running away from the building just before the fire started. He failed to stop when challenged and according to procedure they fired shots and think he was wounded but he ran off before the police could apprehend him. An intensive search was underway. Fellows told Rowley it was a matter of priority to secure the safe.

'We will check it out as soon as we can enter the building,' he said.

It was an hour before the fire was brought under control and they could safely enter the building. To their horror they found the safe had been opened and the contents removed. The fire must have been started as a distraction, which then went out of control. Fellows and Rowley looked at each other in silence. Only two people had the safe combination and Jones was dead. How could it have been opened unless Jones had done it prior to the fire? Unknown to Rowley, Fellows had copies of the software and computer codes Susan had developed. She had been suspicious of Mueller so had given copies to Fellows. Elements for the initiators were already being made in a special workshop but now a stolen one in the hands of the enemy could diminish their value.

Fellows knew this latest incident was too serious to conceal from the public. The loss of life and injuries coming so soon after Smith and Snow's deaths would have grave consequences for him and Halborn. It wouldn't take the investigators long before they discovered the fire was arson and the most secret part of the Establishment had been attacked. The area would be crawling with police, reporters and bereaved relatives demanding to know what had happened. The Prime Minister, the Home Secretary and MI5 would be demanding statements. It was going to be a long day and night.

Mueller was supposed to be working in the building with Susan but his body was not found. Was he the running man? Fellows asked Rowley for a copy of Mueller's file and any more information on his background that was not listed.

Rowley said, 'Wherever he is, Mueller cannot leave the Establishment.'

Returning to his office, Fellows first concern was for Susan. He called the hospital to find that she was in a critical condition with first degree burns. He was told she was not expected to survive. Two laboratory technicians who were just slightly burnt were conscious and able to speak about what had happened; fortunately Briggs was one. He said, 'I saw Dr Jones opening the safe to get out some samples when he seemed to collapse. Another man, whom they assumed was Dr Spicer, went to his assistance when suddenly there was an explosion and the whole space was filled with a cloud of gas. It was like the kind used by the SAS to stun people. The technician went on to say, 'We all passed out until the heat of the fire woke us up. Black smoke from a fire in a nearby laboratory started to choke people. Those of us who could walk ran to the nearest exit. There was panic and I believe some people didn't recover from the gas and smoke so died from asphyxiation before help arrived.'

The police asked, 'Did you see anybody else at the time the safe was open?' Briggs replied, 'Just before I passed out I saw Dr Mueller in the background.'

Fellows called David Simons to tell him about the disaster, knowing soon that he would have to report to the Prime Minister who by now would know about the incident. Simons answered immediately as if expecting a call. 'I just found out from a newsflash. It didn't take long for the media to sense a big story unfolding. This looks like the work of The New Order. If they have stolen the initiator and codes to sell to the Soviets then serious damage will be done. You must be careful, Henry, since you are likely to be next on their hit list. Their objective seems to be to compromise Blue Star and embarrass the Government. Trust nobody and check out Mueller yourself. If he is the perpetrator then he must have an accomplice in the Establishment. So far the FBI hasn't come up with anything but further checks have been carried out on his background with the help of your MI5. His family came from Germany after the war but there are apparently some gaps that need to be filled in when he seems to have disappeared from the university. I have asked our Inner Sanctum members to assist in finding the names of New Order members who might be responsible for the fire at Halborn.'

Fellows interrupted him because the blue phone was ringing.

'I must ring off as the Prime Minister is calling. Let me know when you have further news.' Fellows lifted the receiver to hear a high pitched tone. The Prime Minister didn't disguise his concern.

'How bad is it, Henry?' he asked.

'We have two leading members of the Blue Star team dead, one critically injured and seven others badly injured. The initiator and computer codes have gone missing, presumed stolen by the person or persons responsible. There is evidence one member of the team might be that person. He was able to get past our security checks and so far has evaded capture. He may have an accomplice. I have placed a tight security cordon around Halborn. There has to be damage limitation and a clamp down on media reporting to protect Blue Star and the national interest.'

There was a brief silence before the Prime Minister replied. Fellows knew the conversation was being recorded and copied to MI5 and others.

'Henry, please convey my personal condolences to the relatives of those killed and injured. The Government sees this incident as an attack on the UK and every step is being taken to find and bring those responsible to justice. The timing of this is politically ominous. I had arranged a private meeting with the American President next week to discuss your results from the Blue Star tests. Please continue with the Pacific trials at all possible speed and let the Government know if you need further resources.'

Fellows thanked the Prime Minister, saying that although the losses were a setback, the team had what was required to ensure the success of Blue Star. Deep down he felt a sense of despair. He was devastated by the news about Susan. They had become very close. He had hoped one day they might have even married. Fate had dealt him a cruel blow.

Rowley called to say the police had found a tunnel under a cupboard in a building used by building contractors close to the perimeter fence. It led out to an entrance concealed by trees in a small wood outside of the Establishment. Spots of fresh blood were seen on the floor near the cupboard. Fingerprints sent to the forensic laboratory on site confirmed a match with Robert Mueller. A manhunt was now on for him. Fellows thanked Rowley and told him about the Prime Minister's message.

'We need to get out a staff notice as soon as possible but avoid mentioning the loss of the secret material.'

Special Branch Police went to Mueller's flat in Swindon. No one answered their call so the door was broken down. Inside they found Mueller dead, hanging from the ceiling with an electrical cord around his neck, similar to the way Smith was found. A poorly written note was found near the body confessing to the fire and regretting his actions that were personal and didn't involve anyone else. It was meant to look like a suicide note but not convincing. The flat looked disturbed. Someone had been through his desk. A drawer was left partially open and a file not pushed back in place. The police removed its contents and checked for fingerprints and signs of other occupants. There was no sign of the girlfriend he claimed to have been living with him. It was a single-bedroom apartment.

Next day the national newspapers carried a muted story about a fire at the Halborn Atomic Weapons Establishment. It did report that some people had been injured but the on-going work programme was not disrupted. It was clearly a Government statement that would not satisfy eager journalists, who would be pursuing their own stories. The police had orders to arrest anyone acting suspiciously near or on the site.

Fellows met with his Division Heads and arranged for staff transfers to be made to replace Jones, Spicer and Smith. Dr Charles Barton would now take charge of the Blue Star trials programme, assisted by Richard Jenson since they were part of the original team. Barton was a brilliant scientist but being a maverick, disliked rules and conventions. He tended to take risks but since he understood what he was doing and got results constraints were not placed on him. The programme had suffered delays and now the stakes were higher so risks might need to be taken. No further disasters could be afforded. It was still assumed that Mueller had an accomplice on site but there was no direct proof. Everyone was on high alert and mistrust of colleagues was causing a lack of morale. This was heightened when the team heard that Susan Woods had died early in the morning. Fellows was broken-hearted. Her parents were dead but he knew she had some relatives who lived in the country. He would speak to them personally.

Paul Fields called to say he had spoken to David Simons and two other members of the Inner Sanctum. They were concerned that the inevitable security investigations by MI5 and the FBI might reveal their membership of The Brotherhood which would threaten their jobs. Fellows told them about the suspicious death of Mueller and an active search was being carried out for his accomplice. It was imperative he or she was caught to find out who was controlling the cell before everything escalated out of control.

It was late and Fellows was tired. Maud had left the office. He was about to call for his car when he noticed a light flashing on the internal telephone. He picked it up and a man's recorded voice just said, '*You're next.*'

It confirmed that the accomplice was a man. Fellows called Rowley, who was still in his office, and told him about the threat. The message was recorded only thirty-five minutes previously so whoever made it might still be in the Establishment. Rowley confirmed that all outlets from the Establishment had been sealed and the buildings were being systematically searched by armed police. No more tunnels were found.

Fellows took out a bottle of brandy from his locked cupboard and poured himself a triple. The last two days had taken their toll. He felt utterly depressed having lost his best staff, his friend Susan, the secret bomb initiator and vital computer codes. He was responsible for the nation's most secret weapons' programme and the five hundred staff at Halborn. A lot depended on the success of Blue Star, the nation's security and standing, the Government's defence policy, the careers of many of his staff and his own reputation. Now, he too, was under direct threat from his enemies. He knew he alone would have to shoulder the responsibility for all that had happened during the last few days.

The enemy was his enemy not the Government's. People believed Soviet spies were to blame but this was a private war between The Brotherhood and The New Order. The latter might be a client of the Russians or anyone else who was willing to pay a high price. Fellows knew he had to deal with it himself. Now that MI5 was involved, which also meant the FBI and CIA, it wouldn't be long before his membership of The Brotherhood would be exposed. Perhaps the time had come for The Brotherhood's Inner Sanctum to talk to the security services of both countries and combine their knowledge to defeat the common enemy. It would mean resigning from his post at the worst possible time. He felt sorry for his Brotherhood colleagues who would also lose their jobs. They had come a long way since 1939 in achieving their objectives. Members had advisory positions in most European Governments and were well-placed in the American political infrastructure. David Simons was an advisor to the US Department of Defence and respected by the military chiefs, so he had the most to lose. Paul Fields was an official advisor to the Prime Minister and the Minister of Defence. Since 1945 the temptations of self-indulgence and making money had been too much for some Brotherhood members who had gone over to the dark side. They had grown powerful under the cover of The Foundation and had learned how to infiltrate Government agencies.

It had been a long day so Fellows called for a car to take him to his flat. The police provided an armed escort and Rowley insisted he had a twenty-four hour bodyguard. A manned police car would be stationed on the road outside. Fellows' apartment was on the third floor of a converted house located on the outskirts of a small village, five miles from Halborn. It was chosen by the Atomic Energy Authority for its remoteness. Apartments on the other floors were unoccupied. The previous tenants were moved out before Fellows had been assigned the accommodation. Only the Establishment's police and the Personnel Office of the Atomic Authority in London knew his address.

The two cars arrived at the house. Fellows thanked his driver and went over to speak to the driver of the police car whose duty it was to protect him. He noticed the sergeant's stripes on the man's uniform and his pistol in its holster. They had sent an experienced person.

'Hope you're not too uncomfortable out here,' Fellows said. The driver looked at him without smiling giving the impression he had not volunteered for the task.

'My name is Sergeant Alan O'Leary. Call me on this phone if you need anything,' he said, with a slight detectable accent, more European than Irish. He handed Fellows a small handset fitted with an alarm button.

He added, 'A relief car will arrive early in the morning, probably before you are awake.'

Fellows found the man's demeanour rather strange. He did not have the militaristic bearing normally seen in Authority policemen who were usually ex-military. He was the most unfriendly policeman he had ever encountered. Alarm bells started to ring in Fellows' head.

Fellows entered the security code at the entrance to the house and opened the door. He went upstairs and was faced with another set of push buttons to use before he could gain access to his apartment. They required a different entry code, known only to himself and the cleaner. He entered the room, turned on the light and pulled the curtains across the window. The police car had moved further along the road and was parked out of sight in the shadow of a tree. Something was not quite right. Fellows had a bad feeling about his bodyguard. David Simons warned him about the assassin's hit list, the mystery phone message confirmed it. Yes, tonight they might try before the police tightened the ring. Fellows' adrenaline was running high. It raises the body's protection by alerting the brain and stimulating the senses. He knew there would be little sleep tonight although his body cried out for it. Planned murders usually take place at night when the victim least expects it. Unknown to the bodyguard below, he kept a loaded revolver in a locked drawer beside the bed. Although it was an old Second World War relic, it did work.

It was eight o'clock and way past dinner time. During the day, Mrs Johnson, the housekeeper and cleaner, always kept the refrigerator well-stocked. Being one of the few people who knew the entry code to the apartment she had undergone extensive security checks so could be trusted. Fellows put on the radio to hear the news. The fire at Halborn had been headlines for a few days, but was now only mentioned briefly at the end of the news bulletin. The Government had done a good job handling the media. Every policeman in the country would be looking for Mueller's accomplice without knowing the background to his murder. Fellows thought it was a little strange that the police had only assigned one man to protect him since he possessed one of the country's most valuable secrets.

Fellows cooked himself a sirloin steak, frozen chips and peas. He opened a bottle of Chablis, making sure he didn't drink too much. Normally he ate with friends at a small pub restaurant in the village. But this was not a time to be socialising. His mind was full of the events of the last few days. He could not shake off the horrific vision of Susan's burnt body. It would live with him for the rest of his life. He had watched her develop into a brilliant young lady. Her contributions were pivotal to the success of Blue Star. The nation had a debt to pay. Revenge for her death filled his mind. Someone would have to answer for it. He almost welcomed confronting his would-be murderer. It looked like Mueller had started the fire but those who controlled him were the real culprits and he would dedicate himself to bringing them to justice.

After dinner, Fellows wrote up the week's events in his diary. One day someone would know what really happened. He had already written a detailed account of the Trinity experience and the history of The Brotherhood Foundation. When time allowed, he would convert his diary into memoires. The Brotherhood Foundation would take its place in history. If it was to end then at least they had achieved a measure of success in what they had set out to do in 1939. Science and technology had been the agents for change in the world. They had brought new products and laid the foundations for wealth and prosperity but with these had come new frightening weapons of war. The world would go on changing, that was in the nature of things. Organisations would come and go but the quest for discovery and new knowledge, the basis of science, would never die. There would come a time when enough knowledge would be acquired to release humanity from the chains of its past and the boundaries set by nature. That was not now, but it would come.

Fellows felt so tired he could not resist the overwhelming desire to sleep. It was nearly midnight when he turned off the light to go to bed. Before doing so he peeped through the curtains and saw the police car was still in place. By a lucky coincidence or a chance of fate, just at that moment he saw the driver of the car walking with another person into the woods that lined the road. They were on the edge of his vision; only dimly lit by intermittent moonlight as clouds scurried across the sky. Perhaps it was the relief policeman, but why so soon and why hide in the woods? Tiredness turned into anxiety. His heartbeat increased as if preparing for a race. Instinctively he reached for the revolver in the drawer. There were only two bullets left over from a previous firing practice he did some months back. He was a good shot and while at Los Alamos had taken advantage of some army training in weapons. The gun gave him some measure of protection.

Many things raced through his mind. In such situations various scenarios spring into being. Was the police bodyguard one of the conspirators? A site policeman would certainly have access to the buildings at Halborn and would have been well-placed to assist Mueller. He and Rowley had suspected a cell was operating at Halborn. Cells usually comprise of at least three persons. If that were true, it was an unforgiveable failure of security for a policeman to have escaped detection. Who were the persons he saw from the window and what were they doing? Very few people knew the security code to enter the building and the apartment. Any attempt that failed would automatically trigger the alarm system.

Fellows decided to call the policeman on the intercom phone to say he was going to bed. He watched as the man, who was still out of the car, walked swiftly back to the car to pick up the phone.

'Hello,' he replied. Fellows inquired if everything was OK. 'Yes, it's all quiet out here, nothing to report.'

A dark figure could be seen moving across the road while the policeman spoke.

Fellows said, 'Good night,' and rang off.

They would know he was still awake so perhaps that would delay any attempt to break in. Fellows dialled Rowley's telephone number. The head of security did not like being disturbed late at night but this was an emergency. The number didn't ring, the phone line was down. Fellows was on his own. He took some cushions from the settee and placed them in the bed and pulled up the bedcovers to make it look like he was sleeping. With the gun in hand, he waited. An hour passed and Fellows found it hard to stay awake. Then he heard what sounded like a depressed thud like footsteps on the stairs. Someone was in the house. They obviously had a means of bypassing or taking out the security system.

Fellows sat on a cushion on the floor behind a chair in a corner of the bedroom, which gave him a clear view of the door and the bed. He would see whoever came through the door. He carried a torch in one hand and steadied the gun in the other. Sweat ran down his forehead as the intruder came closer to the door. A horrific thought crossed his mind. The gun in his hand hadn't been used for some time, would it work or would it jam? It was too late now to find alternatives. Seconds ticked by, nothing happened. Silence. Then the door burst open, a tall black-coated figure pointed a gun at the bed and fired three successive shots that resounded in dull thuds on the pillow. The gun was fitted with a silencer. Fellows immediately responded. He shone the torch into the intruder's face, causing temporary blindness, and fired a shot. Knocked back by surprise, the intruder doubled up, regained control, turned and fired a round at the source of the light. After Fellows had fired, he dropped the torch and moved from behind the chair just in time to see the torch disintegrate in a shower of sparks as the bullets hit its metal case. The room was in darkness except for a glimmer of moonlight coming through the semi-transparent curtains. The intruder had been hit and was incapacitated and, being unsure of what was in the room, fled down the stairs and out of the front door, disappearing into the darkness of the woods.

Fellows felt relieved to have survived and made no attempt to give chase. Surely the policeman would have heard the shot and would be responding? Looking out of the window, he could see the police car was still on the road but there was no sign of him. Suddenly there were loud sounds of shouting and gunfire in the woods. Through the window Fellows saw a bewildering sight. Police cars with lights blazing and men running everywhere.

Two plain clothes men with pistols cocked in the ready mode and a uniformed one rushed into the house and up the stairs to confront Fellows.

'Are you alright?' they shouted in unison.

'Yes I'm alright,' he replied. Adding, 'What the hell is going on?'

The older plain clothes man, who Fellows assumed was a senior detective, asked him to sit down after taking the revolver from his quivering hand. 'I am Superintendent Bob Fuller and this is Inspector Richard Adams. We are from Special Branch of the London Metropolitan Police.'

Another uniformed man came rushing into the room, saying the suspect had been shot and killed. The detective swore,

'Bloody hell, I told them not to kill her. We needed the woman alive.'

Fellows looked at the detective. 'Woman?' he said.

'Yes, the assassin who tried to kill you was a woman named Anna Fischer, she was Mueller's accomplice and an East German. We believe she was the controller and headed up the cell. She probably killed Mueller.

'Your shot wounded her enough to make her flee. It was a good shot. I only wish she had not shot at our policemen who returned the fire in self-defence. But I think she wanted to die rather than be captured. She was probably about to shoot herself anyway.'

'What about the policeman, Alan O'Leary?'

'He was dead when we arrived. I think she shot him in the head before she entered the house. We are dealing with ruthless people who don't want to be caught and leave any evidence. O'Leary was the insider of the cell at Halborn who assisted Mueller. It was Rowley, with help from us, who tracked him down. We found papers at Mueller's flat that had only partially been burned. They gave us the information to identify his accomplices. It looks like Fischer left in a hurry and fortunately for us didn't do a good job at destroying the material. Your name was next on her list so we took the opportunity to set a trap. We tracked her to this house but unfortunately lost her on the road here and had to make a detour. Sorry we arrived late. Glad you had a gun otherwise the end result may have been different.'

Fellows was furious. 'You mean I was set up as bait? I could have been killed.'

'Yes, we are sorry about that but we were acting on orders. It was the only way we could catch these people.'

'On whose orders?' Fellows asked.

'I cannot say now but you will be given an explanation later. The papers we found in Swindon have wider implications. I have been asked to take you to London at the request of the Home Secretary.'

Still angry, Fellows said, 'I need some rest.'

'We appreciate that so we have booked you a room at a hotel in London. You have an appointment to meet with the Minister and the Chairman of the Atomic Energy Authority tomorrow morning at ten o'clock. A helicopter will be arriving soon to take us to London so please pack some clothes.'

'You will not be returning here, it's too dangerous,' said the other detective.

Fellows insisted on calling Rowley from a phone in the police car but he did not answer, probably too embarrassed, knowing his complicity in setting up the operation.

The silence of the night was broken by a police helicopter landing on the road. The local villagers must have wondered what was happening in their normally undisturbed haven of England. Fuller and Adams accompanied Fellows into the plane and they sped off towards London. Fellows used the opportunity to find out how Anna Fischer had found him and been able to overcome the security system and enter the building. He was told she had called O'Leary who had connived to be his escort. Fuller, rather embarrassingly said, 'That's being investigated. O'Leary also knew the security system in the house and how to immobilize it. He did that after you went in so the way was clear for her. Our GCHQ traced a telephone call she made to him so we were able to locate her exact position in Swindon. We also knew from the papers we found that you were the next on the assassination list. We followed her car to the house but she parked in the woods about a mile away and then went on foot. It was at that point we lost her. We did not wish to alert the woman by arriving too soon since we knew O'Leary would be waiting. It was hearing your shots that told us she was in the house. When we arrived O'Leary was dead in the car. She had shot him before going into the house. You know the rest.'

Fellows replied. 'If I hadn't had a gun, you would be looking at a demotion and I would be dead. Fischer was a professional and would certainly have killed me. How did the cell, as you call it, manage to operate for so long without detection? They must have had other help, either from outside or inside Halborn.'

Fuller told Fellows that Special Branch was carrying out a thorough investigation of the security at Halborn. 'It will be tightened up and a new professional will be put in charge. Your Brigadier Rowley may have to take early retirement.'

As they flew over London in the early hours of the morning, the capital city seemed to be alive. 'London never sleeps' came a reply from Fuller who saw the scientist looking at the sights below. The machine passed over the Thames and the Parliament buildings to land on a hard standing on the South Bank of the river. A car was waiting to take them to a small hotel located a few blocks away. There was a strong police presence around the hotel; this time all precautions were being taken. The assassins had been killed and the cell broken up but they were no nearer to finding those who controlled it.

The next day Fellows was taken to the top floor of the Home Office to be met by a portly man with a balding head. He looked like a cross between the comic character Billy Bunter and a James Bond film villain. The fat man asked a woman, who was physically his opposite in stature, and presumably the secretary, to fetch some tea and biscuits. He introduced himself as Charles Rigby-Smith, Personal Director of the Atomic Energy Authority. Rigby-Smith led Fellows to an office overlooking Whitehall. He introduced him to two men sitting at a table in the centre of the room. One was Sir Donald Fielding of the Ministry of Defence and the other, Martin May from the Cabinet Office. Rigby-Smith started by apologising to Fellows for bringing him to London so soon after the ordeal he had just experienced. He said they had been asked to convene the meeting by the Prime Minister and the Home Secretary. He went on to say the meeting was private and no notes would be taken. Fellows knew whatever assurances were given, the meeting would be recorded and filed; that's how the Civil Service operated. This wasn't going to be just a routine meeting.

Rigby-Smith did the standard speech on how invaluable the work being carried out at Halborn was to the nation's security and standing in the world. The Prime Minister was determined that nothing would stop Britain from achieving its goals in becoming a leading military nuclear power. He went on to say the business at Halborn was unfortunate but it must not prevent the success of Blue Star.

Fellows looked around and saw the other two men looking down at the files in front of them. So far they had not made eye contact with him. Rigby-Smith suddenly changed from his friendly rather whimsical manner. He told Fellows that certain information had come to the Government from reliable sources about a secret organisation known as The Brotherhood Foundation, run by a group of people, who called themselves The Inner Sanctum. Some held senior positions in certain Governments. In fact, whatever their motives, they were spies who used their privileged positions to access confidential and sometimes secret information for their own purposes. Looking directly at Fellows with his piecing brown eyes, Rigby-Smith reminded him of the Official Secrets Act that he had signed when accepting the post at Halborn. He told Fellows they knew he was the Vice President of The Brotherhood Foundation and its Inner Sanctum. They also knew the names of other members, including its President, David Simons, who at this moment was being interviewed by the FBI. Paul Fields' name was not mentioned which surprised Fellows. Rigby-Smith continued to tell Fellows that because he had failed to declare his association and interests, he had contravened the Act. This carried a substantial prison sentence and automatic dismissal from his post at Halborn. Noting Fellows' distress, Fielding interrupted Smith, who seemed to be enjoying the interrogation.

'We know you have personally suffered losses at Halborn. Your leadership and professionalism have guaranteed success of the Blue Star Project for which the Government is grateful. But in view of the seriousness of the offence, your case will have to go to the Office of Public Prosecutions. The Atomic Energy Authority is left with no option than to replace you as Director of Halborn since you have broken the terms of your contract. The risk of further disruption to the programme by further incidents is too great at this time.' Fielding paused to give Fellows a chance to speak.

It was now his opportunity to tell them why The Brotherhood Foundation was founded back in the 1930s, and the reason why an element of secrecy was necessary. Fellows told the three men that no member had ever broken The Official Secrets Act and given away the nation's secrets to anyone. He admitted he had deceived the Government and apologised for that but had never broken the law. He and his colleagues had always worked hard to protect the national interest as was evident by their work at Halborn and elsewhere.

The men listened. Fielding, a typical professional civil servant and probably a member of the same club as Rigby-Smith, asked

Fellows why it had been necessary over the years to keep The Foundation's activities secret if its intentions were honourable. Fellows told him that most scientists had the knowledge but without the power to use it since they were never part of the decision-making process. He cited the development of the atomic bomb and nuclear energy as examples where the scientists that made them possible had no say in their use and applications but were blamed by society for the consequences of their use. It was a question of understanding the long-term consequences rather than the short-term benefits often referred to by politicians. The three inquisitors looked at him without comment and almost contempt. It was obvious they were the type of people who were at the root of the problem. Rigby-Smith continued talking.

'The Government knows your life's in danger and the exposure of a trial, much of which would be held in secret, would not be in your or the Government's interest. The proposition is: the Government would announce you have been killed in a car accident. You will be given a new identity. It might be possible for you to take a visiting professorship at a little-known university or just retire and remain anonymous. This would avoid a trial and a prison sentence and your enemies would not be able to find you. The Government will provide you with a house which you will own, a pension and security for the rest of your life. But you will never talk or write about your work at Halborn to anyone. You will resign from The Brotherhood and never associate with any of its members. MI5 and the FBI are currently investigating the Foundation and prosecutions could follow for some members. If you accept the proposition you will be guaranteed immunity from prosecution.'

Fellows interrupted to say that the real enemy was The New Order, not the Brotherhood. He would be prepared to accept the proposal on the condition he could be unofficially permitted to help the security services bring to justice those New Order members who were responsible for the deaths of his colleagues at Halborn. Rigby-Smith said he would talk to the Prime Minister and Home Secretary who wanted the situation resolved quietly as soon as possible. Meanwhile Fellows was told to return to the hotel where police protection would be provided. The three men thanked him and said they hoped a satisfactory conclusion could be reached for everyone concerned.

Fellows was distraught at the predicament in which he now found himself. He wondered what David Simons was experiencing. They still had their secret telephone number unless that had also been compromised by the police. Their enemy, The New Order, had dealt a fatal blow to The Brotherhood. But not every member's name was necessarily revealed. Fellows did not want to change his identity and throw away everything he had worked for all his life, but if it meant he could escape the ignominy of prison and be allowed to fight The New Order, then he was left with no alternative. After what had happened he could not go back to Halborn anyway, so losing his job was not such a great disaster. Losing The Brotherhood gave him much more grief.

Later in the day Simons called Fellows. Their encoded telephone number was still active so nobody could listen into their calls. He had apparently been through the same experience as Fellows, except the FBI and State Department wanted his help in tracking down New Order members in exchange for giving him an amnesty. They were more appreciative of the work of The Brotherhood and although he had to officially resign his Government advisory post, the FBI was prepared to pay unofficially for his services. He would also be given a new identity and a chair at the University of Arizona in Tucson. Simons told Fellows that he should come to America. Fellows liked that idea but didn't think he would be allowed to leave the country as he would then be outside the jurisdiction of English Law.

David Simons did not know the names of other members of the Inner Sanctum that had been revealed. He still had his contact who was a member of The New Order, but for the time being, he had gone to ground. Before doing so he revealed the material stolen from Halborn had been sold to an American client. Part of the plan had been to discredit Fellows and put back the Blue Star programme. In that, they had partially succeeded. The name of the individual who was actually behind the Halborn attack was unknown but was thought to be either American or German. Fellows knew the police possessed papers taken from Mueller's flat which had helped their investigations and eventually led them to the cell leader and killer, Anna Fischer. What else did they know? It was obvious there had been an exchange of information between MI5 and the FBI and CIA. He felt there was a bigger political game being played out in which they were only just small fry.

Early next morning Rigby-Smith called Fellows to say the Prime Minister and Home Secretary had agreed to Fellows' request. They would make arrangements for Henry Fellows to be killed-off in a car accident so there could be a public announcement and new Director appointed at Halborn. Meanwhile a safe place in the country would be found where Fellows was not known. He reluctantly agreed to the terms. But Fellows was curious about why Paul Fields' name was not mentioned. He seemed to have gone to ground. Had he escaped detection or was someone covering for him? Did it mean other Brotherhood members' names may not have been discovered? Fields must have known what had happened to Fellows which was probably the reason why he remained silent. Fellows rang Fields using their encoded number. The number failed to ring; it had been disconnected. That left him with mixed feelings. Had the Brotherhood survived or was he betrayed by his old friend and colleague? He would have to find out.

PART 3
THE CONSPIRACY

CHAPTER 7

The New Order

I know no safer depository of the ultimate power of society but the people themselves.

Thomas Jefferson

Background

A Greek democracy based on a form of government in which governing power is derived from the people, either by direct referendum or by means of elected representatives of the people was widely established in the twentieth century. Over the centuries it has developed and replaced Feudalism and Dictatorship in many countries. Democracy is enshrined in the American Constitution and is now central to most European political systems.

Democracy is continually challenged by other systems. These include: Absolute Monarchy (rule by hereditary individuals), 'Dictatorships' (rule by an individual supported by a political party), Fascism, Communism (state rule by single party), 'Oligarchy' (rule by an elite) and Theocracy (God – religious autocracy – Islam).

After the Great Depression of the 1920s, some of countries in Europe, Latin America, and Asia turned to Fascism, Communism and Dictatorship as a form of Government. The Second brought a reversal of this trend in Western Europe.

The International Brotherhood Society, created by a group of scientists in the early 1930s, was seen by many as an attempt to build an oligarchy of scientists. It was certainly in the minds of the early founders, who based their ideas on what H G Wells envisaged in his book, *The Shape of Things to Come*. They had to make it a secret organisation otherwise democratic institutions and Governments would have seen it as a threat. In principle, the secrecy element was no different to that practised by the Freemasons and many other secret societies. The aims of The Brotherhood were actually the opposite of what oligarchies usually represent. A constitution was written in 1938 and the Society was converted into an International Foundation.

At the end of the Second World War, some members of The Brotherhood used its veil of secrecy to further their personal gains. A number of like-minded members formed a secret inner group, encouraged by an industrialist, who offered two members a million dollars for confidential information. It was the start of a new era in profitable industrial espionage. Simons and Fellows suspected existence of the renegade group operating within The Brotherhood. It was confirmed when they discovered that secret documents, relating to the design of the first atomic bomb, had been passed to people who were in contact with Soviet agents. One Brotherhood member with others was thought to be responsible for the murder of Peter Petrovitch. But later all met their deaths in suspicious car accidents.

The post-war era opened up new global markets for goods and services. Increased air travel, the rapid development of radio communication and advanced world trade helped those with insider knowledge to accumulate wealth. This extended to the stock markets where millions of dollars could be made from just a few selected transactions. Most of the money came from deals in commodities such as oil, coal, and precious metals required by the new industries. At the time, an extensive black market existed for goods that were in short supply. Sales escaped tax, so goods could be sold directly to the customer at prices well below the market rate. This was particularly lucrative in European countries whose economies had been devastated by the war.

Under the cover of The Brotherhood Foundation, the renegade group grew strong. It attracted people with political ambitions with a desire to become rich. They called themselves The New Order. The name had political connotations. It was used in the early works of Wells and Szilard. As time passed, the more active members accumulated large bank balances. A code of silence, intimidation and bribery, similar to that practised by the Mafia was established. Those who broke the code were usually quietly disposed of; road accidents were the most common but later more sophisticated methods of murder were employed using drugs.

The FBI and similar agencies in European countries had been fighting an underground war against criminal organisations since the 1920s but new technology and the possession of the greater wealth meant they were losing the battle. This subterranean war was as dangerous as the more open Cold War that existed between the Soviet Union and the West from the 1940s up to the 1990s. Now at the close of the twentieth century, The New Order emerged as the strongest and most dangerous of all the groups because its growing membership extended across borders, governments and politics. Power breeds corruption and fuels ambition. The name New Order implied a replacement of democratic government by an elite-led authoritarianism.

Eventually, The New Order disconnected its members from The Brotherhood Foundation and became autonomous. A governing Cabal of seven leading members was formed. In the 1960s they become millionaires from their clandestine activities, enabling them to offer generous bribes to politicians, judges, senior civil servants and even members of the police and security services. Following The Brotherhood's methods, The New Order became well-embedded into the fabric of the societies in their respective countries. The companies they controlled employed millions of people. This gave them economic and political power. They became the new barons of the twentieth century. The New Order dominated the criminal underworld and soon found itself in conflict with the Mafia and other well-established criminal organisations. But unlike these, it did not need to depend on the loyalty of family members, trade unions or professional societies because many of its members were in influential positions in companies, state institutions and agencies. Some were coerced into membership by the use of blackmail and the inducement of large sums of money.

When it suited them, The New Order avoided conflict with the long-established criminal fraternities by negotiating mutually beneficial arrangements with them. For example, it agreed not to become involved in drug or people trafficking. It was a win-win situation and preferable to the turf wars of the past which resulted in murder and mayhem amongst those involved. During the 1970s, New Order members had infiltrated into governments and security agencies and the board rooms of many key multinational companies. A fatal chasm existed between The New Order and The Brotherhood Foundation. Things came to a head in 1959 when The New Order became responsible for incidents at the Halborn Atomic Weapons Research Establishment in England. A number of key scientists working on Britain's top secret hydrogen bomb programme were killed. The whole operation was bungled, resulting in the deaths of all The Order's agents. But a fatal blow had been done to The Brotherhood Foundation. Papers recovered by the police at the flat belonging to the leader of the Halborn cell revealed names of The Brotherhood's Inner Sanctum. This resulted in Simons and Fellows losing their high-ranking Government jobs and virtually destroyed the Foundation. But it brought The New Order to the notice of all the world's leading security agencies. The names of members of the Cabal were not revealed and they remained a powerful group.

A secret nuclear device, computer codes and other documents stolen from Halborn were sold to an American client for an undisclosed sum of money. Someone didn't want Britain to have a lead in hydrogen bomb design. The success of the British hydrogen bomb trials that took place in the Pacific in 1959 eventually led to a workable partnership with the American Atomic Energy Commission. At last, Churchill and Roosevelt's original agreement was realised. It opened up a new era in Anglo-American relationships. This strengthened NATO and was a key factor in preventing Soviet aggression in Europe. It marked a turning point, a stalemate in the Cold War, since now each side had similar weapons and delivery systems. But who had the will to use them first should a conflict arise? This was to be put to the test in 1962 when the Soviet Union shipped missiles to Communist Cuba. Jack Kennedy, the American President, reacted by threatening to physically stop Soviet ships from entering a blockade that he set up around Cuba. It became known as the Cuban Missile Crisis and exposed the vulnerability of the world to nuclear annihilation by the two superpowers. The two countries came close to a nuclear war but a last minute secret deal with the Soviets prevented such a disaster.

After the Cuban Missile Crisis, The New Order took advantage of the unpopularity of the Kennedys. The Soviet Union's leaders never forgave the American President for making them lose face. Some ultra-right wing elements joined The New Order since they were opposed to the liberal policies of the Democratic President and his brother, Robert. The Russian member of the Cabal was not a communist but he saw an opportunity to discredit the Communist Soviets. He linked up with some of the disenchanted American members to plan the assassination of the Kennedys. They hired people to carry out the acts who would be traced to the Soviets and their Cuban allies. The Order made sure they had members on the official Warren Commission, set up after the President's assassination in 1963, to establish who was behind the act. Nothing was actually proved but suspicion fell on Soviet and Cuban agents. There were some who thought right-wing elements and even the CIA were involved in a conspiracy. The New Order made sure that those expressing such views met premature deaths in car accidents.

The Order's Cabal was the equivalent of The Brotherhood's Inner Sanctum. The difference was this breakaway group of extremists were intent on taking control of the world's sources of wealth. Now near the end of the twentieth century, they also wanted political power. In 1982, the Cabal decided to elect one of their members, Jean Dupuis, the Head of a French Industrial consortium of arms manufacturers known as FAM, to be its first

Chairman. He was rich with extensive worldwide contacts. He was also one of the founders of a right-wing French political party that initially supported the Gaullists but later became disenchanted with their coalitions with the left-wing socialists.

The Cold War had reached its height in the 1960s and initiated a massive arms race that divided the world into armed power camps, led by America and the Soviet Union. These two super-powers represented the ideologies of Capitalism and Communism. It was an ideal situation for some members of The New Order to exploit the needs of both camps and accumulate vast wealth for themselves from the sales of military equipment. The millionaires became billionaires.

The seven members of the Cabal created symbolic aliases to conceal their identities. They were: Eaglestar (America); Lionheart (Britain); Wolfman (Germany); Fox (France); Bear (Russia); Serow (Japan); Tiger (India).

Membership of the Cabal was for life. Members could not resign or retire since they knew too much. There was only one way to exit. The number seven was chosen owing to its religious and mythological associations. According to Genesis, the world was created in seven days. There are seven deadly sins and seven wonders of the ancient world. In Japanese mythology there are seven gods of good fortune and seven principles in the Bushido Samurai code.

The first British member of the Cabal was Professor Paul Fields. He was also a member of the Inner Sanctum of The Brotherhood Foundation and trusted friend of Fellows and Simons after their experiences at the Trinity site so he had a serious conflict of interest. After the Second World War, owing to their unique experience of the Manhattan Project, Fields and Fellows were given top Government jobs in Britain. Fields did not change his Brotherhood allegiance until the late 1950s. After his wife's death, he started to drink and gamble. Unknown to his colleagues, he became in debt to a number of unscrupulous financiers. His life was threatened. He was desperate for money. Knowing he would lose his job in the Civil Service if his debt was discovered, Field sought help from a fellow member of The Brotherhood, who, unknown to him at the time, was also a member of The New Order. The member gave him the name of a contact who offered to pay his debts and a large sum of money in exchange for secret information.

Fields was a Senior Scientific Advisor at the Ministry of Defence and had access to Britain's secret weapons programme. At first he refused, but after receiving death threats from his creditors, he agreed to copy some classified documents for the man who had given him the money but whose name he did not know. Secret papers were passed to the client in library books. It was a classic blackmail situation and Fields had fallen into the trap. Being a senior and trusted member of staff, he was able to carry on spying without being caught. At the time he took great risks because MI5 were active in seeking out spies within the Civil Service. A number of notable people were caught after being blackmailed by the Soviet KGB. Within a year, while still pretending to be working for The Brotherhood, who were pleased to have one of their members in an influential Government position, Fields became very rich from his clandestine activities. He maintained contact with Henry Fellows at the Halborn Research Establishment and other members of the Inner Sanctum, including David Simons. He was able to do this in his official capacity as a Government Advisor on Weapons. Up until the time of the incident at Halborn, Fields and Fellows had regular contacts involving the Blue Star Project.

In late 1958, Fields was elected to the Inner Cabal of The New Order on the condition he worked to destroy The Brotherhood and its founders. At first, he was reluctant to accept their proposition since he still owed his position to Fellows and Simons, but refusal was not an option. They had made him rich; they possessed him and could destroy him by making one phone call. He had no choice but to accept their invitation. Assurances were given that his secret would be protected. They had people in very powerful positions in the Government whom he did not know. He knew what they could do to him and his family.

After Fields agreed to join the Cabal, he found out what they really wanted. It was the secret device that researchers at Halborn were developing to make a Super H-bomb. They wanted him to use his position to protect a cell of people the Cabal had placed at Halborn. Their mission was to steal the device and the associated top secret files. It was the most daring project The New Order had undertaken but the stakes were high and Fields was promised two hundred thousand dollars in advance and the same amount on a successful delivery. All the resources he required would be made available. He was told not to try and find out the identity of the client but was assured it was not the KGB, the Soviet Secret Service, the declared enemy of the American and British security agencies. It was purely a commercial deal being done for money. The amount of money being offered for the task was too great to refuse. But some members of The Order had other ambitions. Possessing such a nuclear device would buy a lot of power.

After the disastrous incidents at Halborn, Fields was retired from his Government advisory job to take up a professorship at the University of Oxford. It was a normal path taken by senior Government scientists. When the names of The Brotherhood's Inner Sanctum were revealed to the Government, Field's name had not been included. At the time, Fellows thought it strange. It raised his suspicions but knowing that MI5 was watching, he decided not to try and make contact with Fields. Clearly someone high-up in the Civil Service had protected Fields and arranged his timely exit. That meant The Order had another highly placed person on their payroll.

It was a year later when David Simons found out from a contact he had who was a confidante of a senior member of The Order, about Fields' dark secret. Simons passed the information to Fellows, who was living under the assumed name of Malcolm Walker, a retired bank manager, at his Cotswold home. A few months later, when the opportunity arose, Fields met his justice on the road outside his mansion near Abingdon, when his car collided head-on with a van which happened to be on the wrong side of the road. The coroner declared accidental death by persons unknown. Fellows, the driver of the van, felt a sense of satisfaction that his friends and colleagues had, at last, been avenged. But he knew someday someone would find him to seek retribution.

Fields had married late but his wife had died of cancer some years back, leaving a daughter from a previous marriage. His step-daughter, Diane Hunter, was a brilliant business woman. After graduating from the London School of Economics, she went to America and took an MBA at Harvard. She managed Fields' many business interests and helped to make him a multi-millionaire. After his death, she inherited his estate. She knew about his dark past but, being even more ruthless, admired what he did.

Diane had political ambitions. Driven in the early 1970s by a disastrous period of socialism the country had ever experienced, she started a right-wing faction within the British Conservative Party. During that period she was one of the few Conservative members to be elected. It was a safe west-country seat vacated by the retirement of the existing member. By coincidence, the constituency also covered the Halborn Establishment. At the time, Fellows lived only forty miles away. It was an ironic twist of fate when he learnt that the step-daughter of the man who had betrayed him and The Brotherhood was his Member of Parliament. Some thought that her selection as candidate for the seat was rigged as no alternative person was put forward by the Party. Perhaps The New Order had used its influence. She was the ideal person to replace her father on the Inner Cabal and was automatically elected as the first woman member. At first, some members resented her election until they discovered how ruthless she could be.

Diane was one of the leading candidates for the leadership of the Conservative Party in 1975 and only missed the vote by a small margin. After Margaret Thatcher's election she became one of her closest supporters. Nobody knew about her membership of The New Order but her close associations with high-level people in Government proved very useful. She was strongly opposed to the European Union and favoured closer links with America where she had many friends and contacts. She wanted stronger immigration laws and hated socialism. She inherited her Cabal codename, Lionheart, from her father. It should have been Lioness but the others didn't want to accept the female version. Diane was, in Greek mythology, the hunting goddess. In the years that followed, the appropriateness of the name would become apparent. Their new British member more than lived up to her symbolic names. She left the Conservative Party after not being re-elected at the next general election and formed her own right wing nationalist party.

In 1998, the leaders of The New Order observed that global events were converging to a point where their power and influence could be used to change the economic and political structure of the world. The seven billionaire members of the Cabal, who represented some of the world's richest multi-national companies, had never physically met. They were phantoms who hid behind aliases and false addresses. They made their own decisions and created their own strategies. They owned international businesses and companies and secretly exerted a lot of power over governments.

Cabal members protected their identities by distancing themselves from those lower down in their companies. It was virtually impossible to weave through their intricate webs to find who made the top-level decisions. Only a few trusted people could identify them. Most criminal and terrorist networks operate on the same principle. Global business, including banks, had always operated in this way. Governments come and go but the power brokers are always in place. But each member was limited in what could be achieved. Global power would require the players to have a collective strategy.

Known billionaires are listed by the American Forbes directory. Members of the Cabal were not listed by Forbes as they took steps to safeguard their anonymity. They were, however, on the Boards of many companies as secret benefactors under aliases, since their names had to be legally recorded.

The American member, who started his career in science, was now a banker with controlling shares in the three largest American banks. He had advanced his political connections by being a major, but unknown, donor of the American Republican Party. Some leading politicians owed their positions to him. This gave him the control over people. It was like an aphrodisiac every time he used it. He enjoyed the power to make people obey his wishes. Coming from a poor farming family in the Mid-West, he had suffered the indignity of having to do what others wanted because they had the money. Now it was his turn and he was taking full advantage of it.

The banks owned large tranches of American real estate and had investments in almost all industries, including military equipment, telecommunication, automotive, aerospace, pharmaceuticals, food and tobacco, retailing and energy companies. Eaglestar's wealth grew each year and with it his power to control the lives of millions of people.

Fox had a global network of arms dealers. At a high-level arms meeting in Saudi Arabia, one of Fox's dealers recorded a conservation made by an associate of a wealthy Islamic fundamentalist named Osama Bin Laden. Further investigations indicated that Bin Laden was funding a major Al-Qaeda bombing campaign planned to take place in America, Britain and France. Fox communicated this information to other members of the Cabal. They collectively decided to break their basic rule and plan a secret face-to-face meeting to discuss a strategy to deal with this threat as it could seriously damage their global interests.

Bin Laden was the spiritual leader and funder of the Islamic Terrorist group, Al-Qaeda. The group used suicide bombing as one of its tools of terror. Suicide bombing was not an Islamic phenomena. It has been used by atheists, anarchists and other sects over many centuries. Such people who want to kill themselves do so more because of their allegiance to their associates in the group rather than for the cause they represent. Al-Qaeda usurped and distorted the Islamic faith for its own purposes by preaching that the killing of non-Muslims, or non-believers as they were called, and sacrificing themselves at the same time, was expected by Allah. It was surprising how many converts they made. Many were young, impressionable Muslims being taught at Madrasa schools in Islamic countries such as Pakistan. The fundamentalists were building an army of extremists to service their political and military ambitions. They were basically a nebulas network of fanatics who believed in a narrow mediaeval way of life based on a distorted interpretation of an ancient religion. In many countries their followers came from poor disadvantaged people who were easily brainwashed. They were controlled by a network of handlers. In many countries sleepers, who could be activated at any time by a single phone call, worked and lived amongst the population. Suicide bombers had already proved how effective they could be in the Middle East against unsuspecting members of the public.

The New Order was close to achieving its ultimate aim, to become The New World Order. Now was the time to take action. In the late twentieth century, America dominated the world. It had both economic and military power. After the break-up of the Soviet Union into a fragmented loose federation, that power was unchallenged. A power vacuum existed that many wanted to fill. Communist China was posed to make the challenge but it was too early for them. It was currently struggling to build up a new economy and prove that Communism with a capitalist face could bring prosperity, unlike the dismal failure of the Communist Soviet Union. The growing threat of Islamic fundamentalism, stimulated by the Gulf War and the hardened Israeli stance against the Palestinians, presented America with real problems, but the Islamists with an opportunity.

Fox, who first brought Bin Laden's intentions to the Cabal, took the bold step to approach a high-level contact in the French Ministry of the Interior to secure a one-day use of The Château de Rambouillet as a venue for a Cabal summit. A very large sum of Euros was exchanged. The summit was to be put under the guise of a one-day high-level conference of leading bankers to discuss the growing crisis in global trade. The Ministry controlled the national police service and only its head would be notified about the date and purpose of the summit. They were told that total secrecy was vital because it was important not to raise alarms in the stock markets since it would threaten share prices. Nobody would suspect that a group of the world's leading bankers would dare to use such a prominent location to hold a nefarious meeting to discuss how to replace the world's democracies. It was Fox's symbolic way of demonstrating the heights to which The New Order had risen. Past kings and leaders had met at the Château to take important decisions.

The Château de Rambouillet was a castle with a long history of ownership and use by kings and national leaders since its origins in the fourteenth century. On August 1944, prior to the liberation of Paris, General Charles de Gaulle arrived at Rambouillet and set up his headquarters. The next day he left by car to enter a liberated Paris. In November 1975, the first "G6" summit was organized in the Château by the French President for the heads of the world's leading industrialized countries. Since then, it had been used as an occasional residence by French Presidents. Security would be provided by the French police but arrangements would be made by the delegates' own organisations. No media would be allowed and the date of the conference would be kept a secret.

At the end of the twentieth century, those who controlled cyberspace had a strong influence in the world as was evident by the power of The Internet. Early start-up companies were already setting up websites and trading. The success of The New Order's operations relied on being able to communicate with its members but at the same time protecting their identities. They employed the very latest generation of sophisticated satellite encryption telephone and computer systems for this purpose and the best experts to maintain and operate it globally. Encryption of data was not new and used by every security agency wanting to protect its files. With such equipment, wiretapping was not possible because the encryption key is never transmitted. All intercepted calls were scrambled and could not be decoded without knowledge or possession of the code.

An all-digital satellite communications system used by the Cabal had specially made and encoded cryptochips. Each time the phone was used, the encryption system changed and never repeated itself. Without an exact replica of the cryptochip, it was impossible for anyone to identify or trace the caller or their location. Most of the criminals, spies and terrorists were caught because they used conventional telephone transmissions or less sophisticated enciphers that could easily be picked up and decoded by the security agencies. Even the military who had access to the most advanced technology, still relied on experts to programme their systems, but only paid a fraction of the salaries offered by The Order's Cabal. It was a new technique for encrypting information based on quantum encryption technology that gave the Cabal members an advantage.

Dr Colin Niedermeyer received a call from his sole client, Freiburg Engineering, a German satellite communications company requesting an upgrade of the software used on the satellite communications system. It was only the second time such a request had been made so he knew something important was being planned. Niedermeyer was an expert microchip design engineer with a distinguished career as Chief Engineer for IBM until he found working as an independent consultant made him a multi-millionaire. His expertise in quantum cryptography and software development linked to customise microchip design was unique. He had to sign a confidentiality clause with the company and give them exclusive rights for use of the software. He was worried that his client wanted him to re-design and programme a special new silicon cryptochip processor for one of their satellite communications systems under the strictest security, without allowing him to know who owned the satellite system and to what purpose it was used. He was paid so well that he didn't bother to ask any questions.

After gaining his first degree in Electronic Engineering at the University of Michigan, Colin Niedermeyer did his PhD at the University of Arizona in Tucson on data encryption for communication satellites, as part of the space programme sponsored by NASA. The University of Arizona undertook research in space science. It was where he met Professor Stanley Rheiner, alias Dr David Simons, who told him about The Brotherhood Foundation that he and Henry Fellows had founded and how it had been taken over by another secret body who called itself The New Order. Rheiner did not reveal his real name or give away any secrets since it was one of the conditions the FBI placed on him after the incident at Halborn when the names of members of The Brotherhood were revealed. He warned Niedermeyer about the actions and aims of The New Order organisation. It had set up companies to recruit people for their nefarious projects. There was a forty-year difference in their ages but with both families originally from Germany they had a common bond so the two men became good friends. After the war, David Simons found out his parents died in a concentration camp. The same fate had befallen Colin Niedermeyer's grandparents, who were half-Jewish. Simons had never met a woman whom he wanted to marry so did not have the benefit of a son that he always wanted. Colin was like the son he would have liked. Rheiner kept in contact with Niedermeyer after he went to work at the IBM Research Centre at Alameda in California.

A few years later, Niedermeyer met Ludwig Menzies, the Director of the Freiburg Engineering company, at a conference in Berlin. Menzies was so impressed with Niedermeyer's paper that he offered him a job with three times the salary he was being paid at IBM. With family roots in Germany, Niedermeyer wanted to return so the offer was too good to refuse. After the successful design of the first encoded cryptochip, Menzies suggested Niedermeyer set up his own consultancy and offered him a long-term contract to be their sole client. It wasn't long before he became a multi-millionaire and was able to acquire a lavish lifestyle.

Freiburg Engineering was among the many hundreds of high-tech communication companies owned by Heinz Kluge, alias Wolfman; they included TV companies and newspapers. He became the world's satellite communications mogul. Cabal members relied on him for their secure telephone and media outlets. Wolfman was unaware that Niedermeyer, being a highly intelligent man, had made copies of the customised cryptochips and the encryption codes he designed. The confidentiality agreement forbade him keeping any material so he kept them locked away securely in a home safe. It was his form of protection insurance. He had checked out his client's company with an FBI contact. They did not have the company on their files as a supplier or any knowledge of them. His suspicions were raised when he was asked to attend a meeting at Freiburg to discuss an extension of his contract. When he discovered that past consultants had mysteriously disappeared after working for the company, he thought the time had come to invoke his insurance policy. He told his fiancée, Anna Bacher, about the work he had been doing for Freiburg and the cryptochip designs and codes that were secured at his Heidelberg home. In the event of something happening to him, she was to take them to Professor Stanley Rheiner in Tucson who would know what action to take. Noting his apprehension, Anna begged her fiancé not to go to the company. But refusing his client without giving a good reason would only make them suspicious and more determined to see him since he held the software key to their most important product. He was a prisoner of his own success.

Menzies wanted Niedermeyer to programme new cryptochips and take them to the Château de Rambouillet in Northern France for testing with a new satellite communication system being used by a client at a conference. He was not allowed to know who the client was or what the conference was about. Menzies told him it was in the interest of national security and so secret that only a limited number of people knew about it. Niedermeyer was led to believe Freiburg must be working for NATO or a Governmental body. He agreed to take on the task and accompany Menzies. It was to be a fateful decision.

Before starting work, Menzies showed Niedermeyer around the company's laboratories. He was amazed at the number of Cray computers with teraflop processing power they had installed. White-coated men sat at numerous work stations around the building. Menzies told him they were connected to high speed fibre-optic lines around the world and to satellites in geosynchronous orbits. Each had a data storage capacity of terabytes. High definition 3D pictures could be transmitted. Freiburg Engineering was more than a small German company; it was the heart of a global network giving those who controlled the systems huge power. They designed large satellite dishes and had a number of them set up around their buildings. Niedermeyer was not allowed into one room which he was told belonged to a client. He assumed that the Government must be paying for all this latest technology and secret Government work was in progress so didn't bother to ask any further questions. He thought it strange that the FBI new nothing of its existence.

Menzies led him to a work station and told him to use it to programme the new cryptochips for installation in the satellite data control units. He knew hidden cameras would be watching so it was going to be difficult to download a copy of the software. Menzies told him they needed to leave within the next two hours, asking if that was long enough. He told Menzies he would need more time as the cryptochips had to temperature stabilise before they could be made active in the circuits which were operated at liquid nitrogen temperatures to reduce noise levels. Their handling and operation required special skills.

Niedermeyer lied, since most of the programming had already been done, but the tests with the new chips required careful work that could not be rushed. He had a plan to copy the software and keep some spare cryptochips. There was a chip for each quadrant of the satellite data box and a complete set of spares was needed. He would actually programme extra ones to keep. He could easily adjust the software to make it look like four instead of five or six. Nobody would be able to check the chips were missing. The biggest problem was passing through their security search system and taking them out of the Freiburg works. Since he was not suspected of any wrong-doing and was well-known at the factory, any search would not be too rigorous, particularly as he would be with Menzies. Wolfman made a call to Menzies. He simply replied, 'Yes, it's done'.

Three hours later Niedermeyer and Menzies were on the road to Rambouillet in France. Menzies told his consultant he would be well-rewarded for the work he had just completed. It was the cynical tone in his voice that made Niedermeyer sense something was not right. He wondered why he needed to go to France since the data boxes they carried had all been tested. All the client had to do was use the phones. Any conversation would be scrambled and impossible to decode without the chip.

After driving for about an hour they pulled over to a roadside cafe for a break. Menzies ordered some coffee. Niedermeyer excused himself and went to the toilet to get away from Menzies. He took the small encapsulated cryptochips from the battery compartment of his mobile phone and placed them in an envelope and addressed it to his fiancée. He replaced the battery and called her number. She answered immediately as if waiting for the call.

Speaking in a muffled voice he said, 'I have to be quick. I'm sending you the cryptochips. If anything happens to me, send them and the papers that are in my safe, you know the combination, to Professor Stanley Rheiner in Tucson. He will know what to do with them. The address is in amongst the papers.'

'Are you all right? Where are you? What's happening? Are you in danger?' she asked in an anxious voice.

He hastily replied, 'Yes everything is alright but I am on a mission with Menzies and he is behaving a little strange. Don't worry; I will call you again tomorrow.' He had to find an opportunity to post the letter without Menzies seeing it. They were about to leave the cafe when Menzie's phone rang. He turned away so Niedermeyer could not hear the conversation. It was after the call when Menzies dropped his bombshell.

'Colin, something important has come up that needs my urgent attention and I must return to Freiburg. I want you to continue to Rambouillet in a hire car. I see there is a garage next to the cafe that might be able to rent us a car.'

He hastily walked over to it. Niedermeyer could see him talking to what looked like the owner. Menzies took out his wallet and many Euros were passed over. He came back to say they didn't rent out cars but had one he could buy. Pointing to the car which looked as though it had already been made available, he said, 'So we own a three-year-old Renault Megane. It should get you to Rambouillet.' He went over to his Mercedes and transferred the boxes to the boot of the Megane.

'When you arrive tell security you want to see a Monsieur DuPont (it was another alias for Fox). Give him the data boxes and telephones. Wait until he calls you to confirm they work before you leave. You will not be allowed into the Chateau. I suggest you then drive to the nearest railway station and take a train home. Please call me when you get back. Leave the car at the station. I will arrange for someone to collect and dispose of it.'

He then shook hands with Niedermeyer and drove away. Something didn't seem right. It looked like it was a pre-planned set-up. Rambouillet was about three hundred kilometres away and it was late in the afternoon. He was supposed to make the delivery today. It would be a fast drive.

As Niedermeyer drove out onto the autobahn, a black Mercedes, similar to the one Menzies had but larger, also pulled out behind. It stayed with him for about five kilometres then sped past. He looked to see the driver but the car had darkened windows. Seeing a post box in a small town en route he stopped and placed the envelope in it. He was worried about using the postal service for such an important delivery but in the circumstances had little choice.

The Megane did the journey in about four hours and arrived at the Chateau at seven in the evening. Niedermeyer knew he would have to take a train to Strasbourg, the nearest central station to where he lived. It was unlikely he would be able to get a train until the next day. He called Anna and explained what had happened.

It was dark when the Megane stopped at the security gate of the vast Rambouillet Estate. The security barrier forced him to stop. A call was duly made to DuPont. Twenty minutes later a tall, rather sophisticated, grey-haired Frenchman drove up in a black Citroën. He approached Niedermeyer with an outstretched hand and thanked him for travelling so far to deliver the equipment. He apologised profusely at not allowing him to enter the grounds of the Chateau and made utterances about tight national security around the distinguished visitors who were expected to arrive at any time. He did suggest that Niedermeyer had a drink in the small security hut. Taking out the data boxes from the boot of the Megane, the Frenchman placed them in his own car. Niedermeyer told him to test the phones and call back when that was completed. DuPont said he would have to go to the Chateau to do the test and agreed to call. He sped away disappearing into the distance.

Niedermeyer was given a coffee by the security guard. He needed the caffeine to stay awake. It had been a long drive. The feeling of anxiety had not left him. 'Expecting some important VIPs today I understand?' he said to the two guards who looked at him and nodded with a grunt. 'We can't go home until they all arrive,' one of them said. The other, looking very miserable, added,

'And we're not getting extra pay.'

Trying to tease out more information, Niedermeyer asked, 'Is it a large delegation?'

'No, that's the problem, all this secrecy and security is for seven people,' said the other.

'They must be very important then,' Niedermeyer exclaimed.

'No one tells us anything, we have no names just individual passwords they have to show us to gain admittance.'

Niedermeyer's phone rang. 'The test showed all boxes are working. Thank you for your efforts. I'm sure you will be well-rewarded.' The Frenchman then put the phone down. It was the second time he had been told he would be well-rewarded. Niedermeyer looked at the guards and asked, 'Where's the nearest hotel located?'

They told him, 'There is an expensive hotel called the Hotel Mercure Rambouillet where all the high level visitors stay, but they've closed it for a few days. Further along the Rue D'Angiviller there are a number of small hotels near to the Gare de Rambouillet where you can catch a train to Paris tomorrow.' Niedermeyer thought it strange that they knew he needed a train since he had said nothing about going to Paris. He resisted the temptation to ask and instead thanked them and drove back along the road around the park. As he went out onto the road, he noticed the black Mercedes speeding past. He couldn't be sure but it looked like the one that had tailed him from the cafe. It brought him new fears.

The road was not well-lit but a sign for a hotel could be seen just off the road. As the Megane pulled into the car park in front of the hotel, the Mercedes was waiting in the shadows. Two men emerged from the trees carrying guns. One approached Niedermeyer. Before he could lock the car, they pulled him out, placed a hood over his head, and then bundled him into the Mercedes. His hands were tied and a gag placed over his mouth. They searched his pockets and every possible place in the car where something could be hidden. He had an uncomfortable feeling. The end he feared had finally come. He hoped it would be quick. His employer, or the client, must have decided he knew too much or maybe they had seen him take the spare chips. Whatever the reason, this had been planned.

The Mercedes drove off. From his position on the back seat, he detected there was only one man driving the car. There was no talking, nothing to indicate who they were or where they were taking him. After about an hour's drive, the car stopped. It was quiet except for the sound of running water, no sound of traffic. They must be off the main road but near a river. Some time passed before he heard the sound of another car. The two men were back in the car. He then found himself being dragged off the seat by the two men and placed in the front seat of another car. It had a familiar feel; it was his Megane.

Suddenly he felt a jabbing pain in his neck as the syringe discharged its deadly liquid into his blood. Within seconds he was unconscious. Those few seconds of his life seemed much longer. He thought about his mother and father, his fiancée, but like a dream that vanishes when the sleeper wakes up, the images faded. Colin Niedermeyer was dead. Murdered by the same people who had made him rich and because he knew too much and might be become a security risk.

It was some time before the submerged Megane was found complete with its occupant. The crash had been made to look like an accident. The skid marks on the road and the broken fence on the road bridge over the deep river were the only evidence the police could find. The obvious body injuries to the occupant indicated he died as a result of the crash. The inquest recorded accidental death so no police enquiry was carried out.

Niedermeyer's fiancée honoured his wishes and sent the cryptochips and codes to Rheiner in Tucson with a note explaining the circumstances of his death. Two weeks after the funeral, Anna was looking through Niedermeyer's bank account and she saw that Freiburg Engineering had placed a million Euros into his account. He had been well-rewarded. She was suspicious of the circumstances of her fiancé's death but the one million Euros was clearly meant to buy her silence. Menzies did not attend the funeral but sent one of his secretaries to represent the company. He clearly did not want to meet her. She agonised about what to do but realised without proof and further knowledge of those involved, nothing would be gained. Her life and that of her family might be in danger. Those who were responsible for Colin's death were ruthless people. She prayed Stanley Rheiner might be in a better position to do more.

Rheiner opened the package and immediately knew why he had received it. The death of his young friend troubled him greatly. The letter from Anna Bacher gave full details about Freiburg Engineering and the mysterious delivery that Colin Niedermeyer had to make to Rambouillet where a secret meeting had taken place. It also explained the codes and the function of the encryption chips that were carefully wrapped in a sealed box. He soon realised The New Order was involved in planning something big. Reverting to being David Simons, he decided to write to Henry Fellows in England using a secure post office box, about what had happened to Niedermeyer. They had kept in touch over the years using this method. Simons saw the importance of the encryption chips. It would enable him to break into The Order's communication network. But did anyone know that Niedermeyer had sent him the cryptochips? If so, he would now be on their hit list. Before contacting the FBI, who was protecting him, Simons decided to wait and see what happened. Why had Freiburg or The Order murdered Niedermeyer? That was the question he needed answered. Could anyone be trusted? He knew from his contact that The New Order had moles in the FBI and CIA.

The Meeting of the Cabal

The seven members of the Cabal would, for the first time, meet face-to-face in a secluded room at The Château de Rambouillet. During the morning they arrived individually in black limousines with darkened windows. Each was quickly taken to a large room in the basement by two black-suited men wearing dark glasses, who could have been mistaken for FBI agents. The French police were instructed about the need for utmost secrecy of the meeting and the security of those they would be protecting. Police cars discreetly shadowed the limousines as they made their way from the private local airfield. Armed guards were placed at all the entrances and exits to the Chateau. No one would enter or leave once the meeting started. All communication would be done by cell phone and the guards would take their orders from a man named Jacques Dupont, the Head of Security at Rambouillet. The Minister had authorised him only to speak to Fox.

The basement room was furnished in a traditional eighteenth century style. It had been used by Napoleon on his way to exile at Saint Helena and General de Gaulle before he set out to celebrate the liberation of Paris in 1945. Over the centuries, the exotic murals and paintings on the walls had witnessed many scenes that were now part of history. In the centre of the room a large round table was set out with all the paraphernalia needed for a conference. Special satellite encrypted telephones were installed so individuals could talk securely to their consultants if they wished.

Members of the Cabal only knew each other by their given code names. But now their anonymities were about to be destroyed. It was a price they had to pay to be together and agree on the plan that was about to be revealed by the Chairman. Except for the Russian member, most were over the age of sixty. Diane Hunter was seventy-three. She was the head of the new right-wing national party in Britain and she longed for power.

Jean Dupuis, 'Fox', the French billionaire international arms dealer, and chairman of the Cabal welcomed each member entering the room, on what he called an historic occasion, with a glass of

Dom Perignon champagne. Dupuis was the real intellect in the Cabal and the most globally connected member. His international arms business made him rich and brought him into contact with most of the world's terrorist groups. Whilst attending an illegal arms deal in the Middle East Dupuis' agent secretly recorded a conversation between two Saudi businessmen about a group called Al-Qaeda and their sponsor Bin Laden. He overheard plans to blow up American and British cities. The Saudis wanted to buy tanks, rocket launchers and small arms such as Kalashnikovs, indicating they were equipping for a war. This stimulated enough interest for Dupuis to instruct his agents in the region to investigate further. He found out more about Al-Qaeda and its well-established global links to other terrorist groups, including Islamic groups in the Russian republic of Chechen. It seemed that their combined efforts were targeted towards America and its Gulf War allies. A bombing campaign had already started in some Middle Eastern countries. Dupuis suspended any further arms sales to these groups. Having persuaded members of the Cabal to meet for the first time in the history of The New Order, he now had the difficult task of getting them to agree with his plan to deal with the terrorist threat and at the same time put The New Order in a controlling position in the world.

Heinz Kluge, 'Wolfman', from Germany was first to arrive since he didn't have so far to travel as the others. Fox and Wolf had been in close contact for many years and actually knew each other. Each had combined interests in their companies. Both knew Diane Hunter, the British member, personally through her stepfather Paul Fields, who Fox had recruited to the Cabal with help from another British member known as 'Belog'. All three had voted Hunter on to the Cabal because of her political astuteness and being a leading figure on the right wing of British politics. She was a forceful woman who knew what she wanted and removed anyone who stood in her way.

The next to arrive was the Russian, Boris Superkov, 'Bear', whose identity was unknown by the others. He was the wealthiest and most dangerous of the members. Survival and success in the post-Soviet Russia required a ruthlessness and ability to destroy enemies. Before agreeing to the meeting he had wanted his own bodyguards to be admitted to the room but this was refused. At first, he was reluctant to show his face. A lot of people wanted him dead. Anonymity was his real security. A short time later the remaining members of the Cabal arrived.

All members took a chair around the table. Fox explained the security he had in place and the arrangements with the French police. He continued, 'They think we are international bankers discussing finance. Rambouillet is often used for secret meetings so our presence has not raised any suspicions. I have called this meeting because we are faced with a grave situation which could become an opportunity if we make the right decisions. Al-Qaeda, who is now one of the more organised of the many Islamic fundamentalist groups, is planning something big in America and Europe.' Fox observed the worried look on the faces of his members.

He continued. 'My intelligence sources inform me that Al-Qaeda is planning to explode stolen atomic bombs in American and British cities, probably New York and London, on the eve of the millennium. If the terrorists are successful, it will start a Third World War, with devastating consequences for everybody. It is the nightmare scenario we have feared since the spread of nuclear weapons. Some of you may have read Tom Clancy's book, *The Sum of all the Fears* in which terrorists exploded an atomic bomb in an American city to start a nuclear war. Maybe that's where the terrorists got the idea from but after the Gulf War there are a lot of angry people out there who want to punish America and its allies. They see a weak American President, a divided Europe and an ineffective United Nations who may not strike back, coupled to the iconic beginning of the new millennium, as a good time to make history. We don't know of any other motives.

Unfortunately, our organisation may have helped Al-Qaeda to acquire the material to build atomic bombs. Back in 1945, one of the three plutonium atomic bombs that were made by the Manhattan Project was stolen from Los Alamos by two of our members. Japan surrendered after the second bomb was dropped on so one bomb was left. It was hidden away in a cave in New Mexico for many years. Only three people knew about its exact location. After the war, most of the active Soviet spies at Los Alamos were caught. This and other events at the time prevented the intended customers from buying the bomb. Two of our members were murdered but the other individual involved disappeared taking with him the secret of the bomb's location. That individual was not one of our members and we believe he may have eventually sold it to a terrorist group in America. No one knows for certain but it may still be hidden in America.'

He paused and looked at Diane Hunter, then continued, 'As our member Lionheart knows, a revolutionary nuclear bomb initiating system was stolen from Halborn in 1959. It was purchased by an American client who was assumed to be working for the CIA or Atomic Energy Commission. Even a small bomb comparable with the power of the early weapons could obliterate major cities like New York, London or Moscow. Imagine the chaos such a bomb would cause if it destroyed these cities, with millions of people dead and even more injured, the destruction of the world's financial centres, resulting in economic ruin and social disorder, national chaos and political instability.'

The Cabal members looked at him in silence. The American member, Eaglestar, looked particularly grave at the references to New York. Being from Tennessee, with roots firmly in the South, he had no love for that city or its inhabitants. In fact, he hated the Rockefeller family who practically built New York and still owned a lot of its real estate. One of his ancestors was a general in the Confederate Army during the Civil War and being a right-wing Republican he loathed the incumbent in the White House but still believed in his country. The thought of Islamists destroying an American city filled him with rage. Fox noticed this but before allowing him to speak, asked members to listen first to his plan. He said with a serious tone,

'We cannot let the terrorists succeed in blowing up cities and starting a nuclear war but can use their threat to our advantage. We must find out exactly where the bombs will be located, even if we have to offer them our help. Before they carry out their evil deed and explode the bombs, we leak it to the media. Various Governments' own intelligence agencies may already know about Al-Qaeda's plans but my guess is they may not know that they intend to use atomic bombs. Even if that is suspected, they are unlikely to make it known to the public for fear of doing the very thing it would do, create panic on the streets and chaos in the world markets. They will hope the terrorists can be found before they strike.

If they are planning to strike at the start of the new millennium, probably near to midnight when everybody will be at celebrations, you can imagine how many people will be in Manhattan's Central Park and in London's Trafalgar Square at that time.

We need to agree on a strategy that would give us the maximum financial and political benefit from the Al-Qaeda threat. As soon as we inform the media, all hell will break loose and it will cause panic on the streets and on the world's stock exchanges. Share prices will drop dramatically, there will be a loss in public confidence in their Governments and leaders will fall. It will be our chance to buy up shares at rock-bottom prices and take control of more industries. Stocks, bonds, commodities and metals exchange markets will be ours for the taking. Once we have these, the world will be ours.

The Governments of America and Britain will be held responsible for deceiving the public. This will likely trigger early elections. It will be our chance to place our people in Governments. Eagle said that he already had a candidate in-waiting for the White House. Elections are due in America and Britain in the years following the millennium anyway. There will be hatred towards Islamic groups and retaliatory measures will be taken in countries like Iraq, Iran, Afghanistan and Pakistan. We may even persuade Israel to do some of the dirty work. Our Russian member will ensure that his fellow countrymen join in the sweep against the fundamentalists in exchange for oil and gas shares. I know he already owns most of these but with disruption and high prices of

Middle East supplies buyers will turn to Russia for their needs. This will bring billions of dollars to the suppliers.'

Fox sat down expecting a lively discussion. Silence filled the room. It was the English member, Lionheart, who spoke first. She complimented Fox on his bold plan but was worried about manipulating Al-Qaeda.

She said, 'They may have a crazy philosophy but, like us, they want to own the world. Using an age-old religious war between Islam and Christianity as a basis for political power means they can't succeed but they should not be underestimated. Remember they have a lot of followers and a wealthy Saudi backer, Bin Laden. They exploit the religious gulf that exists between Jews and Muslims related to the Israel-Palestine situation which also divides the West and the Middle East.

The New Order will only succeed if its members are in top decision-making positions in Government and Industry. We must make sure that fundamentalist religious groups never get political power or take control of the world's material resources. The Western world will face a confrontation with the Asian countries, in particular China and India, who will continue to grow economically strong. These countries have nuclear weapons and China has vast military strength. The Russian Republic has to unite with Europe and the Americas to be in a position to face the Asian challenge. The democratic systems under which our governments are elected and operate are not right for the challenges that face us. The West needs The New Order but it cannot be imposed, it has to be wanted. That will only happen if the existing systems are shown to be inadequate. Sometimes a disaster scenario is necessary to accelerate the change. The Al-Qaeda threat provides such a scenario. Will we succeed in preventing the disaster at the right time to discredit the Governments of the countries under threat? For us that is the crucial question.

We could consider another possibility. If Al-Qaeda succeeded in obliterating some capital cities and killing millions, then a global conflict would follow. The New Order could move in after the devastation and chaos and take control. Remember this was the theme of Wells' book, *The Shape of Things to Come,* when a powerful, educated elite rebuilt a world devastated by local wars. It inspired the founding of the Science Brotherhood back in the 1930s from which our movement evolved. We have been responsible for many events that shaped the history of the twentieth century, often motivated by greed and the need to make money rather than political ideals but we learnt that politics and wealth creation are inextricably linked.'

The American member, Jonas Gould, 'Eaglestar', owned banks, airlines, ships and had investments in most of the large electronics and computer companies in Silicon Valley. He was known as Mr Valley. He said, 'I want this Cabal to instruct its members to use all their resources to find out more about Al-Qaeda's bombing intentions. I find it inconceivable that even crazy terrorists would want to use atomic bombs to destroy capital cities as had been suggested.'

Looking angry, he added, 'I will only support the plan if the safety of the cities is guaranteed. I will not allow New York to be bombed. We have members in the FBI, CIA and MI5 so intelligence is available to us. We must take action at the appropriate time to stop the terrorists from carrying out their threat.'

Eaglestar was rich enough not to care about making money from shares due to panic selling, but saw the value in taking control of major industries and banks. America needed a new Government that followed what the nation's founders envisaged.

Dr Heinz Kluge, 'Wolfman,' said, 'My company has put in place the most advanced satellite communications network, better than anything possessed by any of the security agencies. Our new encryption system gives us complete secrecy. Without possession of the same cryptochips and the codes, no one can intercept or unravel scrambled telephone calls. We can listen into conversations on any other networks without them knowing.'

Wolfman gave every member a small black data box to which was attached a miniature telephone earpiece. He told them it was their encrypted connection to an international satellite network.

They could use it to communicate with their members by using a special coded number sequence. It was impossible for anyone to tap into or record speech since the codes continually changed. Members could only respond to calls and not make them, unless they used a special number. Wolfman told members that nobody except his staff must attempt to interfere with the system. Continuous global monitoring of every telephone call made using the system ensured security. He added that the CIA had a similar system which was also impossible to penetrate.

Boris Sudakov, 'Bear', was the most powerful member of the Cabal. Physically built like a bear, he was typically Russian. During the 1990s, when Boris Yeltsin took office after the fall of Communism and the break-up of the Soviet Union, Sudakov was one of the first oligarchs to emerge. He started from nearly nothing, coming from a poor farming family. Using his connections with old communist officials, he became a member of one of the many Mafia type organisations and became rich by exploiting the connections he had in the corrupt, but democratically elected, Government of Russia during the transition to a market-based economy. Many post-Soviet business oligarchs were relatives or close associates of Government officials, even Government officials themselves, as well as criminal bosses who achieved vast wealth by acquiring state assets very cheaply during the privatisation process. They exploited the new freedom to own assets which, in the absence of law, opened the way for the criminal pursuit of money and power. They assigned front men to serve as executives or legal owners of the companies they controlled to avoid state tax.

Bear was an ideal member for The New Global Order. He embodied what it stood for and became one of its Russian founders. With investments in oil and gas fields, refineries and real estate in cities like St Petersburg which was undergoing massive modernisation, he became one of the new billionaires. Real estate was being sold by the Government for very low sums. With appropriate back-handers to officials they were practically given away. Bear ran one of the many Mafia-type organisations and learnt how to bribe government officials. In the post-communist Russia they controlled most of the cities. Russia's Federal Security Service (FSB) that emerged from the Soviet-era secret service, the KGB, turned a blind eye to these criminal organisations since many of their agents were also receiving financial benefits.

Bear was one of many rich men to set up a private investment bank in Moscow. He was voted entrepreneur of the year and listed alongside Roman Abramovich as one of the richest men in Russia. He provided some of the money to re-establish Russia's most famous shopping arcade, Gum, located near Red Square. Other interests included steel and vodka production.

Boris Yeltsin, the Russian President, was losing control of the country and the man expected to succeed him was Vladimir Putin. Bear saw problems in the future as Putin was an ex-KGB hard man. Like other oligarchs, Sudakov re-invested much of his wealth in England and countries outside of Russia. After its defeat in Afghanistan, Soviet Russia faced continuing hostility from the Islamic factions. These continued during the Federation years, with threats of terrorism being made on Russian cities, including Moscow and St Petersburg. Bear thought that Chechen and Mujahedeen rebels were the most likely candidates. They had the support of Al-Qaeda and used similar tactics. He believed the time had come to rid the world of the Islamic fundamentalists and liked the idea of using the Western democracies to do it. Blaming Al-Qaeda for the start of another war in the Middle East would help to establish a New World Order and, although it would be difficult, could produce politically the wrong changes in Russia. Unknown to other members around the table, Bear also had a plan of his own since he knew more about Al-Qaeda's intentions than he declared. He saw himself and his friends as leaders in a new regime in Russia and making it the new power in the world, but first, the American power base had to be destroyed.

The Japanese member, Dr Takaki Tobata, 'Serow', was the latest member of the Cabal. He owned many companies and had shares in most of Japanese industry. Much of his immense wealth came from the boom days of the Japanese economy which had been consistent throughout the 1970s and 1980s. It was the financial crisis, after the bubble burst in the 1990s, that affected his companies with the fall in share values. Takaki blamed his Government and its resistance to change for the current problems. He and a number of industrialists started secret negotiations with China for their help in changing the Japanese constitutional monarchical system of Government. Japan still ranked high in the world owing to its high quality technology products but was being overtaken by its larger geographical neighbour.

Serow's ambition was to be Prime Minister and he had already built up a strong political base. He was a scientist and had agreed with the original aspirations of The Brotherhood. But he now saw The New Order as a more effective structure for achieving change. His parents and grandparents and many family members had perished in Nagasaki. He only escaped because as a young child he went with family members in another city. Naturally he had an abhorrence of atom bombs and a deep rooted resentment of America for what they had done to his family and country. For them to suffer the same experience would in his mind serve justice. He liked Lionheart's suggestion that rapid change would only come about after major cities were bombed. But he didn't voice that opinion to fellow members of the Cabal. He supported The New Order because he felt that change was needed.

If Japan was to survive as a dominant industrial power and rise above its Asian neighbours, it had to adopt a new system. China might become the largest economic power but its billions of people would eventually want freedom which could ignite another revolution. It was a problem The New Order would need to confront China at some time in the future since it would have to be part of any plan to change the world's political and industrial infrastructure.

Daman Khan 'Tiger' was the Indian member and next to Bear was one of the richest on the Cabal. He was a banker with interests in Tata Steel and the Indian Oil Corporation and had extensive investments in America and Europe in key industries such as textiles and chemicals. As his Christian name suggested, he liked to be in control. He was a Christian and hated the Muslims. But he had no political ambitions. His power quest was to control India's growing industry. Next to China, India was expected to be the world's largest economy in the future.

Fox asked everyone to test the data boxes using their codes because once activated they could not be changed. He said, 'As we approach the millennium next year, the world could be faced with the danger of a nuclear war, greater than anything since the Cuban Missile crisis. We must take every step to stop that while retaining our anonymity. The security agencies will be on red alert when they find out what Al-Qaeda is planning. They are likely to have early intelligence on their activities from their many field agents. Most of Al-Qaeda operatives are amateurs so many will make mistakes and get arrested.'

Turning to the Chair, Lionheart said, 'I believe that some ex-members of The Brotherhood are still active and might be working with their Governments. It had been a condition for them to receive immunity of prosecution. I am particularly referring to David Simons and Henry Fellows. I learned from one of my members in MI5 that after the Halborn incident the Government offered Fellows immunity if he changed his identity and allowed them to kill him off in a car accident. I now know after all these years that he is living in a Cotswold village. It was when I learned recently about exchanges taking place between him under the name of Malcolm Walker and a man called Stanley Rheiner, a Physics Professor in Tucson, that I knew our old enemy, The Brotherhood Foundation might still be active. I also believe Fellows killed my stepfather Paul Fields. She told members it was time to finish the job and eliminate Fellows and Simons and secure any documents they might possess that could expose the names of the Cabal.

Fox told her she had the Cabal's support to finish the job her father had started. Bear looked up and offered her the services of one of his best KGB-trained agents. After Communism many KGB agents looked for new employment. Some found jobs with Mafia type organisations or set themselves up as freelance spies or assassins. Bear owned one such group and used them to eliminate his enemies. Lionheart accepted the offer. Bear made a note and gave her a contact number to call. It was now her chance to revenge her father's murder. But she was oblivious to her father's betrayal and the reasons why Fellows killed Field.

Wolfman was also concerned that Simons might know enough to identify the members of the Cabal. It was likely he possessed incriminating documents. He was concerned that one of his employees might have stolen the encryption codes and passed them to Simons with whom he had a friendship. If so, they must be retrieved as soon as possible.

Lionheart replied, 'I will do what is necessary.'

Fox returned to the strategy they needed to adopt to deal with Al-Qaeda in making sure America and Europe knew what they were planning, so the terrorists would be blamed for causing the inevitable disruption. He emphasised, 'We will prevent them from actually carrying out their threats and make sure the people involved are caught before the bombs are detonated. It will require meticulous coordination. Failure to stop them would be disastrous for us and the world. If we succeed then the Americans, with European help, will wage war on those countries deemed responsible. If we make the public aware of what is happening just before the bombs are due to be detonated then there will be panic in the streets and on the stock market. When the public find out they have been deceived by their Governments, even though the bombs will be found and those responsible caught, it will be too late for them to redeem the trust of the people. Governments will fall and elections will be held. It will be our chance to make sure the new people elected are New Order members, particularly when they know it was us who stopped the bombs from being detonated and gave the warning.'

Eaglestar said, 'Al-Qaeda and the fundamentalist regimes will be finished and we will be able to solve the Middle East problem. Russia will follow a similar path. We shall have to deal with China and other Asian countries but that will be for later. No one will know about us or our plan since we shall just be providing a new way forward after the Al-Qaeda bomb threats. Secrecy is imperative to our success. We must protect our anonymity whatever it takes. A threat to one of us is a threat to all. Members would have to rely heavily on resources, intelligence and infallible communication.' Wolfman, Eaglestar and Fox said that they had all of these in place but members had to be ruthless in stopping anyone who got in their way. All the intelligence agencies would be on full alert. 'Al-Qaeda, who would rigorously sought.'

Lionheart disagreed saying, 'Al-Qaeda is a network with a powerful strategic purpose and although led from the Pakistani tribal areas, it has recruited some well-trained and capable people, many of which have been educated in the West and know how the security services operate.' Fox looked angry that someone should challenge his remarks. She added, 'Like our organisation, they might have placed their members in the security services so would also have access to intelligence. We should consider them as the enemy and seek out their agents. We must not under-estimate the British police, MI5, the FBI and CIA. They have vast resources and might find the bombs and bombers before we do.'

Fox thanked Lionheart and agreed that Cabal members must not be complacent about Al-Qaeda. He went on to say, 'When the public find out they have been kept in the dark about the atomic bomb threats they will still react in the way I have suggested, even if the security agents catch the terrorists before they carry out their mission. We are in a win-win situation so long as none of our members are identified and the conspiracy is not divulged. We want a quiet revolution that will rid the world of social democracy and religious theocracy. The millennium event will not give us total power but if we can take control of governments in America and Europe and the essential industrial and financial infrastructure, then our aims will rapidly advance.

All seven members of the Cabal agreed the strategy and promised to use their resources to find the terrorists and compromise their plans and ensure their members were not caught by Government agents. Fox would coordinate all operations and individual members would only use the system to communicate with each other if it became essential.

Each member separately left the room with their satellite data boxes and walked down a long tunnel that opened up onto a courtyard. Covered in cloaks, one by one, they boarded waiting black chauffeur-driven limousines. All had private planes hidden away in hangars at a local airfield. Like ghosts in the night they faded back to their prosperous existences, to their families and businesses. In the weeks that followed the seeds of the conspiracy started to germinate.

The Lear jet took off for Washington. Eaglestar strapped himself into a seat beside a pretty blonde woman who was his secretary, flight attendant, and lover. She was twenty years younger than his wife and knew how to please her boss. She wore a low cut dress, pulled tightly around her slim waist, to accentuate her well-rounded breasts. He knew the seven-hour trip would be a pleasurable one since the plane was furnished with everything, including a double bed.

Bear's Eclipse 500, a twin-engine private jet, sped to Moscow while its two passengers discussed the situation they now faced. Leon Seperkov was a Russian Jewish émigré and Bear's closest confidant. Like Bear, he was also worried about his future in Russia. Jewish businessmen were facing a growing antagonism from certain ex-communists groups who frequently used threatening behaviour. Two of Seperkov's friends were murdered but the police failed to respond.

Seperkov looked after a number of Bear's security companies who employed ex-KGB agents. Bear told him that Lionheart needed their services and asked him to contact her to make appropriate arrangements. Bear made numerous calls to New York, Moscow and London. His army of people were put on alert.

Diane Hunter travelled alone. She preferred it that way. Her mind was troubled by the plan for the millennium event. She knew they were up against formidable enemies. Her stepfather had been well-connected and had made friends in high places with people who shared his views, but most were either dead or long-since retired. MI5 had files on him and his friends. She had a lot of support for her own right-wing party from the wealthier aristocratic and upper-classes and a significant number of working-class people who opposed the Government's immigration policy. The New Labour Party had been in power for six years but many of its traditional followers felt betrayed by its policies since they were seen to be more Conservative than Labour. New Labour, however, were re-elected for a second term in 1997 with a landslide victory over the Conservatives.

Many of Hunter's supporters were keeping a low profile so even the millennium threat might not produce the result The New Order members wanted. But it would raise British public opinion against Muslim immigrants who were flooding into the country. New Order members were widely spread throughout British society. Hunter had their names on a secret list. She had a daughter from a secret love affair with a high-ranking person called Lord Globe back in the 1970s. She discovered under the code name 'Belog' that he had protected her father many years ago when the names of The Brotherhood were revealed after the Halborn incident.

Some months passed before Hunter received a call on her encrypted telephone from a Russian woman known as R2. Bear's man, Leon Seperkov, had selected her to carry out the task required by Lionheart. She was given Fellows' address and a date when the work would be carried out. Unknown to Lionheart, R2 was the Seperkov's best operative. Bear had recruited her from the old KGB. Having successfully executed twelve assignments with no traces left at the scene, she was totally reliable. Her services came at a cost but Lionheart had no problem paying her fee.

PART 4
THE THREAT

CHAPTER 8

Washington DC
December 1999

London quickly faded away into the distance as Concorde shot up through a thick cloud base. I tried to relax and not think too much about the events of the last few weeks but more on what awaited me in Washington. I had spent most of Monday and Tuesday reading Fellows' memoires and trying to understand the significance of what he had meticulously written. Much of the text must have come from handwritten diaries started in 1933 when he first met David Simons in London. These diaries were probably placed with the original papers in a bank depository box. In the copies I recovered from the cottage, some chapters covering years in the 1990s were missing. I had made notes on my laptop computer of the missing years because I thought they might be significant.

The clouds below seemed almost stationary as we flew over them through the stratosphere, faster than the speed of sound. Stretched out below, as far as the eye could see, was the vast blue-grey Atlantic Ocean, full of life, oblivious to the world above. Cruising effortless at 50,000 feet it was just possible to see the curvature of the Earth and the blue rim that merged the atmosphere with the blackness of space beyond. The power of Concorde's four Rolls-Royce engines was barely audible in its sleek aluminium body. I felt like a Greek god looking down on my kingdom. We had come a long way from hiding in caves and chasing game across the Savannah but it was only the first part of the long journey we had yet to make.

Strapped in an aircraft seat knowing there is nowhere to go

produces a relaxing effect on the mind, after the initial fear of what could have happened on take-off, had passed. Most aircraft accidents occur on take-off and landing, not when actually flying. Surprisingly the seat next to me was empty so I was able to avoid indulging in conversation. Being alone so high above the earth is a good time to reflect on one's personal life.

I thought back to my recent experiences with women in Kuwait and London. They made me think the time had come to find a permanent girlfriend. It might keep me out of trouble. I liked women; they were important in my life but I never let them have a controlling influence over me. Over the years I had satisfied my physical and emotional needs through a number of temporary relationships. Some women saw me as a one-night stand, James Bond type character, something I hated but probably deserved. Like everyone, I did have an ego to fill but I was not pretentious, always myself, never acted a part. I valued my independence, liked to work alone and enjoyed making my own decisions. These, however, were not the best qualities to sustain a long-lasting relationship. If I did settle down and get married one day, it would probably mean giving up the job I loved, unless the woman could accept my lifestyle. Investigative journalists are often required to go, at a moment's notice, on unpredictable assignments to anywhere in the world. I was lucky to have a well-established reputation and not wanting for money so could choose my jobs. But failing to respond to a client quickly erodes a reputation and good jobs are difficult to acquire.

Before I became a successful journalist I did have a close relationship with a girl named Anna who was half-Malaysian and stunningly beautiful. She was a nurse in a London teaching hospital. Initially the attraction was physical, but after the fiery passion of physical love-making declined, I think I started to fall in love. Being more English than Asian, she became possessive and wanted me to settle into a normal life and stop accepting overseas assignments. At the time I did not know the meaning of a normal life. I had travelled the world and went wherever the job took me. Our breaking-up was an upsetting business. It left me feeling depressed and I vowed never again to get involved. But never say never. Fortunately, following the break-up, successive overseas assignments in war zones helped me to overcome my depression. Work is a good therapy.

After a well-served lunch and too many gin and tonics, I drifted into an oblivious doze. Before I was fully conscious the plane was landing at Dulles airport. On arrival I was ushered by a flight attendant through the VIP channel followed swiftly by my suitcase. Somebody high up on Capitol Hill had done some string-pulling. It did make me feel important but I wondered why I was getting the diplomatic treatment. Security at airports had recently been stepped up owing to the deteriorating situation in the Gulf and the ever-present danger of terrorist attacks. I was met and greeted at the VIP arrival gate by Robert. He had a chauffeur-driven black limousine with shaded windows waiting on the road outside with its engine running. It took us towards the Hay-Adams Hotel located in Lafayette Square just a few blocks from the White House. Most Government officials and politicians stayed at this five-star luxury hotel when in Washington. On the way our limousine pulled over to give way to a number of similar vehicles accompanied by a police escort of flashing lights and sirens. Our chauffeur told us it was the President's limousine and escorts. He was leaving the country on Air Force One for some clandestine overseas meeting. A police car surreptitiously followed us from the airport but disappeared before we arrived at the hotel.

Robert, who had been very quiet since we left the airport, broke the silence and explained that we had been invited to a formal evening reception in the hotel that night. It had been arranged by the White House Press Office. The journalists' conference was not due to start until tomorrow afternoon so it would be a chance to meet some politicians, media moguls and White House staff before it started. I told Robert I had not brought a tuxedo.

He smiled and said, 'Don't worry I have arranged for one to be brought to your room at the hotel. There are likely to be a lot of senators and Government officials at the reception so that means the FBI and secret service guys will be there guarding them. These receptions are common in Washington. I've been to them in the past. They provide an intelligence gathering opportunity for the people close to the President. It also gives them a chance to leak to the press. Likewise, the press can unofficially lobby politicians. It's a game everybody likes to play here. Washington is a hothouse for information exchange and gossip. Be careful what you say and to whom you say it. Your name is well-known from the articles you write about Middle Eastern affairs. Everybody here reads the Global Economist. Don't say anything about your recent visit to Kuwait. It's likely the events have been leaked and that's why you have been invited, so beware.'

'I will certainly be careful after what happened in Kuwait. We have a contract with Gulf Oil anyway,' I replied. Robert ignored my last statement and continued,

'Anyone who wants to move up the political ladder and be an insider has to get an invite to these meetings. Some say you have to be on the invitation list to get on the first rung of the ladder. In politics, it's who you know not what you know, that matters. These meetings also provide the opportunity for large companies, mainly multi-nationals, to meet with politicians; such companies have real power. They can move capital around the world and employ large numbers of people and so can exert considerable pressure on politicians. Here in the US, as in many other countries, they control the multi-billion dollar arms and oil industries. In fact, they are often wealthier and more powerful than the Governments of the countries in which they operate. Some people say they actually encourage wars to increase sales of their products.' I interrupted and asked, 'Will Houseman be at the reception?'

'I don't know, his office has not returned my calls,' he replied rather unconvincingly.

Quickly changing the subject, Robert said, 'After the reception there are some people I want you to meet. I have booked the Lafayette Room for a private dinner.'

Before I could ask who they were, the limousine arrived at the hotel. A frock-coated doorman promptly opened the car door and ushered us to the reception desk. Robert had registered earlier so agreed to meet me in the bar in thirty minutes.

I checked in at the desk. A smart looking man took the keys and led me to my room; a converted Federal Suite with a view of the White House. I was certainly being given the VIP treatment. I took a shower and dressed. The tuxedo was already hanging in the wardrobe. It was a perfect fit; someone had gone to a lot of trouble to size me up. After my Kuwait experience, I warily scanned the walls for any hidden cameras or bugs. I was becoming paranoiac.

Robert was standing at the bar with two large Rémy Martin cognacs. I had the feeling I was being pampered, softened up for something. People were assembling in the meeting room where the press reception was being held. I noticed many were accompanied by their wives, girlfriends, partners or secretaries. Their body language helped to distinguish the differences. Robert said the Vice President was expected to give an opening speech. The President was elsewhere – his current location was covered by security. It was known some secret negotiations were in progress in South America. The secret service people stood out like candles on a Christmas tree even though they tried to surreptitiously surround the senior senators in their care. Their oversized suits, probably concealing Magnum type handguns like the type used by Clint Eastwood in Dirty Harry, couldn't go unnoticed. I was only surmising. These days they were more likely to pack less conspicuous smaller weapons. Some of them did look trigger-happy. After what happened to the Kennedys in the 1960s, they could be forgiven for being ultra-cautious.

Someone was about to talk, so Robert suggested we moved into the room. At the door we were frisked for weapons and had to show our invitations. Fortunately, Robert had them ready. The Vice President had not arrived. A Washington senator presented the Vice President's apologies and gave the welcome address. It looked like a planned event. Presidents and Vice Presidents rarely expose themselves at such gatherings. Robert introduced me to a number of newspaper editors and then moved away, leaving me to ward off any awkward questions about Kuwait but fortunately none were asked. It was obvious that I was being observed by a number of black-suited men standing around the room. I was talking to the sub-editor of the Washington Post when my eyes caught sight of a woman standing just a few yards away, speaking to a group of what looked like senators.

Her high cheekbones, sparkling-green eyes and honey-blonde shoulder-length hair, made her stand out. She was about five-feet ten tall and wore a figure-hugging, dark grey business suit which looked like it came straight from Fifth Avenue. But it was her engaging smile and bubbling personality that first caught my attention. I had never before seen a woman who, on first sight, was capable of raising my adrenaline.

I knew instinctively this was a very special woman. She was stunningly attractive and not surprisingly surrounded by men, buzzing like bees around a honey pot, trying to engage her attention while other women looked on with envy. I caught Robert's eye and asked him who she was, 'That's Valerie Day. She is the Personal Assistant to Bill Lopez, the Head of the Office of Foreign Affairs. I've met her a few times.' Noting my interest, he added with a wry smile, 'Do you want an introduction?'

'Yes, if you can get her away from the man she's talking to.'

For an instant, I wondered what I was going to say. I had a number of well-rehearsed opening gambits for introductions but as often happens, my adrenaline was up but my brain was not engaged. Her physical beauty had temporarily stunned me. In the few seconds it took Robert to push his way through the guests to reach her, I started to gather my thoughts.

'Valerie, it's great to see you again. There's someone I want you to meet,' said Robert, taking her arm to move her away from the man she was talking to, after giving him a rather soft apology.

'Valerie, can I introduce you to my friend and colleague Paul Cane, who has just flown in from London on Concorde,' hastily moving aside to give me full contact space. I looked straight into her green eyes. Eyes can send out all-important messages.

'Delighted to meet you but haven't we met before?' I asked.

It was an old cliché.

'I don't think so,' she replied with a smile, showing she had heard that line before.

Detecting her English accent, I added, 'Perhaps in London.'

She paused before saying, 'Possibly, I am English. After leaving university, I worked in London for a few years before coming to Washington. I go back at least once a year to visit relatives and friends and so try to keep my English accent. It's very easy to lose it working here in Washington.'

Good start, I thought, we've engaged in conversation. I remarked on her clothes and asked about her work. The compliment about the clothes was well-received but she was less forthcoming about her work. The second opening gambit was more old-hat than the first one, but it worked.

The waiter came to us with a tray of champagne. He provided a convenient gap in the conversation for me to think of what next to say. Normally I didn't have a problem, but I was still trying to get my brain to regain control of my emotions.

I took a glass and gave it to her before taking one myself. I didn't actually like the stuff but this was not the occasion to show it. She looked at me and said, 'It's nice to meet an English gentleman.'

'Thanks for the compliment, I am not often called a gentleman,' I replied.

I noticed a number of people in the room were watching me. Robert was doing a good job keeping the people who she was first with occupied in conversation.

After some further probing she told me she was the Personal Assistant to the Head of Foreign Affairs in a Government Department in Washington and lived in Georgetown. That gave me a hint she was not living with anyone and the absence of a ring on her finger confirmed that she was not married.

My flirting was making good progress. That mystical, unexplainable chemistry which can exist between two people was being activated. I experienced a warm feeling. It was time for the direct approach. I was about to ask her out to dinner, but was cut-off rather abruptly by an elderly, overweight man with a dome-shaped bald head. He grabbed Valerie's arm and turning to me, said, 'Sorry, but Miss Day has to meet the Mexican Ambassador before he leaves.'

She apologised to me for having to leave and in a quiet voice, excused herself. She walked away but turned back and gave me an encouraging smile. I knew by her body language that I had been a hit.

Valerie left the room with a group of men. I instinctively knew I would see her again. No other woman had affected me so much in such a short time. I did not have her telephone number and was sure that working for a Government Department as a Personal Assistant, she would be ex-directory. At that moment Robert appeared from behind a waiter carrying a tray of food.

'How's it going?' he uttered in a half-English, half-American accent. He had been in America just long enough to damage the English part.

'See you've got on well with Valerie Day,' he replied casually.

Robert knew most people in Washington so he had to know more about her. His immediate reaction to my request for her telephone number was, 'Lay off, she's involved with a very high-ranking politician.'

I knew that such a good-looking woman had to be married or be in a relationship in a town like Washington. I was disappointed, but not surprised. I was determined it would not deter me. Robert offered to get her telephone number from one of his sources in exchange for a favour. Before I could enquire about what that was someone came to speak to Robert and I moved away.

At the reception I spoke to a number of people, mainly newspaper editors, but had to be careful not to say too much about my recent exploits. Many had read my articles so were keen to find out if another Iraq war was likely. I could see Robert was getting anxious. He strolled over and asked me to go with him to the private room he had booked for dinner.

We entered the room. Already sitting at the table were two well-dressed men who had not been at the reception as they were not dressed in tuxedos. On seeing us they both stood up. Robert advanced toward them and shook their hands.

Turning to me, he said, 'Paul, this is Mark Brooks and Gary Stevens, two friends of mine.'

'Glad to meet you Paul,' said the taller of the two men holding out his hand to me in a friendly gesture.

Gary, the smaller, but more aggressive looking man, had dark penetrating eyes. He refrained from looking directly at me, suggesting he had something to hide.

We exchanged the usual niceties like London versus Washington and the merits of living in England and America. Robert ordered two bottles of wine and after surveying the menu ordered steak and fish – it's called surf and turf in America and one of the more traditional dishes. Unlike the fast food restaurants, the up-market ones served at hotels have the best Kansas steaks and Maine lobsters. After a dessert of Key Lime pie, and American coffee, the talk became serious.

Mark started by saying, 'We've heard a lot about your problems in Kuwait, Paul. I gather you had a rough time. But we were pleased with your report. It was just the kind of information we wanted.'

I just smiled. From their remark, I assumed they were executives from the Gulf Oil Company. I was about to ask about Richard Houseman when Robert looked at me and said, 'Paul, there is something I need to tell you. It was not possible before tonight since I only found out a few days ago myself but the reason why I asked you to come to Washington was... '

He was interrupted by Gary, who said, 'Robert, perhaps it would be better if I explained to Paul the real reason why we are all here.'

It was now obvious these men were not from Gulf Oil. Gary stopped talking and asked Robert to lock the door and switch off his cell phone. He went on to say, 'Paul, first I need to say to you that everything we are going to tell you is in the strictest confidence. We need to apologise for misleading you but we are Government agents attached to a special Task Force set up by the President. The Gulf Oil Company has been helping us with a matter of extreme national security. Their CEO, Richard Houseman, agreed to allow us to use their company as a front for an intelligence gathering operation. Your contract with them is officially valid and our arrangement with them does not affect that, except the mission you were on was strictly secret. Nobody knows or will know about it, except the President, Vice President and designated members of the Task Force. We needed someone who was independent and seen to be acting for a private company on a business visit to Kuwait. Since we believe there are security leaks in our agencies, the President decided to form a special investigative Task Force to ascertain the validity of certain bomb threats being made by Middle Eastern groups to our respective countries.'

It suddenly explained everything that had happened to me in Kuwait. My assignment had been a CIA cover. I had been used as a pawn. I needed some answers. The question in my mind was: why me and why was I here?

I looked at Robert who was holding his head down in embarrassment. I pretended to look surprised but was not. Looking at the two agents I asked, 'Why was the information I obtained in Kuwait so important for the President to set up a special intelligence Task Force rather than use trained CIA agents?'

Showing anger, I raised my voice. 'What is going on? Why am I involved? Why was I set up in Kuwait? Who was the girl in Kuwait? Why did I get arrested and then released?'

Seeing my anger, Gary raised his hand, stepped in and said, 'We can understand your anger, Paul, so I will try and answer your questions. First, let me say that your friend and agent Robert had nothing to do with this and didn't know anything until he was told the day before you arrived. He couldn't tell you on the telephone for security reasons which is why we brought you here. The conference provided a convenient cover. If we had told you before you went to Kuwait you would have probably declined.'

I interrupted and repeated, 'But why me?'

Gary, who I perceived was the more senior agent, continued. 'Paul, you have inadvertently uncovered a missing link in our intelligence on Middle Eastern fundamentalist groups who we believe are planning more attacks on Americans and Britons but this time on our countries.' He stressed the plural.

'We have suspected for some time that a group, probably Al-Qaeda, have been operating in the US and planning an attack of some kind. Unknown to the general public there has been an increased security alert at ports, airports and all entry points into the country. Terrorists can only succeed with help from American sympathisers. Such people could be at high-level in Government, in the security agencies or in the military. We need to find out as a matter of urgency. It is because our intelligence sources in the Gulf have been compromised that it was necessary to carry out the Kuwait mission. Abdel had found people whom he thought had valuable information to attend your interviews.'

Now everything that had happened to me while in Kuwait was beginning to make sense, except the girl. In my report which the CIA now possessed, I did mention the connection between Al-Qaeda and The Brotherhood Foundation without naming Fellows directly. The intelligence services would know about him and the connection anyway. Anything I could find out on the Internet, they would also know about. But did the CIA know about Fellows' diaries and papers? More importantly, that I possessed copies of them. What knowledge did I possess that they didn't? It was now imperative I found out how much they knew. Gary looked at me for a response. I obliged by asking him the obvious question again. 'Why me?'

'Before I answer I need to give you some background information. We have known for some time that the US is a prime target for Islamic terrorists, now heightened since the Gulf War. Conflict in the region amongst the various religious and political groups had been raging long before the Gulf War. The Arab-Israeli wars are well-embedded in history but our lasting support for Israel makes us unpopular with most countries in the region, even those we have helped, like Kuwait and the Emirates. We know many of our agents in the region have been compromised and some assassinated. Our own agencies here have been infiltrated by Islamic sympathisers. Much of the intelligence gained in the past was false and led us in the wrong directions.

The weakness of our own intelligence meant we were caught by surprise in the recent attacks on US property and personnel. Part of the problem is the fragmentation of our worldwide intelligence services and the lack of coordination and management of information. The President took a serious view of our shortcomings and has appointed a commission to review all intelligence operations both inside and outside the country. It involves the FBI, CIA and many other agencies who work for individual Government departments. This brings me to our urgent problem and the reason why we need your help.'

I now began to feel apprehensive and wondered what was coming next. It was now Mark's turn to talk. In a softer, less aggressive tone, he revealed the problem.

'The Islamic fundamentalist movement, Al-Qaeda, has risen to the top of our hit list and we think they are now behind most of the current bombings. Our recent intelligence, which has to be verified, indicates that American and British cities are on their target list. There is talk of a plan to carry out what is being called a Big Event. We think a weapon of mass destruction may have been smuggled into the country for an attack on one of our major cities like Washington, New York or Los Angeles.

The information you brought back from Kuwait has been carefully studied for clues. You actually acquired more intelligence than we had ever obtained from our agents. We believe that some of it was deliberately given to you and was a disguised warning about the planned attacks. One of your interviewees clearly wanted to tell us more but did not go far enough to identify any actual plan. We did check up on the guy and found that he was the brother of a known businessman who had sold arms to Al-Qaeda. There was no indication of where or when any act will take place. We do have the name of a person who may be one of the planners. His name is Rashid Youssef, thought to be an Iraqi but he has collaborators in other countries.

Paul, you're knowledge of the region; the fact that you are known as a journalist, gives you access to people that we don't have. Any moles in our agency will not suspect you. We would like you to identify people on our suspect list. They could lead us to the conspirators and any weapon, if there is one.'

Robert, who been quietly listening, saw the worried look on my face and interrupted Mark. 'Paul, our friend Abdel was working for the Agency and we think someone found out and murdered him. You would be doing his memory a service by helping to find those responsible for his death.'

Mark continued. 'We will give you all the protection and help you need. The names of members of the special Task Force set up by the President and chaired by the Vice President are only known by the members themselves. Gary and I have been co-opted from the FBI and CIA to assist the Task Force. The President has made this a top priority mission. The lives of millions of Americans may depend on us finding these bombers before they strike. It would be a moral victory for them to succeed. Nobody has successfully attacked and killed Americans in their own country. The underground garage bomb in the World Trade Centre in New York in 1993 was a warning of how easy it is to attack a free society. We believe if this attack succeeds it could escalate into a global conflict since the Government would be left with little choice but to respond with force to the country that supported the terrorists. The disruption of Middle East oil supplies, already reduced and at record high prices, could wreck many Western economies so the stakes are high. We will pay you half-a-million dollars if you can help find those responsible for the planning of this supposed attack. In addition, you will have all the resources you need and armed protection.'

I saw Robert's eyes widen and thinking – remember I am your agent and got you the job. I wondered what he was being offered. The offer was tempting. I would receive a fee of half-a-million dollars, tax free and be given armed protection. In addition to the fee, I would have access to top Government officials. I would not have any official status, which meant I would be an independent operator, basically a free-lance spy. There were obvious dangers and I did not want to get into the same trouble experienced in

Kuwait but the opportunity was too good to refuse.

I decided to play hard to get and told them I needed more time to consider their proposition. Detecting my concern about acceptance, Robert suggested that we talked in private. He excused us from the table. The two agents said they needed an immediate answer and looked concerned after having brought me into their confidence that I needed time to reflect on such a generous offer. I was surprised how far they went before being sure I was going to accept it.

Robert said to them, 'Have some more wine, we will be back shortly.'

Outside the room, Robert told me I had little option as we both knew too much. He didn't think a lot of my chances of staying alive if I walked away. I was angry at being trapped into something way beyond anything a journalist should be doing. Robert said, 'Look our enemies have already tried to have you locked up and made death threats. At least now you will get some protection. Professionally this could be the greatest story ever written – I can see the headlines *British Journalist Saves the World.*'

I looked at him, 'Yes, but it will be you reading it as I am likely to be dead.'

I decided it was time to tell Robert about the memoires I found at the Cotswold cottage and about Fellows' niece, Ruth Goodman, the possible link to Al-Qaeda and the present threats. He listened intently and agreed I should not tell the agents about what I possessed until we knew how they were linked to Al-Qaeda. Robert was always thinking about making money. He asked if anyone else had a copy of the memoires. I told him there was reference to the original papers and documents being held in a bank deposit box in Swindon. Since Ruth was Fellows only surviving relative he had nominated her to take possession of all his belongings. If he had told her about the papers then she would have access to them. I also told him I tried to call her from my apartment in London before I left but had to leave a message to call me back. So far she had not responded. She was selling the cottage so I was calling on the pretext of the sale. I did let my estate agent, Jeremy

Simms, know I was interested in the property and to tell Ruth to call me. He seemed reluctant for her to speak directly with me. Estate agents believe clients do deals behind their backs so try to keep buyers and sellers apart until their commission is guaranteed.

Robert was getting excited; his facial veins were turning scarlet.

He said, 'You must talk to the girl as soon as possible to see if she has retrieved the papers. If what you tell me is true then what we have' – I corrected him – 'What I have is a goldmine of information. It's very hot stuff. We could rewrite the history of the twentieth century.'

He cited what I had told him about the stolen Los Alamos Bomb in 1945. If it was still in the US, it may have been in the hands of terrorists.

I said, 'Hold on – that's making a lot of assumptions.'

'But if the Brotherhood or this offshoot, The New Order and Al-Qaeda did relate in some way, then is it possible, even after all these years, for a cell in the US to have acquired an atomic bomb or those parts of it that could be used to make a bigger one?' he asked.

It did make me think whether Robert's perceptions could be true. The whole thing was shaping up like a good story and, as a journalist, was whetting my appetite. I told Robert I was prepared to work for the Task Force but on the condition we both shared the responsibility and worked together. In fact, I realised that I had little choice if I wanted to sleep safely in my bed at night. We returned to the room to find only Gary.

'Well, guys have you decided to work for us?' He replied in a demanding way. In unison, we said, 'Yes.'

Gary said, 'Good, Mark had to leave but since you are both on board, let me welcome you to our team. Go to the conference tomorrow as planned. We don't want anyone raising suspicions about the two limeys who left the room with two suits.'

We shook hands and he left saying we would be invited to a briefing at the White House in a few days time and not to plan to return to England. It was late and I needed a drink so suggested to Robert that we retired to the bar. He agreed. We downed a half-bottle of brandy. I returned to my suite slightly drunk but my consciousness was awakened by the CNN news report about the situation in Iraq which was worsening day-by-day. Concerns were being expressed about Saddam Hussein's threatening behaviour to the weapons inspectors who were being asked to leave Iraq. Suspicions were being raised that Iraq was building an atomic bomb or some other weapon of mass destruction. We already knew they possessed chemical weapons. Israel was in the firing line and demanding action from the UN. They were threatening independent action if the UN did not take it. Hussein had already contravened the UN resolutions and seemed hell-bent on taking the world to the brink of another war.

The brandy was making me have illusions. Was there any connection between Iraq, Al-Qaeda and the supposed threat to the US Homeland? Saddam Hussein would certainly have the motive but did he have the support of the Islamic Fundamentalists who were mainly Shiite not Sunni Arabs? These two tribes hated each other as much as they hated the West.

There was a knock on the door. I turned off the TV, quickly put on a bath robe and opened it to a porter who handed me a padded envelope that had been delivered earlier by courier. I signed for it.

I anxiously opened the package which contained a letter and a computer tape. It was from Ruth Goodman.

Dear Mr Cane

I am sorry I was away when you called my telephone at the flat but I have only just returned to Cambridge. Jeremy Simms called me on my mobile to say you were interested in buying the cottage. We need to talk further about that when you return. I am writing this letter in response to what you stated in your message concerning my uncle and for security reasons am sending this letter by courier to your hotel. I am also doing this because I know from what Jeremy Simms told me, you are an investigative journalist and may know more about my uncle than you state. If this is your real objective then you should know certain things. First, his real name

210

was not Malcolm Walker but Henry Fellows. He was living in the cottage under an assumed name on a Government protection scheme. I will not go into the reasons for that now. I am probably already breaking the law by telling you.

When I last met my uncle, he confided in me about his Government work. As you probably know, during the war he was a member of Oppenheimer's team on the Manhattan Project. His work since then at Fort Halborn, up to his forced retirement in 1959, was of extreme national importance. It is because of that and what is happening now in the Middle East, a region in which I see you are an expert, you will see the relevance of what I am sending you.

My uncle told me that everything was written down in his memoires. These, together with diaries and copies of official documents, he had placed in a bank deposit box. He told the bank that in the event of his death, I was to be the sole beneficiary of the contents of the box that was essentially his will. He was in an agitated state when I left him last year. Clearly something or somebody had caused it but when I questioned him further he told me it was better for me not to know.

I was only informed about his death three days after it happened and was never allowed to see the body. It had been identified by someone unknown and he was cremated without an autopsy since the death was stated as being natural due to a heart attack. It was all hushed up by the Government, probably because of his change of identity. At the time of his death, as far as I know, nobody else knew about his papers.

I did withdraw the safe deposit box and took possession of the papers. After reading them, I believe he may have been murdered by people who thought their identities would be exposed. If this is true, and I have no proof, then his enemies will stop at nothing to acquire the papers.

My uncle left instructions that in the event of his death, I was to send them securely to a retired American physicist, named David Simons who lived under the alias of Professor Stanley Rheiner in Tucson, Arizona. He was an old colleague and a founding member of his Foundation. I have not so far been able to do that since

Rheiner has not yet returned my letter from the address my uncle left. I have therefore returned the papers to the Bank. But I am sending you a computer disc on which I have copied a coded list of names of what I assume are past Foundation members; those underlined may have a special significance. These names may not be the real names of the members as The Foundation had a secret Inner Sanctum that issued members with aliases to protect their identity. In the papers, a group known as 'The New Order' is mentioned. Apparently it became a breakaway group from The Foundation. This group of people have a different set of aims to that of The Foundation which was originally dedicated to giving more power to scientists to promote peace and stability in the world. 'The New Order' seems to embrace an opposite set of objectives. These people could be responsible for my uncle's death as he blames them for the death of his colleagues and his own downfall. Please keep this letter safe, do not share its contents and don't trust anyone, even in Washington. Please do not try to call me until you return to England then we should meet.

Sincerely yours

Ruth Goodman

The letter confirmed my suspicions that I was now involved in something bigger than an historical feud between two opposing organisations. I feared for Ruth's safety and ignoring her request, immediately called her but there was no reply or answer phone on which to leave a message. This was strange since when I rang before leaving England, it did record my message. Perhaps for security reasons she had disconnected it.

Ruth did not know I already had many of Fellows' original handwritten papers so I knew much of what she had explained in the letter. I recalled the name of an organisation known as The New Order which had appeared in the papers. I had to find out more since it could hold the key to the present crisis. If only there was more time. After a sleepless night I finally dozed off, but once again was woken in the early morning by Robert's call.

'Sorry to call before breakfast but Gary just called and said that new information had been received. The briefing has been brought forward. It is now urgent we all meet at the White House this morning. He also wants us to meet the rest of the Task Force team. A car will pick us up at ten o'clock in the morning at the hotel entrance. Incidentally, I have Valerie Day's work telephone number but she may not be too pleased you have it. Callers to these numbers are all monitored so be careful. Don't tell her about our meeting – it's confidential.' I thanked him but before I could tell him about Ruth's letter. He rang off.

I replaced the phone and immediately rang Valerie. She answered quickly. I spoke slowly, carefully selecting each word.

'Hello Valerie, this is Paul Cane, I would love to see you again and continue our conversation that was so bluntly interrupted last night,'

It sounded a bit coy. Before she could reply I quickly added, 'Could we meet for lunch or dinner?'

She replied in a warm soft voice, 'Sorry about last night, how did you find my number, it's ex-directory? I cannot speak on this telephone. I will call you back.'

I gave her my cell phone number and awaited the call. A long five minutes passed before the phone rang. Like an anxious school boy waiting for exam results I placed the phone close to my ear.

'Sorry I had to call you back but my business phone is monitored. We are not allowed to take personal calls. I would like to see you again but things are complicated at present.'

My heart began to slow.

'Can we just meet for a coffee for an hour at lunch time, perhaps tomorrow or the day after?' I asked. There was long pause.

'Alright,' she said. 'Call me tonight on my cell phone.' She then gave me the number.

'I will call you about seven o'clock tonight after the conference finishes,' I said.

'I look forward to it. Goodbye,' she replied.

Well, I had made some progress. I had a date with the most beautiful woman I had ever set eyes on but I had to be careful because of why I was in Washington. The black sedan arrived on time to take us to the White House. In the car I showed Robert the letter from Ruth Goodman. I saw the nervous vein in his face start to twitch. A sign his adrenaline was up.

'Did you call her?' he asked.

'Yes, but no reply. The messaging system on her phone was not operational so I couldn't leave a message.'

Getting excited, Robert said, 'We have to tell Gary and Mark about these papers. Do you have copies with you?'

'No, only a summary but I do have a disc with a list of names that Ruth sent. The names are in code. These were not in the handwritten documents I found in the cottage. What I saw confirmed my worst fears that somehow part of The Brotherhood Foundation became a breakaway group, known as The New Order. Some members of this group may hold high level positions in Western Governments, security services and key industries.'

'What about the list of names?' Robert asked.

'The names are jumbled sets of letters,' I replied.

'Surely the CIA or FBI could break the code?'

'It's not as easy as that; members have evaded identification for over forty years.'

The short ride to 1600 Pennsylvania Avenue, just around the block from the hotel, terminated at the security gate where we had to go through vigorous checks. Various phone calls were made until finally we were escorted to a ground floor office in the West Wing, close to the famous Oval Office of the President. The White House is actually a huge complex of offices and suites. Gary and Mark greeted us at the door to the room. Seated inside, around a large oval table, were five people, three men and two women. One chair at the far end was occupied by a man I recognised as the Vice President, Victor Adams. We were ushered to two chairs facing him. I sat between one of the women and a fair-haired man, who had an almost albino complexion while Robert sat between the other men.

The other woman was obviously a secretary as she seemed to dash about with a laptop in one hand and a cell phone in the other. She was dressed in a business suit that would go unnoticed in a crowd. The woman next to me, by contrast, was an African-

American with short black hair. I could not see all of her since she was seated close to the desk but she wore a loose-fitting white blouse and charcoal grey trousers. I gave her an assuring smile but only got a blank look in return. Her oval brown face and cold black eyes portrayed little emotion. Her name was Alicia Garcia. The fair-haired man's name was Henry Schmidt, whose parents probably would have preferred Heinz but wanted to emphasise their American citizenship. He was an Assistant Director in the Office of Foreign Affairs.

Sitting either side of Robert, the other two men were totally opposite in appearance. One was an olive-skinned man of mixed race, probably Arab-African. The other, a smart-suited guy looked like a military person or a civil servant. So this was the Task Force.

Gary spoke first to make introductions around the table and confirming my assumptions. The suited man was from Homeland Security. The other was a scientist from the Office of Secretary of Defence. Gary emphasised the need for absolute security and asked the Chair to address the meeting. The Vice President, looking nervous as though he had just come out of another difficult meeting, apologised for bringing the meeting forward at short notice, and welcomed everybody. He had a grave look on his face. Looking directly at Robert and me, he thanked us specifically for accepting the invitation to join the Task Force. He referred to us in a rather condescending way as 'our friends and allies from Britain.' He justified our presence by referring to my report on the Middle East as providing invaluable but disturbing intelligence that others had failed to get.

He said, 'America and Britain have a crisis because most Western agents in the Middle East have been murdered or compromised. Terrorist groups are now operating in complete freedom. We don't know when and where their next attacks will take place. I have called this emergency meeting sooner than was intended because a suspected Islamic terrorist was apprehended crossing the border with Mexico this morning in possession of what is thought to be a vital component of a nuclear bomb. It is currently being examined to find out its origin. The person who so far has not been identified is being rigorously question by the FBI at a secret place. (*I wondered* what *rigorously being questioned meant*). Taken together with other intelligence, we now believe an attack on the US using a nuclear weapon is being planned. It's something we have feared for a long time. The President has ordered all security agencies to be on full alert but we must act discreetly to stop those planning the attack from going underground.'

I raised my hand. 'Mr Vice President, if we have taken out one of their people, have we not already signalled to them we know about the plan? Also may I ask how could a nuclear bomb be smuggled into the country with all the strict controls you have in place?' Showing a slight sign of annoyance at my question, he hesitated before replying.

'We have put steps in place to make sure those who are planning an attack don't know that we have arrested one of their men. Yes, we have very well-protected borders and its unlikely anyone could bring such a bomb into the country, but it doesn't exclude the possibility of them acquiring the components here to make one.' It seemed a strange but an obvious answer.

'What do you mean acquired the components?' I asked.

'The US has many thousands of nuclear weapons stockpiled. When the war ended in 1945, a nuclear weapons research and development programme was initiated and limited production of low yield bombs like the ones made at Los Alamos was started. We knew the Soviet Union had also developed nuclear weapons since they had been given our secrets by spies such as Ted Fell, Fuchs and the Rosenbergs.

Records of all weapons and their components are scrupulously safeguarded but discrepancies have been known to occur and the theft of parts cannot be ruled out. A working nuclear bomb is a very sophisticated device and would require expert skills to make it.'

He paused and I raised my hand again and said, 'But the Hiroshima Bomb was not that sophisticated.'

He looked at me and smiled. 'Thank you for that observation, Mr Cane, but you have a lot to learn.'

I inwardly smiled, because I knew more than he did about the Hiroshima bomb from what I had read in Fellows' papers. I wondered if he knew about the theft of the fourth Los Alamos bomb. It was at that moment I was reminded of something Ruth Goodman said; *don't trust anyone, even in Washington.* I looked over at Robert hoping he would not say anything since I had decided to keep the Fellows' papers a secret, at least for the time being. Alicia turned her head towards me. A wry smile cracked her ice-cold countenance. Had I found a chink in her shield? Others around the table gave me a disdainful look for breaking the protocol and interrupting the Vice President.

The meeting, which lasted for about another thirty minutes, was mainly a history lesson on the FBI, CIA, terrorism and how after the Second World War, Moscow had seeded the United States far and wide with spies and sympathizers whose theft of secrets and influence on policy, damaged US national security. It was decided to go after the enemies in their own countries before they entered the US so the CIA was established in 1947 by President Truman. In Britain, MI6 had a similar function. But now that policy was not working.

I was still puzzled why Robert and I were asked to join what looked like a normal committee of people that Presidents and Vice Presidents like to have around them when a crisis was looming. Then something unexpected happened. The Vice President specifically asked me, Gary, Mark and Alicia to stay behind. I noticed a rather surprised look on Robert's face as he left the room with the others. Now, perhaps I would find out what was really going on and why I was involved in the so-called clandestine Task Force. Fresh coffee was poured by the secretary who then left the room. Victor Adams had returned to his desk and was on the telephone. This meeting was going to be informal with no minutes taken. It was time to get to know more about my three colleagues. I fired the opening shot to draw them out. I said, 'Guess you both have a lot of experience in this kind of thing?'

Gary looked bemused.

'You might say that, I am an Assistant Director in the CIA and on secondment to this Task Force. For years I've had to deal with bomb threats to American personnel and properties overseas. We get them all the time from white supremists, Nazis, left-wing activists, anarchists to religious fanatics. They all have a similar aim-to destroy the US and its democratic institutions. We have to take them seriously because their madness often puts lives in peril. Most are beyond any kind of reason and offer no alternative to the system that they despise. The religious nuts are the worst because they are brain-washed to believe we should all go to a heavenly paradise on their terms. Even some of the fundamentalist Christian groups are trying to bring the day of salvation close to us. Unfortunately, we sometimes get it wrong. The warnings from Islamic fundamentalists were ignored and the World Trade Centre was bombed in 1993. The President doesn't want that to happen again so has set up this Task Force to bring together the CIA and FBI and others involved in national security.

Mark interrupted and said, 'Like Gary, I am an Assistant Director with the FBI responsible for tracking down people suspected of planning terrorist activities inside the US. By nature we have to be very secretive and that sometimes leads to distrust and a lack of intelligence sharing. We have made big improvements to our respective structures to eliminate some of the liaison problems that Gary spoke about. We have been working well together since the President set up this unit.'

I looked at Alicia, expecting her to say something and was not disappointed.

'I am the Head of Intelligence for the National Security Agency and brief the President's National Security Advisor. I'm the bridge for the Task Force. I am also a trained CIA agent and have direct links into Langley.'

At that moment Adams came over to us having finished his protracted call. He turned to me and said, 'Paul, you deserve an explanation as to why I brought you here.'

I saw the faces of the others harden.

'First, let me say, the President and the British Prime Minister, after consultations with their respective agencies, have given their approval for your membership of this special Task Force. The security services in the UK seem to know you very well.' That last statement worried me. He continued, 'They wanted to put their own man on the Task Force but owing to the moles that have infiltrated their organisation, and after some persuasion by me, and because of your knowledge and experience in the Middle East, they agreed to loan you.' I thought that very generous of them since I was not consulted and knew nothing about what was going on until now. I began to doubt that he had even spoken to the Prime Minister or MI5 who would certainly have objected my involvement over one of their trained agents. I was more disposable.

Adams paused to sip his coffee then continued with his dialogue.

'The current threat seems to be directed at the United States but MI5 believes Britain cannot be excluded. The British Ambassador rescued you from the prison in Kuwait because we were concerned it may have been the work of a terrorist group. We now know a criminal gang set you up with the woman purely for financial gain. But we think they may have chosen the wrong man as the girl was sent to a room with the same number on the wrong floor. The police are corrupt and would have been paid for their services. We are not sure but don't believe politics was involved. The timing was unfortunate because Abdel had planned the whole operation so meticulously; he was one our best operatives. We believe one or more of the men he selected for you to interview were responsible for his murder. We are not sure if they are members of Al-Qaeda or some other fundamentalist movement since now we have no reliable agents in that part of the world. You are a well-known journalist and open about what you do so these people have no reason to suspect your involvement with Governments or security agencies. This places you in a good position to help us find those people behind the current threat.'

I interjected, 'Why do you think I can be more effective than all your trained agents? I am not trained to be a covert agent and will likely become a liability.'

He replied, 'No, that's not true. Simply because you can move freely as a journalist and are expected to ask questions you will not be suspected. Anyone that checks you out, and we think they have already done it, will not find anything that connects you to our agencies or the British ones. Also you actually spoke to some of the suspects. We did find a way of installing a small video camera in the interview room in the hotel so we will give you copies of their photos. We know one has been to England and spoken to people who are known to be Al-Qaeda sympathisers. He is being investigated.'

I now began to feel uncomfortable about the information I was holding back.

'Do you really know who is behind these threats?' I asked.

'No,' he replied.

'We know there are moles in all the agencies, both here and in Britain and the crisis that I referred to at the earlier meeting results from a concern of who to trust. A severe dearth of reliable intelligence exists at the present time. There is an unproved theory that the fundamentalist movements which have grown up during the last two decades are being used by more powerful people for their own purposes. Business is global and run by a relatively small number of international companies. They can move capital around, buy the best experts and easily operate outside of national laws. Since the fall of communism, the wealthy Russian oligarchs exert massive influences and have both political and industrial power. They own and have major investments in many industries which are the backbone of the new Russian economy. Many are ex-senior KGB people so are well versed in the clandestine methods of gathering intelligence and coercion. In many ways they are similar to the great American business entrepreneurs like Rockefeller, Carnegie and Ford who built up oil, steel and motor empires that made the American economy boom in the nineteenth and early twentieth centuries.

The international arms business is worth hundreds of billions of dollars so some companies have a vested interest in wars. It has never been proved they actually start wars but they can encourage

220

them by selling arms to belligerent countries. The US government did support the Taliban in their fight against the Russian occupation of Afghanistan. We did the same thing in Iraq for Saddam Hussein in the war with Iran. In these conflicts as with others, the arms companies were the real beneficiaries.'

I thanked him for the history lesson. Later, I discovered Adams had a degree in Politics and History from Harvard and before becoming a Democrat politician, was a lecturer.

'What do you want me to do now?' I asked.

'I will give Robert funds to provide you with an office in Washington to write a set of articles about *Life in the City*. This will serve as a cover for being here. Alicia will be your contact. She will lead the investigations and give you all the relevant intelligence we get from our agencies. With her, you will follow up any leads that look worthwhile. We have a budget to cover all your costs. I believe Gary has spoken to you about fees etc. It is expected our enemies will use the millennium celebrations as the time to strike but that's supposition, we are not sure. The stakes are high. It's imperative we find out and catch those behind these threats. Let me emphasise you must not take any risks. You are here to seek out intelligence not to be a James Bond. Report everything to the agents and let them deal with it.'

Adams had an anxious secretary trying to get his attention and a backlog of appointments, so he left the room saying Gary would fill in the details. Gary took control and said, 'Code names have been set up for us. These will automatically relate to special telephone numbers that must be used at all times. It will enable an encrypted messaging system so all information can be securely transmitted. Someone will always be on station to answer and relay calls. That number cannot be used by anyone except the three of us and the Vice President who generally will not use it. All messages will be automatically recoded. Prefixes with the code name 'Falcon', which if, preceded by the word 'Merlin' means act immediately, must only be used in emergencies. Use the word 'Peregrine' to signify, don't act, but wait for further information. The operator, who is located at a desk in Langley, will know what to do. If you are in extreme danger and cannot use your phone then peel back the strip on this device to make it active.'

Gary gave me what looked like a plastic shirt button. He said, 'Sew this onto your shirt or use it as cufflink then it will be with you when needed. It has a long range and its transmitter will connect to a receiving satellite that is always on station. Langley constantly monitors its transmissions. Don't wash the shirt with it on otherwise it will stop functioning.'

It made me realise how far microtechnology had come to enable such a tiny transmitter to be manufactured. I asked, 'Are agents in Britain or elsewhere also being assigned to finding the terrorists and any bombs?'

Mark replied, 'Some trustworthy agents are involved but with limited briefs since we don't want to make our enemies aware we even know or suspect anything. We don't want them to go underground. We are very much on our own.'

Gary and Mark shook hands and left the room while Alicia, who had started to warm to me said, 'Just call if you need anything.'

The black ice-maiden actually smiled as she shook my hand with a tighter than normal squeeze, but my mind was elsewhere on another woman. Robert met me in the hallway outside the offices where he had been reading some papers. The black sedan was waiting to take us back to the hotel. We didn't speak in the car as we knew whatever we said would be recorded. Our lives had now changed. Absolute privacy would be hard to secure.

At the hotel we went to the lounge bar and ordered a light lunch and felt free to talk. It was unlikely the FBI would bug the bar, even in a hotel used by politicians. Robert was bursting to ask questions.

'What the hell have we got ourselves into?' he exclaimed.

'You mean what have you got us into,' I briskly replied.

'I didn't know that Gulf Oil was being used by the White House and the CIA to gather intelligence about terrorists otherwise, even for the large sum of money, I would have refused. But you can't say no to these guys once they have you. Doing so means you end up in a cemetery.'

'You're lucky; it's me they've pulled into their inner circle. I didn't tell them about Fellows' papers although The Brotherhood Foundation was raised. They are looking at its members to find any connections to Al-Qaeda. One of the people who I interviewed in Kuwait went to England to see a member. First question – who was it? I need to find out. It could be a useful lead. We need to decipher the membership list.'

Robert looked worried.

'If the bad guys know we have a copy then we will be on their hit list. Ruth Goodman thinks Fellows was murdered for that list so they are very desperate to protect their identities. I think it's urgent for us to find the identity of the people on that list. We need to find someone not connected with the CIA or FBI to crack the code. The problem is then they will also have the knowledge which places them in danger.'

I thought about Robert's suggestion and said, 'Do you remember there was a student named Alan Masters in our year at Oxford who studied the history of code breaking and wrote a paper on Enigma and Alan Turing? I think he became an expert at codes and went to work in banking.'

'Could we contact him?' said Robert.

'Possibly, but let's think the implications through. Why do we need to know the names and what would we do with them if we did?'

Our discourse was interrupted by the waiter bringing our lunch and the sudden appearance of the chair of the journalists' conference who came to our table to introduce himself. His name was Clive Porterhouse, a tall bearded Australian with a friendly disposition, who was a foreign correspondent for CNN and had covered the Gulf War. I wondered if he was checking up on us to ascertain we were actually going to attend the conference. I was conscious of having been seen talking to politicians at the reception and with people who knew about my work. After a few niceties he left us. I checked my phone. No one had called. It was early in the morning in Cambridge but I called Ruth's number. This time there was a continuous dialling tone which indicated the phone was not operational.

I said, 'Robert, I think something is wrong. In a few hours Jeremy Simms should be at his office so I will check with him.'

The conference for which I had originally come to Washington to attend was about to start. Robert and I made our way to the conference centre located on the opposite side of the hotel. Our badges and documents were waiting. I told Robert I would sit at the back so I could go out to make phone calls without being noticed. I made sure that I was visible to the other delegates in the reception area.

The Chairman opened the conference with the usual welcome speech. Journalists from many countries were registered. Topics covered increasing problems about the neutrality of journalists when reporting from war zones. More were being killed and when taken prisoner, were treated like soldiers or spies and executed. The Iraq war had highlighted many problems. Public opinion could be quickly influenced by what was presented almost as it happened. Satellite television took the atrocities of war straight into the living room. It became like a daily soap opera, often exaggerated, and sometimes played down by those doing the broadcasting. The enemy would often show the devastating effects of bombs on civilians, particularly women and children. Saddam made great play of it in the Gulf War when he put civilians in deep bunkers which he knew would be targeted by missiles, since they were designed and used for storing weapons. Journalists were actually given frontal views from hotel rooftops of the bombardment of Baghdad so they could be transmitted around the world. He thought the pictures would influence public opinion to stop it, but the reverse effect took place. It became like a daily TV drama. Gone were the days of sending home belated reports of events, now they were live on TV.

The conference organisers had to select presentations that did not promote propaganda but were about genuine issues. There were many critics of the Gulf War and the way the press handled reporting. One Arab presenter raised the issue about countries using journalists as spies. This touched on a sensitive area for me in view of what I was about to do. I took a note of the speaker and was alarmed to see he was from Pakistan.

During some of the more boring talks my mind went back to Fellows' papers and what I was going to do about them in respect of my new assignment for the White House Task Force. I knew eventually I would have to tell the FBI and CIA about their contents. But I had to know whom I could trust.

I slipped out of the conference and called Jeremy Simms. He answered immediately as if expecting my call. Before I could speak he said, 'Paul, I am glad you called, you were on my list to call this morning but I have only just arrived at the office. You may not have heard the terrible news but Ruth Goodman was found dead in her flat early this morning. It was on the early news but will be in tomorrow's newspapers. The police believe she was murdered sometime after midnight. The police apparently are looking for the driver of a black BMW seen in the street where she lived in Cambridge about the time she was murdered. It's a quiet part of the city and usually deserted at that time of night.'

I was stunned to hear the news and replied, 'Have the police suggested a motive?'

'They didn't say. The sale of the cottage is now on hold for the time being.'

'Do you know if anyone else had been to see it or made enquiries about seeing it?' I asked.

'Gladys Cook told me that a man and woman in a car were seen driving slowly past it a few days back. Before you ask, the car was not a black BMW but a Mazda. Nobody has called me.'

I thanked him for the news and asked to be kept informed about the property. The coffee break was about to start so I took the opportunity to tell Robert about Ruth's murder. Like me, he was shocked and worried that someone might know I had possession of Fellows' papers and could be next on their hit list. It was now looking like there was a connection between the Brotherhood Foundation members and the terrorists. Finding that connection, if there was one, must now be our priority.

I told Robert I had a lunch date with Valerie, even if it had yet to be arranged. I knew what he was thinking by the look he gave me. My encounters with women always brought trouble. He reiterated the warning he gave me at the reception. I was so excited at my prospective date that I ignored his misgivings.

In London a computerised voice on the telephone said, 'We have a problem that needs an urgent solution.'

The receiver replied, 'The solution package is on its way.'

Unknown to me, Anna Kolzak alias Olga Petroitch was just boarding a British Airways Boeing 747 in London, bound for Washington.

After the conference I went to my room and called Valerie. She answered immediately. 'Hello Paul,' she said.

'You must be keen to call me so early, just as I had come out of the bath.'

I resisted making an obvious comment but told her the conference had finished early and I wanted to make sure our date was still on.

'Can we meet at one o'clock at a small bistro called the Potomac Bar, just across the river in Arlington? Most taxi drivers know its location. It's about a twenty minute drive from your hotel. They do a good seafood lunch,' she said.

'That sounds great. I will get a taxi,' I replied.

'Are you at home?' I asked.

'Yes, I am in my apartment in Georgetown and expecting some friends to arrive at any time,'

I heard what sounded like a door bell.

'I won't keep you then and look forward to seeing you again tomorrow.'

I couldn't believe my luck. I had to tell Robert, but then had second thoughts, perhaps it was better for him not to know. Robert called and we went to dinner in the hotel restaurant. I noticed two men and a woman sitting on a corner table watching us. I told Robert who said with a smile on his face. 'Now you're their celebrity spy they will be looking after you.' He was obviously enjoying the whole experience but I liked my private life to be private. It seemed as though while I was in Washington that was a sacrifice I would have to make. Then I thought about my date with Valerie. Would that be watched and recorded? Robert was not married and didn't seem to have much interest in women but devoted himself to making money. We discussed the day's events and the sad news from London about Ruth. I warned him not to trust anybody. It was going to be difficult to separate the goodies from the baddies. We couldn't understand why Robert was excluded by the Vice President from the meeting with the FBI and CIA people when we had met them the night before.

Trying to reassure Robert, I said, 'Perhaps they wanted to keep you out of danger.'

'But they know we are associated. Any assassin will go after us both,' he retorted.

'Remember it was me who did the interviews in Kuwait and I got arrested.'

'That's because you couldn't keep your hands off the girl,' he quickly snapped.

I smiled back at him. 'I know, but she was worth it,' I replied.

We finished our drinks and decided to have an early night. Before being overcome with tiredness, I booted up my laptop to look again at the coded names list Ruth had sent me. I began to wonder why the list was coded. Why was it so important to protect the names of The Brotherhood's members? Suddenly, I realised the one person who might hold the key was David Simons. He was with Henry Fellows back in 1933, the co-founder of The Brotherhood and a life-long friend. There were so many unanswered questions; Simons might have the answers.

David's name was mentioned dozens of times in the memoires, but like Henry, he had been forced to change his identity. Simons must also be on the hit list. He probably wouldn't have heard about Fellows' death since he officially didn't exist.

I started a search using Google, a new Internet company that had just been established in Palo Alto in California. It was fast becoming the most advanced Internet search engine. I had a lot of references from the memoires so was able to make progress in tracking Simons down. I found hundreds of David Simons since it was a common German Jewish name but none fitted the profile. Eventually I found a reference using The Brotherhood for Peace as key words. It brought up hundreds of sites about Islam. It was interesting that on one site similar words were used to describe the Islamic religion as could be found describing the objectives of the Fellows' Brotherhood. *Islam is a religion of brotherhood, justice, forgiveness, peace and love that promotes universal peace and brotherhood.* Was it this that led to the connection with Al-Qaeda? The Brotherhood didn't have a website since it existed long before the Internet was born so references were mainly from publications or reported news items. Everything found on the Internet has been put there by someone, usually historians or researchers. I searched publications associated with The Manhattan Project and since Fellows and Simons had worked together on it, I came up with a publication from the University of Arizona in Tucson which thanked Dr Henry Fellows for his talk. As indicated in Ruth's letter, David Simons' alias was Stanley Rheiner.

He would now be in his eighties and certainly retired. Many of the scientists in Oppenheimer's team took posts after the war at universities or Government establishments. Most were long dead. But they were good places to start searching. The hunt had begun, but I wondered where it would lead me?

CHAPTER 9

A Date with Destiny

On my third day in Washington I attended the final session of the conference at the hotel, primarily to meet some people who wanted to talk to me about working in war zones. I heard some harrowing stories about experiences in the Balkans war, in Iraq and Afghanistan. As lunch time approached, I excused myself, went to my room, changed my shirt and splashed my face with Armani aftershave.

The taxi arrived and took me over the Potomac River via the Arlington Memorial Bridge and around the famous cemetery, then turned south along the bank of the river. The journey actually took less than ten minutes so I arrived early for my date. I paid the taxi and was about to enter the bistro when a tap on my shoulder made me turn around to see Valerie's smiling face. I wanted to reach out and kiss her but it was too early to make such a gesture.

I could not resist telling her how good she looked in her light grey business suit. She wore matching high heeled shoes. Her long blonde hair was tied neatly back with a red bow. The restaurant was not busy so a reservation was unnecessary. We chose a table in the rear which looked out onto the river. This was my first date so I had to use it to find out more about the woman I felt an overwhelming desire to know. But I had to be careful how much I told her about myself at this time.

Valerie knew the restaurant so recommended the seafood salads which I then ordered. We had soft drinks because she was driving. She had to return to her office within the hour as some important meeting was being held later in the afternoon so it did not leave us much time.

'How long have you been in Washington?' I asked.

She replied, 'I came to Washington with my father in1989 when he was appointed the first Secretary at the British Embassy and with his help I got a job as an administrator in a Government Department in Washington. I moved from my flat in London to share an apartment with father. My mother died when I was seven. At the time, father's job took him to different countries so I was brought up by my aunt, who was my mother's eldest sister. In 1996, father had a heart attack and was then forced to take early retirement from the Diplomatic Service. He returned to London and now lives there with his new wife. After father left, I was offered a new job in Washington as a Personal Assistant to Bill Lopez, the Head of the Office of Foreign Affairs and personal friend of the President. It was through my father that I got the job since he knew most of the senior politicians and civil servants in Washington.'

She looked at me expecting me to say what I was doing in Washington.

'I am a freelance investigative journalist and receive commissions from multinational companies, journals and newspapers to write reports and articles. Currently I am a regular contributor to the Global Economist on Middle Eastern affairs. Robert, who you know, obtained a commission for me to write about politics in the capital, which is why I was at the reception and fortunately able to meet you.'

I detected a slight blush of embarrassment and don't think she believed my reason for being in Washington. She was too politically astute to think I had obtained a pass for the White House reception based on writing about Washington but her face showed no expression of disbelief. I expected to see a dubious look but instead I got a loving smile.

Eagerly she said, 'I know a lot of people in the city so I can help you with introductions should you want to interview anybody.'

She noticed me looking at her hands. Instinctively, I was looking for a wedding ring but covered it by telling her what beautiful nails she had. It was a little coy but they accentuated her long fingers. She had a gold ring on her right hand middle finger. She placed her fingers over it and told me it had been her mother's wedding ring. I asked her directly if she had ever been married. She paused before answering. The question seemed to trouble her.

'I have had some bad relationships and have been let down a number of times so am still waiting for the right man,' she said with a smile.

She looked away and quickly changed the subject without asking me the same question. The ensuing silence was interrupted by the salad arriving. I perceived she was hiding something but now was not the time to pursue it. I cracked a few jokes and found Valerie had a great sense of humour. We began to warm to each other. I was looking beyond her physical beauty and saw an intelligent sensitive woman. Our exploration was abruptly interrupted by her telephone ringing. She turned away to answer the call and I could see by the expression on her face, something was worrying her.

After putting the phone down she said, 'Sorry, Paul, but I'm needed urgently back in the office.'

I replied, 'OK, I understand but will you have dinner with me tomorrow night so we can continue to get to know each other, hopefully without interruption?'

She smiled and said, 'I would like that but I'm not sure I will be free. Call me tomorrow on my cell phone and I will let you know.'

I kissed her on the cheek as she got into her car. I said softly, 'I can't wait until tomorrow night.'

She squeezed my hand and gave me a smile. At that moment I knew this was the woman I wanted. In the taxi back to the hotel I thought about the events of the last week. All I wanted was a quiet house in the Cotswolds and instead had become a freelance agent for the CIA, a member of a secret Task Force set up by the most powerful man in the World and a carrier of secret files. I had also met a woman with whom I could fall in love. The other positives were that if I survived I would be half-a-million dollars better-off and Robert would have a great story for his book.

Back at the hotel I called Robert but he was out, so I decided to take a sightseeing walk to the Mall. It was a bright sunny afternoon with a clear blue sky over the city. I walked across to the centre of the Mall to get a view of the Washington Monument which was on my right and the Capitol Building on my left. The latter is the very heart of America where all the Presidents are inaugurated and the nation's decisions are made by the Senate and House of Representatives. The sweeping lawns and tree-lined paths leading to the Capitol create an elegant view when seen from the Monument.

It seemed to me this would be the natural target for any attack on America rather than New York, which is essentially the commercial capital. A bomb detonated here would wipe out the White House and centre of Government with a devastating impact on the country. Perhaps the bombers wanted to keep the Government institutions for their own purpose which indicated they may not be Islamic extremists. Could we be facing a group of Western extremists who wanted to take-over America?

I made my way to the end of the Mall to the steps of the Lincoln Memorial on the banks of the Potomac River. The nineteen-foot high statue of Lincoln enshrined in a massive marble Greek temple with Doric columns is not only one of the most impressive monuments in Washington but the most symbolic. It contains inscriptions of the two best known speeches by Lincoln, *The Gettysburg Address* and his *Second Inaugural Address*. In 1963, the Lincoln Memorial grounds were the site of one of the most significant political rallies in American history when 250,000 people came to hear Martin Luther King deliver his memorable speech *I have a Dream* as part of the 'March on Washington for Jobs and Freedom' for the black people. It reminded me of the turbulent history of the country since the colonial days of the 'Boston Tea Party.' Since then it has enjoyed freedom and prosperity and upheld the basic rights and democracy throughout the world. Now for the first time, outside enemies, and perhaps some from within, were challenging the very democratic principles on which the nation was founded. From the Memorial I could see

232

the famous Arlington National Cemetery across the Potomac River. It was a heart-stirring sight to see where all the American heroes were buried, including the Kennedys. Their deaths, caused by extremists who wanted to change the political structure, served only to strengthen it.

I walked past the White House and through the park towards Lafayette Square where the Hay-Adams hotel was located, being conscious of CCTV cameras in the surrounding streets. Somebody in the FBI might actually be tracking me at this very moment. Alicia said I would be protected which meant be under surveillance. Was I being followed by a human being? I wondered. Like a scene in a Hollywood film, I decided to test the theory. I suddenly turned around and walked back along the road, to see who might be walking towards me. Sure enough, a smartly dressed woman walking towards me suddenly crossed the road to avoid passing. I then crossed the road to follow her, only to be eclipsed by a taxi coming around the corner and picking her up on the opposite side of the road. As it sped away I waved to the occupant, hoping she would see me. I was taking a risk as it might have been an innocent pedestrian, like me, taking a walk around the sites or an employee from one of the many Government offices close by who decided to take a taxi home. But the taxi seemed too readily available and in haste. Perhaps paranoia was clouding my brain.

I was about to enter the grounds in front of the hotel when a black van with darkened windows passed slowly by on the opposite side of the road. I didn't think anymore about it until it turned around and drove deliberately straight at me. I managed to just jump out of its path and run into the grounds of the hotel. It missed me by only a few feet. Fearing the worst, I ran into the hotel lobby. Looking back I saw the van had disappeared. I hoped it had been captured by the street cameras.

Robert was in the bar in a rather agitated state so I joined him for a drink. I told him that someone had just tried to run me down. He poured me out a brandy from a bottle he had on the table. I rang Alicia using the special number. She answered immediately. I told her about the incident and that I was now with Robert in the hotel. She told me to stay in the hotel. Ten minutes later she called back, 'Switch on your laptop, I am sending you the video clip from the CCTV camera outside the hotel. Look carefully at the van's rear window.'

I went to my room to get my computer and plugged in the radio adapter. I received a clear picture of the van turning towards me; obviously with intent to run me over. What was more worrying was there was something sticking out from the partially open rear window. It could be a gun but it was too dark to see. The van moved away but its number plate was easily visible. I continued talking to Alicia on the phone.

'Was that a gun barrel sticking out of the van's window?' I asked.

'Yes,' was her reply.

'Can the van be traced?' I asked.

'It had false number plates, but we've tracked it going into a garage five miles away and a swat team are on their way to it now.' she replied.

I detected excitement in the tone of her voice.

She added. 'It looks like our enemies have made their first clumsy move but it may give us our first lead. I am sending over two agents to the hotel. Don't leave the hotel. It looks like you are their next target, Paul.'

The last statement was not conducive to my well-being or my planned date with Valerie. I went back to the bar where Robert was sitting and told him everything. I took another sip of brandy to steady my nerves.

It was interesting that the FBI had immediate access to the pictures from the TV monitors. It meant they could monitor the whole city. Not surprising being so near the White House. The age of Big Brother was certainly with us.

Being able to track the van and its passengers to their hideout could provide Alicia and Gary with the lead they wanted. I visualised a group of FBI agents getting excited, scanning CCTV outputs all over the city. I forgot to tell Alicia about the suspicious woman who I thought was following me, but she might have been one of her agents.

Robert and I went on to discuss the surreal situation we found ourselves in. He was concerned about how it would affect his agency business. It was impossible for him to contact other clients because of the security restrictions placed on us. He had called his office and told his secretary to cancel all his engagements until further notice.

'Do you think we are on their hit list? Robert asked.

'Somebody knows that we're working with the Task Force. That information must have come from within one of the agencies because few people outside know about us.'

'There has to be an informer. How else could the killers know?' asked Robert.

'I'm sure Alicia is doing her best to find these moles,' I said.

'I cannot understand why such people would want to help the enemies of their country, even for money,' said Robert.

'People do it for a variety of reasons. Some get trapped in religious cults, some are blackmailed and do it for money or to save their reputations, others have personal grudges against the Government,' I replied.

We ordered dinner and then retired after an eventful day.

Georgetown

After breakfast with Robert, I called Valerie. She was busy and had no time to chat but confirmed we could meet for dinner and suggested a restaurant called '1789' since it was located on 36th Street in Georgetown close to her apartment. I knew Georgetown was a fashionable district of Washington with a number of beautifully restored town houses owned by the wealthy and political elite. It's where you have to live to be close to people who matter. She declined my offer to pick her up from her apartment in a taxi. I did not mention my experiences on the previous day but leaving the hotel without the FBI agents seeing me was not going to be easy.

I scanned the newspapers which were again full of speculation about Iraq's weapons of mass destruction. There was little coverage of any British events except a small paragraph indicating the Government had been alerted about possible terrorist bomb attacks. A government spokesman denied any credible evidence existed to justify the rumours. This was the first time I had seen such a reference. Somebody must have leaked it to the press. I was reminded that the MI5 and FBI were exchanging information so the Government should be briefed on events. It was going to get increasingly difficult to keep the press and public out of the information loop.

The hotel desk rang to say two men were asking to see me. I went to the lobby where I saw Robert standing with two black-suited guys, obviously FBI agents. We shook hands and went into a small private room. Robert said they were our bodyguards and would keep surveillance at the hotel. This time no names were mentioned and the two men said very little. Both were well-built and could have been clones of Arnold Schwarzenegger. They looked like they were trained to kill, to shoot first and ask no questions. It was some comfort to have such men as protection. Alicia was determined to lock us down. I hadn't told Robert about my date with Valerie and certainly wasn't going to tell Alicia so I needed an escape plan. We thanked our new minders who were going to be stationed at some inconspicuous location in the hotel and then left them so we could talk about our own strategy.

I told Robert I was not going to be a prisoner and confided in him about my evening date with Valerie. He warned me again about seeing her but agreed to help me with an escape plan. We assumed our confinement was for our protection and temporary until the FBI had caught the would-be killers. My cell phone rang. It was Alicia.

'We found the van in a lock-up garage but no sign of the occupants. It had been hired by a man yesterday morning and then stolen. Forensics are going through it now. So far we have only some DNA samples and they are being checked but the people involved are professionals and left no obvious clues.

'We are checking out the person who hired the vehicle since that could be a hoax. Hope you've met my two agents. They will look after you both.'

I said, 'I am letting you know that Robert and I are going out to dinner tonight in Georgetown with one of his clients. We will keep our phones on and be discreet.'

After a long silence she spoke, 'I can't protect you outside the hotel. Let me know immediately if you see anything suspicious. I will tell the agents you are going out of the hotel tonight.'

I agreed to be careful and thanked her for her concern. I now had my escape plan.

I put on my best suit and sprayed on the Armani body cologne. It was always difficult to understand those experts who say that natural body odour was more attractive to women. It's true that the male pheromone androstenol found in sweat is attractive to woman when fresh, but as soon as it becomes oxidised it becomes a female repellent. Most scents contain chemical pheromones designed to activate the sexual senses but many fail. I always use those that have proved helpful but they are no substitutes for mental and physical attributes. The hotel desk rang to tell me that the yellow cab booked for seven-thirty to take us to Georgetown had arrived. Robert and I made sure the agents saw us leave. We knew the CCTV cameras would also be recording our departure. Robert arranged to visit some friends who lived just outside Georgetown so the taxi would drop him off and then take me to the restaurant.

The '1789' restaurant was a quintessential federal townhouse restaurant with distinct dining rooms. It was furnished and decorated with traditional American antiques and period prints; a large glowing wood fire created a warm atmosphere. The Head Waiter escorted me to a table in a private room. A number of elderly couples already eating looked curiously at me as I walked past them. Not surprisingly, a well-dressed stranger would be noticed in this traditional restaurant, frequented by local Georgetown residents. I felt a little uncomfortable at being on my own. Sensing this, the waiter told me that Miss Day had sent a message saying she had been delayed but hoped to be at the table within ten minutes.

I ordered a bottle of Moet Chandon to be put on ice and a large brandy. The waiter closed the door to ensure privacy. Within five minutes, the waiter opened the door and Valerie walked into the room. She was dressed in a short, figure-hugging black dress with a low-cut neckline that accentuated her cleavage. Her long-blonde hair was tied back in a single bow with a blue ribbon. She greeted me with her engaging smile and apologised profusely about being late. Something at the office had apparently stopped her from leaving. She did not say what it was, so I did not ask.

The waiter brought the ice-bucket with the champagne and gave us the menu. On Valerie's recommendation, I ordered crab chowder for the first course. It was her favourite soup and although she did not know, it was also mine. Valerie told me she often came to the restaurant with her friends, sometimes male ones from the office, so being seen with me wouldn't raise any surprises with familiar on-lookers. Government people often booked private rooms and no questions were asked. She had a special arrangement with the Maître D. I was curious about what that meant.

Over dinner we continued with our previous conversation about our lives and jobs without giving too much away. Valerie was more open about her life than me. She seemed to have a therapeutic need to talk about herself. I sensed in her a feeling of insecurity. She was born in Guildford and educated at London University, initially studying for a degree in chemistry but changed the course after one year for Political Science. Her interest in politics was raised after attending a talk given at the university by the then Prime Minister, Margaret Thatcher, who coincidentally had also started at university taking a chemistry degree course and then changed to law. After graduating with a second-class degree, Valerie decided that she wanted to work in politics. Her professor suggested she should work in London to gain experience. With help from one of her father's friends, she acquired a job as a Research Assistant at Conservative Central Office. It gave her useful experience. She did talk to Thomas Donald, the Vice

Chairman of the party and the man responsible for recruiting new people onto the parliamentary candidates list. He advised them on the procedures for being selected for parliamentary seats. Valerie even had an interview with the Chief Agent, Alan Laker, who had the ear of the Party Chairman. Alan couldn't resist beautiful women so she had no difficulty in winning his support, but repelled his suggestive advances to take her out. But the Government was unpopular and various changes occurred after the fall of Margaret Thatcher's premiership that made her decide on a change of career. It was an opportunity to move on so she left England to join her father in Washington. Thatcher had established good relations with the American political classes, both Democrat and Republican, particularly the latter through her friendship with Ronald Regan, thus renewing the so-called special relationship.

During the time when her father worked in Washington, Valerie accompanied him on social occasions. With her good looks, knowledge of politics and contacts, she was an excellent substitute for a wife. Having met most of the key people in American politics, she became well-known within the Washington political set. Occasional return trips to London to visit her aunt helped her to overcome bouts of homesickness.

She told me her boss, Bill Lopez, was a self-made millionaire and a typical American Democrat class of politician. They had a good working relationship. Being half his age she became a substitute for the daughter he would have given anything to have had, but his wife Sophie could not have children.

I told her about my family, my life at the University of Oxford and how I became a journalist, adding some of my experiences in the Middle East writing articles for the Global Economist. She seemed content not to know more about my current work which was a relief because I did not want to tell her lies.

After a main course of Maryland chicken, a dessert of Key Lime pie and consuming most of a bottle of Moet Chandon followed by two large glasses of liquor brandy, we were getting slightly intoxicated. The chemistry between us was being activated again and my physical body was responding. Soon it was time to leave. I summoned the waiter and asked him to order a taxi. We continued for a while with our small talk.

A smart black limousine, probably one on contract hire to the restaurant, arrived. It drove us slowly along the poorly lit tree-lined Wisconsin Avenue. The mix of the Moet Chandon and brandy was having its affect on both of us. I felt the leather seat move as she snuggled up close to me. I squeezed her hand and felt the warmth of her body transfer to mine. Our driver must have decided to take the long way round as he drove slowly through many streets lined with rows of large Georgian houses. The limousine eventually stopped outside a modern five-storey apartment block that looked incongruous alongside the more traditional style residences in the street.

I helped Valerie out of the car and asked the driver to wait. We walked along a well-maintained garden path to some white marble steps leading to a porticoed entrance of the apartment block. It was very quiet; no lights where showing at any of the windows. It looked as though none of the tenants were at home but then I realised the windows had shutters. As we approached the front door I began to feel aroused. I turned to look at her face, now lit by the moonlight. She gave me an encouraging smile.

'When shall I see you again?' I asked.

The long silence that followed my question filled me with dismay. Was this to be just a one-night date? What had I said that made her pause before giving an answer? My anxiety was quickly terminated when she squeezed my hand and replied, 'Do you want to come up for a nightcap?'

'Yes,' I said.

I went back to pay the driver and gave him a very large tip. Noticing my excitement, he smiled and gave me a wink.

Valerie placed a card in the security lock and we entered a well-lit hall area. There was a second door leading to the inner part of the building and the lifts. She placed her face into a recess in the wall. She explained it had an iris scanning security system to give additional security. It was similar to the one I had in my own apartment block in Knightsbridge. She dialled in some codes which then allowed me to also enter. I knew the system could be programmed to accept visitors by the card holder.

Once inside the lift, she pushed the button for the fourth floor. The lift moved quickly and quietly. In the confined space of the lift we looked into each other's eyes. I had subconsciously been thinking about what I would do. I wanted to make love to her and believed she felt the same way. But we hardly knew each other and this was only our second date. She did not seem to be the sort of woman who would have sex with a relative stranger so soon after meeting him. But I didn't feel like a stranger. Our chemistry was overcoming such inhibitions. The primitive physical urge was greater than societal conformity. Thousands of years of civilisation had failed to suppress the genetic desire to mate. It sounds crude but is basically true.

As the lift ascended to the top floor, I felt an irresistible and uncontrollable desire to bring her body close to mine. I kissed her gently on the lips. Her response was more passionate. She flung her arms around me, bringing our bodies into intimate contact. The lift came to a gentle stop and we stepped out into the corridor. She took my hand and almost pulled me across the floor to her apartment located a few yards beyond the lift. Nervously she fumbled in her bag for the key. The door opened into a room lit only by silver moonlight shining through the open curtains. Avoiding the light switch, she moved away from me. I could see the shape of her body silhouetted against the pale light as she moved across the window.

I noticed she still wore high-heeled shoes which compensated for the two inch difference in our heights. We were now face-to-face, cheek-to-cheek. She unbuttoned her blouse. The pale light reflected her shapely curves beyond anything I had ever seen before, and I had seen many. She undid her hair so it dropped lazily over her shoulders. Placing her arms tightly around my waist she drew me towards her. My arousal heightened to bursting point. Sensing my desire, she whispered softly.

'Relax, we have all night.'

She slid her hands inside my shirt undoing the buttons one at a time, then unzipped my trousers which dropped to the floor around my legs. Feeling my hardness, she brought her leg up and wrapped it around me so I could feel the warmth of her inner body. At that moment we both lost control and spontaneously ripped off the rest of our clothes. We dropped onto a white rug on the floor beside the bed. We kissed, almost consuming each other until fighting for air to breathe. I had never experienced such passionate love-making.

After, the physical passion was transformed into that gentleness experienced afterwards by lovers. Something I had never felt before.

We lay for a while to regain our strength. Then, I picked her up and gently laid her on the bed. I did not want the night to end. We clutched each tightly and made love again before falling into a blissful sleep.

I was woken up by bright sunlight streaming through the window. I felt good, very contented. Reaching out across the bed for the girl of my dreams, I was surprised to find an empty space. Glancing at my watch, I saw it was 9.15 am. Valerie had left quietly.

Memories of past experiences raced through my mind and temporarily numbed me. Then I saw a hastily scribbled note on the bedside table. It read,

'*Sorry Paul but we overslept and I could not wake you. I had to go to work for an early morning meeting. Please call me later this morning from your hotel.*'

I was still surprised she did not wake me. But I was so tired, the jet lag, the events of the last few days and last night had left my body in a state of exhaustion causing me to sleep so deep that I did not hear her leave, but it left me with a disturbed feeling. This time I had hoped that the woman I slept with would be there in the morning. At least this time I was left a note of explanation.

I took a shower, dressed and made a cup of coffee. The apartment was well-furnished and had every convenience. It looked over-sumptuous, for a single woman. Something was not quite right; the furnishings didn't seem to match the personality of the woman with whom I had just made love. There were no personal artefacts in the apartment. It was like a hotel suite. I wondered if it belonged to her. I did notice what looked like a man's robe hanging on the door of the bathroom but saw nothing else indicating a male presence. Resisting the temptation to pry further, I locked the door and left.

Walking along Pennsylvania Avenue, I had an uncomfortable feeling that Valerie still hadn't told me everything. I kept thinking about what Robert had said, warning me to keep clear as she was involved with someone very powerful in politics. If that was true, why did she make love to me on our second date? Just as I was beginning to become melancholy, a yellow cab passed. I waved it to stop, got in and directed it to the Hay-Adams Hotel.

When I arrived at my hotel room there were two call messages on the phone. They were both from Valerie. Her voice sounded anxious.

'Can we meet? I need to speak to you urgently? I will come to the hotel before lunch. Please don't call me. I will come to your room.'

The call added to my concerns. I called Robert. There was no reply so I went to breakfast. The room was full of senators and journalists who had stayed on after the conference to do some lobbying. I found a small table in the corner of the room. Newspapers hid the faces of those who did not want to be disturbed. Not having a paper meant the vacant seat at my small table was soon occupied. A round-faced well-built man, displaying a broad smile, suddenly appeared and asked, 'Do you mind if I share your table'

'No,' I answered.

I shook his outstretched hand without saying my name.

'My name is Darrel Edmunds. Aren't you the guy at the reception the other night with that gorgeous gal?' he asked.

'I think you are mistaking me for someone else. I was with my agent Robert.' I replied.

Not wishing to engage in a conversation, I excused myself to get some toast from another table, hoping it would stop the guy from asking any more questions. But when I sat down he continued.

'Were you at the Journalist conference?'

'Yes,' I replied.

I hoped my short answers would deter him but he was determined to talk.

'How long have you been in Washington?'

'Just three days,' I said.

'I run a political consultancy business here in Washington. We are helping with the Republican Presidential Campaign,' he said.

He paused, expecting a reply. When he didn't get one, he stopped talking and went over to the buffet table to fill his plate with a pile of food. He returned and started to eat. Just when I thought I would be spared more questions, he said, 'Would you mind being interviewed by one of our researchers on public issues?'

'I'm British, so my opinions would be of little value here,' I answered.

'No, you would be ideal. We want to find out how you Brits see us.'

I was becoming frustrated with the man when I noticed a copy of the Global Economist in his brief case. I looked at him and said, 'Let's cut the crap – you know who I am.'

Unperturbed, he smiled and repeated the question.

'Mr Cane, I apologise for not immediately recognising you.

We would pay you well for an interview on your thoughts about another Iraq war following all the rumours about terrorist threats to America.'

I was astonished he knew about the terrorist threats. It was time to get away from this man. I expressed my apologies and told him I was too busy to give interviews. I quickly left the table. He put up his hands and continued eating his ham, eggs and pancakes and a load of other stuff that filled his plate. I collected some newspapers from the hotel shop and returned to my room to read them. Again, they were full of Iraq and the UN sanctions.

An hour later there was a knock on my door. I opened it to a woman who looked upset, a more serious woman than the one I had been with the night before. With tears in her eyes, she said,

'Paul, can I come in? I am sorry I left so early this morning but there is something I have to tell you. It can't wait.' I sat her down on the couch and held her hand.

'I received a call on my cell phone this morning from someone I didn't know. He apparently saw us together last night at the restaurant and followed the taxi to my apartment. He is threatening to tell the man with whom I have a relationship that I slept with you unless I pay him ten thousand dollars.

I am sorry I did not tell you before but I am not completely free, I have a friendship with a man. He owns my apartment and thinks he owns me. I do not love him but he was very kind to me when I needed someone after my father left and we became very close friends.'

'Who is the man?' I asked.

I can't tell you, but he is a very senior ambitious politician. It would be dangerous for you to know his name at this time. Being well-known in Washington and married, a scandal would ruin his political career if the public found out about us.' I looked at her and knew what was coming next.

'I cannot go back to him. I have been trying to break off our relationship for a long time but he is a very possessive man.'

She placed her arms around my neck and I could feel her intensity. I held her tightly and said, 'Is he in love with you?'

'No,' she replied.

'If he knew about us, would it make things more difficult for you?' I asked.

She replied in a soft voice. 'Yes, it would. Since he is in a position to know everything that goes on in Washington. He will probably find out anyway. I should not have taken you to that restaurant, as too many people who know him go there. Washington is a gossip town. I was late arriving because he called me from Long Island where he lives with his wife and two daughters.'

The revelation made me feel slightly depressed. She continued,

'I am sorry about last night. You must think badly of me for allowing it to happen but I couldn't help myself. For the first time in years it felt right and made me realise that I have to break off my relationship with Alan.'

'Alan who?' I asked.

She hesitated before saying, 'It's Senator Alan Sherman.'

'Isn't he the Republican's front runner for the Presidential nomination?' I asked.

'Yes, that's why he will stop at nothing to protect his name and reputation.'

'Then you have what you need to stop the blackmailer. Call his bluff, take the offensive, deny the allegation and say if he bothers you again you will report him to Sherman, that should frighten him off. Anyway if Sherman does find out, he can't do anything for fear of it becoming public. That would end his chances of getting the nomination.'

'Paul you don't know him. He is a jealous and ruthless man. He has a lot of bodyguards and friends who do all his dirty work. We would both be in danger. I usually only see him once a week when he stays in town. He wants to come to the apartment tonight. I don't know how I'm going to cope.' She started sobbing.

'I cannot see him after last night with you. My life has now changed. I am sorry I shouldn't be putting you in this position.' She gripped me tight. I held her for a while and gave her a kiss. I tried to think rationally about what do, while emotionally I wanted her and couldn't let her return to the man who clearly was using her for his own selfish purposes. But I also wondered if she was using me as an escape route? Were my emotions clouding my judgement?

'Do you have anywhere you can stay, like at a friend's house?' I asked.

'Yes, I have many friends but I do not want to involve them, particularly in Washington. I can go to a beach house that I own in Martha's Vineyard, an island off the coast of Massachusetts, near Cape Cod. I sometimes use it as a retreat from Washington. I have a pilot's licence and fly myself using a small 172 Cessna Skyhawk aircraft, located at a flying club twenty miles out of town. The house originally belonged to my father but he gave it to me when he returned to England.'

246

Appearing to be more composed, she said, 'I will go to my house for a few days to sort things out but there is the blackmail threat to deal with.'

'Don't worry; I have a plan to deal with it.' I said.

'Paul, can you come with me to Martha's Vineyard?'

I hesitated, then said, 'Since we are being honest with each other there is something I have to tell you. In the interests of national security what I am about to say is strictly secret but because of our situation you have to know why I am really in Washington.'

She looked anxiously at me. I told her about my recent experiences in Kuwait and England, the President's Task Force set up to deal with a terrorist threat and how Robert and I became inextricably involved.

I said, 'Being part of a secret Task Force under the direction of the Vice President gives us White House and FBI protection. Only a limited number of people in the agencies know about it because we believe the organisation behind the terrorist group have moles in both the agencies and probably in the Government. As cover, I have been given an office in a building close to where your Department is located, to write some articles about Washington so that part of what I told you yesterday is true.'

Valerie was stunned by my revelations and was holding my hand so tight that it went white.

'What am I going to do? You have a serious job to do and cannot leave Washington to come with me,' she said.

'I will work something out and promise to protect you. I hate to say this but try to carry on as normal. Go back to work and stay in your apartment tonight. Tell Sherman you are unwell. That should stop him from coming, or say you are visiting a sick friend. If he believes you then he will not have to know about us.'

Valerie seemed reassured and agreed.

I told her I would have to tell Robert about us since he knew we had dinner together and was my friend and confidant. She knew and liked Robert but did not want him to know about her affair with the politician. I promised to keep it to myself but Robert knew anyway. I told her that I would call her tomorrow. We kissed and hugged each other before she left.

I was afraid to tell Robert about my problem. He wouldn't be pleased when he found out. My track record with women was not admired by my dear friend, but this one was different. Her predicament was now mine and I intended to rescue her. What had passed was gone. It was our future that mattered now. I knew the job I agreed to do for the Task Force would require my total dedication and leave little time for a love affair, but I was now infatuated with Valerie. There was no way back. I wanted to be with her as much as possible and didn't care about the consequences.

Robert had just arrived back at the hotel when I called. I asked him to come to my room immediately. When I told him about Valerie and our problem he was, as expected, very displeased; perhaps furious would be a better description of his reaction. It took a few glasses of brandy to calm him down. I asked Robert about Alan Sherman since he was more knowledgeable about American politicians than me.

He said, 'Sherman is a very wealthy guy with a lot of high-level political connections. He is favoured to be the Republican nominee to run for the Presidency next year and so could become the next President. His second wife, who is much older than him, lives with their three children on Long Island. Like so many politicians he has a flat in Washington and only goes home to New York at weekends. Nobody knows about his other apartment in Georgetown. After Valerie's father returned to England, Sherman helped to get her a good job in the Department of Foreign Affairs. They started secretly dating. When the lease ran out on her father's flat, he set her up in one of the Georgetown apartments he owned. Georgetown is full of aspiring young women living in luxury apartments provided by wealthy politicians and businessmen. Valerie was not the only woman he saw. Sherman is a bit of a womaniser. Such guys collect young beautiful woman like trophies to fulfil their egos. I am surprised that such a nice English girl like Valerie got caught in his trap, but like London, Washington can be a lonely place. She became lonely when her father went back to England who, without her knowledge, married an old friend of her mother. She felt let down when another woman entered his life. I believe she also suffered a failed love affair in London so had no desire to go back to England. Sherman came along just at the right time and, I suppose, filled the gap.

A public admission of having a mistress would ruin his political career so the stakes are high for him to keep it a secret. People like him can make dangerous enemies. They will stop at nothing to protect their interests. At present, we have enough enemies hunting us outside of Washington, so you must be extra careful and very discreet about your relationship with Valerie. Don't let our FBI and CIA friends know. It will only add to our problems.'

'How do you know all this Robert?' I asked.

'You mean about Valerie's involvement with Sherman? I had my suspicions but until last night I didn't know very much. The friends I went to see know Valerie. They saw you with her at the Bistro in Arlington a few days ago and told me to warn you about Sherman. Rebecca is a close friend of Valerie with whom she confided after her father returned to England.

James King, Rebecca's husband played golf with her father and promised he would keep a fatherly eye on his daughter. He tried to dissuade Valerie from getting involved with Sherman. But the man can be very charming and persuasive. Unfortunately, one of Sherman's many companies bought the real estate company that employs James. Sherman found out that James and Rebecca knew Valerie and tactfully warned them to keep his arrangement with her confidential. Fearing the consequences and in Valerie's interests they have done so. James hates the man and knows how ruthless he can be to people who cross him. It is rumoured that his political campaign is being bank-rolled by the billionaire, Jonas Gould. Now you have another potential enemy who may yet be more formidable.'

Robert then changed the subject.

'I have been trying to locate Alan Masters whom I believe might be working for an American Bank in New York but was unsuccessful. We may have to reveal what we know to Alicia and get the CIA at Langley to help since they have all the experts.

We had just about finished off a bottle of our brandy when my cell phone rang. A voice said 'Merlin Falcon is flying.' It was Alicia wanting to see me immediately. She was on her way. I told Robert, who ran back to his room where he had left his phone. A similar voice message was on it. Within ten minutes there was a knock on my door; it was Alicia. She walked passed me without speaking and went over to look out of the window, then went around the room with a hand-held scanning device looking for bugs. Having found none she turned and smiled, 'You're clean,' she said.

Jokingly I replied,

'I hope so; I've just had a shower.'

Alicia was a hard professional with no sense of humour so my joke was not appreciated.

'We have just checked you out of this hotel,' she said in a demanding voice. 'Intelligence has come through to us from your MI5. They have picked some telephone chatter which indicates new terrorist cells have been set up in London and New York. We are taking this to mean these cities are likely to be the targets for the bombs. MI5 are sending over one of their top agents to work with our team and, likewise, Mark will go to London.'

I listened intently and said, 'But why do I have to check out?'

This time with a wry smile she added, 'On a separate intelligence line we have been informed that a Russian free-lance assassin is on her way to this hotel to kill you. Her name is Anna Kolzak. We don't want to lose you just yet so we are putting you in a safe house in Georgetown, just a few miles from here and close to Langley where we can keep an eye on you.'

Playing her cool game, I said, 'Thanks, I appreciate your concern. Can I ask why she wants to kill me when I was told nobody knew I was working for the Task Force?'

'It has nothing do with that, it's your knowledge of Henry Fellows which they are concerned about. It is believed this assassin murdered Fellows and Ruth Goodman and now you and Robert Carville are the next targets but Robert's name was not mentioned so we are leaving him at this hotel for the time being to find out.'

'You mean he is bait. He will not appreciate that,' I said.

'Don't worry he will be protected. We want the assassin to lead us to her employers and the moles in the CIA and MI5. She is unaware we know her identity. Your MI5 have done a great job but now it's up to us to catch her,' she replied.

'What is the connection, if any, with the bomb threats?' I asked.

'That's what we want you to find out,' she replied.

It was time to tell her about my ventures in England and the Fellows memoires as she seemed to know about them anyway. I told her about my visit to see the cottage and how accidently I came across the documents and the subsequent letter and disc with names on from Ruth Goodman.

'Why didn't you tell us this before?' she said.

'Because I was not sure of the connection,' I replied.

Alicia was a highly intelligent woman and was probably not convinced by my weak explanation. She spoke to me like a teacher talking to a pupil.

'From now on you must tell me everything, however small, since it could have a relevance to the terrorist threats. You must realise we are at war with these people and the consequences of failing to catch them will be catastrophic for us all.'

I felt embarrassed and apologised, quickly realising apologising was a mistake. Alicia was not a person you apologised to; she would take it as a sign of weakness. Now she had a hold on me which I knew she would like. I could imagine her being the dominant partner in a love session. Not a role I would like, but some men would.

She went to the corner of the room and bent down for reasons that were not clear. I noticed her shapely figure just showing through an oversize business suit. A small bulge appeared around her waistline, no doubt produced by a revolver. It was a sexy pose, probably meant to tease me. In an authoritative manner, she said, 'Pack your case quickly as there is a car waiting at the rear door of the hotel. You must not be seen leaving. The hotel bill has been paid and the hotel management informed.'

I thought it prudent to obey and guessed the hotel management was used to such clandestine activities being so close to the White House. I was not allowed to even talk to Robert who was currently being briefed in another room.

So I was going to Georgetown. It was a strange coincidence that Valerie's apartment was also in Georgetown. Alicia probably knew all about her but hopefully not about last night. I wondered if she knew about her relationship with Alan Sherman. Alicia asked for my cell phone. She took out the Sim card, plugged it into a machine she had concealed in a small case, entered some new codes and then replaced it. She also took my laptop, switched it on and to my surprise was able to circumnavigate my password then typed in some data. When I asked what she was doing she looked at me with a smile saying, 'Now you are protected and nobody will know when you use these devices or be able to access them without our knowledge.'

Without giving it too much thought, I thanked her and zipped up my suitcase.

'We must go now,' she said in an anxious voice.

A black-windowed limousine like the one used by the President took us swiftly along Pennsylvania Avenue. People looking could have thought the President was passing. I did feel a sense of importance and momentarily forgot about the reasons why I was being secreted away from a murderer.

We arrived at a Georgian-style house in a tree-lined avenue similar to the one where Valerie lived. Alicia told the driver to wait. I collected my case and followed her into the house. It was well-furnished with every convenience, an upgrade on the hotel room. Alicia said it would be safe to use my cell phone and computer. The house was secure which probably meant it was under constant surveillance.

I showed Alicia the list of coded names on the disc Ruth had sent. I also asked her for help in finding David Simons, who might be able to help us identify the names. She switched on her phone, extracted a small optical sensor from it and scanned the list. Looking at it, she shrugged, saying, 'It shouldn't be difficult for the guys at Langley to decode it. Who is David Simons?'

That was a surprise – so she was unaware of Fellows' memoires. 'He was a close friend of Fellows and co-founder of The Brotherhood Foundation. I think he could be living in Arizona under the name of Stanley Rheiner,' I replied.

She seemed a little puzzled but responded, 'I will get a check done and call you when I have some information. Meanwhile until I do, don't communicate with anyone. There are plenty of books to read and you have a TV set. The fridge is well-stocked. If you need anything call my number, it's always active. I sleep with it. You can use your phone but be careful who you call. Your location cannot be traced but whoever calls will know you are alive.'

It was ironic that a woman was coming to Washington to assassinate me. Perhaps it was the revenge of the opposite sex for all my misdemeanours over the years. My adrenaline surged. I was now the hunted not the hunter. I had an instinctive desire to meet her, to confront her, to test my masculinity. This was not a sexual thing but a deadly confrontation. I did wonder what a female assassin was like. Would she show any emotion when our eyes clashed at the moment she pulled the trigger? Then I remembered that Fellows and his niece had been killed more subtly, not even seeing the killer or knowing the nature of their deaths. I would want to face mine.

It was getting late. It had been a long day so I decided to raid the well-stocked freezer and watch some TV. I chose a large succulent steak to cook for dinner and placed it on the grill. I was worried about Robert who might also be on the assassin's list or mistaken for me. But my new friends in the FBI would protect him. I recalled from films and TV plays they sometimes failed. I decided to call him but his cell phone was switched off so I rang the hotel desk. They told me he had gone out with a man and woman. I assumed it was Alicia and another agent taking him to safety somewhere. A bad feeling came over me so I rang Alicia using the Merlin Falcon call sign. As expected, she answered immediately.

'Are you with Robert?' I asked.

'No, I am at Langley,' she replied.

I told her he had left the hotel with a man and woman.

With anger in her voice she said, 'He was told not to leave. Our agents are at the hotel but there is no other woman agent. I will call them immediately. Stay on the line. I told you not to call anyone, but maybe this time you did the right thing.'

In a few minutes she came back. 'Something is wrong, I am on my way to the hotel.'

I forgot about my steak on the grill which was getting burnt. I rushed to remove it just in time. I took a few bites but lost my appetite. I was now very worried about Robert. My reaction was to go to the hotel but knew that would be wrong. I was feeling helpless, trapped in a situation not of my making. Despair was taking me over when my phone rang again. To my surprise it was Valerie.

'I need to see you immediately,' she said anxiously.

I explained what had happened since we last spoke and that I was now located in a safe flat not far from her apartment. She seemed pleased I was so near.

'Where is it?' she asked.

I knew I would be breaking the rules but I gave her the address.

'I thought your friend Sherman was returning tonight.' I retorted.

'I cannot speak on the phone so will explain when I see you,' she said.

Ten very long minutes passed before there was a knock on the door. I opened it to view a woman whose head was covered in a dark cloak with a round white face peeping out. Seeing her transformed my despair to joy. I closed the door and we kissed. I took her into the living room. She told me that Alan had been called away on urgent business and would not be back for at least a week. There had been another phone call from the blackmailer. As I suggested, she told the caller that she was informing Alan Sherman and the FBI if he bothered her again. The man put the phone down so hopefully was scared off.

Valerie looking upset said, 'I am giving up the apartment and

254

breaking off my relationship with Alan. I have been considering it for some time so it's not just because of you. I have decided definitely to go to my house in Martha's Vineyard before he gets back.'

She looked at me in silence.

'When are you going?' I asked.

'In a few days' time when I have cleared up some things in the office. I am taking a week's vacation.'

'Stay here with me tonight,' I pleaded.

'That may not be a good idea in view of your problems,' she said.

I told her about the woman assassin who was coming to Washington for me. She put her arms around my neck and with a smile said, in a very English way, 'Serves you right for all the women you disappointed. Where's the kettle? I'll make a cup of tea'

She took off her cloak and explored the kitchen. I told her of my concerns for Robert and about Alicia's warnings.

'Do you trust this Alicia?' she said with a jealous look in her eye.

'I have to; she is the Task Force's co-ordinator of all the intelligence on these bomb threats. I have given her the names list that Fellows' niece sent me to get decoded. She thinks the Langley experts can fathom it out.'

Changing the subject, she asked, 'Do you think I was seen coming into the flat?'

'There will be a CCTV camera somewhere outside,' I replied.

'An agent will be looking at the screen at this very moment. He will be sending it to Alicia so we can expect a phone call at any time as she will think you are the assassin unless she is chasing her now.'

Before I finished talking my phone rang.

'Are you alone?' the voice said.

It was Alicia.

'No.' I replied.

'I have a friend with me. It's alright; I let her into the house.'

Her tone became angry.

'I told you not to let anyone into the house. You must not keep disobeying me. Who is she?'

'Just a friend, I can't tell you her name.'

I realised instantly it was the wrong thing to say. She would now try and find out.

'Robert is safe. He is on his way to a safe flat in downtown Washington.'

'What happened?' I asked.

'I cannot tell you over the phone, it's too complicated but you are both in danger so be extremely careful and get rid of your friend. We don't allow visitors to our safe houses.'

It was not a polite gesture but a command. I had a gut feeling she knew about Valerie anyway. I asked to speak to Robert.

'It may be better for you to remain out of contact for a while until we can catch the suspect. She arrived at Dulles this evening, took a taxi from the airport, but then we lost her in the heavy traffic so she could be anywhere.'

I asked if the list had been deciphered yet and was there any news about David Simons.

'Good progress is being made with the list. David is living in Tucson, Arizona. He was given an amnesty and a new identity in 1959 by the Government after discovering he was a co-founder of the Brotherhood Foundation. At the time he was a senior advisor to the President so held a very influential position. It was arranged for him to have a position as a Professor of Physics at the University of Arizona under the name of Stanley Rheiner.'

'What are we going to do?' I asked.

'It might be wise not to contact him until we have caught the Russian assassin. Let me think about it,' she replied.

I had an uncomfortable feeling about Alicia knowing too much. But it was her job to know everything. After a short pause, she added, 'Your MI5 knew about Fellows. It seems you have caused quite a stir in England. Their agent will be arriving in a few days and may want to see you.'

She abruptly terminated the call. I was left not knowing what I should do next. I related what Alicia had told me to Valerie. She was pleased that Robert was safe. I told her that Alicia had asked who she was but I refused to say.

'I know she will be trying to find out. I think it would be better for you to go back to your apartment and I will call you in the morning.'

She reluctantly agreed and after giving me a goodbye kiss put the cloak over her head and went out. I ignored Alicia's order and called Robert. Surprisingly, he answered immediately.

'Paul, I was about to call you although Alicia told me not to. Why we shouldn't talk is a mystery but we must keep in touch during this crisis. Where are you?' he asked.

'In a safe house in Georgetown,' I replied.

'Good, Alicia wouldn't tell me where you were, I'm in a safe flat downtown,' he said.

'I was told you were seen going out of the hotel with two people. What happened?'

'They were FBI agents with orders to take me to a safe house. I asked them for their credentials which were shown, so I packed, checked out of the hotel and went out with them without calling Alicia which I now know was a foolish thing to have done. They told me it was urgent so I left immediately. We had only walked a few yards towards their car when another group of men, probably CIA agents, rushed up demanding I be handed over. These guys looked desperate and already had their hands on their guns. There was an exchange of documents and phone calls were made. The FBI agents, a man and woman, apologised, saying there had been a mix-up. Red-faced, they hurriedly left me with the other agents. More apologies were exchanged and I was led back into the hotel. It was not until Alicia arrived in a panic about ten minutes later that I was told about a confusion from orders high up in the Bureau. She was in a furious mood and made a phone call to the White House. She then explained that because an assassin was coming to kill you they were also moving me as a precaution to a safe location. I was to be guarded and protected around the clock so nobody could get near me.'

Two FBI agents made themselves comfortable in the lobby of the

Hay-Adams Hotel. The manager had already been told about the need for their presence. It was late morning when the desk clerk at the welcomed her guest.

'Please sign in, your room is ready. Can I have your passport? Do you have any luggage?' she asked.

The old woman placed her stick against the desk and handed over her passport.

'My daughter will be arriving later with my luggage from the airport. She is not staying at this hotel as she has some business out of town.' Seeing her walking disability, the clerk asked if she needed any assistance.

'No,' was her curt reply.

She walked towards the elevator, watched by the two CIA agents who were reading newspapers in the lobby. She was the ninth old lady to register, but the others had husbands or were accompanied by younger people. They thought it strange such an elderly lady with a walking stick was on her own. They approached the desk, showed their ID and asked to see the woman's passport.

Elena Tolstoy was a seventy-three-year old American citizen whose white Russian parents had emigrated to America just before the Stalinist repressions. She lived in Connecticut with her two daughters. The CIA men decided to put a check through to Langley. The result came through quickly, indicating the passport facts were correct and a full family record showed no associations or connections with terrorist groups. They returned to their observations of the visitors to the hotel.

Photos of Anna Kolzak had been circulated to all officers but she would almost certainly be using a disguise. The real face of her Avatar, Olga Petrovitch, was not recorded anywhere. One of the CIA men noted the only tentative connection with the old lady was that she was of Russian origin. During the Cold War many émigré Russians were investigated for Communist sympathies. Some were interned while others fled the country. There was little doubt that Stalin had a network of spies in America formed by such people. It was one such group that helped to secure secrets of the Hiroshima atomic bomb.

Alicia was scanning the file on Elena Tolstoy but could not see any suspicious connections. The Russian connection to their assassin was purely coincidental. But she would place Elena on the watch list, now with a dozen people on it. None had any suspicious connections.

The experts at Langley found the names on the list were not written in any known language. When the individual letters were changed to numbers related to their position in the alphabet then some sort of coded sequence emerged. Someone with a mathematical mind had gone to great lengths to protect the information. It became obvious that there were two lists. One was short and looked more precise and written in a different code to the longer one.

While Alicia was pondering the data, a call came through from the FBI. They had lost Anna Kolzak at the airport. It was thought she had disguised herself. Cameras scanning all the stations had picked up a strange-looking old lady being helped by a porter at the station. She eventually boarded an Amtrak train to Phoenix in Arizona. The porter who helped with her luggage described her as having a young face that didn't fit the body. Alicia immediately called Gary using their call code and asked him to come over to Langley for an urgent meeting.

Gary arrived within thirty minutes.

'I think our Anna Kolzak is after Rheiner,' she said.

'Who is this guy Rheiner?' he asked.

'His real name is David Simons. He was Henry Fellows associate and the founder of the Brotherhood Foundation. They also worked together in Oppenheimer's team on the Manhattan Project. He would certainly know all what Fellows knew and is our best lead. I want him placed in a safe house until we can get to Tucson.' Alicia ordered.

'OK, do we know exactly where he lives?' Gary asked.

'Yes,' she replied.

Alicia told Gary about the coded list of names.

'Why is it so important?' he asked.

'We are not sure but we believe there is a connection to the terrorists. The list could contain the names of others who may be involved with helping them. They may be members of an international group who are using Al-Qaeda to do their work.' she said.

'Since we have the information why kill those who also possess it?' Gary retorted.

'But the terrorists and whoever is behind them do not know we have the list, unless we have a mole in our organisation,' she replied.

'How would Fellows and Simons have known about these people unless they were part of the conspiracy?'

'That's what we need to find out from Simons, or Rheiner as he is now called. I think we must take Paul Cane with us to Tucson since it was he who uncovered the whole thing,' she said. Gary agreed.

Alicia requested the names of all known Al-Qaeda members, particularly those known to be in America and Britain. She also asked for lists of the Mafia and similar criminal groups. It was horrifying how many such groups existed in the United States. Such was the price for having a free society. Ironically many of them wanted to destroy the very society that gave them those freedoms.

Surprisingly, Langley could not find any telephone records for Rheiner in Tucson, at least under that name. They had been purposely removed. Paul had just gone to bed when the phone rang.

'It's Alicia. I have Gary with me. We think the Russian is going to Tucson to kill David Simons. Gary has asked the local FBI to protect him until we arrive tomorrow. I have booked us on the nine o'clock flight tomorrow morning. A car will pick you up and we shall meet at the airport.' I had little choice but to say, 'OK'.

I immediately called Valerie and told her that an emergency had arisen and I would be in Tucson for a few days. But when I returned I would go to Martha's Vineyard with her if she still wanted me. I could detect the joy in her voice.

'I will call the airfield and asked them to get my plane ready. Be careful, Paul, you're now part of my new life,' she said.

'I am in safe hands; see you in a few days,' I replied.

At least I wasn't the assassin's next target. My new safe residence gave me some privacy, which I needed at the moment. Things might start to become dangerous as we moved closer to finding the people behind the terrorist threat. David Simons might hold the key that unlocked the door to the secret organisation controlling events.

CHAPTER 10

Tucson- Arizona
9 December 1999

Dulles airport quickly vanished as the Delta 737 climbed above the clouds en route to Phoenix. Gary, Alicia and I believed that David Simons could hold the key to the secret organisation which could be masterminding the terrorist threats.

Fellows' memoires did paint a sinister picture of The New Order's intentions. They were not the first group who thought they could take over the world. History is littered with people and groups with such aspirations. But what made this one different is that it had been in existence for over fifty-five years. Its members had infiltrated Governments, security agencies and some exerted control of powerful multinational companies. What disturbed Alicia was that very little was known about them. Even the FBI, CIA and British security services lacked intelligence or knew more than they were admitting. Over the years this secret group had been able to conceal the identity of its leaders and actions by using other organisations as fronts. Having some of its members in high places in Governments, the security services and probably the military, made them a dangerous adversary. We were up against a group of power-seekers who were conspiring to dismantle Western democracy. If they were using Al-Qaeda to carry out the bomb threats, what sort of deals had they struck with them?

I asked myself why The New Order would want to initiate another Middle East war by blowing up American and British cities and placing the blame on Arab extremists. The reason had to be political, but why now? Was it the perceived weakness of the capitalist system? Was it the economic collapse and breaking up of the Soviet Union after the fall of Communism? Was it concerns about China being the new power, having adopted a form of authoritarian capitalism? Was it the world dependence on oil giving economic and political power to those nations possessing most of it? Or was it the unchallenged military power of America that made them the target? All or some of these could be factors in the minds of the men and women who sat around a table deciding on how they would destroy Western democratically elected Governments. We had to look for the Achilles heel. Since no plan is perfect, there had to be one. Usually it resides in the personality of leaders. All the great dictators in history eventually failed because of defects in their characters. Hitler, because of his belief in the superiority of the Aryan race and hatred of the Jews. Napoleon, because of his megalomania and desire to control. The ambitions of such people were often formed in their early childhood, dictators and power-crazy people are usually motivated by greed, envy or revenge or some of the other deadly sins. In today's world such people can hide under aliases but eventually they have to emerge. It's in their nature. They need to be recognised, to be acclaimed by their followers. The New Order had wealthy leaders. They may all be ruthless but each must have a weakness which ultimately would destroy the collective ambition of the group. That would be their 'Achilles Heel'. If we could identify one, then it could lead to the others.

The flat colourless landscape of the wheat belt of America seemed to go on endlessly below. I thought of the green lush pastures of central England where I grew up. I wondered what David Simons was like after reading so much about him in the memoires. A strong enduring relationship had existed between the two founders of the Brotherhood since 1933. They shared some dark secrets so it was not surprising they had many enemies lurking in the shadows, just waiting for the chance to remove them. Alicia was depending on Simons for leads to finding the people behind the bomb threats. I was more pessimistic about how much he would know. The man had been in hiding for decades; he was out of the loop and could not know today's people, who would, by age, be at least two generations younger. It really depended on how much he might know about The New Order and its members.

We touched down in Phoenix in the late afternoon. When the door of the aircraft opened it was like being exposed to the heat of a blast furnace. At midday the temperature had reached a hundred-and-five degrees Fahrenheit, it was still about ninety-five. Gary had organised a chauffeur-driven car to drive us to Tucson so fortunately it wasn't long before I was sitting in a comfortable air-conditioned environment. Phoenix was supposed to be a mecca for wealthy senior citizens who wished to retire from the big cities. My guess was many died early from dehydration or liver disease after drinking too much in the persistent dry desert heat. The population of Phoenix has grown significantly owing to the wealthy people leaving California for a retirement in a less polluted atmosphere.

Gary told us that David Simons was now in a safe house at a secret location in the foothills around Tucson and was being very cooperative. He was aware we were coming to talk to him but had been told little about the reasons. My guess was he probably did know what we wanted and was even expecting us. Being taken to a safe house was a giveaway to a man who had been party to the Second World War's greatest secret.

Soon we were speeding along a flat road through the Sonora Desert towards Tucson. Groups of Saguaro cacti, some over twenty feet high, stood like sentinels along the roadside. Over thousands of years these desert trees have adapted to the harsh environment. They have been known to live for three hundred years or more and were unique to the region.

Seeing that Alicia was deep in thought, I asked, 'What are you thinking about, Alicia?'

She replied, 'Organising a major bombing of cities requires a sophisticated communications network and a highly developed organisation. Electronic methods are easily detectable so the plotters would have to be using a very sophisticated one of their own to avoid us picking up their phone messages. Spies still use conventional notes in bottles and coded scripts in newspapers. But even these are only easy to find if you know where to look or possess the cipher keys to the codes used. Spies are very often the unexpected people; the ordinary citizens going about their daily business. A lot of people must be actively engaged in this bombing threat even if most of them do not know the ultimate plan. If we can catch one, then it may lead us to the planners.'

Gary responded, 'Time is running out. I believe we should concentrate on finding the ring-leaders but since they will be well-hidden it's imperative we find and arrest those in the field who have to do the dirty work.'

After about two hours we entered Tucson city. I asked Alicia and Gary what we were going to say to David Simons. I suggested if we wanted his full cooperation we should tell him all we knew.

Alicia replied, 'I will do the interview. Then let's see where it leads.'

'What about the names list?' I asked.

'I assume your people have not broken the code yet?'

'I meant to tell you about that,' she replied.

'It is a transposition cipher. Langley believes the letters that make up what we think are the names are actually symbols used for the hundred and two elements of the Periodic Table. Using their positions in the table they have converted the letters into numbers. Without the key, it is impossible to relate these numbers to names or letters of names that could be hidden anywhere in a text. They have tried substituting the numbers for positions of text in *Who's Who* and the *Oxford Dictionary* and a variety of other sources used by code breakers but so far, none has produced a coherent set of names. If Simons knows about this, he may have the key. We are up against the same problems that were experienced by the code breakers at Bletchley during the Second World War. Our more sophisticated computers can speed up the process but the basic problems are the same. It was only when the Royal Navy captured an enigma machine and German code books that it was possible to break the codes. Fortunately our problem is much simpler than the ones they faced as our code will not change.'

I thought using the Periodic Table as part of the cipher was typical of a physicist like Fellows. He must have found a similarly clever way of hiding the rest of the information. Alicia gave me one of her wry smiles and continued.

'It doesn't necessarily mean the people whose names are on the list are behind the current threat. Langley thinks there are seven names that matter. These are probably the leaders. The other information is mainly historical.'

'What do you mean historical?' I asked.

'We don't know the names but they are linked to the people who were the original members of the Foundation, since they are listed under the date 1945.'

'Why did Fellows go to so much trouble to conceal the list with a cipher code, particularly when he hid it with his memoires?' I added.

'That's a question I hope Simons can answer,' she replied.

The car came off the Interstate 10 and moved slowly through the town of Tucson. Like so many American towns, the streets were built on a grid system, numbered and given familiar names, like Broadway, Speedway and Grant. We passed the large University of Arizona, sprawled out over many blocks, leaving behind streets of single-storey houses with well-kept gardens and then headed north to the Tanque Verde area at the base of the foothills.

It was early afternoon and the sun was moving away from its zenith. The temperature must have been in the ninety degree plus range. The streets were deserted, except for a few cars like ours passing through the city. Sensible people were sheltering from the heat of the sun; it was siesta time, as the Mexicans called it. As we drove further north, the Catalina Mountains loomed up in front of us. The desert city of Tucson is surrounded by mountain ranges, the land in-between being flat except the area close to the foothills.

I asked Alicia why Simons had been taken to a safe house.

She replied, 'We believe the person who has been sent to kill you may have also been tasked to kill Simons. If she does come it will give us an opportunity to catch her so a false trail has been laid. It is assumed that whoever is giving the orders knew where Simons lived. If we have a security leak at Langley, then she will also know that we moved him. Just before we left Washington, I ordered him to be moved again to another house. Only Gary and I, and the two local FBI agents know that new address. I know all the people at Langley who knew about the first move. If she turns up at the first address, I will know the source of the leak. If we are lucky the leak at Langley will be identified.' I began to see why Alicia was Head of the Intelligence Unit.

She added, 'I've just received a reply to the text message I sent on my phone a few minutes ago, confirming that everything is going to plan. All the addresses, including Simons' ranch, are being watched by FBI agents.'

The day before, Olga Petrovitch, alias Anna Kolzack, boarded the Amtrak train at Union Station in Washington. Her disguise would detract the onlookers at Langley whom she knew would be scanning the CCTV cameras dotted about the station. She had only survived through the decades in her business by becoming a master of disguise. They were looking for a younger fair-haired Anna, not a plump dark-haired old lady with a walking stick who had just asked a porter to help with her luggage. Wearing dull grey clothes made her blend in with the other passengers. Cameras always focus on colourful images. She had successfully evaded the watchers at the airport by changing in the ladies restrooms. They had seen someone else getting into a taxi, but they lost it anyway. She then took the train from the airport to a downtown hotel for the night. Going to Tucson by train was less likely to attract attention as she knew all the airports would be watched. She had been told a car was parked at the station car park for her use. The key would be fastened with a magnet under the rear wheel arch.

Olga was pleased that her English assignments had been successful. She was hardened to killing, but had not enjoyed murdering the young Cambridge graduate whose only crime was having an uncle who confided in her. Maybe she was becoming soft but her mind was troubled, eliminating traitors, informers and the enemy was all in a day's work but killing innocent people seemed to serve little purpose. She knew her employer wanted to eliminate Stanley Rheiner before he could talk to the FBI. The fear was the FBI already knew about Rheiner and wanted to talk to him. She had not secured the memoires and coded names list while in England so had failed in one part of her mission. Her employers were now looking for complete success from the next assignment. She could not fail again. If she did, she knew the consequences. Failure or being captured was not an option. She knew the location of Rheiner's ranch in the foothills above Tucson and that he was about to be moved to a safe house by the FBI. The encrypted information was sent to her cell phone before she left Washington. It was a race against time to kill Rheiner before the agents could interview the man. She could not understand why he had to die now. But then Olga was not part of the millennium conspiracy. She was just a contract killer and had no knowledge of why she was killing her assignments.

At Phoenix station, Olga collected the car as arranged and drove to Tucson. She checked the boot to make sure it contained the equipment she had requested. On the outskirts of the town she booked into a cheap motel under another name, paying in advance with cash. Afterwards, she drove to the Catalina foothills to find out if the FBI were guarding the ranch house where she had been told Rheiner was staying. Using a local map she took a road that climbed above the ranch and found a suitable observation point. It was late in the afternoon and few cars were on the road but to avoid looking conspicuous she parked in a gully between some tall rocks from where she had a direct view of the ranch below. Looking through binoculars, she spotted an FBI agent sitting in a car about one hundred yards away. They always used black 4x4 vans and wore dark glasses. She had to know if Rheiner was with a guard in the house. It was now clear the FBI knew he was being targeted. She returned to her car and drove back to the motel to wait for nightfall. A plan to deal with the guards was already formulating in her mind. Olga did not know at that very moment David Simons was being interviewed at another location and revealing all he knew to the agents.

We arrived at a large secluded hacienda-style ranch house tucked away between some rocks and a field of Saguaro cacti. Two FBI men, who had been alerted to our arrival, jumped out of their car and came towards us. Alicia and Gary got out, shook their hands and introduced me. We all walked to the house. The door was opened by another well-dressed agent. Passes were shown and we were taken to a traditionally South Western style furnished room at the rear of the house.

Sitting on a comfortable settee was a small grey-haired man. He was physically quite different to what I expected from the description in Fellows' memoires. He didn't look very surprised to see us. I expected him to be angry at being confined but his calm nature obscured any display of such an emotion.

Before Alicia could say anything, I advanced towards Simons, shook his hand, introduced myself and briefly explained my reasons for being at the meeting. Looking puzzled, he turned his attention to Alicia and Gary. I knew that Alicia wanted to ask the questions but her rather aggressive nature tended to put people on their guard. Surprisingly, she apologised to Simons for placing him under confinement outside of his own ranch but emphasised it was being done for his own protection as they believed an assassin was on her way to murder him. Still saying nothing, he looked at Gary who had been busy giving orders to the FBI agents, presumably to ensure our safety.

David Simons invited us to sit down. He had a polite and quiet manner. He thanked the FBI for their protection saying that since Henry Fellows' death he was expecting to be the next victim. Alicia told Simons about the terrorist bomb threats being made to the American and British Governments. Intelligence gathered suggested that atomic bombs might be used. The mention of atomic bombs made Simons wince.

Alicia asked him about The Brotherhood Foundation, its membership and associations, and its relationship with The New Order. He gave her a surprised look, saying, 'I assume you have seen Henry Fellows' memoires and will already know about The Brotherhood Foundation and the reason for forming it back in 1939.'

Alicia replied promptly. 'Yes, and we have an encrypted names list that was sent to Paul by Fellows' niece before she was murdered. We believe it contains, in code, the names of leading members of The New Order.'

Simons looked a little unsettled at the last statement. He regained his posture and addressing all of us, said, 'I think before answering any questions, I need to give you a brief history of The Brotherhood Foundation and what happened to it. You can then draw your own conclusions about any connections with the current crisis.

In 1959, when Henry and I lost our jobs and had to dissolve the Foundation, members more interested in acquiring wealth and political power joined The New Order. Some were black-mailed into giving their support. A few remained true to the Foundation's cause and passed information to us. After the incident at Halborn we found out that our trusted colleague, Paul Fields, had betrayed us. He had been working for The New Order for some time and was a member of their so-called Cabal. It was he who had been responsible for the deaths of the people at Halborn and the eventual demise of the Foundation when our names were revealed. Later Henry dealt him the justice he deserved. After his death, we believed, but were not sure, that his place on the Cabal was taken by his stepdaughter, Diane Hunter. Being an astute businesswoman, she took over all her stepfather's business interests. She was also a right-wing radical and became the leader of a political party in Britain.'

I interrupted and asked, 'Does MI5 know about Hunter's possible membership of the Cabal?'

'I am certain they do. She has been investigated many times. But we believed she was being protected by someone high up in British Society to have avoided being charged or prosecuted,' he replied.

Alicia said, 'I will ask Mark to check her out with MI5.'

Simons continued, 'The seven members of the Cabal control the New Order. Using our contact, Henry and I thought our best protection was to let the Cabal know we had their names. We sent a message to them through our contact who told them that if anything happened to either of us, their names and evidence of their crimes would be sent to MI5 and the FBI. It was a hollow threat but it worked for some time. It was the only way we could survive. For some time, Henry had been writing his memoires which gave an account of our lives and work since the formation of the Foundation. I know he included a lot of incriminating material in them. We did not physically meet after 1959 but kept in touch through a secret post box. It was crude but the secret code we used for the telephone conversations over many years had become compromised so it was our only option. Much later, when digital portable phones became available, we tried to set up another confidential link. But we knew any calls would be monitored by the security services so we were forced back to the post box. My last postal contact with Henry was a few months before he was murdered. Someone, and I don't know who, sent him a list of the names of the Cabal members and information about an event they were planning. He told me he was going to code the list and place it in the text of his memoires. These would be put in a safe deposit box in his bank and he would send a copy of the list to me. Unfortunately, he didn't send me that list or the code. He probably believed it would be too dangerous for me to have that knowledge or was murdered before he could do it.'

I asked, 'Do you have any idea who gave that information to Fellows and who was your contact?'

'No, I don't. I think Henry had a code name but I don't know it. The contact ceased to supply information shortly before Henry died. I guess he or she was discovered.'

For the first time Simons showed emotion and had to pause to compose himself before continuing. 'A young friend of mine, named Colin Niedemeyer, worked for a German company, who I think were owned or contracted by The New Order's Cabal, as their expert on encryption technology. Colin was my PhD student back in 1989. I told him about The Brotherhood Foundation and how The New Order had evolved from it. He was a brilliant young man but was lured away from a good job at IBM in California to work for the German company. They make communications equipment, including satellite dishes. They actually run a global network which is financed by a private consortium, which was probably set up by The New Order or one of its companies.

Colin was sent on a mission by Freiburg to Rambouillet in France and was murdered on his return home. The car he was driving was found in a river with his body inside. The local coroner declared it to be an accident so there was no police investigation. I'm sure it was a cover-up and the police were compromised.

After Colin's death, his fiancée sent me his notes, some encryption chips and the codes he had designed for Freiburg. Apparently they were made especially for a contractor who he was not permitted to know or meet. The chips were given to a man at the 'Château de Rambouillet,' where a high level conference was taking place. They were to be fitted to telephones and satellite communications system to allow encrypted calls to be made by the delegates attending the conference. I believe the conference was convened by The New Order for its Cabal members. Colin overheard a conversation at Freiburg about a Big Event being planned. The Cabal could have met at Rambouillet to discuss their strategy for it.'

'Do you still have the chips and codes?' Alicia asked.

'Yes. I will give them to you since they might help the FBI monitor telephone calls and give access to the Cabal's communication network. Your people will know how to use them.' He handed Alicia a padded envelope that was lying on a nearside table.

Alicia said, 'These will help us decode their telephone calls.'

Simons looked cautiously at Gary and Alicia.

'Before our contact disappeared we were told the Cabal had an informant working in the CIA at Langley under the codename *Catseyes*.'

Alicia replied, 'We are aware the security services have been infiltrated and investigations are underway to find the moles. It's the reason why the President set up a special Task Force.'

Simons said, 'You see why I did not reveal what I knew to the FBI or the CIA.'

Alicia asked Simons about the missing bomb at Los Alamos.

'Was there really a fourth bomb and was it stolen and by whom?'

'Yes, by three people, two were members of The New Order and were part of Oppenheimer's wider team, and an unknown outsider,' he said.

'Do you know what happened to the bomb?' I asked.

'No, but an extensive investigation took place after our two members were killed in road accidents. The other person was never identified or caught. The Government and the Los Alamos directors were embarrassed by the theft. At the time, it was denied that a fourth bomb had been made. Records were never found and so there was nothing to investigate. Somebody may still be alive who knows the truth of what happened. Enough plutonium was produced and processed for a bomb which I know had been assembled. The history of the events of those times is well documented but no reference to a stolen bomb was ever made. Just after the war ended, the Russians were desperate to get their hands on a bomb and used spies to get information. Many, but not all, were caught and tried. Two, Julius and Ethel Rosenberg were convicted and executed. At the time the Russians would have done anything to get their hands on a real bomb so it was assumed they were responsible for the theft. I personally think that whoever stole it, did so purely as an investment. Years later the value of that investment rose steeply'.

Alicia asked, 'Would the stolen bomb still work?'

'In the last fifty years huge developments in nuclear bomb manufacture have taken place. The Los Alamos bomb was a crude weapon by modern standards but, yes, it would still work but people with expert knowledge would be required to make it possible. The principles are the same even if the detonation techniques have changed. Plutonium, the most toxic material known, does not deteriorate much in fifty years. The nuclear core would still be viable. The explosive charges required would be different to what we used for the Trinity bomb, but today anybody could acquire the appropriate materials required. Detonators can be remotely initiated by radio signals from almost anywhere, unless those wanting to explode a bomb want to light the touch-paper and vaporise themselves.'

Alicia had been listening intently and said, 'Today we are faced with Islamic extremists who have armies of trained suicide bombers. They would find doing what you suggested as a quick path to their heaven so there would be no shortage of volunteers for such a task, particularly as they could kill tens of thousands, even millions of unbelievers with one bomb.'

Simons, looking thoughtful, said, ' I recall a year ago a report was logged by the local police in New Mexico about a Mexican quarry worker who told the police that he saw men out in the desert near Silver City moving a heavy object onto a lorry. The next day deep car tracks were found close to an old copper mine, but nothing further came of it. The local police believed it was a gang of thieves moving stolen goods, quite common in those parts. It could be worth visiting the mine to see if any traces of the bomb are present as it would have been a possible hiding place. But it's just a guess without any real evidence to back it up. The police would not have bothered to search the mine at the time as they had no knowledge of a stolen atom bomb.'

Alicia looked at Gary and said, 'Find out from the New Mexico Police the exact location of the mine and get them to send over a copy of their report of the incident. Also we need to speak to the Mexican so get his address.'

'Let's get a team over there and see what we can find,' she said excitedly.

'Will do,' said Gary, dialling a number on his phone.

With a smile on his face, Simons said, 'You certainly don't waste any time.'

'It's the one thing we don't have,' she said.

Simons' expression changed and he said, 'When can I expect my visitor?'

Alicia reassured Simons that everything was being done to protect him. 'Until we catch the person you will need to remain in this house.' He looked at her and said, 'I would like to help you track down the terrorists. If they do have the Los Alamos bomb then we have a very serious problem. I was a physicist on The Manhattan Project and helped to build the bomb so have some responsibility for what happened at Los Alamos.'

Gary looked at us and said, 'Professor Rheiner should come with us to the mine in Silver City and assist the team.'

Alicia agreed. Simons said jokingly, 'It's better than waiting here to be murdered.'

Ten minutes later, Gary's phone rang. He was told that an FBI search team was on its way by helicopter to the mine. They had a map reference to its location.

Gary said, 'A helicopter will pick us up at Tucson airport and take us to the site.'

Later we arrived at a small airport called Whiskey Creek in Silver City where a Ford 4x4 was waiting for us. The car drove for miles into the wooded mountains above the Chino open caste copper mine. It left the road and travelled over rough country for about five miles to the edge of the Gila Forest. The forest covered a large area and was less than 100 miles from the old Trinity site and 200 miles from Los Alamos. Up ahead, I saw two military type Apache helicopters with a number of army personnel and armed FBI agents swarming over the area near the mine. I couldn't help thinking how appropriate it was to have such machines in a place once inhabited by the Apache Indians. Gary had told the military personnel there might be stolen explosives and possible nuclear material hidden in the mine and wanted appropriate equipment and trained personnel sent immediately to the area. We were met by the leader of the detachment, a young army Captain who looked like he had just come out of West Point and an FBI agent. I wasn't sure what brief he had but this was a real show of strength.

David Simons, Alicia, and I left the vehicle and walked towards the entrance where a barrier had been set up. Three army men and two white-coated guys with what looked like Geiger counters were about to go into the mine when David called them back. He introduced himself as Professor Rheiner, a nuclear physicist. The two scientists immediately shook hands with him and smiled showing relief that one of their kind had arrived. I couldn't hear the conversation but Simons returned and said quietly to us so the others couldn't hear.

'This site should be treated as a crime scene and forensic analysis techniques used if we are to find any traces of a bomb having been stored in the mine. Soil and rock samples need to be taken for traces of plutonium and radioactivity. If the bomb had been stored here for many years they should be found using the sensitive analytical equipment now available.'

Alicia told the man leading the team to do what Professor Rheiner asked. The men in white coats started to collect samples in and around the mine entrance. Rheiner told us to stay outside. He then put on protective clothing from a box brought by the team. He took a torch and went inside the mine with the others following. The evening was fast approaching and the temperature dropping fast on the mountain.

Gary spoke to Alicia and then made a phone call to the agents guarding Simons' first safe house. They reported so far nobody had been seen. It was now dark so he told them to execute the agreed plan.

Olga Petrovitch checked the pistol and placed it in the box with the other items in her rucksack. It was fitted with a silencer and specially designed to only fire small poison-tipped darts, shaped like bullets. Poison was her kill weapon. She disliked conventional guns and bullets. Her masters had done a good job of leaving all she had requested in the car at the station.

She dialled the code into her cell phone to see if any new instructions had been issued. None had, so she would proceed with her instructions to kill Stanley Rheiner. Darkness descended quickly as the sun set behind the mountains. Petrovitch drove to the foothills and parked at the spot above the house she had selected earlier in the day. She took out a pair of small powerful binoculars from the rucksack. They were fitted with night-vision sensors so everything came up green. Stealthily she crept down the mountain to the rear of the house and concealed herself behind a bush to get a better view of the living room.

An uncanny silence filled the air that was beginning to cool as convection currents took it up the mountain. She noticed the black Ford belonging to the FBI agents was no longer in front of the house. The window shutters were partially open so she could see Rheiner sitting in an armchair reading a book under a dim table light in the living room. Nobody else could be seen but the assassin thought if the FBI agents were still guarding Rheiner, then they would be somewhere in the house. She had seen two men in the afternoon. The fact that Rheiner had been moved from his own ranch and had FBI guards meant they would be expecting her. Because they didn't know when, she had the advantage of surprise. First, she had to find out if the men were still in the vicinity. Their absence would simplify things and her diversion Plan B wouldn't be required. She checked the garage; it was empty. Further searching didn't reveal any sign of the FBI agents. Perhaps they had gone away thinking Rheiner was safe.

Now it was time to act. Petrovitch decided to go into the house through a rear door. The key-lock didn't present a problem. Once inside, she made her way toward the living room. The room was dark except for a small reading light being used by Rheiner. The silence still bugged her – even Rheiner's breathing could be heard. She edged her way through the partially open door of the room and crouched down behind a large settee from which she could get a full frontal shot at her target. Her adrenaline was now up. It was the body's way of preparing the hunter for battle. With her finger on the trigger and both hands clasped around the barrel she stood up to face her quarry. Suddenly, a blinding flash of light and a deafening bang, preceded a searing pain in her chest. It was immediately followed by a second and a third bang, by which time her vision had narrowed to seeing down a long tunnel of light, then darkness. She lost all sense of the world around her and slumped to the floor. Olga Petrovitch was dead.

The agent rose from the chair and made a call. His partner checked the body for signs of life and removed the rucksack from it.

Gary answered. 'Plan executed successfully, the Russian is dead. We have possession of her phone and other equipment. What are your instructions?'

'You were told to take her alive,' Gary said.

'I had no choice, she aimed her gun straight at me with the intention of firing it, thinking I was Rheiner. I only just got my shot in first,' said the agent.

'Transport the body and everything she had with her back to Washington. Operation here is still in progress,' Gary replied with a broad smile on his face.

'Well we have eliminated the Russian assassin so for the time being, Paul and David, you are safe.'

Alicia said, 'Didn't we give instructions to arrest her not shoot her? She would have been a valuable lead to the terrorists.'

Simons, the two scientists and three of the soldiers had been given handsets to communicate back to their team leader. It was a little worrying to see his men still carrying loaded weapons as though they were expecting the enemy to come out of the mine. Gary also noticing this, asked the Captain to order his men to stand down. None of the team knew really why they were there. They were told that some explosives had been stolen from an army barracks and there could be a terrorist link. An atomic bomb was not mentioned but they must have wondered why two scientists carrying Geiger counters from Los Alamos were now being led by a nuclear physicist in the mine.

We waited anxiously for a report from Simons. He was not a young man and clambering in the dark through a disused mine with hidden dangers, put him and us at risk. Suddenly the intercom came alive.

'We've discovered an inner chamber which looks like it was once fitted up to be some kind of workshop and although attempts have been made to remove the evidence, it's clear this is where the bomb was stored. There are high readings of radioactivity in one part of the chamber. There seems to be a brick wall across the end of the chamber blocking it off from the rest of the mine. I am looking through a small hole in the wall and can see what looks like a skeleton. Please send in men with excavation equipment. We are coming out with some material.'

After twenty minutes the men came out. Simons was holding a polythene bag containing what looked like rusty nuts and bolts and some other metal parts. He said, 'These are the casement fittings we used at Los Alamos for the bomb. There is no doubt the stolen bomb was stored here. It may have been modified using today's technology, but it's the plutonium core that really matters. Everything else can be replaced. What's in the bag needs to be analysed. It may give us some clues to what has been replaced or changed.'

Thirty minutes later, the skeletal remains of a man were brought out. Simons believed it could be one of the men who stole the bomb from Los Alamos in1945. Alicia ordered the body and all the other materials to be flown immediately to Washington to the FBI's forensic laboratory.

She thanked everybody and said, 'I think we're done here. Let's return to Tucson. The big question now is – have the terrorists got the bomb?'

Alicia walked away from us and made a telephone call using the coded call sign 'Falcon' and adding more numbers that took the call straight to the Vice President's Office. The Vice President picked up the call.

'Sir,' she said, 'We believe we found the location of the atom bomb that was stolen in 1945. It was stored in an old copper mine in New Mexico but five years ago was removed by the people who may be involved in the bomb threat. A lot of material has been found in the mine and has been taken away for analysis. The Russian sent to assassinate Professor Rheiner, has been killed by FBI agents. The Professor, whose real name is David Simons, the Founder of the Brotherhood Foundation, is safely with us. I know the identity of the CIA informant. We want to keep him under surveillance in the hope he will lead us to the terrorists and their supporters. The professor has given us what he thinks could be the satellite telephone encryption codes used by The New Order. I am taking them to Langley to install in one our satellite systems so we can decode their telephone conversations. This is a significant step forward. I want permission to bring David Simons to Washington to help us with the investigations.'

He replied, 'Excellent work, Agent Garcia. I will re-convene the Task Force as soon as you get back so you can give us a full report after the material has been analysed. Keep me briefed. We also plan to set up a video meeting with the Brits to coordinate their activities with our own. Good luck and well done.'

Gary called the New Mexico Police to enquire about the Mexican worker who had seen the lorry being loaded at the mine and their report on the incident. He was told the worker had been killed shortly after the incident in a mining accident and the report could not be found.

Alicia was furious when Gary told her about the lost report. Clearly another crime had been committed. Somebody in the police was working for The Order. She told Gary to instigate a full FBI enquiry. The bomb had been removed about five years ago so those responsible would have had plenty of time to rebuild it and find a new hiding place.

Alicia asked Simons if he was prepared to help the team further with the investigations and go to a safe house in Washington. He agreed. We all flew back to Tucson in one of the modified Apache helicopters. Simons was driven back to his house to collect some belongings and then returned to the airport to join us on a specially chartered aircraft to Washington. It was very late when we arrived at Dulles. Cars were provided to take us to our respective homes. Simons went with Gary to an unknown location. We had made some significant discoveries but they raised the threat level. For the first time in its history, it looked like America, and possibly Britain, faced the ultimate horror of an atomic bomb attack.

Leon Seperkov's phone rang in Moscow. The voice said, 'The R2 package arrived but was not delivered to the customer successfully who has now left the house. We believe it's lost and not recoverable. Should we send another package to a different address?' Seperkov told the caller to await further orders.

CHAPTER 11

Martha's Vineyard, Massachusetts
13 December 1999

It was late at night when I arrived back in my flat in Georgetown after two gruelling days in Tucson. I called Valerie to let her know that I had arrived back safely.

With a sound of relief in her voice she said, 'I'm glad you're back, I was very worried about you. What happened in Tucson?'

'I will tell you later. Is everything OK? Did you get any more calls from the blackmailer?' I asked.

'Yes I'm fine and no more calls, your suggestion seems to have worked,' she replied.

'What plans have you made for us to go to your house in Martha's Vineyard?' I asked.

'It's all arranged for us to go tomorrow morning. A taxi will pick me up at ten o'clock from my apartment and take me to the club airport. My plane is in the hangar. You could do the same and meet me in the hangar. No one will see us there.'

I reminded her that Alicia probably knew who she was anyway.

'That doesn't matter. I am not worried about her. We must not talk now on the phone. I will see you at the airport tomorrow,' she said and rang off.

I had difficulty sleeping. My mind was still full of the events of the last few days in Arizona and New Mexico. Added to which I was about to go away with a woman who was escaping from a relationship with a powerful politician who could be ruthless enough to come after her and me. I tried to formulate a plan to deal with such a situation but couldn't. The atom bomb threats to New

York and London were much more troubling, not just for America and Britain, but for the world. In the days of the Cold War, the enemy was identifiable and nations could take steps to protect themselves. International terrorist groups were stateless moving targets and very difficult to identify with any particular country. The problem that would face our Governments if attacked by atomic bombs, would be who to blame and retaliate against. It put emphasis on possessing good, reliable intelligence. With Iraq being the current pariah it would be too easy to blame them, but the events unfolding were beginning to show they may not be involved in the current bomb threats.

I eventually fell asleep but had some unpleasant dreams. Nobody is sure what constitutes dreams. They can be unconscious virtual representations of our darkest fears, deepest secrets, and most passionate fantasies. I certainly had my share of these during the last few weeks. It seems as though in my mind, the bad things were overtaking the good ones. Perhaps my brain was preparing its defences.

After eating a large breakfast from the store of food in the refrigerator, I called Robert and told him about the events in Tucson. He was relieved the assassin had been shot but reminded me we still had the same enemy and the reasons for killing us were still valid. I also told him David Simons was joining the team since he had vital knowledge about the bomb and the possible terrorists. I suggested he spoke to Alicia to arrange a meeting with him.

He was not surprised when I told him Valerie and I were going away to her house in Martha's Vineyard for a few days since she had decided to give up the apartment in Georgetown to escape from Sherman. He warned me the man was ruthless and would likely try and find us.

My next call to Alicia was going to be difficult. I had already prepared what I was going to say. Using the secure number, I called her. Alicia answered immediately.

'I need to tell you I am leaving the safe house for a few days and taking a vacation with a friend. Our successful mission to

Tucson provided a lot of evidence to analyse. You now have Robert and David Simons to help you.'

She reacted as I expected.

'You shouldn't be away at this critical time. We have a national emergency. You know I can stop you, but I guess you would find a way out anyway. I must be able to contact you at all times so keep your phone active. In the interests of national security you must not divulge what you know to anyone. Be careful. You are still on the enemy's hit list.'

There was a pause.

'Where and when are you going?' she asked.

'We are leaving this morning.' I said, omitting where.

I was not going to say any more so shut the phone down expecting her to ring me back. She didn't, so she understood my message.

I packed some clothes in a small bag including my laptop, the special cell phone, Fellows' memoires and my Beretta pistol. The taxi driver knew the address of the private airport on the outskirts of Washington. It took twenty minutes to arrive at the airfield which was located in a secluded clearing in a wooded valley. It had a very short runway. Looking at the numerous light aircraft parked around the hangar, it was obvious the rich of Washington used it for a quick getaway to avoid the larger commercial airports. A number of aero-clubs had their logos spread around but there was only one hangar. The control tower was only just visible on the opposite side of the airfield.

I knew the taxi driver would expect a large tip. His usual clients expected to buy his discretion. I realised they now included me since nobody else, except him and Valerie, knew I was here. He dropped me outside the hangar and waited why I fumbled in my wallet. I gave him a hundred dollar bill for the fifty dollar ride and picked up my case. He frowned, didn't say anything and drove hastily away. Had I underestimated the cost of discretion? The airfield was deserted, so unless I was being watched through binoculars by some distant FBI observer, my arrival and presence would go unseen. I went through a side door of the hangar expecting to find people and aeroplanes but it was empty except for a small plane with its occupant. Seeing me, she stepped down from the aircraft and ran over. Valerie was dressed in slacks and a lightweight red anorak covering a tightly-fitted white jumper. Her hair was tied back up in a pony tail. She greeted me with a hug and a kiss and said, 'I'm glad you made it. I was getting worried when you didn't call from Tucson.'

'Sorry, but Alicia banned all telephone calls. I will tell you about the trip later. Where is everybody?' I asked.

'I made sure nobody would be here to see us so I filed my flight plan with the control tower yesterday. We are expected to leave very soon.'

'Who helps you with the aircraft?' I asked.

'I had it checked before I arrived and the maintenance engineer left me his check list. This airport is used by people who don't want to be recognised or seen. That's why they pay a lot of money to the owners. I can handle the plane. Get your luggage aboard and we can go,' she said, in an authoritative manner.

I now knew why my tip to the taxi driver fell short of his expectations. Valerie had already prepared the small Cessna 172 Skyhawk for take-off. There was little space for luggage in the small cabin. After making the necessary flight checks and a brief conversation with the control tower, the single engine plane with its two joyful occupants, roared along the runway and soared into the bright blue sky, levelling out at about ten thousand feet. Some contrast to Concorde I thought, gazing at my pilot. I had never knowingly flown in a plane piloted by a woman. It was a new experience for me. Now we were airborne I switched on my RT button to talk to her.

'How long have you been flying?' I asked.

'I acquired my licence three years ago so haven't flown many miles. Mainly trips to Martha's Vineyard and the local area. We should be there in less than three hours if the weather is kind. The forecast is good and we have a tail wind so should land with plenty of fuel left above the reserve. I have had an extra tank fitted anyway so the plane can fly beyond the Island. I flew to Cape Cod to visit a friend two years back without any problems.'

I was surprised how far Martha's Vineyard was from Washington. Actual distances across the American continent are always longer than they seem from the maps. It was difficult to talk much during the flight so I switched on the laptop to again read Fellows memoires and notes. After what David Simons had told us I might have missed something. I puzzled over the coded names list and wondered why it had been sent to him.

My life had certainly taken some leaps in the last few weeks. Here I was in an aircraft piloted by the most beautiful woman I had ever met, to be taken, almost kidnapped, to her secret house for a purpose that was yet to be revealed. It had happened so quickly. Was I being used for some nefarious purpose? Without doubt I was being blinded by love and fleeing from a supposed killer. They had failed to kill David Simons so perhaps I would be spared. It could end up like a Greek tragedy where pleasant dreams turn into nightmares.

We flew low over the coast for part of the flight then out into the Atlantic towards the famous Chappaquiddick Island which is linked to the island of Martha's Vineyard by a narrow strip of land on the south side. Chappaquiddick was where Senator Ted Kennedy drove his car off a bridge in 1969 resulting in the death of his passenger, Mary Jo Kopechne. He was cleared of responsibility for her death but lied about the incident in court, which destroyed his chances of ever becoming President. He was prosecuted for a misdemeanour charge of leaving the scene of an accident.

Martha's Vineyard is a popular retreat for the rich and famous of New England. It's an island located six miles off the coast of Cape Cod in Massachusetts. Many wealthy people, including senior politicians and Presidents, often retreat to the island for their short summer breaks. Lesser mortals like writers and artists go over from the mainland using the ferry at Woods Hole. It's a place that became well-known in the Kennedy era. The family went on holiday there frequently.

As the plane veered north-east towards Vineyard Haven and the West Chop lighthouse, the ferry terminal to the mainland became visible. Below, foam-crested waves rolling over a clear grey-blue sea broke onto a long stretch of sandy beach fringed with sand dunes and the occasional white clapboard beach house. A straight narrow road running parallel to the beach seemed to fade away as if dissolved by the sand dunes. I spotted a flight of sea birds in perfect formation below us, quite oblivious to the sound of our single-engine plane overflying them. Our technology has yet to match the dexterity of these natural flying machines. I could see many small power boats moored in the Vineyard Haven harbour but no luxury yachts. They had been sailed away to warmer places. It was now December so all the holiday-makers had gone.

Valerie had been concentrating on flying the plane so we didn't talk much during the flight. She did smile at me a few times as we banked to make a turn towards the runway. We had a slightly bumpy landing at the tiny airport. Later she admitted that landing was something she always dreaded. Her flying hours and, therefore, take-offs and landings were somewhat limited. We came to a halt on a grassy verge only yards from a small building which I guess served as the control tower. The journey had taken longer than anticipated and the fuel gauge was showing close to empty. It was only then, when the engine was switched off, I appreciated the pleasure of silence. After making the aircraft safe and secure, Valerie told me to take the luggage to the edge of the field while she completed some paperwork at the office and hired a car. I noticed a large number of similar aircraft parked on the edge of the landing strip.

A few minutes later she drove up in a grey 155 hp, four-litre, Ford Explorer SUV. I loaded our two suitcases and we sped off along the coast road. I expected her to have a sleek more stylish convertible. Anticipating my thoughts she said,

'I like this vehicle because, as you will see, we need to travel off the road over some rough ground to reach my beach house. There is no paved road to it. It's not too bad in the summer but in winter an ordinary car would get stuck in mud and sand whereas this four-wheel drive vehicle has never given me any trouble. I hire it from the aero-club every time I come to the island.'

After driving for about thirty minutes along a tarmac road, she pulled off onto a dirt track which eventually narrowed to be a sandy path, edged with green turf. In a slightly raised position overlooking the sea was the beach house. Valerie stopped beside it, looked at me with her enticing smile and beckoned me to see her beach hideaway. The house was of a white clapboard design and a tiled roof, no bricks were visible. She undid two locks, took my hand and almost pulled me through the door. A small hall opened up into a large but cosy room lit by light streaming through a large bay window which looked out onto the sea. It was so different to the apartment in Washington. Between the house and the sea was a grassy bank, beyond which small white sand dunes with tufted-grass tops acted as wind breaks and barriers to any waves crashing in from the sea. I was mesmerised by the view. In the room was a wide stone fireplace used for burning wood. Comfortable armchairs and a long sofa were placed around it as if expecting their occupants to share the warmth of an evening fire. The house reminded me of a holiday cottage I once stayed in as a boy in Cornwall. It had a warm, cosy feeling, perhaps more appreciated on a cold winter's night with the howling wind coming in from the sea.

Valerie was busy taking our cases, including a hamper from the car. She came over and interrupted my seaward gaze.

'Do you have any neighbours or friends nearby,' I asked.

'Yes, you can see why I like this place, it's quiet and private. My nearest neighbour and friend, Carol Johnson, lives about a mile along the coast but usually only comes to the island in the summer. The coastguard keeps an eye on us and patrols the coast line every week. This is the quiet side of the island and rarely gets any visitors. Daddy bought it from a writer, a novelist I think, he came here to write. He needed the solitude and beauty of the place. It's what I do when I come here.'

'Have you written any books?' I asked.

'I am trying to write one,' she replied.

Before I could say anything else, she changed the subject and invited me to see the bedroom. At the door of the room she turned, put her arms around me, and in a soft voice, said, 'I'm sorry I was a little sharp with you on the phone. I am not worried about the FBI or the CIA knowing about us, they probably do anyway, but if others knew, it would place us both in danger. Nobody knows about this house. My father never disclosed its existence to anybody so we should be safe here.'

I felt an overpowering urge to make love to her. I knew she felt the same. We both felt the tension lovers have after being parted even for a few days. Within a few minutes, and before we had time to remove all our clothes, except for the necessary articles, we were locked into each other on the bed. Suddenly all the tension drained away. It was quick, but fantastic. We lay in each other's arms for a while. Her long blonde hair hung down over her shoulders. She was at home, relaxed and happy and looking at me whispered, 'I feel so safe with you.'

I sensed an anxiety in her voice. It was time to find out what was worrying her. Taking her in my arms, I said, 'Please tell me what's worrying you.'

She looked away. A moment of silence ensued. I knew she wanted to say something but the words wouldn't come out. The time was not right to say it. I was pushing her too soon. I held her hand and said, 'OK love, let's have dinner.'

She said, 'Yes, but we have at least three days before I have to return to Washington so let's not talk about bomb threats, terrorists, politics, or anything else but you and me.'

'I agree, but you have to know what happened in Tucson on our visit to David Simons because the threat level has now been raised. Like it or not, we are both involved in this, since I'm probably still on the enemy's hit list.'

I showed her the Beretta pistol and the alarm button that Gary gave me for protection after the car incident in Washington that I had to use if threatened.

I told her about the events we experienced in Tucson and warned her I could be called back to Washington at any time. She looked at me in dismay and asked, 'Do you know how to use the gun?'

'Yes, I had some training some years ago, but not with a Beretta. But Alicia showed me how to use it. I only have one magazine of bullets so cannot do much target practice.'

She gave me that curious look that women give when there is a spark of jealousy.

'Alicia seems to have looked after you.' she said with a wry smile.

I smiled back saying, 'You know she is married to the job.'

Her face relaxed and Valerie said, 'What do they expect you to do?'

'I'm not sure but I'm one of their team. The FBI has a lot of evidence to check. They must find the location of the bomb and track down the terrorist suspects before the eve of the millennium. My guess is they will be checking out their extensive list of suspects. One member of Al-Qaeda was caught crossing over from the Mexican border with a bomb component. No doubt he is being vigorously interrogated. The British MI5 and police will also be carrying out a search of suspects in Britain. There is a code red alert, although the general public have yet to be told. It won't be long before the press get hold of something. There is certain to be a leak since too many people know about it. We don't want the terrorists to know too much about our intelligence so it's imperative we identify and catch the informers in the FBI and CIA. Alicia has already identified one at Langley who is currently under surveillance. He was giving information to the assassin sent to kill David Simons. I suppose much of the original intelligence originated from my trip to Kuwait and from Fellows' papers. That's why I am in this whether I like it or not.'

My explanation didn't reassure her.

'Paul, why can't we both disappear? Go back to England together and get away from all this,' she said.

'That wouldn't be so easy. We would be tracked trying to leave the country and raise suspicions that we were part of the conspiracy. Sorry my love – we're trapped. Once the FBI has you, there is no way out until they let you go.'

'But I have to be sure Alan Sherman doesn't find me.' she said.

'You told me nobody knows about this house,' I replied.

She looked worried.

'You don't know him. He has agents everywhere and if determined, he will find me. He has an army of people who do his bidding and I wouldn't be surprised if that included some criminal elements. I know he once arranged for a Mafia gang leader to be released early from prison so that man owes him a debt.'

'Why would he do that and risk his career?' I asked.

'I don't know,' she replied.

'Why would he want to find you now he knows you don't want to be with him anymore?' I asked.

She didn't reply so I changed the subject.

'I'm getting hungry, let's prepare some food,'

Valerie took some steaks and other foodstuffs from a hamper and placed them in a refrigerator. Looking at me with her large sparkling eyes, she said, 'Before we have dinner and it gets too dark, let's go for a walk along the beach.'

She took my hand, pushed open the sliding door of the room and led me out onto a beach-facing patio. A light refreshing sea breeze caught our faces as we ran out onto a strip of grass. Large sand dunes, heaped-up like ant hills, separated the beach from the land. We climbed up onto one and saw a grey-blue ocean ahead of us with its foam-crested rollers gently crashing onto the shore. I could taste the salty air. Bare white sand stretched for miles along the shoreline. This part of the island was only easily accessible by foot so visitors did not spoil its serenity. Valerie had certainly chosen an ideal place to be alone with nature and for now with me. She was in her element, dragging me over the dunes until, exhausted, we both fell over. She rolled over on top of me. We kissed and kissed until we became breathless. She snuggled up into my arms. It was uncannily quiet except for the sound of the breaking waves and the occasional seagull squawking overhead. I was looking up to a clear blue-orange sky, only broken by a few cirrus clouds, as the sun progressively set in the west. We just lay there enjoying the solitude, knowing that it would not last. Out beyond was a restless noisy world.

Valerie sat up on the soft sand and looked out to the ocean. Light from the setting sun lit up her hair, giving it an orange tint. I put my arms around her. It was a pity to spoil our moment of bliss but I had to know what was worrying her. I could feel her shaking, trying to say something but the words failed to emerge. She looked at me and said, 'I'm afraid that something terrible is going to happen to me.'

'Not as long as you're with me,' I said.

She started to talk, 'I was seven when my mother died. I felt lost. My father's diplomatic job took him to many countries so I saw very little of him. He was not part of my early life. I loved him but was never close to him. Fortunately, my mother's sister, Flo, and her husband looked after me. I became their surrogate daughter. Flo was close to my mother and could not have children of her own so she gave me all the love and affection any girl could expect. It helped, but I missed my mum for years. She would sometimes come to me in my dreams. In my dream we would meet on a sunny hillside and talk. She was my guardian angel. She was near when I needed her. Then one day she disappeared from my dreams. We no longer met on the hillside. I tried but could not reach her. It was like she had abandoned me. I was so unhappy and cried night after night trying to find her but she never came back.

Thanks to my aunt and uncle I had a normal childhood. My father visited when he could and provided all the money the family needed. I actually did not want for anything physical but I needed love. When I became a teenager I met a boy. He was my first boyfriend. Like all teenagers, we fell in love. I was vulnerable so it was easy to fall in love. After a while he became interested in other girls so we parted company before the relationship became physical. At first, I was broken-hearted, and then got over it. After, I decided to devote myself to study. Later, I had a number of other boyfriends, but nothing serious. It was then my mother came back in my dreams. I don't know why but I was feeling low after breaking up with a boyfriend one night. Again, I saw a vision of her on the hillside. She was smiling and holding my hand. I woke up feeling on top of the world. My guardian angel was back with me.'

She was almost in tears and paused to compose herself before continuing. I held her hand tightly. 'One of the pitfalls of childhood is that one doesn't have to understand something to feel it. By the time the mind is able to comprehend what has happened and why, the wounds of the heart are already too deep to heal. I obtained a scholarship to go to London University to study for a degree in chemistry, mainly because there were more places available in that subject. I had also got distinctions in German and French in my A-levels, which I felt were wasted doing chemistry. I became interested in politics and participated in the university's debating society. As I told you in the restaurant in Georgetown, Mrs Thatcher came to give a talk to our university student society. I was so impressed with her speech that I made up my mind to change my course and study political science. I had made friends with a senior lecturer in the Department. He took a fancy to me so arranged the transfer. We did go out together for a while but he became boring so we stayed just good friends. After graduating I took the job in Conservative Central Office as a research assistant.

Whilst working there I met many influential people, including ministers, and attended conferences and meetings. It was all good training for my ambition to eventually become an MP. At that time there were a number of scandals involving MPs and their secretaries. It was an occupational hazard for members living in flats in London during the week while their wives lived in the constituencies. The higher up the political ladder, the easier it was for those who wanted to conceal their clandestine activities but the consequences of being discovered were devastating. You may remember the affair between John Major and Edwina Curry. He was the last person anyone would have thought could do such a thing. It made nonsense of all his political speeches about family values. After that was discovered, he lost his credibility.

I became disenchanted with British politics and decided to look for an alternative career. That's when my mum, my guardian angel, came back to me in a dream. She told me something good would happen. It did, my father was appointed to be the First Secretary at the British Embassy in Washington. Through his contacts I got a job at the Department of Foreign Affairs. You know the rest.

After you called last night, I packed my case and went to bed. I had another dream. My mother came and warned me of impending danger, saying I must escape before it was too late. I had already arranged our trip here before the dream so was confused about what she meant.'

She paused and, sobbing, she got up and ran down the beach. I followed, grabbed her hand. The beach was still deserted and apart from the crashing of the waves, I could only hear the occasional sound of distant seagulls. It seemed this place was meant for us. It belonged to us. We walked hand in hand without saying anything but I knew she had more to say. I could almost read her mind. It's said that lovers become of one mind when they are close. I could feel her heartbeat, her anguish, as we strolled along the beach. Then she started to talk again.

'Paul, I am worried that Alan Sherman will try to find us. I don't think he knows about my house here but he has the resources to find out if he really wants to use them for that purpose. Did you know he is likely to be nominated as the next Republican Presidential candidate? But there is something going on with him that really scares me. I don't know what it is but he had many telephone conversations with people in New York who are not involved in politics. I had become his distraction in Washington and I know he will not want to lose me. If he finds out I am with you, he will be jealous and will try and find out who you are.'

I swung her round and kissed her. 'Don't worry, I will protect you. I have my Beretta and the whole of the FBI behind me,' I said rather naively.

'Does anybody in the Government, in your Department know about you and Sherman?' I asked.

'I don't think so, but if they did, it would be kept quiet. It's an unwritten rule in Washington. Even the Vice President has a mistress.'

'Does Sherman have any close friends in the FBI?' I asked.

'He has his own bodyguards. Some politicians use them like

private armies. They don't ask questions but just do what they're told. Strictly, until he is officially accepted as the Republican Presidential candidate, he is not entitled to Secret Service protection. In reality, he has friends in the FBI whom he relies on for information. Like all politicians he receives death threats which are passed onto the Bureau. He has powerful associates in the Party; some have nefarious connections to big business and criminal elements.'

Remembering what Robert told me, I asked, 'Do you know Sherman's relationship with the billionaire, Jonas Gould?'

'I only know what I overheard from a telephone conversation. They do have some business arrangements outside of the Party. I think that's who he makes the calls to in New York. Did you know that Gould is one of the Party's greatest financial supporters?' she said.

I was beginning to think Sherman might be a more dangerous person than just a jilted man. My thoughts were broken when Valerie suddenly looked up.

'I think that's my friend Carol coming towards us.'

I saw a short dark-haired woman walking along the beach a short distance in front of us. As we approached, Valerie said, 'Hello Carol, I thought you were overseas.'

The woman looked at me somewhat surprised before Valerie introduced me as David, a friend.

'Hi Valerie, I came here just a few days ago. I'm hoping to bring mother here next week to recover from her operation. Just thought I would take some exercise,' she said.

'Nothing serious, I hope,' said Valerie.

'No just a fractured arm. She is eighty-two and fell over in the garden. Since Dad died and, being an independent woman, she still tries to do everything herself but her mental abilities exceed her physical ones. I am hoping to see Kara in a few day's time. Her father Ted has not been well. I thought you were in Washington,' she said, giving me a curious look.

'Just taking a few days off from a busy time at the office' replied Valerie, squeezing my hand and appearing to be slightly embarrassed.

'Well, we had better get back as the light is fading.'

Carol didn't stop eyeing me the whole time.

'Come over some time, that is, when you're on your own,' she said, turning to walk back along the beach.

'Will do,' said Valerie.

I looked at Valerie and said, 'That's blown our little secret.'

She replied, 'Kara is Ted Kennedy's daughter. They live at Hyannis Port on the mainland just over that strip of water. People who live here or who come here for short breaks have a culture of being discreet. You know it's the place where politicians, business people and writers come to escape.'

'Will curiosity get the better of her though? I assume I am the first man you have brought here?' I asked.

It was my turn to give a wry smile. She smiled back.

'Yes, of course you are.'

'Come let's run back, I'm starving and want that steak.' I said.

We arrived back at the beach house and wasted no time in cooking the dinner. Valerie placed the two beef steaks and a bottle of wine on the table. It was red so needed no cooling.

Reluctantly, I switched on the television to see some breaking news on CNN. A reporter had found out about bomb threats to American cities by extremists. It didn't give details but just said the FBI was investigating. It would remind people of the terrorist attack on the World Trade Centre underground garage and the FBI's shortcomings in discovering it too late. The news item didn't mention atomic bombs or give any dates but the report would only heighten public fears of further incidents. I couldn't get any news from Britain but the police and security services would have known about the press leaks. Such news quickly becomes international. It would put our enemies on their guard and make the job of finding them more difficult. The new millennium was less than a month away so this report was certain to stir things up in the media.

Valerie called to tell me to change into something more comfortable and went over to switch off the TV.

'You know what we promised ourselves – no politics, no bombs threats.'

'Yes, but you should know the cat's out of the bag. A CNN reporter stated that bomb threats have been made to American cities,' I said.

She replied. 'But you said that was inevitable – it just puts people on their guard. Is that not a good thing?'

I went to the bedroom and unpacked and came across the shirt button Gary had given me to use when in danger. All I needed to do was peel off a tape on the rear side and press it hard to activate an alarm call to Langley. I wasn't sure what would then happen except my identity and location would probably come up as a warning blip on someone's computer. Perhaps a swat team would then arrive with guns blazing. I put the button carefully away in its box and stowed it in my case.

I put on a tee shirt and jeans and went back into the living room. It was now dark so I closed the curtains. Valerie came over and pulled them open.

'Look' she said, 'We have a full moon coming up. Let's enjoy the good luck it will bring.' She lit some candles on the table which now displayed an array of cutlery, wine glasses and food, fit for a king. This had been planned and not just happened. This lady knew what she wanted. I was the prize. It made me feel special, but that was the intention. The steaks and trimmings were excellent, it proved she could cook. I opened the red wine and filled our glasses. She gave me one of her looks. I raised my glass and said, 'I want this to be a toast to celebrate our being together at this very special moment.'

She came over and put her arms around my neck. 'I have never wanted anyone as much as I want you. Promise you will never leave me,' she said in a soft voice. It was another plea not to be left alone.

I looked into her eyes and felt myself dissolving, 'I promise.'

After dinner we talked again about our lives, our ambitions and hopes for the future. We did not talk about marriage but Valerie clearly wanted children. She was basically a lonely person who needed someone to love. I had never thought of myself as a family man. It was a new dimension I had to consider having at last found the woman I had always wanted.

I had one of the best nights of my life, including a relaxing sleep. Early in the morning we were woken by the sound of an aero-engine over the house. At first we ignored it, until we heard the same sound for a second time. Valerie said that no aircraft ever flew low in the area as the airport was some distance away. I ran to the window just in time to see a light aircraft similar to the one Valerie owned flying low over the beach just in front of the house. It looked like someone was taking photographs. I pulled Valerie down onto the floor behind the couch to avoid being seen. The plane then turned and flew over the ocean towards the mainland. I could just see some numbers on the tail which I quickly scribbled down. It looked like someone was trying to see who was in the house.

We stood up realising our quiet rendezvous may no longer be a secret. But who was it? I could see that Valerie was visibly shaken.

'I think it's him,' she said.

'You mean Alan Sherman.'

'Yes, he is using his people to track us down.'

'It could be me they are after. Remember I am on the hit list.

We have to leave here as soon as possible. At least we had one unforgettable evening and night together.'

'Don't say it like that,' she said, with tears in her eyes.

Taking her in my arms, I said, 'That's why we have to find another safe place,'

'But this is my safe place,' she said, now sobbing.

'It's my entire fault. If you hadn't met me then it would still be your safe haven. Let's think who would know you were here.' I said.

She thought. 'There is only one person who saw us together and that was Carol Johnson. If she called someone to enquire about you then it may have linked back to Alan. She is a gossip and knows many of the politicians in the Washington set. But she knows the rules. I don't think she would do that as we have been friends for many years. She knows about Alan and that this is my secret hideaway. Many people come here knowing they can escape from their lives in Washington. Even Carol has her own reasons for being in the Vineyard. I will call her and find out.

Alan might have returned to Washington early and now be checking up on me. He would have read my note saying that I was giving up the apartment and returning to England but it wouldn't have taken him long to find out I wasn't on the London flight. He was already suspicious and knowing his contacts and resources he could have chartered a plane to look for me.'

'But why would he come here if he didn't know about your house?' I asked.

'I don't know. If Carol is the source, then he would deduce I was on the island and now I was with a man. This is only speculation but I cannot think of anyone else who would be able to provide that information.'

'But why would it be so important for him to find you anyway?' I asked.

Now showing anxiety in her voice, she replied. 'He thinks I am his possession. Finding out I had left him for another man would fuel his anger. He would also lose face with those who know about us.'

Trying to reassure her, I said, 'Don't worry, we have FBI protection. Anyway I'm sure Alicia knows about us.'

'He will have influence with the FBI which he could use,' she said.

'I doubt whether he would risk his position by doing anything like that.' I retorted. Deep down I was worried. I didn't tell Valerie everything that David Simons had revealed. Her ex-boyfriend could be on the list of names. David didn't know the names on the coded list but he had given us useful information that could help trace the people associated with it.

Using her cell phone Valerie called Carol. Her anxiety showed in her facial expression. It didn't change when she put the phone down. 'No reply, I will call her later.'

I decided to take action. 'I suggest we do nothing. There is nowhere to go on the island. Our only alternative is to return to Washington and pretend you changed your mind about going back to England and came here to think things out. Would that work for you?'

'No, I don't want to see Alan again. I brought you here so we could spend time together and get to know each other.'

'Good,' I said, 'Let's get off the island, hire a boat and go for a sail. It's a little cold but a sunny day.'

Her eyes lit up and she gave her irresistible smile.

'First, I´m starving. I will make the breakfast.'

'OK' she said, 'I will pack.'

I went into the bedroom and I called Alicia on my cell phone. She answered immediately.

'Any news?' I asked.

'We are still working on the information David Simons gave us. Autopsies are being carried out on the bodies. London's been in touch. They are watching terrorist cells who may be involved.'

I interrupted, 'Alicia, I guess you know where I am and who I'm with.'

There was long pause.

'Yes, I do. Be careful,' she said quietly in a very protective voice.

'I think someone is after us, or after me. A light aircraft flew over the house taking photographs. Valerie is worried about Senator Sherman.' I gave her the details of the plane. Again there was a long silence.

'Don't worry, we know all about the Senator but be careful. You know what to do if anyone comes for you. Use your button but don't do anything yourself.'

'Your cell phone is secure. I can't say anymore at present,' she said, and rang off.

I put the Beretta 92 pistol in my coat pocket and continued cooking the scrambled eggs for breakfast. Valerie came in saying, 'I rang a boat house at Vineyard Haven. We can hire a boat down at the harbour.'

'Have you done any sailing?' I asked.

'Yes, when in England I once went out in a small sailing dinghy with an old boyfriend. He taught me how to tack and jibe, but it was on a lake, not out at sea.'

'Is there anything you can't do?' I asked.

'I cannot pick up spiders or any insects. A boy at school put one down my blouse and ever since I have a fear of them,' she replied.

'Well I'm not, so can protect you against such creatures.'

She looked at me with a slight frown.

'Paul, I saw you put the gun in your bag. Is that wise?'

'I said I would protect you, the gun will help if any one does come for us.'

I felt guilty not telling her that I had called Alicia. I had some bad feelings about what might happen and didn't want to spoil our day. It was comforting to know I had a guardian angel at Langley.

We drove down to the harbour at Vineyard Haven and walked to the boat house. Unfortunately they only had a twenty-foot motorised launch available for hire. All the sailing boats were stored away for the winter. I paid a very suspicious looking man a hugely elevated sum of money as a deposit for a day's hire of a boat. He asked for my passport seeing that I was a stranger from across the pond. Valerie didn't want to show herself in the current situation so kept out of sight. I had to sign an insurance document for both of us to cover a whole range of liabilities that were embedded in the small print. I guess my enthusiasm must have made him suspicious. I didn't want him checking up on me which is why I paid in cash. In the US where credit cards are the normal currency, anyone who pays large sums of cash for services are immediately under suspicion since they cannot easily be checked on.

The weather was good and the ocean looked unusually calm for the time of year. I steered the boat out of the harbour, passing numerous private moorings and jetties. I could see the ferry boat to Woods Hole on the mainland docked at the jetty. The well-sheltered harbour was truly an ideal haven for small boats and their owners.

I stowed my bag containing my laptop, phone and pistol in the cabin. I never went anywhere without my computer since it contained copies of Fellows' documents that were now being sought after by those who wanted to kill me. Valerie was busy finding her way around the cabin and making some tea. She was familiar with the satellite navigation equipment since it was similar to the one on her aircraft so we could easily locate our position. At least on the boat we were safe from terrorists and Valerie's ex. Before we took possession of the boat, she had bought some food and drink from a local shop. She came out of the cabin with some sandwiches and sat with me on the upper deck. Being at sea on a boat with the woman you love is as good as it gets. There was just the two of us, alone on the ocean with only the sound of water lapping against the side of the boat and the gentle purr of the engine. I broke the rules and switched off my cell phone. Seeing me do that, Valerie also switched off hers. We both laughed out loud like two kids who had just run away from school and thrown away our books.

As we moved out of the shelter of the harbour the sea became choppier and I had to take greater control of the vessel. It was December and winter on the island can be bad and the sea rough. So far we had been lucky experiencing almost summer weather. We sailed around the coast and came within sight of the beach where Valerie's friend Carol's house was located. The house was just visible from the boat. Valerie found a pair of binoculars in the cabin so started to scan the beach. She saw a small inflatable dinghy with an outboard motor attached pulled up onto the beach. There was no sign of the owner. It was rare for visitors to approach by sea this time of the year. Most visitors had long since left. I could see it concerned Valerie so she asked me to take a look. I took the glasses and focused on the area around the boat. Footprints were scattered where the boat was beached. It also looked like something had been dragged across the sand and placed in the sea.

'Does Carol own a boat?' I asked.

No, she can't swim so certainly wouldn't go out in a dinghy this time of the year. I have her number in my phone so will call her again.'

Valerie switched her phone back on and dialled Carol. The phone rang for some time but there was no reply and no messaging system. Our motor cruiser passed the beach and headed further west around a rocky point. It took us most of the day to navigate around the island before landing back at the harbour. It was getting dark so we decided to have dinner in a hotel restaurant near the harbour. The island specialised in seafood so we indulged ourselves with a locally caught lobster.

I was conscious we were being watched by a couple sitting at a table on the opposite side of the room, particularly by the middle-aged man. But he would be looking at Valerie not me. It was strange that his wife or partner, who looked older, didn't seem to mind him ogling her. I was staring back at them when I noticed a man, sitting two tables away reading a newspaper. The position of the paper showed that he didn't want to be noticed. There was something not quite right about him. He was dressed in a formal business suit that didn't quite fit with the environment we were in. He was obviously a recent visitor. The overriding factor was he did not look up from his newspaper. When Valerie walked into a room, even dressed casually, it was impossible not to notice her. The man on the next table certainly proved it. After we finished the meal, I paid and deliberately passed close to the man before walking out. Still, he refused to look at us. His behaviour was strange, almost threatening. I made a mental note of his face.

It was dark as I drove back to Valerie's house. For most of the journey she was quiet, displaying a worried look. As we turned off the road onto the sandy path to the house, I saw lights and people walking about. Suddenly we were confronted by an array of police vehicles with flashing lights. Two uniformed men approached our car and asked who we were. Valerie told them her name and that she owned the house.

They looked very concerned and told us they had found a body washed up on the beach close to this house. Two people were placing a body bag into an ambulance. The policeman led Valerie over to the stretcher. He pulled back the zip exposing Carol's white distorted face.

'Do you know this person?' asked the policeman

Valerie gasped and grabbed my hand.

'Oh no, I can't believe it.'

'Yes, she is a friend and my nearest neighbour, Carol Johnson.'

The policeman looked at me, 'Who are you sir?' he asked.

'My name's Paul Cane. I am a friend of Valerie. We've been out in a boat all day sailing around the island,' I replied.

Valerie nodded and burst into tears. I put my arms around her. At the policeman's request we went into the house. The policeman said, 'We received a phone call in the afternoon that a woman's body had been seen in the water. By the time we arrived, it was washed up on the beach. We have to confirm the cause of death but on first examination, it looks like she drowned.'

'Who made the call and when was it made?' I asked.

'The caller didn't leave his name. It was made at three o'clock,' replied the policeman.

We told the policeman about the dinghy we saw on the beach about an hour before that time.

Valerie said. 'Carol couldn't swim and would not go out alone in a boat.'

The policeman took notes. I wanted to tell him about the suspicious man at the restaurant but decided not to become too involved. We had enough problems. I was reluctant to be drawn into Carol's death. I had a feeling there might be a connection to our meeting with Carol on the beach yesterday and the possibility she might have called someone in Washington. Her drowning, the boat on the beach and her meeting with us were too much of a coincidence to be ignored.

The police asked more questions about Carol, her next of kin and other personal stuff. It seemed they didn't know much about her since she was only an occasional visitor to the island. They left, after asking us to go to the station in Edgartown the next day to give statements and not to leave the island. We had no choice but to agree.

It confirmed by belief that Martha's Vineyard was no longer a safe haven for us. Valerie was very distraught about the death of Carol. She had political connections and friends but no enemies and was enjoying the seclusion the island gave her. What was the motive for killing her? Did it have any connection to those seeking us? These were the questions that worried me.

I suggested to Valerie that we returned to Washington after we had given statements to the police, assuming they would let us. There we would have FBI protection and anyway I would soon be needed by the Task Force. Valerie reluctantly agreed, stressing she wanted to stay with me but a flight plan would have to be lodged with the airfield in the morning.

I checked my Beretta 92 and locked all the doors and windows before we went to bed. It was quiet outside except for the sound of waves breaking on the beach. The wind was light and coming across the sea in the same direction meant the sound was constant.

It was about three o'clock in the morning when I was awakened by a noise that sounded like a thud. Valerie was fast asleep so I quietly crept out of bed, put on my dressing gown and shoes, took the gun from my case, and went to look out of the window. Seeing nothing and with gun in hand, I cautiously opened the bedroom door. This time I heard a floorboard creak. My heartbeat raced. Someone was in the house. I wasn't sure what I would do if confronted with an intruder. American law, unlike British law, was clear, shoot the intruder first and ask questions later. I knew there were people who wanted to kill us. I had to protect the woman I loved and the secrets I carried in my computer so my British instinct to give the intruder, if there was one, the benefit of the doubt, was quickly dispelled from my mind. As I had never actually killed anyone before I wasn't completely sure how quick I might react. Hesitation at such times can be fatal. I recalled the saying: *He who hesitates is lost*. It was going to be him or me; there was no middle ground, no compromise, no holding back.

I stood very still, hoping Valerie would not wake up and, finding me out of bed, put the light on and come looking for me. It was too late to wake her now. I closed the bedroom door and moved into the living room but unfortunately forgot about the catch, which in the silence, made a loud 'click' as it closed. If an intruder was in the house then I had just lost the element of surprise, so had he. Now we both knew of each other's presence in the room. There was just enough moonlight in the living room to see that no person was lurking in the shadows. For a fleeting moment I wondered if paranoia had replaced my reasoning to the extent that a single noise had made me believe an intruder had broken into the house. I went to the side window that looked out onto the driveway just in time to see a shadow moving across it. My worst fears were confirmed. Were there two people? A sense of panic came over me. Our lives now depended on my actions.

I gripped my pistol, removed the safety catch and waited in the far side dark corner of the room. The only sound was the continuous swishing of the sea on the sandy shore. I waited and waited for whoever was in or outside the house to make their move. Suddenly, the sound became louder and a cold draught of air circulated around my feet. Someone had opened a door or a window on the sea-facing side of the house where the sun room and patio were located. I crouched down to reduce the possibility of being seen. The bedroom door was now on the opposite side of the room from me. I prayed Valerie would not wake up now the noise level had increased. Then I spotted him walking stealthily towards the bedroom. I had to act quickly. Remembering some earlier training, I held the Beretta with two hands and aimed at the centre of the dark blob approaching the door, and squeezed the trigger until the gun fired. A blinding flash illuminated the room, momentarily showing a shocked expression in the eyes of a masked man.

What happened next was an unbelievable sequence of events. Valerie must have woken up just before I fired the shot. At the same instant, she switched on the bedroom light and opened the door so I could see the man I had shot crouched on the floor. He was still moving and had a gun in his hand now elevated and pointing at Valerie since I was still out of sight. I instinctively fired another shot into him. His weapon clattered down on the floor. I rushed to Valerie who hadn't put any clothes on and pushed her back into the bedroom putting my hand over her face to prevent her talking. I then turned back to the room only to see the shot man staggering back towards the opening he had made in the patio door. I fired a third shot but missed. Leaving a trail of blood on the floor and across the sand he disappeared into the darkness. I gave chase in the darkness but stopped when I heard two shots coming from the direction of the beach. I rushed to a cupboard in the kitchen where earlier I had seen a flashlight stowed. Fortunately it worked. Adrenaline was now pumping into my bloodstream so all reason was being replaced by excitement. I was now the hunter. With my pistol in one hand and the torch in the other I ran out onto the beach. It didn't immediately occur to me that the two shots might be from another person's gun. Before I had run twenty feet I saw the body lying on the sand with a man standing over it. In one hand he had a large smoking revolver that looked like a Glock 22 pistol, the type used by the FBI, pointing at the corpse now looking very bloody. I stopped, pointed my gun and torch at him and said, 'Raise your hands and don't move.'

I had heard that phrase many times in TV plays and films so it was a natural thing to say. I detected a slight smile on his face as he turned and with a swift blow to my arm, made my hand release my gun. With his other hand he took an FBI badge from his pocket and flashed it in front of my face, saying, 'Relax I'm here to help. FBI, Alicia sent me.'

I was now very angry and still in a fighting mood. I shouted, 'You idiot I could have killed you. Why didn't you stop this killer before he came into the house?'

Seeing my anger he suggested I went back inside the house. He searched the body for identification but found none. The dead man was a professional and clearly came prepared. But where did he come from and who sent him were the questions that had to be answered.

Valerie emerged from the house with a terrified look on her face. I hugged her and said, 'Everything is OK. Go back and put the kettle on.'

In the circumstances it was a stupid thing to say. Meanwhile the stranger was making a phone call and shining his own hand torch on the victim, describing the man to whoever was on the end of the phone. I could see that my shot had found its mark on the man's chest. All the other shots had blown off parts of his arms and legs. They looked like the ones fired by the stranger. Fortunately his face, now unmasked, was untouched so a good description was possible. He was dressed in what looked like army battledress and had a black woollen balaclava that had fallen around his neck. He was a young and had a tattoo on his left arm.

When the FBI agent walked into the house through the patio door, I saw to my astonishment he was the man from the restaurant who had tried to avoid eye contact with us. So Alicia had sent over an agent to protect us. The man wouldn't get an endorsement in my report.

'My name is Agent Ben Carter, from the FBI's Terrorist Division in Boston. Sorry I arrived late but I was chasing the other suspect who got away. This one came in by the sea; the dinghy is out there on the beach. It was probably him that killed your friend this afternoon.'

He paused and then explained, 'Washington sent an urgent message that two men suspected of terrorist activities had crossed over on the ferry from Woods Hole with orders to kill a Paul Cane, a British agent working for the FBI. They said you were with a girl and staying at a beach house. I was given the exact satellite location. One of the two men made a phone call to Washington which our people picked up so we were able to locate his exact location. It was relayed to me so I tracked the two suspects to a hotel in Vineyard Haven. It was situated on the opposite side of the road to the restaurant which is why I was sitting there. By coincidence you both walked into the restaurant so I had to avoid contact. At first, I wasn't sure from the description I had been given that it was both of you but there was no other good-looking blonde in the town.

When you left the restaurant, one of the two men who were sitting in a car outside the hotel got out of the car. The other started up the car and followed you, so I followed him. It was the wrong decision since it was the other one, now lying dead on the beach, who intended to kill you. I'm not sure but I may have been spotted since the man in the car took me along a different road to the one you were travelling on. Eventually he did a circular trip and came back to the boat terminal where he boarded the ferry for Woods Hole. It was then I realised my mistake, so I then proceeded to your house. I parked my car out of sight, further along the path leading to the beach with a good view of your house and waited, believing the killer would have to come that way. I had no idea where the other suspect was so they effectively put me off the trail. These men were professionals and seemed to have inside information. I think I was compromised before I even started my surveillance.

It was only when I heard your shots that I knew the killer had succeeded in breaking into the house. I rushed to the beach in time to see him fleeing to the dinghy he had left on the sand. It was dark and I didn't know he had lost his gun or that you were still alive, so I had no other option but to shoot. We always aim for legs rather than kill shots to the chest unless directly confronted. I would have liked him alive but you had already done the chest shot so the man was almost dead when he fell on the beach.'

Valerie and I listened intently to his story.

I asked, 'Why didn't you warn us in the restaurant? Why didn't the FBI call me from Washington since they have my number?'

'I was given specific instructions by Washington not to contact you,' he said.

I asked the agent if he would call the local police since they had already been to the house earlier in the evening about Carol Johnson's murder. He had instructions not to involve them as it was now an FBI case. I said, 'We have to report to the police in the morning to give statements about Carol Johnson's death and since it is likely to be linked to the man on the beach, wouldn't it be the same FBI case?' He made a phone call to Washington. After a brief conversation handed the phone to me. It was Gary.

'Paul, I understand you've had some trouble. You were warned. We have been keeping an eye on things on the island. I want you and your girlfriend to be at the airfield tomorrow morning where a charter plane will bring you both back to Washington. Don't worry about the local police; we are dealing with that under our national security emergency measure. There has been a lot of progress and we need you here. Please let me speak to Agent Carter.' I handed the phone to the agent.

Carter told us to get some sleep. He would take care of everything with the local police, including the body on the beach. We had to pack up and drive to the airport in the morning to board the aircraft at eleven o'clock.

The agent apologised, shook our hands and left the house. Valerie was still in shock and I did my best to console her. She was more upset about having to leave her house than the events of the last few hours. We still didn't know how the killer found us or who sent him. I could see it was important for her to know if Alan Sherman was behind it or the terrorists. Our colleagues in Washington would probably have the answers. It was impossible to go back to sleep so we spent the time talking until the sun rose and the dawn began.

The drive back to the airport was in total contrast to the one we had made a few days earlier. Our happy frame of mind was replaced with a sombre mood of uncertainty and worry about what we would learn in Washington. We were met at the airfield by an FBI agent who had been instructed to accompany us to Washington. The aircraft was a Lear jet so the journey would not take long. They certainly weren't taking any risks. We strapped ourselves into our seats. I held Valerie's hand and managed to get a smile from her and said, 'You know we have the highest level of protection so we shall be safe. I know Alicia will make arrangements in Washington for you to be with me. I will insist on it.' She didn't seem very reassured and buried herself in a magazine.

As I always do on air flights, I thought about the events of the last day to try and make some sense out of them. I wasn't sure if Carol's death and the attempt on my life were linked. There was no possible motive for killing her in the way it was done. Clearly, whoever was behind it wanted to make it look like an accidental drowning but didn't know the lady couldn't swim so hadn't any background information. She was linked by friendship to Valerie not me. A thought came to me. The killer was hired to kill us but Carol, who may have inadvertently got in his path saw him trying to break into Valerie's house. She may have walked to the house along the beach and seen him. He couldn't risk her telling us and being recognised sealed her fate. Since it was in the afternoon, he must have seen that we were out. Was he looking for the memoires or hoping to conceal himself in the house until we returned? It must have been when he forced open the door of the conservatory so the lock would not work. I was not too fastidious about locking it so wouldn't have noticed any malfunction. It seemed unlikely any terrorist group would take the trouble to hire a killer for such a purpose. It was not their style since there was nothing to be gained. By this time their masters would know the FBI and CIA had copies of it. Unfortunately, it pointed back to Alan Sherman. I recalled Alicia's comment *'we know all about Sherman'* which indicated he was mixed up in something they were investigating. I was hoping the CIA had decoded the names list. It could lead us to the villains. My excitement rose when I saw Dulles airport coming up towards us. Valerie was just waking up from a sleep when I told her.

Return to Washington

The agent swiftly took us through the VIP channel and into a black stretched limousine. Sitting inside were Robert, Alicia, Gary and David Simons. It was certainly a welcome I didn't expect. I introduced Valerie who looked a little embarrassed. Robert gave her a kiss and exchanged some niceties with her. Alicia welcomed her to the team and, showing a feminine side I hadn't seen before, made some jokes about getting involved with a man who was being followed around by woman assassins. It broke the ice and created a friendly atmosphere. Gary told us that everybody had safe houses for the time being but some re-arrangements might be necessary. He knew about Valerie's predicament and said she could stay with me in the safe house.

Alicia told us the Vice President had called a Task Force meeting to take place in two days' time so wanted everybody updated on events. The President and British Prime Minister had spoken on the telephone the previous day and had agreed on a strategy to deal with the crisis. Both were concerned about the media finding out too much but speculation was fuelling the newspapers. It was decided to give out a press statement about bomb threats being made by certain terrorist organisations owing to the situation in Iraq. No mention would be made of atomic bomb threats on the eve of the millennium.

Alicia said, 'The President wants a full briefing from us about the current level of our intelligence. I have instructed one of my female agents to stay with Valerie at the safe house in Georgetown while we have briefing meeting at Langley this afternoon. A car will pick you all up at your respective houses at two o'clock in the afternoon.'

Valerie and I were the first to be dropped off at the house. It was sad to be back so soon after our short and eventful visit to Martha's Vineyard. It was thoughtful of Alicia to be providing protection for Valerie in my absence. I feared she might have some bad news for me about Sherman. We made ourselves some lunch, the freezer and refrigerator were still packed with food. At one-thirty a young, rather good looking woman knocked on the door. She showed her FBI badge and introduced herself as Chloe Rogers. She shook hands with us both and looking at Valerie, she said, 'Alicia has asked me to provide protection when you are alone. She insists that I accompany you when you go out. I have a car that we can use.'

She took Valerie's cell phone and inserted a new SIM card.

'This will stop anyone from locating you. Any call can be monitored by pressing the M on the keypad which puts the call through to our monitoring station at Langley. All other calls are private and no one can listen in or tap into the phone.'

Observing their body language it looked like the two women would get on well together. I kissed Valerie and went to the car that was waiting to take me to Langley. Now I might find out the truth about Sherman and perhaps the names of the conspirators.

CHAPTER 12

CIA Headquarters, Langley
18 December 1999

David, Robert and I were met by Alicia at the entrance of the CIA headquarters at Langley. After taking us through a complex of security stations where we were photographed, scanned and searched, we arrived at a building somewhere in the interstices of the site. It had its own security system but this time our host was able to lead us through the barriers. She escorted us along a narrow corridor to a conference room where Gary was already seated at a table with three other agents. The atmosphere was tense. Alicia welcomed me back and told the group about my experiences at Martha's Vineyard. She congratulated me on my first kill in circumstances that even a trained agent would have had difficulties. The three other agents, who had been working in the back office at Langley and at the FBI's Hoover Building in Washington, were introduced to us. She told us the bomb threat had been given the codename Whirlwind. There were now hundreds of agents in America and Britain working around the clock on it. Both Governments had given Whirlwind the highest priority and a top secret security rating.

Alicia said, 'Before the Task Force meeting with the Vice President, scheduled tomorrow, I want to update you on our latest intelligence. David Simons gave us the most important lead by supplying the telephone encryption codes used by The New Order's Cabal members. We have already monitored some of their calls; one was made to an Al-Qaeda operative in New York. Al-Qaeda's American cells may have been made active to prepare for what they call the Big Event. There is no doubt that an association exists between these two organisations but as yet we don't know the basis for it.

A call was made from Paris to someone in a company owned by the billionaire, Jonas Gould. We found out that Senator Alan Sherman is a shareholder in that company. In addition to Gould's financial support for Sherman's campaign, the two men have a business relationship involving investments in Asia. The connection is tenuous but David and I believe Gould is a member of the Cabal. He is on the short list of the world's billionaires who could be Cabal members.

David knows that two of the individuals who made the calls were once members of his Brotherhood Foundation. They are Jean Dupuis and Heinz Kluge. He thinks they became members of The New Order after the demise of the Brotherhood in 1959. If so, Gould, Dupuis and Kluge are also likely to be members of the Cabal. What is difficult to understand is why they would support, or be involved in, an Al-Qaeda plan to destroy American and British capital cities. There have to be good reasons why they would be helping the terrorists. It's just not in their interests to do it. These people are politically opposed to the Islamists and anyway have secure positions in their respective countries and industries.'

I asked, 'Have you decoded the names list so we can confirm the names of the Cabal members?'

Alicia replied, 'We had reduced the names list to a matrix of letters but without the key it's difficult to make further progress. David believes the key is in the Fellows' memoires, which may be the reason why The New Order is trying to kill the people who they believe have copies. Paul, since you have the original copy of the memoires you must be their prime target. We need to scan the text into our computer to see if the matrix can be matched to any parts of it.'

'OK, I will work with the coding expert to see if we can find a fit,' I said.

Gary took up the briefing. 'We interviewed some of the Mexicans in New Mexico after obtaining the police report on the accident that killed the man who witnessed the removal of the atom

313

bomb from the old mine. The police chief and local sheriff have been dismissed and are charged with corruption and the misappropriation of police files. They were paid large sums of money to destroy the files but being greedy and realising their value, they kept them to extract more money. Instead they received death threats but it has not been possible to trace the people who made them. When we became involved they admitted to what they had done and handed over the papers. The information we obtained, particularly the description of the van, eventually led us to a private warehouse a few miles from New York. A team was sent to search it and other buildings where a bomb might have been stored but no evidence was found. The warehouse is currently owned by a company that provides services and storage facilities for the Port Authority of New York.'

'How long have the company owned the building?' I asked.

'About twenty years, but in the last five it has been used for storing equipment for the Port Authority,' replied Alicia.

'That's a coincidence. What was it used for previously?' I asked.

'We don't know,' she answered hesitantly.

'Has the company been checked out?'

'Yes, thoroughly, it's clean,' she replied.

'What led you to the warehouse?' I asked.

'We checked hundreds of CCTV records of vans with the description we had from the police report that cross the boundaries of large cities on specific dates. Fortunately, after the 1993 garage bombing in the World Trade Centre in New York, all vehicles entering and leaving the city were monitored. Normally these are not archived for long but in February 1998, about the time when the bomb was removed from the mine, there was another bomb threat in the city. It was the fifth anniversary of the attempt to blow up the World Trade Centre so fearing another attempt might be made, camera records were kept. On studying these we saw what looked like the van travelling along a road in the vicinity of the warehouse. It didn't appear at camera sites two miles further on, so no further sightings were recorded. The warehouse was the only significant building in the area so it became the focus of our attention. But as I said, after a thorough search nothing to suggest a bomb had been worked on or stored in the building was found. But there was an area in the basement near the river that had been extensively refurbished. Apparently it had been used to store some environmental monitoring equipment. But the owners were not given any information since it was part of a Government project. We later found no such project existed.'

I looked at everybody and suggested, 'Perhaps we should take another look at the building and the owners. The bomb cannot just disappear. It sounds like Al-Qaeda has been very clever at subterfuge.'

David agreed and said, 'I should go there with another team and take a look.'

I suggested, 'It might be better for just two of us to go instead of a team since another visit by an FBI team would raise suspicions.'

David continued, 'Before the bomb could be made ready for use, appropriate laboratory or special workshop facilities and expert nuclear physicists or technicians would be required. It's unlikely any American would do the job knowing the intended target so we should be looking for Muslim or foreign scientists who may have recently entered the country or ones that are studying here.'

Gary replied, 'Current checks are being made on all foreign entries, especially from the Middle East, and on nuclear scientists working on weapon projects in this country.'

David warned, 'The plutonium bomb we are looking for may have been upgraded to be a fusion-boosted fission bomb. If they had possession of initiators like the ones stolen from Halborn together with tritium and deuterium gas pressurised containment in the core and the expertise to build such an assembly, then it would be a possibility. The yield of such a bomb would be at least a hundred times greater than the Hiroshima one. It would obliterate Manhattan with an area of devastation that could extend up to two hundred miles. To use a product of the wartime Manhattan Project to destroy Manhattan would appeal to the twisted minds of fanatic terrorists.'

Alicia responded, 'It looks like, as we expected, they are going for New York and probably Manhattan, so we should concentrate our search in that part of the city. Can I remind you over seventeen million people work and live in the New York area.'

Robert asked, 'How long would it take to evacuate New York?'

'Many days, but even if we did, the terrorists might strike somewhere else. Our only hope is to find the bomb without raising an alarm,' said Alicia.

I asked, 'Do you think they would try and hit the World Trade Towers again since the garage bomb failed to knock them down?'

David replied, 'It doesn't matter where the bomb is placed, it will completely obliterate Manhattan even if it was detonated outside the island. The terrorists will use a secure site that's less likely to attract attention. It could be miles outside the city.'

Alicia sighed, 'We have one hell of a job to do and little time left.'

I repeated, 'I cannot understand why the leaders of The New Order would want to help these suicidal maniacs. There is no gain for them from the destruction of the commercial centre of the richest country in the world. It simply doesn't make sense.'

Everybody agreed but no suggestions were put forward so I changed the subject.

I asked, 'Did you find out anymore about the person that was sent to kill David in Tucson?'

Alicia replied, 'Yes, we were able to confirm it was Olga Petrovitch. We traced her back to Russia. She had been a trained KGB operator in the days of the Soviet Union. She was not on our primary search list because she had a number of aliases which made it difficult for us to find her connections. Eventually we did connect her with a man called Leon Seperkov who is the personal assistant to Boris Sudakov, the Russian billionaire. Seperkov runs a security service for Sudakov's many global interests. It's really a front for a Russian mafia type organisation. They hire contract killers to people willing to pay. We think Olga was one of his best operatives. But Sudakov hates Muslims and the Islamic fundamentalists so cannot be supporting Al-Qaeda. If he is a member of The New Order's Cabal, then this connection to Al-Qaeda also gives us a problem.

As far as we can ascertain Petrovitch had been working undercover in Britain for many years. It was likely she murdered Henry Fellows and Ruth Goodman. She flew from London to Washington last week on her kill mission. We tracked calls made to her from Langley and London. We know who made the calls from Langley and that person is under surveillance. The Directors of the CIA and FBI, and the Vice President have been informed. It is a high-ranking FBI officer working under secondment at Langley whose name I cannot give you at this time. He has not yet been arrested but his access to further intelligence on Whirlwind has been restricted. The telephone encryption codes given to us by David are proving invaluable in decoding the calls he's making and receiving. Some have originated from Moscow and London although the people speaking haven't yet been identified. David was right, he is known as *Catseyes*.

The old Soviet Union was our enemy in the Cold War years so no Russians were members of David's Brotherhood Foundation. Sudakov is one of the new rich men who flourished when Yelstin came to power after the fall of Communism. He is a political person and opposes Putin so the man has an interest in making Russia a leading power again. He may be using the Al-Qaeda Islamists to weaken America. If the terrorists succeed there will be a war which could spread across the whole of the Islamic world and America would be blamed. This is just a theory but it could explain why he could be helping Al-Qaeda. The only problem is Sudakov has extensive financial investment in Britain, particularly hotel chains in London. There is no way a man who hates Islam will permit the terrorists to destroy London. He may be our best weapon to use against them.'

Following Alicia's statement, I observed the stunned look on the faces of the others in the room.

Robert looked up and said, 'You mean the Russians could be using both The New Order and Al-Qaeda to start a war in which they would benefit?'

'Possibly,' replied Alicia.

Someone came in and asked for Gary. Alicia and the other two agents excused themselves and left the room.

David Simons had been put in a flat close to where Robert was staying so the two men had become friends. They had been worried about us in Martha's Vineyard. Robert told me Alan Sherman had been seen in Washington. He had returned sooner than expected from his home in the Hamptons and would have seen Valerie's note in the apartment. I told them about the attempt on our lives, the killing of Carol Johnson and our suspicions of Sherman's involvement.

Robert told me about an article on Sherman in the Washington Post. The Senator was ramping up his campaign for the Republican Party's nomination. He vehemently criticised the President and Government's foreign and domestic policies. The Party's election would be in early 2000 and since there was no viable opposition, he was likely to get the nomination.

In another article about the rising power of billionaires, Jonus Gould was, with a number of other rich businessmen, seen to be backing him. They wanted to get rid of the Democrat President because of his perceived weakness in dealing with the terrorist threats. With all this publicity and a high public profile, Sherman was unlikely to become involved in murder, too much was at stake. He was publicly criticising the President's foreign policy and his stand on terrorism so was also unlikely to be involved in the current terrorist threat to America. But for Valerie's peace of mind I had to find out for certain if he was connected in any way to the gunman sent to kill us.

By coincidence, Alicia and the others returned to the room. Her face displayed one of her more serious expressions. She looked directly at me and said, 'We've just found out that the gunman you shot in Martha's Vineyard was an ex-member of an army commando group. He worked for a private security company in Boston which looks like a front for hired killers. He was a highly trained operative named Alan Garbo. You were lucky, Paul.

We tracked a phone call made to the company from England.

It relayed the following message: '*arrange for package to be delivered to Paul Cane and the girl in Martha's Vineyard.*' The same company chartered an aircraft to fly around the island on the pretext they were carrying out an aerial survey for a holiday company. A very large sum of money was paid over to the aircraft charter company before they agreed to do it. The police and other authorities were alerted but nobody thought to challenge the request. It seems like the same people who contracted Petrovitch had you next on their list.'

It was looking less likely thatAlan Sherman was involved, which would be a relief to Valerie.

'Why was Carol Johnson killed?' I asked.

'The police found her cell phone on the beach. She had made a call to Valerie Day in the afternoon before the police received a call from someone saying they had seen a body floating in the sea. Since her footprints and phone were found on the sand dunes near to Valerie's house, we can assume she was on her way to the house when the killer struck. Carol was killed by a blow to the head not by drowning. Her body was taken back to the beach close to her own house and then put in the water. Her killer believed it would be taken out to sea by the current. What he didn't know was that the tidal currents in the afternoon flow in the opposite direction, so her body was washed up on the beach near Valerie's house.

The only explanation was that Carol's call must have been made at the same time that Valerie called her from the boat, so hers didn't get through. But no message was left. Perhaps she saw the killer and he struck before she could leave one. She was in the wrong place at the wrong time.'

'Did she make any other calls?' I asked.

'The police are still investigating but she did make a call to Washington the day before. I don't know to whom at this time. I have asked for a full report from the FBI. They have taken over the case since the attack was linked to you. The local police are not pleased since we wouldn't give them a reason why we had to take over the investigation. We've placed a press clamp down on the

319

incident. To the relief of the tourist board it will not be in the local newspapers.'

Alicia asked me to put up on the screen the last part of the Fellows' memoires so everybody could see them. I switched on my laptop and opened the document files. One of the agents plugged my computer into a projector and displayed the text on a screen set up on the wall of the room so David and Robert could see it. I had already copied in the material from the disc sent by Ruth Goodman so the names list and additional text written by Fellows just before he died could be displayed. It read like an epilogue. Fellows had tried to sum up his life and kept making references to the impending doom facing the world. It was as though he had a premonition of what we were now facing. David had tears in his eyes when he saw what his life-long friend had written. On the last page Fellows mentioned the valuable information he had received from Paris by someone he called 'Butterfly', obviously a code name. It was a person, assumed to be a woman, who had been employed as a secretary to Jean Dupuis, a wealthy and legitimate French arms dealer. She had access to Dupuis' computer files because she arranged most of his meetings and travel arrangements. Butterfly was also one of Dupuis' many mistresses so knew more than most about his private life.

Butterfly had made the arrangements for the meeting at the Château de Rambouillet in 1998. When she discovered what Dupuis and the Cabal were planning she decided in her own interests to keep a copy of the names of the people attending the meeting. She found out about the threat to kill Henry Fellows and David Simons from the files. Appalled by this she posted a copy of the names of the Cabal members to Fellows, warning him about the plan, and asking him to keep them secret unless she was found dead. Henry honoured her request and coded the names into his memoires. It also provided protection if anyone tried to kill him. Butterfly's last message indicated she feared for her life after Dupuis had replaced her for a younger, married woman with whom he was also having an affair. They had a row and he accused her of reading his private letters and stealing money. He may have suspected her correspondence with Fellows. No further letters were received so Fellows didn't know the fate of his informer but assumed she was dead. David was clearly upset by what he saw on the screen but it did reveal some vital clues as to why his friend was murdered.

Alicia asked us to accompany her to Langley's computer complex. I saw booths where young men were hard at work peering at screens showing large maps of terrains. It was where the CIA kept watch on terrorist camps and other would-be enemies. We were led into a basement room which had an eye scanner on the door. It recognised us, and allowed entry to a room which housed the latest mainframe IBM supercomputer. I was introduced to a computer technician who could have easily been a young Bill Gates. He had already been briefed so no discussion was necessary. The new supercomputers worked quickly and silently, unlike their ancestors that displayed rows of flashing lights and banks of magnetic tapes spooling away in the background. This was the culmination of twentieth century technology.

The computer expert showed me the analysis he had done. A number matrix had been derived from the letters in the names list by fitting them to the symbols used for elements in the Periodic Table.

He said, 'Seven separate matrices have been derived from the way the list was formulated. Each has five rows across with the following numbers of rows: 3, 4, 5, 5, 7, 9 and 9. The computer will scan the memoires to determine what format best fits the matrices. The programme will look for a fit of the numbers to the following: the first number is the page number in the document, the second is the position of the paragraph on the page, the third is the position of the sentence in the paragraph, the fourth the position of the word in the sentence and the fifth is the position of the letter in the word, then that letter will be the first one in the hidden word.'

He illustrated the search routine shown below for a 5 by 3 matrix, assuming a 1000 page text, 10 paragraphs per page, each with 100 sentences and a maximum of 100 words per sentence. In practice the computer had no limits on the maximum. He showed an example by putting a series of numbers.

1	2	3	4	5
Page,	paragraph,	sentence,	word (1-10)	letters etc.
1-1000,	1-10,	1-100,	1-100	letter in word

Number Matrix

95	5	6	2	1
45	3	3	5	3
33	2	8	6	2

The technician said, 'It's very likely that, unless Fellows had a powerful computer, he would have used this simple format to hide the true names.'

David had told us that Fellows did have a desktop computer which he would have used to construct the code.

I watched with excitement as the computer scanned the text. Within a minute the results were displayed on the screen. The first word that came out was: FoxF M1, followed by six other names, EaglestarA M2, WolfmanG M3, SerowJ M4, BearR M5, LionheartB M6, TigerI M7.

The technician looked at us and said, 'These are the actual names that were coded in the text of the memoires.'

Alicia had already realised they were coded names for the leaders of the so-called Cabal. Unfortunately, they didn't immediately identify their actual names but gave significant clues. Her face glowed with satisfaction because one of the code names, Eaglestar, had been used in one of the monitored telephone exchanges between Russia and America.

David thought that Lionheart was Diane Hunter, the stepdaughter of Paul Fields, whose place on the Inner Cabal she took after he was killed. He thought Bear was Boris Sudakov, the Russian member, Wolfman was Heinz Kluge the German member, and Fox was Jean Dupuis, the French member.

Alicia believed it wouldn't take long to find the identity of the other three members. She said, 'Gary and I will make sure these people are placed under close surveillance but we shall also need to find others who work for them if we are to establish links to the Al-Qaeda terrorist cells. These people have gone undetected for decades owing to the networks of protectors they have employed, so finding actual evidence that links them to the bomb plot will be difficult.'

She added, 'A decision will be jointly made by the President and Prime Minister on the evacuation of New York and London before the eve of the millennium. But the exact date and reason for the evacuation will be a closely guarded secret until a final decision is made. It's imperative the press and public don't know to prevent a widespread panic. If the terrorists find out we know about the timing and planned targets they may change them.'

'I said 'Why don't we make contact with the people who we believe are members of the Cabal and find out what they want and why they appear to be supporting Al-Qaeda? They may be in a better position to stop the terrorists since they must know who they are and have knowledge of their plan of operations. It would call their bluff.'

'How would we do that?' asked Robert.

'Letters could be sent to each one of the suspected members of the Cabal informing them we know their identities. In exchange for their help in finding the bombs, we could offer them immunity from any prosecution.'

'But that would virtually destroy The New Order,' said Robert.

'Exactly, if they know we know who they are, then they are finished anyway and a deal with the Government could be their only way out. If we could persuade even one of the seven members to agree to help us then the others are likely to follow. I suggest we target Jonas Gould and Diane Hunter, since they have most to lose if exposed and I cannot believe they want their cities destroyed and millions of their citizens killed.'

My suggestion gained the attention of everyone in the room. David Simons said, 'Paul's suggestion would be the best way to smoke out the Cabal members but I doubt whether the President would offer them immunity from prosecution if it was proved they were part of the conspiracy. If that became public it would finish the President and the Government.'

Alicia said, 'Such a proposal would require approval of both the President and Prime Minister. But it's worth floating the idea to them. I will talk to the Vice President to get his view first. He is likely to see it as the last resort if we fail to find the bombs before any evacuation deadline is set.

We will increase surveillance on the people who are suspected to be Cabal members and try and find the identity of the remaining members. All the companies and businesses owned by these people will be checked out, including recent bank transfers. Since the code names relate to their countries, finding the remaining members should just be a process of elimination once we get the lists of all the politically motivated billionaires.'

Gary added, 'We are dealing here with very powerful and influential people, most of whom are outside American and British jurisdiction so alerting them to what we know would only put them on their guard and almost certainly make them more difficult to bring to justice even if we could prove their involvement in Whirlwind. They would have to be dealt with by their own Governments and security services. You know the problems that would bring, particularly with the Russians at this time.'

David said, 'Gary is right. The Brotherhood Foundation successfully operated for many years in different countries by placing its members into Governments and on the boards of large companies. As you know, our purpose was to prevent Governments from using science and knowledge against the interests of their people. The New Order has been even more successful and, as we have already witnessed, corrupted people at high levels in Government and the security services so there is little chance of them being brought to justice by their Governments. Our only chance is to find the Al-Qaeda terrorists and their bombs and find indisputable evidence that links them individually to The New Order. Being able to identify these members will help that process. It's taken decades to track down and convict Mafia bosses and we haven't succeeded yet in doing that with the drug cartel barons in South America.'

Alicia said, 'We have to listen to the views of the British team. They are sending over an agent whom we expect to meet at the next Task Force meeting. As you know, Mark has been assigned to liaise with the London team. They have made good progress in identifying Al-Qaeda cells and have placed the known ones under surveillance. With a large number of Muslim immigrants, mainly from Pakistan, MI5 is able to track most of them. The British are expecting a bomb to be brought into the country so most efforts are being devoted to monitoring all entry points.

Our immediate task is to check the New York warehouse again. David and Paul should go there and discreetly ask some questions. If we find anything suspicious then we should send in an expert team to examine the evidence. The silver mine in New Mexico certainly provided valuable leads.'

Alicia closed the meeting and asked everybody to await further instructions for the meeting of the Task Force at the White House. We were all escorted out of the building and taken back to Washington by cars.

Alicia returned to her office, locked the door, picked up the telephone and called her boss, the Director General of the CIA, to report on the successful decoding of the names list and her meeting with team members. She asked his permission to brief C5 on Whirlwind.

'Are you sure this is absolutely necessary?' he asked.

'Yes, to retain complete secrecy, total elimination is the only solution, whatever happens on 31 December,' she replied.

'I will call the Vice President. He may want to have the emergency meeting of the Task Force scheduled for tomorrow before talking to the President,' he said.

'I appreciate what you say, sir, but C5 would only be activated on an order. Time is short and we need him to track down the key people involved so he can be in a position to act immediately when ordered. He did find the Russian assassin and warned us in time to save David Simons.'

Sensing Alicia's anxiety, the Director added,

'Agent Garcia, do you believe C5 can be trusted to act only when ordered? From his record I see he is a maverick who doesn't like taking orders. He is British and an independent contractor so he may decide his allegiances lay elsewhere.'

Alicia didn't say anything. She also knew the Director was a maverick and hated waiting on politicians for decisions. He would also know the CIA and FBI would be blamed if everything went wrong because they were charged with protecting the country. Removing the main players would certainly save a lot of anguish if it could be achieved.

The silence was broken, 'OK Agent Garcia, brief C5 but he is your responsibility. If he fails you fail and it's on your head. Is that clear?'

'Yes sir, very clear. There is one further item. Can I put *Catseyes* on the hit list?'

'Yes,' he replied.

She then re-dialled a unique number. The receiver would know who it was. Within seconds, a voice said, 'I will meet you at the rendezvous place in one hour.' She checked her Glock and left the room.

Sean 'Curly' O'Brien was one of a handful of hit men unofficially used by the CIA. He went under the codename C5, his identity was known only to the Agency's Director and Alicia Garcia, his contact. Such people worked alone and often outside the law of the countries in which they operated. If caught, or captured, they were on their own, not protected by the Agency who would always deny their existence. They were the unknown foot soldiers who dispatched the enemy's assassins and undercover agents, using any means at their disposal. No questions were asked. Rewards for success were high. Success was all that mattered. Failure was sometimes fatal. Their names never appeared on records or in files. Their actions were listed as the unexplainable in case histories.

Born in Belfast of an American mother and Irish father, Curly had served as an army SAS officer before being recruited as an undercover agent for MI5 in Northern Ireland during the IRA troubles. He resigned after the Northern Ireland Peace Agreement was signed because he could no longer play by the rules when many terrorists whom he had put behind bars were released. As expected, revenge killings on both sides followed. He was involved in tracking down the IRA people who were responsible for the Warrenpoint massacre near Newry, in Northern Ireland in 1979 where eighteen British soldiers were killed in an ambush; it made him many enemies. He was about to retire and live a quiet life in obscurity when the murder of his parents by the IRA forced him to return to his former life but as a free agent.

MI5 agents are never really free. A number of transatlantic phone calls were made. It wasn't long before Curly was recruited by the CIA as a freelance agent. He was contracted to their Russian station in Moscow to seek out ex-KGB agents who would make useful contacts. After the fall of Communism in the Soviet Union, many such agents became highly paid gunmen for the variety of private Mafia-type organisations that controlled much of the business in the cities.

Curly was a curious mix of Len Deightons's Harry Palmer and Clint Eastwood's Harry Callahan from the 'Dirty Harry' films. He was intelligent, self-centred, ruthless, hated rules and liked to work alone so had the right qualities for the CIA job. He only accepted assignments if they involved removing his country's enemies. Coming from a family with a military background he had a strong sense of patriotism. Using his Russian contacts he had found out about the organisation that employed Olga Petrovitch and had warned the CIA about her intended mission. Curly knew about Leon Seperkov and the identity of some of his other employees including the link to Boris Sudakov. He was supposed to be on the same plane as Petrovitch but because of a delay in Moscow he missed the Washington flight from Heathrow. FBI agents were assigned to track her from Dulles airport but they lost her in Washington.

Alicia drove into an underground car park of an office block located six miles outside Washington. It was the second time she had used it as a rendezvous. Normally meeting places were changed to avoid suspicious eyes but time was too short to set up a new one. Curly knew the meeting place and time from a code on her earlier telephone call. She was early, so she waited. In those minutes of waiting things can happen. Things not planned for can occur. She sensed movement, and then a black Ford SUV slowly came alongside. Its passenger, dressed in jeans and leather jacket, smiled as he opened the door of the car and sat next to her. She thanked him for delivering Olga and updated him on the Tucson incident and then went on to explain the nuclear bomb threat now facing New York and London. She told him that the situation was unique and there was no set of procedures to deal with it. America and Britain were facing national emergencies. Even if those responsible were caught and arrested they could not be brought to trial. It would jeopardise national security and have far-reaching political ramifications. There was only one solution. Curly listened with interest.

'Do you know who these people are?' he asked.

Alicia replied, 'Our analysis has produced a set of assigned names from which we have deduced the true identities of most of them but cannot be absolutely sure. They are written on the sheet in this envelope.'

Curly took out the paper and gazed at the names. Without emotion he said, 'I know most of these people. It will be a pleasure to carry out your contract. For most, it's long overdue.' Alicia continued, 'Our agents are trying to find the location of the bombs and the Al-Qaeda cells involved. The terrorists must have nuclear experts supervising the whole operation. It's too big a job for ordinary bomb-makers. They must be found and stopped. After the bombs are found and the involvement of the people on that list is confirmed, we want you to administer the final solution but not until I give you the order. This is a highly delicate situation politically and before any further action is taken, the CIA Director General has to get Presidential approval.

The public must never know. If it was found out the President and the Government would lose all their credibility, the Stock Market would slide and chaos would ensue. The media are already getting suspicious that something big is about to happen.'

'Perhaps that's exactly what The New Order members want. They can then put their candidate into the Presidency and at the same time buy up shares if the Market collapses. This would give them strong political and economic power,' said Curly.

'That's something we have considered,' said Alicia.

Alicia gave Curly another cell phone encrypted with new codes and said, 'The millennium threat has been given the codename Whirlwind. Use only this phone for all communications with me. It has an encryption chip that makes it impossible for anyone to tap into your calls. No other person in the Task Force team will know your identity or your task. You're a ghost. You don't exist. Only the CIA Director and I will know about you and your work.'

'Can he be trusted?' asked Curly.'

'Absolutely,' was her reply.

He grimaced and said wryly, 'I've heard that before.'

But Curly trusted no one, particularly agency directors who would sacrifice anybody to save their own skins. He had survived because he always took steps to protect himself. He was more dangerous to his employers dead than alive. Momentarily, Alicia detected a look of satisfaction on Curly's face as he got back into the SUV. She felt a sense of relief when it drove out of the car park. She knew whatever happened in the weeks ahead, C5 would carry out the task efficiently with or without the President's approval. He was a big risk but that was balanced by his patriotism and fair sense of justice. The people he would go after were democracy's greatest enemies because they knew the law couldn't touch them. Sometimes democracy has to be protected and needs people like Curly to sustain it.

The day had been long and we had made good progress but it was now only one week before Christmas and two weeks to the new millennium. As the car drove to the safe house my thoughts turned back to Valerie. I called her to say that I was on my way back. At least I had some good news for her.

Her FBI bodyguard opened the door with one hand poised

near her gun. That was what she was trained to do. On seeing me she smiled and stood aside. Valerie was sitting in the back room reading a book. She greeted me with a hug but still showed signs of stress from our recent experiences. The agent came in and said she would be leaving and would return in the morning but to call immediately if needed. Valerie thanked her and after making some small talk, the two parted company.

'How did you two get on?' I asked.

'We have become friends and found we had a lot in common so the time went quickly.'

I told Valerie the man sent to Martha's Vineyard to kill us was from the same organisation as the one who sent the Russian to Tucson.

'It has an office address in Boston but we believe its controller is a Russian based in Moscow. They have a mole in the CIA headquarters named *Catseyes* who is under surveillance. It was through him they were able to track us.'

'I am glad that Alan Sherman was not involved,' she said.

'He has a close connection to Jonas Gould who is under investigation by the FBI. We decoded the names list. It didn't give the actual names of the Cabal members but did reveal their assigned codenames. Further analysis has created a list of possible suspects. Jonas Gould's name is on that list.'

Valerie's face changed. A worried look returned.

'Do you mean he could still be mixed up in this conspiracy?' she asked.

'Nobody knows yet. I cannot believe he or Gould would want to see New York blown up. There has to be a very good reason for them to be connected in some way to the terrorist threat,' I replied.

'I'm going to work tomorrow. It's a day earlier than planned but I will try and act normal so as not to raise any suspicions. I've told Chloe Rogers but she will need to be briefed by Alicia Garcia on the current threat level to me which, if what you say is true, should now be lower,' she said confidently. I didn't pursue the conversation but our enemies now knew about us both so Valerie was also a target. Alicia would know this so would want to continue giving her protection.

Colour was returning to Valerie's face. She was looking more like the person whom I met on my first night in Washington.

I told Valerie about the meeting of the Task Force the next day and that afterwards I would be going to New York with David to hunt for the bomb.

'Why put yourself at risk again? Let Alicia's people do it, that's what they get paid for.' she said in a pleading way.

'David needs my help. We believe the FBI and CIA people going there would raise suspicions. We will have full back-up if required,' I replied.

She put her arms around me and smiled, saying in a soft voice, 'Paul, will you take me back to England before Christmas? I want to see my father and aunt and anyway I will feel safer there.'

'Yes, I will. I want to go back myself. But remember London is also under threat. I actually ought to be helping the Government there rather than here,' I replied.

'I'll call Daddy tomorrow and tell him I will be coming home for Christmas.' 'OK but remember to say nothing about what has been happening here. You can stay with me in my flat at Knightsbridge. But the people here may not allow us to leave until the bomb and terrorists are found since we know too much. I will find out more tomorrow at the Task Force meeting.'

My cell phone rang. It was Robert. He told me that MI5 had sent over someone who I knew to act as liaison officer. His name was John Henning. He also told me MI5 were not pleased that we were working with the CIA without their knowledge and agreement.

Henning had been co-opted onto the Task Force as the official British representative. I suddenly remembered it was him whom I spoke to in St James' Park after my return from Kuwait. My suspicions were raised then about why he approached me. He must have known more than I did at the time about what was going on. Henning was a dark horse at university, a loner except he liked gambling but didn't mix well with the other students. He had a sinister side so it didn't surprise me MI5 had recruited him. My guess was he'd been sent to watch me rather than be useful as a liaison with the CIA.

The next day a car arrived and took me to the White House. Valerie went to work after a more relaxed night. The weather had turned cold and snow could be on its way. Washington could get very cold in the winter. People were getting ready for the festive season. The shops and some buildings were showing decorations. Office parties were in full swing and people were preparing for holidays with their families. Nobody knew about the potential horror hidden away in New York that would be unleashed if we failed to find the bomb and the terrorists. The Christian festival had no meaning for them; they hated it and all it represented.

The car drove through the security gate to the East Wing of the White House. We got out of the car to be met by a tall, broad-shouldered secret serviceman at the door. He checked my credentials and escorted me to a room where other members of the Task Force were seated. I noticed David Simons and Robert were sitting next to each other at the table.

Alicia greeted me with a smile. She seemed to warm to me after the events in Martha's Vineyard. Perhaps after the shooting she saw me as one of her kind. John Henning was absent from the room which surprised me. I asked Robert about him but he didn't know anything.

The President and Vice President were seated around the table. They shook my hand, giving me guarded smiles that didn't hide the serious nature of what we were about to discuss. The same people were in the room who had attended the first meeting except Henry Schmidt. The President was about to address the meeting but was stopped by the arrival of John Henning who made his apologies for being late. At the same time a messenger handed the President a note which he quickly read and passed to the Vice President. Their body language showed that the contents disturbed them.

The President said, 'I have called this meeting to update you on the very grave situation that confronts us. Most of you know of the dilemma concerning making the public aware of the bomb threat that we face. Yesterday I had a telephone conversation with the British Prime Minister and we agreed on a joint strategy to deal with it. Just before I came to this meeting my office received a coded telephone call warning us that unless we withdrew all our forces from the Gulf, including Kuwait, within two weeks and release all Iraqi prisoners, a nuclear bomb would be detonated in an American city. I have just been told it came from the border area between Pakistan and Afghanistan where we know Bin Laden and his cohorts are hiding but the language was Western in style. This is the first time we have had confirmation from our intelligence about the bomb threat. I know most of you have been searching for the terrorists and the bomb which we believe is in the New York area. This confirmation places us in an insidious position. As President, I have an obligation to protect and inform the American people. We do not know for sure which city is being targeted or exactly when the terrorists will commit the act. At the present time, evacuation is not an option. If a public announcement is made then panic will break out. You can guess the consequences. We have decided to wait for a week to give time to find the bomb, before taking a decision on making it public but evacuation plans have been made and all necessary steps taken to remove vital assets from the New York area.

This latest information has been sent to the Prime Minister but as yet no similar threat has been made directly to the British Government. MI5 have intelligence that suggests London will also be targeted unless we agree to the terrorist demands. The second problem is they may still detonate a bomb in London even if we find the bomb here. In view of this, all the security and military services in our countries have been placed on full alert and emergency powers have been given to them. The most extensive search ever taken is in progress. The Prime Minister and I agreed that meeting the terrorist demands was also not an option. Only a few people in the Cabinet and the top security chiefs know about the atomic bomb. The threat level was raised and a press statement given out about terrorist bomb threats to cities. This has happened many times in Britain so people are used to it. We receive hundreds of such threats every week but most are from deranged people and have little credibility. This one is different and deadly serious because we believe the terrorists here have an old atom bomb that was stolen from Los Alamos in 1945. An enquiry into the circumstances surrounding this is underway. In view of the latest information I have convened an emergency meeting of the military chiefs so please excuse me at this time. The Vice President will continue with the briefing.' He then abruptly left the room so avoiding any questions.

Alicia and Gary looked at me and smiled. The Vice President took over the meeting. Before he could speak, I asked,

'Do we know with absolute certainty the call came from Al-Qaeda?' The Head of National Security looked at me with a frown and stepped in with a reply before the Vice President could speak.

'We have been tracking these bastards for months. Who else would want to attack America in this way?'

I replied, 'We have had success in identifying the leading members of a global organisation know as The New Order who we believe are involved in some way with the bomb threats. Their motives will be different to that of terrorists but are equally dangerous.'

I could see John Henning looking at me in a disdainful way. Was I raising something that he had not yet been briefed on? Henning caught the Vice President's eye.

'Mr Vice President, Has Mr Cane and the CIA shared this knowledge about The New Order with the British team? It's the first time I've heard about it.' Alicia stepped in to confront the arrogant Englishman.

'It was only late yesterday that, with the invaluable help of David Simons and Paul Cane, we discovered the codenames of the leaders of this New Order organisation. We need to verify their actual names before a full report can be made.'

She knew the Vice President already had the information in his possession since she had called him the day before but she said it to placate Henning. He seemed even more obnoxious than he was back at Oxford. I recalled what David had said and wondered what he would report back to London. We both believed MI5 knew more than they were revealing or probably had made known to Henning.

Alicia gave her report on what we knew so far about the bomb and its likely whereabouts. She omitted to say that David Simons and I were going on a bomb reconnoitre to New York the next day.

Adams asked, 'Are we likely to find the bomb within the deadline?'

Alicia replied, 'We have to be careful not to alert the terrorists otherwise they may move the bomb to another location. Our intelligence (she meant David Simons' prognosis) suggests the weapon could have been upgraded to be a thermonuclear bomb many hundreds of times more powerful than the Nagasaki bomb on which the original design was based.' Adams looked more worried.

'Agent Garcia,' he repeated, 'You haven't answered my question. Will the bomb be found within the deadline?'

All eyes were on Alicia. For the first time this hardened agent looked uneasy. Adams clearly wanted to shift the blame to the CIA. Suspecting her boss had already answered that question and knowing the two men hated each other, she put her neck into the noose Adams had cleverly made for her and said, 'It's very likely but I cannot guarantee it.'

'You had better do more than that Agent Garcia since millions of American lives depend on your success,' he said in a loud voice. I saw his secretary frantically typing away. I knew it wouldn't be edited out of the minutes.

Alicia came straight back at him, 'Can I assume, Mr Vice President, that the President will be ordering an evacuation of New York if we don't find the bomb?'

'No, you cannot make that assumption. Do you realise what an evacuation will mean when we have no firm knowledge of where and when the bomb will be exploded? The President is at this moment conferring with the military to draw up contingency plans. We must find these bastards and nail them to the wall. Do you have all the resources you need, Agent Garcia?'

She answered, 'Yes.'

I looked at Henning who had raised the issue of the exchange of intelligence on terrorist cells and knowledge about The New Order between the two Governments.

'It seems to me, Mr Vice President, it was agreed that I join this Task Force by the British Government who knew much more than I did about the activities of The New Order and their possible involvement with Al-Qaeda. Can I ask John if he has been fully briefed by his masters at MI5 about The New Order?'

Henning looked angrily at me.

'Can I remind Mr Cane that since I am the official MI5 liaison officer to this Task Force I am fully briefed on all the intelligence. We have the known members of The New Order and Al-Qaeda suspects under surveillance. I need to be updated on any recent information since London is on red alert. So far the public have been made aware of terrorist bomb threats but not related to any atomic bomb.'

Adams told us that in America two Al-Qaeda cells were being tracked by the FBI but it was likely that those in possession of the bomb were unknown people since Al-Qaeda seemed to be receiving inside intelligence information.

Henning said, 'We have some agents working inside terrorist cells but so far nothing has been reported about bomb targets in London. All places of entry are being closely watched since we believe they may be bringing a suitcase bomb into the country. During the Cold War a range of such atomic bombs were designed. Our scientists developed an effective detection system back in the 1960s for use at airports. These are now being deployed but parts can be brought into the country in a variety of disguises so the task of detection is still challenging.'

I hadn't considered suitcase bombs since we were focused on the stolen bomb which would be quite large in comparison. I could see that Adams was anxious to conclude the meeting. It was obvious he was not revealing everything he knew. I wondered if the Vice President and the President had different agendas. I suspected the real action was taking place in another part of the White House at the President's meeting with the military chiefs.

David Simons had been quiet during the meeting but I could

see he wanted to say something to the Vice President. Adams was about to conclude the briefing when David raised his hand.

'Mr Vice President, can I assume you are aware that if the bomb has been upgraded to a thermonuclear weapon or an H-bomb and is detonated in New York then Washington will be within an area of some destruction?'

I could see that Adams was visible shaken by that announcement. Clearly that had not been factored into the plan. Not wishing to show ignorance he said, 'Yes, Professor, we have a contingency plan to allow for the evacuation of the Capital should it be required.'

It was obvious to David and me that no such plan had been made. In fact I didn't believe evacuation was on the agenda. Where would people go? During the Cold War many underground shelters had been built and equipped to allow Government to continue but the majority of the population could not be catered for in such an event. Adams, looking even more disturbed than he did at the start, thanked everybody and closed the meeting.

After the meeting, Henning came to me and apologised for the deception in St James' Park but told me he was under orders. MI5 knew about my visit to Kuwait and my problem with the police. They had in fact helped to get me released and sent back to London. It was only later Henning found out from his masters about Henry Fellows' memoires. He pulled me into the corner out of earshot of the others to say, 'London wants you back to help them. The political situation is deteriorating because the public is losing confidence in the Government's ability to protect it. The soft approach of the Labour Government towards immigration is being exploited by the right-wing parties led by Diane Hunter's National Party. She is being watched. We have known for some time that she is a leading member of The New Order but she has some high level protection. But so far there is no evidence that she, or her party, is connected to the bomb threats.'

I told him we believed she was behind the murders of Henry Fellows and Ruth Goodman since the FBI had monitored the phone calls she had made to a Russian named Leon Seperkov, who ran a Mafia group. He knew about the Russian assassin who was sent to kill David Simons and shot in Tucson. I didn't reveal the events that took place in Martha's Vineyard. I told him it was my intention to return to England before Christmas since most of my work there was done. From the look on his face that pleased him, since he clearly wanted to be the only British representative involved. His demeanour changed when I told him that Robert was based in Washington and would continue to help the CIA and FBI.

I asked David Simons to come to my safe house later to plan our strategy for our visit to New York and to meet Valerie. He agreed but suggested we first discuss it with Alicia and Gary but at this stage not include Henning and Robert. The fewer people who knew, the less likely information would leak out.

Henning looked suspiciously at us talking. I was curious about what he would be reporting to his MI5 masters. Knowing they wanted me back in England would help me extricate myself and Valerie from our present situation. But it would have to be agreed between the President and Prime Minister since full protection would be required before and during travel. It was doubtful we would be permitted to use commercial airlines.

After lunch at the White House we were driven back to our respective houses. It was mid-afternoon when we arrived back at my house. Alicia, Gary and David came with me so we could discuss our search plan in New York. It was agreed that David and I would arrange to talk to the owners of the warehouse on the pretext that we urgently required storage space for some equipment being delivered for use in a harbour maintenance programme. Our guise would be Government inspectors from the Department of the Environment who were checking out the security of the building. We would search for signs of the presence of radioactive material using sensitive instruments, particularly in the refurbished basement. Inspecting their records for previous material stored in the warehouse should show us the existence of such material. It was impossible to hide or store and work on a nuclear bomb without leaving traces since special facilities would be required. Alicia had already arranged, with some difficulty because of the time of the year, for us to meet with the manager in the building. He was curious why it was so urgent to carry out an inspection just before Christmas so was told that urgent work had to be started in the holiday week to minimise disruption to the port. Companies did not want to upset Government officials for fear of losing the licences to operate in the port area so tended to be conciliatory to requests.

Gary suggested that one of his agents drove us to New York to provide protection and any assistance that we might need. If we found any evidence of the bomb having been in the building then a full scale search of the surrounding area would be made by the FBI and police. David was still concerned that the terrorists could remotely detonate the bomb if they knew we had discovered it, so absolute secrecy was paramount. It was likely the bomb had now been moved to another location. Arrangements were made to collect David and me at nine o'clock in the morning for the drive to New York.

Alicia checked my cell phone and gave me a new Glock pistol with her compliments. Before leaving, she warned me to avoid using it unless it was absolutely necessary as I might not be so lucky next time I engaged with a professional gunman.

Just after my associates left the house I had a call from Valerie to say she was on her way back from the office. I raided the refrigerator and prepared some steaks for the grill and extracted two bottles of wine. I was beginning to enjoy having a woman to share my life. It seemed like I had known her for years instead of just a matter of days.

I switched on the TV in time to see CNN news. The main feature was that terrorist threat level had been raised. Further attacks on American property in the Middle East were expected. Someone was leaking information to the media and it was affecting the Stock Market. Wall Street was seeing millions of dollars being wiped off the shares of major enterprises at a time when people were withdrawing money for Christmas celebrations and presents. Christmas celebrations were in progress in all the major cities, particularly New York and Washington so the bomb threats were not deterring people. TV news commentators were more concerned with the winter weather affecting travel than terrorist bomb threats. This would please the President because if people started a more than usual exit from New York it could grow into a panic move.

Valerie arrived back to the house with Chloe Rogers. The two women agreed to meet the next day. Alicia still believed we needed protection. Displaying a worried look, I knew Valerie had something to tell me. She produced a letter from her brief case.

'This was given to me by special courier this morning. He tried to deliver it while I was away so had to keep it until today. It's from Alan Sherman,' she said, handing it to me.

> *Dear Valerie*
> *I returned to the flat earlier than planned and found your note. After all I had done for you and what we shared I was very disappointed that you chose to end our relationship by going away with an Englishman. Yes, I discovered you did not go back to England but flew your plane to Martha's Vineyard.*
> *As you know, I am running a campaign for the party nomination and cannot afford any scandal so was going to end our relationship anyway. But I want you to promise not to reveal it to anyone. In your own interests I advise you to leave America and return to England immediately. I wish you well and am sorry that things had to end this way.*
> *Fondest wishes*
> *Alan*

Sherman obviously knew more about our movements than we believed. The question was, since he knew about Martha's Vineyard did he conspire in the attempt to kill us? He was clearly worried about Valerie revealing their relationship. How did he know about me? The tone of the letter implied a threat to Valerie. It was difficult to believe that he would be part of an Al-Qaeda threat to blow up New York, particularly since his family lived at the Hamptons on Long Island. Perhaps Alicia and Gary might know more from their intelligence reports.

Seeing that Valerie was still upset I took her in my arms and said, 'It doesn't matter now because as soon as I return from New York, we will go to England.' I told her about John Henning and the British Government's request for me to help them. She tightened her arms around me and sobbed.

'But remember London is also threatened and we don't know the progress the intelligence services have made in finding the terrorists and any bomb.'

'I know we will be together but am very worried about what you might discover in New York. You could be in danger if you find the bomb or the terrorists,' she said in a soft voice.

'David and I will have an armed agent with us and I will have my new Glock pistol,' I replied.

'That's what worries me because I know you will use it,' she said.

'My pistol did save our lives at Martha's,' I hastily added.

She was not convinced but my intent to go to England did help to console her. I added, 'Alicia will have to obtain Presidential approval for us to leave Washington. As it's Christmas, most of the Government employees would be going away on holiday so we shouldn't have a problem. But, because of my membership of the Task Force and involvement in Whirlwind, I may not be allowed to leave unless the British Government make a formal request and we make progress in finding the New York bomb.'

A burning smell sharply interrupted our conversation. I rushed to save the steaks blackening on the grill and my reputation as a cook by extracting them from the heat before total destruction. Fortunately, we both liked our steaks well-done. Valerie was amused and it seemed to take her mind off the problems facing us. I was happy to have a woman to share my life. For now it was all that really mattered to me. My mind was pre-occupied with escaping with her to a safe haven in England. I started to wonder how I let myself become involved in this millennium conspiracy. There were many things about the validity of the bomb threats that didn't make sense and gave me cause for concern. I was hoping our visit to the warehouse in New York might yield more information and answer some of the questions that needed to be answered.

Alicia called me to say an FBI car driven by one of their agents would pick up David and then me at seven o'clock in the morning. She had cleared our New York visit with her boss. He insisted, however, that we did nothing to raise suspicions and took no actions without FBI approval. David had all the necessary briefing notes and information on the warehouse.

Valerie was still in bed asleep when I got up, showered and dressed. When I finished she had already arisen and prepared breakfast. I discreetly placed the Glock pistol in its holster which fitted snugly inside my suit jacket but she saw it and gave me one of her worrying looks. In the other pocket I clipped my cell phone. These were my protection. I also still had the emergency shirt button Gary had given me.

After breakfast, the car arrived at the house. It was about ten minutes early. I gave Valerie a kiss and told her I would call when I arrived in New York. The black Ford saloon had darkened windows so it wasn't until I opened the rear door that I noticed there were two men in the front and David Simons was sitting on the rear seat. His facial expression displayed a worried look. The two men in the front introduced themselves as John and Andy. Both were well-built men and looked typically like FBI agents. Little more was said as the car sped off in the direction of the Interstate 95. David was clutching a briefcase that I assumed contained the notes Alicia mentioned. He was tense and I wondered why. At first we exchanged small talk being careful to avoid discussing the purpose of our journey. As we drove out of Washington, a flurry of snowflakes blew across the car windscreen. The air-conditioned car gave us a false sense of warmth. I hoped bad weather would not impede our journey since I was keen to carry out the search and get back to Washington.

Valerie had just cleared away breakfast and started to dress when the phone rang. It was Alicia.

'Has Paul left yet?' she asked.

'Yes, the car arrived ten minutes ago,' replied Valerie.

'That's strange, Agent Mallory was supposed to call me when they were about to leave. He didn't make the call and his cell phone is switched off. Did he come into the house?' asked Alicia.

'No, he didn't. Paul went to the car when it arrived. I think there were two men in the front,' replied Valerie.

There was a pause before Alicia continued. 'There was supposed to be only one agent who was also the driver. Are you certain there were two men?'

'Not absolutely, because the car had darkened windows,' said Valerie.

Valerie began to feel sick, sensing an anxiety in Alicia's voice.

'Right, I will call Paul and ask him about the driver. Stay on the line,' she said.

Alicia, suspecting something had happened, decided first to call the Langley control centre since they were able to track the car and its occupants. The car was showing up on their monitor as being en route but Agent Mallory's cell phone was not active. Paul Cane's phone was on so she sent him a text so the car driver wouldn't see it.

I felt the vibrator on my phone and looked at the screen as the text came in.

'*Warning. Suspect driver is not one of our agents. Is there a second person in the car other than David Simons?*'

I noticed the driver looking at me through the rear facing mirror. He must have seen the cell phone in my hand.

I quickly typed, *two tall men in front seats, names unknown. Not speaking. Acting suspiciously.* I pressed the 'Send' button just before the car was suddenly driven onto a side the road and stopped. The two men got out of the car, pulled out guns and asked us to step out of the car.

My worst fears were realised. We had fallen into the hands of our enemies. Were we about to be killed? The taller of the two men pointed his gun at me and demanded that I hand him my cell phone and any weapons.

I didn't immediately respond. Rather than submit I went on

the attack. 'Who are you? Where is our driver? What do you want?' I shouted.

With a gun held to his head, David had already handed over his phone to the other man. Being older he was not prepared to challenge our captors.

'We don't answer questions. You will do as we say if you want to stay alive,' said the taller man.

I did find a modicum of comfort in his reply. It didn't look like we were about to be shot. They would have already done that if it was their orders. I handed over my phone and gun, knowing that Alicia would already be responding to my reply to her question. I still had the emergency button on my shirt to activate if necessary.

Back at Langley all hell had broken loose. Who were the men who had stolen the FBI car? Where was agent Mallory? An armed team was already aboard a helicopter awaiting orders. Another arrived at Mallory's flat to find the agent bound and gagged and tied to a chair. The car was observed to be stationary on a minor road three miles from the Interstate 95. The signals from my and David's phones had stopped. Alicia needed to know what the abductors wanted before taking any action which could put David's and my life in danger.

She sent a text to C5. *Desperate situation. Suspect enemy have abducted Paul Cane and David Simons from their FBI car on their way to New York for bomb search. Take affirmative action. Location can be seen on map being sent to your PDA.*

It was a last resort but she knew C5 had his own way of dealing with situations which would not involve other people. It was vital our mission was kept secret so the situation had to be dealt with without involving a lot of people. If a swat team was sent to rescue us, questions would be asked which could jeopardise the mission.

C5 quickly acknowledged and agreed to take immediate action. It gave Alicia some relief but she still wanted to identify the abductors and for whom they worked. Knowing how C5 operated that might not be possible.

Agent Mallory was questioned. Two men had ambushed him

outside his flat just as he opened the door to the car. They forced him at gunpoint back into the flat, tied him up in a cupboard and then stole his phone and car. But they did not harm him or conceal their faces. Alicia was perplexed and wondered how they knew that Mallory was driving Simons and me to New York. Another person in the Agency must be responsible. She knew everyone who was present when the trip was discussed so it should be possible to identify the culprit.

The two men looked nervously at each other as a black Mercedes, which seemed to appear from nowhere, screeched to an abrupt stop a few yards away. The driver, a well-dressed man in his fifties emerged, and spoke a few words to our abductors in what sounded like Russian.

The two men then prodded us to get into the Mercedes. It was a later model to the one I possessed and had many more accessories like a radio transmitter, a fitted telephone and a satellite navigator which were only fitted on special demand top-of-the range cars as the new technology was only available to certain privileged customers. These people were not terrorists or common criminals. They acted more like security agents. It confirmed my suspicions that we had been abducted by The New Order.

I stepped aside, demanding to know who he was and what he wanted. The new man, staring at me with his deep blue eyes produced a hint of a smile and said in perfect English, 'All in good time. If you do exactly what I ask then no harm will come to you.'

Now feeling less afraid, I blurted out, 'That's not good enough; I want answers before we get in that car.'

For a moment I thought I saw concern in the man's face when he looked at the other men.

With a more demanding voice which sounded like someone who had been in the military, he said, 'I will answer questions only when you get into the back seat of the Mercedes.'

David started to walk to the car and I followed. The other two men looked up as if expecting someone to drop out of the sky to rescue them. I knew it wouldn't be long before a swat team would arrive. Alicia would have easily tracked the car to the location.

These men were professionals and knew exactly what the FBI would do.

I knew Alicia would not want to involve too many people at this time and would be looking for an alternative *modus operandi*. As requested, we got into the Mercedes. It was a new car; the seats gave it away. I memorised the number plate and searched for any giveaway signs of ownership but nothing obvious showed. The tall man pushed himself into the driving seat, turned to us and in what sounded like an Eastern European accent said,

'If you want to find the bomb you must come with me. If you try to escape or if I'm tracked by the FBI then I won't be able to help and you will not find it. You may not believe me but we are on the same side. We are not terrorists. If we were, you would have been shot.'

I stared back at him and asked, 'Who do you represent?'

'I cannot tell you but we must go now as time is short if we are to prevent a disaster.'

The car sped off in the direction of the Interstate 95 to New York leaving the other two men behind. We had only gone a few miles when I heard a bang and saw flames rising from the area we had just left. It looked like they had blown up the FBI car. The distant sound of a helicopter could be heard. The operation had been meticulously planned. But it wasn't a swat team coming to rescue us. Alicia would have noticed the absence of a signal and would now be trying to find a tracking satellite. We didn't have our cell phones so there was no way of sending her a message. If he was genuine, this man was now our hope of finding the bomb. The danger now was the FBI stopping him before we arrived at New York. The car accelerated and was now speeding at nearly 100 mph but the driver was careful to slow down on approaching the Interstate where police would be monitoring speeding cars.

David had been very quiet but like me now believed this man was a member of The New Order who was now playing out its final game plan. One thing was clear, there was a bomb in New York and terrorists were going to detonate it. The big questions were when and where? Hopefully we were about to find out.

I did have my emergency button, which if activated would locate my exact position but I would reserve that option until we reached the New York site.

Alicia and Gary back at Langley saw the screen in front of them go blank and knew that something bad had happened. Alicia ordered a satellite feed but it would be at least thirty minutes before one would be in the right position. She called up the Vice President and briefed him on the situation. She then remembered to update C5. He was travelling on I 95 from New York but had no trace yet on the car in which Simons and I were travelling.

CHAPTER 13

New York
20 December 1999

Niagara Falls

Mohammed Khan, Ahmed Fazi and Vladimir Koslov sat quietly in the back of the truck as it edged its way slowly in the queue waiting to cross over the Rainbow Bridge, linking Canada with America at Niagara Falls. Farah Bell, the leader, confidently drove forward as she had done many times before. She and her companions worked at the Crowne Plaza Hotel and were well-known to the border guards. They were all Canadian citizens but Farah also had an American passport since her late father was American. The others were from Pakistan and Russia but had lived and worked in Canada and America since they were teenagers. There was a daily movement of people across the border to work in the hotels and businesses. The Americans paid better rates above the minimum wage. Miriam was well educated and worked as a deputy service manager.

The two Pakistani men served in the kitchen and Vladimir was the maintenance engineer who looked after the heating and ventilation systems at the hotel. They were actually an Al-Qaeda sleeper cell. Their handler lived and operated in Buffalo on the American side of the border but his name was unknown to them. There was a long-established cell in that city. It was formed by Abul Ala Mawdudi as a sister organisation to the Muslim Brotherhood in Pakistan but he died in 1979 in that city. It was he and others who laid the foundations to the violence that eventually led to the conflicts in Iraq and Iran. The revolution in Iran in 1979, like the French revolution in 1789, became a template for Islamic advance. It was encouraged by the Communist Soviet Union and other socialist regimes. Iran was rich in oil so up until the time of the revolution, money flowed into the accounts of the powerful oil companies and the governments who supported them. Multi-nationals had a vested interest in supporting any political regime if it made them money. Even fundamentalist ones needed to sell their assets to acquire wealth. Iran and Iraq were no exceptions. Iran knew it could hold the West to ransom. It now dominated the seaways in the Persian Gulf and had the ability to stop the export of half the world's oil. This alone prevented any American attack. If the giant wells in Saudi Arabia were destroyed then oil would have to be rationed with disastrous economic consequences for that country and the West.

Farah knew her instructions would come through contacts posing as tourists staying at the hotel. All they knew was the day would come soon when they would be expected to serve Allah in a great event. Nobody had any idea what the event was or when it would take place.

Al-Qaeda cells were made up mainly of US-born Muslims, young male Muslims from Pakistan, the Persian Gulf states, Yemen, Somalia and Indonesia. Deeply entrenched in their communities, working or running small businesses that were covers for their terrorist activities. The FBI knew many but resource limitations made it impossible to watch everybody all the time. In 1995 Abu Moussa Marzook was caught at Kennedy Airport only because he was on an alert list of a money laundering operation for Hamas worth $10 million. His personal telephone directory contained the names of many top terrorists of which 20% were contacts in America. It led to the capture of an engineering professor at the University of Florida who was the sleeping head of an Islamic Jihad group.

Farah and her friends had been checked out a number of times by the FBI but nothing was found to link them to any terrorist group. None of them had ever been to the Middle East, but they were anti-Jewish and hated America for its support of Israel and the attack on Iraq which they saw as an attack on Islam. The men went regularly to their mosques and were indoctrinated by the extremists.

This indoctrination converted many of their brothers. Farah's mother was a Palestinian who had met and married a US soldier who brought her to America. Her grandparents had been killed by a reprisal Israeli air strike on their village at which a Hamas group had set up a rocket firing site. Joining the cell was her way of avenging their deaths. She was not a fundamentalist like the others and was only accepted as their leader because she did not arouse suspicions. The group had been waiting for their instructions. Then, in early December they came. A handwritten letter addressed to Farah told her and the team to go to addresses in New York. They would be contacted and given further instructions.

Members gave short notices to the hotel that they were leaving. Farah was the last to resign. The hotel management was used to a regular turnover of staff but four people who were known to travel together, did raise some suspicions, particularly since they were of foreign origin. Farah had an American passport so was able to enter the country easily but her colleagues, having left their jobs and wanting to stay in America, did not cross the border back into Canada. Three were illegal immigrants so had to avoid contact with the police. New York is a very cosmopolitan city so they would not look out of place in the city. Accommodation was arranged for the three men in a back street basement flat looking over the River Hudson. Farah would be located in a bed and breakfast hotel near the river waterfront.

Their mission would be to provide support to two nuclear experts who had been working on a bomb for months in an improvised basement room in a warehouse on the Hudson River. The specially equipped room had access to a waterway wide enough to accommodate a large barge. Except for the river access there was only one entry point into the room. The company who owned the warehouse was told that sensitive marine environmental equipment, the property of the Government, was to be set up and tested for a new harbour project to be started early the following year. They wanted limited access for safety and security reasons. The door to the room would always be locked and entry limited to two designated people. Over a period, bomb parts were delivered at night so nobody could observe them. A special shipping container was ordered to accommodate the bomb and the high explosive material that would be packed around the nuclear core. A standard container on a barge, a common sight in the dock areas, would not look out of place.

None of the cell members had any of the specialised experience required to prepare and assemble the bomb so their job was to provide manual support, provide security and assist in transporting the bomb to the dockside site. The Pakistani scientists in charge would make all the decisions.

Farah and her members were only told in early December about the nature of the bomb and the plan to obliterate New York and its inhabitants. They were given the choice of being martyrs and dying with the bomb or leaving the area. What they didn't know was that no cell member would be allowed to leave alive anyway. The young cell leader's desire to kill Americans began to wane when she realised the enormity of what was being planned. This act would start another war with devastating consequences for everybody. She didn't want to be part of it and made the fatal mistake of telling that to her cell members. Unlike her, they were enthusiastic at being martyred for such an historic event but when they learned of her decision and lack of commitment they knew what had to be done. She knew too much so they were left with only one choice. The cause was greater than any person. Farah became just another daily statistic in the bodies taken out of the Hudson River. Her badly mutilated body made identification difficult but DNA samples were taken and stored. The police assumed she was just another victim of gang violence since there was evidence of gang rape. Her cell members had to give the police what they expected even though they hated doing it.

New York

It was a cold, bright sunny day with a cloudless sky as the Manhattan skyline just appeared on the horizon when the Mercedes left the interstate and proceeded onto the New Jersey Turnpike crossing over Newark Bay. The World Trade Towers, just visible on the south side, rose like sentinels above the city. They were the symbols of the global market and commercial power of America. The car then took a left turn onto a minor road, near what looked like a container storage area. Beyond was New York harbour with its busy shipping lane. To the north lay Liberty Island with its famous Statue of Liberty. The terrorists had certainly chosen a symbolic site for their attack. Our driver stopped the car in a yard. He then turned to us and said,

'This is where I leave you. You will find the bomb in a container numbered 66 sitting on a barge tethered to a jetty on the dockside. It was loaded last week from a warehouse situated close to the water's edge on an inlet to Newark Bay a few miles from here. Beware, as far as I know it is primed to be detonated remotely. Someone closeby will send a signal at an appointed time probably within the next week, exactly when I do not know. If the Jihadists see anyone approaching the container they may detonate it immediately. They could be watching us now, although I doubt it. Go under the cover of darkness into the container to verify what I am telling you. You will need to find a way in since such containers are designed for loading onto large container ships like the one you can see over on the left, so it will be well-sealed. The door could be booby-trapped so be careful. Dr Simons will know what to do once you find the bomb. I know your intention is to keep this operation secret but if you don't succeed in de-arming the bomb the whole world will know.

Finally, I will answer some of the questions that I know you want to ask. This has been planned by Al-Qaeda since the failed attempt to blow up the World Trade Centre in February 1993. The nuclear bomb in the container is a modified version of the one stolen from Los Alamos in 1945. It was stored away in a mine in New Mexico for many decades because those who stole it were all killed. Its location was passed onto a Russian agent, who, after the collapse of the Soviet Union, sold it to an Eastern European gang who hawked it about to find the highest bidder. Nobody would touch it fearing it was an American set-up. It had to wait until Al-

Qaeda, formed by Bin Laden, the Saudi multi-millionaire learned of its existence. He eventually provided the $5 million to purchase it from the gang. We know the name of the man who negotiated the sale of the bomb. He tried to escape with all the money but his associates found out and killed him. What happened to the money is still a mystery. We think most of the people who knew about this sale and the existence of the bomb have now been eliminated, but that is not certain.

We know that Al-Qaeda recruited some expert nuclear scientists from Pakistan to help them re-build the bomb using the latest technology. It was Bin Laden's secret weapon to destroy Christian America. My organisation found out about his plan last year and decided to exploit the situation but ensure the bomb was found and destroyed before it could be used and those responsible eliminated. We did not want New York or any US city destroyed. The current US President and his Government are seen by the Islamists as weak and after the invasion of Iraq and the continued support for Israel, they believed the time was right to strike. We saw this as an opportunity to bring about a change in the White House and a change in the Government.'

I interrupted him.

'Do you really believe that risking the lives of millions of your own people and starting a world war is the right way to achieve your aims?'

He snapped back. 'Al-Qaeda has to be defeated and when the world knows what they have been able to set up here under the noses of the Government, the FBI and CIA, there will be a public outrage and a real war against them will be started. At present Bin Laden's group are admired and supported by extremists in Pakistan, Afghanistan and elsewhere. The West has to take a stand and stop them.

I am sorry I can't help you further but the ball is now in your court. I am giving you back your cell phones but remember what I said. A wrong move could set off the bomb. The narrow-minded, brain-washed people hiding nearby want to be martyrs. They don't have Western morals about mass murder.'

He got back in the car and left us standing helpless a few yards away from Armageddon. Both David and I were speechless on what had just been delivered to us. My first action was to call Alicia. She answered immediately.

'David and I are in Newark, near the Hudson River in a container yard. The man who brought us here has just left. He told us the bomb is inside a container mounted on a barge at a jetty close to us. It is armed and can be detonated remotely.'

She said, 'Do you believe him?'

I said, 'Yes.'

She continued. 'We have tracked you and the car on a satellite link. Someone is pursuing the car to see where it leads. Can you describe the man?'

'Yes. He was about six feet tall with a dark complexion and spoke with a slight East European accent, but was an American. He knew everything about us, Al-Qaeda's plan to blow up New York with a nuclear bomb, the history of the bomb's disappearance from Los Alamos and most important, the exact location of the bomb. He must have had a good intelligence network to do what he and his friends did. He was certainly well-informed and spoke more like a statesman than a criminal. David is certain he is a member of The New Order since he revealed their plan to bring down the President and the Government. That seems to be their motivation for not revealing the terrorists' plot until now. But there may be other reasons than just political ones.'

Alicia said, 'Yes, there are. Can you hold the line open while I call the President?'

I could hear a lot of excited talk going on in the background.

'The President and Vice President, the CIA and FBI Directors have been informed. They still want to keep the mission secret and beat The New Order's intention to bring the President down so I am going to put in place the following action plan. An armed team will be sent immediately with some nuclear experts. They will arrive in darkness and assemble some distance away from the yard. An extensive search is being made for the members of a suspected

Al-Qaeda cell that is operating in the area; they travelled from Niagara some weeks ago. We are also watching closely the movements of a nuclear specialist from MIT who is known to have Islamic fundamentalist sympathies and visited Pakistan twice in the last year. He recently had telephone calls from that country. The man had been an associate of Abdul Qadeer Khan, the controversial Pakistan nuclear bomb expert who gave Iran and North Korea essential know-how for the nuclear weapons' programme. We think he could be the expert the terrorists are using. Others are also likely to be involved. A bomb project of this magnitude would require an expert team.

Keep the barge under observation until the team reaches you after dark but don't do anything that can put yourselves or the mission at risk. We are putting radio jamming equipment in place to prevent any signal reaching the bomb. The President is adamant about not informing local police about what is happening. Our own FBI agents will carry out the work. The fewer people who know about Whirlwind the more secure it will be.'

C5 had the satellite feed displayed on a screen in his SUV and was discreetly following the Mercedes across New York and onto Long Island. Alicia had fully briefed him about the discovery of the bomb's location and mine and Simons' situation. He wanted to know who the stranger was and his associates. Alicia gave him my description.

The Mercedes pulled up at a large house in the Hamptons in the east end of Long Island. It's an exclusive area where most of the notable celebrities and millionaires have homes. C5 parked some distance away but used his long range video camera lens to observe the man's movements. The Hamptons was also where Alan Sherman lived but he had already left to holiday with his family in the warmer climate of Florida where he had a house. The car's number plate was noted and sent to the FBI. It came back as not known. He would wait and observe.

It was very late in the afternoon. Darkness started to envelope New York. Fortunately, although cold, the weather was fine and the expected snow which often falls, giving New Yorkers a white Christmas, had yet to materialise.

David and I registered at a small local hotel and so had a room for the night. The proprietor was suspicious of two well-dressed strangers arriving without suitcases and a car. We were fearful that he might call the local police, something we didn't need.

Alicia called me at one o'clock in the morning to say that a special forces team had landed about a mile away under the command of a Major Buchannan Jones, known affectionately as 'Buck' by his men. She told us to meet up with them at a warehouse just a few hundred metres away from the container yard. On entering, we were confronted by a small army of men in camouflaged uniforms and armed like they were going into battle. On seeing us, one of their number approached with his FK7 in a firing position. I quickly raised my hand and said, 'Paul Cane and David Simons'

He beckoned us to follow him to a corner of the building. In an authoritative manner he said, 'We have secured a one mile perimeter around the barge so no one can approach it. My orders are to accompany Dr Simons into the container to verify the existence of the bomb then our expert team will disarm it.' I noticed that I was not included.

Noticing my disappointed look, he added, 'Mr Cane, you will stay with the team and help with communications. The President has ordered that owing to his specialised knowledge, Dr Simons will go into the container escorted by my men. Any actions will be ordered by the President. We have set up a direct and secure video link to the White House where the Directors of the FBI and CIA and Security Chiefs will be watching.'

David was looking worried and said, 'How do we know the terrorists will not be watching us and detonate the bomb?'

Jones replied, 'At this moment my men are searching a one-mile area around the dock. There is no direct line of sight but we cannot be absolutely certain that they don't have a distant observer.'

I heard a phone ring. Jones answered.

'Alpha One,' he whispered softly.

I saw his expression harden.

'Red Alert,' he cried out to his men. Others on the line would have also heard the command. I could hear a lot of shouting and the sound of distant shots in his earpiece. Whatever was going on stimulated everybody into action. Jones told us to stay put and went out of the building. My cell phone rang.

'Paul, its Alicia. Tell David to activate his cell phone so he can also hear what I have to say. We intercepted a phone message to a terrorist cell located on a boat close to you. A command was issued to them to detonate the bomb immediately. The receiver of the call was pinpointed to be in a rear cabin. Fortunately, three of the soldiers were about to search the vessel when they received the information in their earpieces. One was able knock down the door to the cabin just in time to shoot a terrorist in the head before he could dial the firing code on his cell phone. Two other terrorists on the boat were also killed in a shoot-out that followed. If you go outside you will see the boat on the quayside opposite the barge. Someone must have known that we had found the bomb so the danger is not over. The container could be booby-trapped. Major Jones and his men will check it out before you go in. Be very careful, David. New York and the lives of millions of US citizens are in your hands.' She terminated the call.

David looked worried. He had been through a lot during his seventy-six years. The man was now being burdened with the fate of his adopted country. He knew more than anyone about the devastation the bomb in the container could bring. He was the only scientist who had witnessed the Trinity bomb explosion; this one could possibly be a thousand times more powerful.

David was kitted up with a nylon and titanium vest, an army jacket and helmet fitted with a video camera. Buck had a bag containing a variety of devices.

I was led to a television monitor and a range of other hi-tech equipment set up on a table in the warehouse. One of Jones' men told me video pictures would be sent back from a camera on the soldier's helmet. Once inside the container they would install portable TV cameras and lighting.

David and four men led by Buck Jones walked cautiously to the container. The night vision cameras sent back incredibly clear pictures. It wasn't certain that all the terrorists had been killed so armed men were posted at key positions. The screen went blank but Buck's voice came over.

'We are entering the container after breaking the two door locks. No indication yet of any booby traps.' An inner steel door confronted the soldiers. Wires emanating from a box fitted above the door could be seen. One of the men scanned it with an instrument. He then melted its contents using a hand-held laser. A dial on the instrument moved to the right. He put up his hand and said, 'It's safe now.'

The door was slowly pushed open to reveal an awesome sight. I had never seen a nuclear bomb but had envisaged a football-sized sphere surrounded by explosive charges. What appeared on the screen was a very large spherical object surrounded by a mass of cables, gas cylinders and instruments. It looked more like a laboratory experiment than a bomb. The whole structure was fitted to a large framework bolted to the floor of the container.

David's voice came over the line. 'As I feared, this is a thermonuclear device or in simple terms, an H-bomb.' He pointed to the sphere and the mass of tubes and cables connected to it.

'Here are the tampers containing the explosive charges and new types of initiators. These are similar to the ones stolen from Halborn back in 1959 and will trigger the fission-fusion process.'

The cameras showed close-ups of the devices. David continued, 'The bomb is a fusion-boosted fission design [5] similar to the one first developed by the Soviets and later by the US in the 1960s. It has a plutonium core with a mixture of tritium and deuterium which fuses to form helium under the high temperature and pressure produced from the primary fission process. The extra neutron yield from the fusion accelerates the fission of the plutonium thus substantially increasing the energy yield of the bomb.

This kind of thermonuclear bomb can produce a yield equivalent to about a megaton of TNT or more. That's enough to remove Manhattan and most of Newark from the face of the Earth.'

A stunned look appeared on the faces of the soldiers around me which would certainly be replicated on those looking in at the White House.

Jones asked, 'How are we going to make the bomb safe?'

'That's not going to be easy,' said David.

He pointed to a digital clock wired into the spherical explosive shell. The twenty-four hour clock showed the exact date and time. It was set to be zero at the end of the year, midnight on 31st of December. The Millennium Doomsday was counting down.

'Fortunately we have time on our side as far as the set point for automatic ignition of the explosives. It's likely the people who built this have made it impossible to change the setting without detonating the bomb so we have to find a way of decoding the mechanism or removing the explosives to prevent implosion of the plutonium core,' said David.

Jones called up his command base. 'We need explosives experts over here immediately.'

It seemed that our problems were just beginning. The only positive thing was that our enemies hadn't planned on us finding the bomb so soon. Time was on our side but the people who assembled the weapon had been experts who anticipated it might be discovered before midnight and probably built-in measures to prevent the bomb from being de-activated.

David continued to examine the bomb and noticed the detonator cables were connected to a box surrounded by sensors making it dangerous to remove or disturb them. It was going to be a long night.

The mile wide exclusion placed around the barge by the Special Forces was beginning to attract local attention. Calls to the police and newspapers were being made about strange happenings on the waterfront. It was four o'clock on a cold morning five days before Christmas. Some New Yorkers were on the move going on holiday completely unaware of the crisis going on just miles from them. The White House knew they needed to act quickly to prevent the public finding out. The President conferred with his advisors and security chiefs. After considering David Simons' comments and the precariousness of the situation they decided the bomb should be moved far away from New York harbour as soon as possible before any de-activation work was started in case it was accidently detonated.

The destroyer USS Kansas was forging its way to Norfolk in heavy seas when Commander Robert Shaw Jr. handed over the watch to his second-in-command, Lieutenant Mark Hamdene, when the bridge's red telephone rang. It was Admiral George Bradley, the Navy Chief. Shaw knew the red phone call meant a serious order usually reserved for war. Various codes were activated then an order was given to proceed at full speed to the jetty in New York harbour to tow a barge to a destination point in the Atlantic Ocean. No reason was given for the order. Kansas altered course but it would take about three hours to reach New York. Fortunately, darkness would be replaced by the light of early dawn over the harbour making navigation easier in the busy harbour. Numerous small boats moved across the river ferrying people and goods during the day.

The President called David personally to inform him of the decision to take the barge and the bomb out into the Atlantic Ocean before work started on de-activating it. I was patched into David's cell phone so heard the President's order. David reacted angrily at the decision being taken without consultation with nuclear experts. He warned the President of the serious implications should the bomb explode on the ocean. The resulting massive tsunami would devastate the East Coast resulting in a loss of life comparable to a detonation in New York harbour. The President and his advisors were still adamant the bomb should be moved.

Clearly the White House considered keeping the existence of the bomb secret was more important than the risks it imposed. David was told that an explosives expert was on the way but because they wanted to limit the number of people involved, asked him if he would stay on board as an advisor to the military team. The seventy-six years old man was very tired and now deeply worried. He was the only nuclear expert available who knew everything about the conspiracy so he was their most valuable asset but, it seemed, also dispensable.

Simons had helped to build the bomb that once again threatened to destroy thousands of people. The long arm of history had reached out to him. He recalled Oppenheimer's words after the detonation of the first atomic bomb 'Now I am become Death, the destroyer of worlds.' It was a saying that had haunted him over the decades. He knew he had no choice; it was now his duty to destroy the bomb and prevent nuclear Armageddon. He recalled why he and Henry Fellows had set up The Brotherhood Foundation. It was to prevent politicians from making decisions on matters of which they had no knowledge and to involve expert scientists. Once again he was now witnessing the very situation he and his colleagues many years ago sought to prevent.

I called David and said, 'You don't have to do this. Let the Government send in their own experts. You have more than done your duty.'

He replied, 'There is no time to brief anyone else and anyway I think I can make the bomb safe with some expert help.'

'But you need some rest,' I said.

'That's not an option at this time,' he replied.

I heard the sound of a helicopter landing nearby. A squad of men in full battledress emerged and ran towards the barge.

Captain John Howard, a Special Forces explosive expert, who had served in Iraq, introduced himself to David. He had armed nuclear weapons and was experienced with the type of explosive charges used. I could see the look of relief on David's face from the camera mounted on the soldier's helmet. They examined the complex structure that lay before them, perhaps momentarily unaware a group of worried people in the White House were also watching.

Dawn was breaking over New York when the destroyer USS Kansas edged its way slowly alongside the barge. Commander Shaw was told there was a large bomb that for safety reasons had to be taken out into the Atlantic Ocean to be diffused. After much discussion, the President ordered the Navy Chief not to disclose the existence of the nuclear bomb to the commander until the ship was out into the Atlantic.

Jones asked for two volunteers from his team of ten men to accompany him on the barge knowing that all would want to go. He selected two who were not married. Manoeuvring the ship in a position to connect a steel tow rope to the barge carrying the container was a difficult task. Those of us left on the jetty watched as the two vessels slid quietly away along the Hudson River towards the ocean.

Alicia called. 'Paul, we want you back in Washington immediately. The helicopter will bring you to the White House. We have all been watching events through the video link in the operations room.'

I was glad to be getting out of New York. As the city lights disappeared into the distance, I visualised people waking up and carrying on with their morning routine, worrying about the traffic problems, the weather, how they were going to find time to do their Christmas shopping. No doubt the morning news might carry an item about some strange activity taking place in the harbour. Hopefully, the security clampdown and removal of the bodies would restrict what any inquisitive reporter might have observed. If the secret leaked out the panic exit from New York was unimaginable.

Back in Washington
19 December

I called Valerie on arrival in Washington but couldn't tell her what had happened in New York, except that everything was OK. It wasn't, but we had found the bomb and removed it from the city so progress had been made. My concern was for David and the awesome responsibility he was landed with by the President who seemed more concerned about his political salvation than the lives of the people involved. Valerie had already called her father in

London and told him she was planning to be back in London before Christmas, even before we had been given permission to leave America. Hopefully, the crisis in America would soon be over but there was still the threat to bomb London and little time left to stop the terrorists. When they discovered what had happened in New York it might make them more determined to be successful in London. I was hoping MI5 and the police had enough intelligence information to prevent the threat from becoming a reality. Very little information on the London threat had been transmitted back to the Task Force. I suspected the exchange of information was limited because of the concern about terrorist moles. Clearly the FBI and CIA still had an unidentified mole who had warned the New York cell members about our presence and who had almost succeeded in detonating the bomb. Alicia and her team would be frantically searching for the person who would have risked their anonymity by making a traceable phone call.

I was taken in an FBI car to the White House and then escorted to an operations room where members of the Task Force, the President, Vice President, their advisors and military chiefs were assembled. A large screen on the wall displayed the inside of the container and the bomb. I could hear the sound of David's voice and some muffled sounds from the others. The ship was only a few miles out into the Atlantic so work had not started on de-activating the bomb. A secure three-way communications link between the destroyer, the container and the White House had been set up. Now at sea, Shaw had been made aware of the cargo he was towing and the implications of failure to de-activate the weapon. He was driving the ship at maximum speed to be as far away from land as possible. If the team could not make the bomb safe it was planned to sink it in the deepest part of the ocean to limit the effect of the explosion. Other navy ships were on the way to establish an exclusion zone around the Kansas. An observer plane sent back a view of the ship and barge leaving a long white trail of surf in the water as they sped out into the choppy winter ocean. The destroyer could only manage about 20 knots with the extra load so it would take about two days to reach its destination. This narrowed the time set on the clock but the greater danger was the rough seas could cause a pre-detonation or the terrorists could send a signal to activate it. This was unlikely without knowing the exact location of the barge; also the electromagnetic screen put up by the escorting ships would prevent any signal from reaching the barge.

I was relieved to be back with my friends in Washington but the events of the past twenty-four hours together with the loss of a night's sleep were taking its toll on my body and mind. Knowing Valerie was close and I would be with her again helped me overcome the fatigue. I noticed the President's worried look as he watched the video coming from the aircraft and the container on the barge. The others in the room displayed similar expressions. Nobody spoke much. It was now a waiting game. America was fighting a secret enemy from within. It was the worst type of enemy because it included Americans who, in positions of trust, were helping Al-Qaeda destroy their own cities. What type of twisted minds these people must possess. I prayed it would be all over before Christmas Eve so Valerie and I could return to London. Alicia had already told me the Prime Minister wanted me back so if Whirlwind came to a successful climax in America we would exchange one crisis for another. I feared for London and was trapped in a situation not of my making but there was no escape, it had to be seen through to the end.

Alicia, Gary and Robert shook my hand and welcomed me back. We all shared concern about David and felt responsible for placing him in such an invidious situation. But he was the only man who could resolve the crisis. Unknown to its citizens the military was on full alert. It was impossible to prevent the media from asking questions and the President was being pressured to make a statement on television. His speech writers had already drafted it. Most of the country was getting ready for Christmas and were not ready to face a crisis but the Administration knew the media would make it one unless satisfactory answers were given, Saying the police and military were on training exercises would not be enough. The existence of a nuclear bomb placed in New York by

Al-Qaeda could not be revealed, particularly when the Government knew about it and failed to inform the public. It was decided that the President would say a high explosive terrorist bomb had been discovered during the night in New York and safely removed. The broadcast would be made live at nine o'clock in the evening

One thing was certain; the day of retribution for those responsible was close. Most of the key perpetrators were known. Their fate was certain. The executioner had been appointed.

It was seven o'clock in the evening when the car took me back to the house. A blurry-eyed Valerie greeted me at the door. She flung her arms around me and held me tight, saying, 'I am so glad you're back. Alicia called to say you and David were safe after the abduction incident in the car and for security reasons you couldn't call me. However, I didn't sleep much last night worrying about what had happened to you in New York.'

'I will tell you everything after a coffee,' I said.

Holding her hand, I told her everything. Once again she looked worried when she knew the man who took David and me to New York was traced to an address in the Hamptons close to where Alan Sherman lived. That irrefutable link made it highly likely he was involved in the conspiracy. It didn't prove he was behind the attempt on our lives in Martha's Vineyard but the association was enough to give concern.

I switched on the television just in time to see the President's statement.

'Many of you will have seen recent media reports about terrorist bomb threats to American cities. The Government has been receiving such threats since the Iraq war and each one is taken seriously and investigated. Last week we received intelligence that a terrorist cell was going to detonate a bomb at a key site in New York. Since we did not know exactly where and when this would happen it was necessary to acquire more information before we could take any affirmative action. I am pleased to tell you that

last night, acting upon information from a reliable source, confirmed by our own FBI; we were able to intercept the members of the cell before they could detonate the bomb. The terrorist suspects were armed and resisted arrest. In an ensuing gun fight they were all shot and killed without police causalities being sustained. The bomb was recovered and removed from the city and is now being made safe.

The prompt action by the FBI and our military has saved the lives of hundreds, maybe thousands of American citizens. I ask each one of you to be vigilant and report any suspicious persons or action since we cannot be sure our enemies will not make further attempts to bring death and destruction to our cities.

I have issued an order to the FBI and all police authorities to step up their surveillance on all suspected terrorist groups to ensure your safety.

I wish you all a Happy Christmas and God Bless America.'

Valerie could see by my facial expression the anguish at hearing the statement. The President had now nailed his political future and that of his Government to a lie. Too many people knew the truth, including our enemies. He had just handed them a victory and played into their hands. The local New York police would be furious when they discovered what had taken place under their noses without having been consulted or asked to be involved. The Mayor of New York and the Senator for the state would be incandescent with rage. I could imagine the heat on the line to the White House.

The truth of the President's statement would be challenged by both his opponents and colleagues so placing him and his ministers on the back foot. He had given the Republicans exactly what they wanted. It would be difficult to prevent the newspapers from publishing the information that they had in their possession. I could only assume the President's advisors were either naive or Republican moles.

Everything now depended on David and the team deactivating and disposing of the bomb in the Atlantic Ocean. Valerie's father had told her that London was on full alert but people were undeterred. Oxford Street was full of Christmas shoppers, traffic as usual blocked all the roads and there was no evidence of large numbers of police. The Prime Minister, in agreement with the President, had not revealed to the public the possibility of a nuclear bomb being planted in the city. But the media had been given more information about the bomb threats and permission to publicise it. After many years of IRA activity the British people were more complacent about bomb threats but strong criticism of the Government's policies prevailed. During the months leading up to Christmas the right-wing parties had taken advantage of the situation and organised protest marches. No doubt Diane Hunter's party would be leading these if what we believed about her being a leading member of The New Order was true. She was certainly on MI5's watch list.

Valerie told her father about me without saying too much about my activities. She had advised him and his wife to move out of London. Being curious, her father was asking lots of questions but not getting satisfactory answers. He still had friends and contacts in the Diplomatic Service so would be trying to find more from them.

After the President's announcement, I went back to bed and slept well into the afternoon only to be woken up by my cell phone. It was Alicia, calling from Langley. A television link had been set up from the container on the barge to Langley with a connection to the White House. It was a highly encrypted channel so nobody could pick it up.

Alicia said, 'I know you must be tired but David and his team are about to start work on the bomb. They are some miles away from the deepest part of the ocean but he feels confident he can make it safe. If you wish to come to Langley I will send a car to pick you up.' I had to watch this final act, so said, 'Yes.'

I could see Valerie looking at me but she said little as I got dressed. I hugged and kissed her saying this was the end. We should be able to escape tomorrow if David succeeded. She smiled and held me so tight that I had a job to breathe.

Getting into Langley was easier since they possessed all my details but I still had to be escorted to the secret operations room. Grouped around the screen were Alicia, Gary, Robert and a tall rather rugged faced person who was introduced as the Director. I guessed it was Alicia and Gary's boss. The only other person in the room was the technician, Mark operating the equipment. I noticed an armed agent on the outside of the door.

In the container, David and the others were dressed in protective clothing with masks and tight-fitting gloves. They were kneeling down working on some cables. Their actions and speech were being continuously recorded. That was standard procedure used by bomb disposal people. The barge was being buffeted by the waves and was rolling and pitching. Not exactly ideal conditions for diffusing an atom bomb. However, everything was secured and the men wore harnesses.

They were working cautiously but I gathered from the conversation taking place, that a problem had arisen as it was protected by a coded lock. David had found a small hollow tube that seemed to protrude from the core. It was not clear what this did since it was open to the atmosphere. A fibre optic light guide with a camera was passed down it to reveal part of the inner core. David had never seen a design like it before but believed it might be possible to destroy the geometry of the core by inserting a steel rod into the tube. The bomb required a perfect spherical geometry to work since the implosive shock wave had to squeeze the plutonium core uniformly to create the exact critical shape for detonation. We could hear an argument in process about this between David and the Army experts. It was clear nobody was sure exactly what to do. At that moment the barge started to pitch severely and the men had to stop and hold onto the guard rails. Being aware of the two cameras someone placed a black cloth over the lenses. We heard some muffled talking. They were finding the pressure of being watched too great and asked for some privacy to confer between themselves.

Gary went to a coffee machine conveniently placed in the corner of the room and extracted four cups. It was a way of reducing the tension which was building up in the room. The air conditioning didn't prevent one's sweat glands from working overtime. The Director, whom I hadn't met before, seemed particularly nervous while Alicia, Gary and Robert looked unperturbed. During the last few weeks our experiences had surpassed what most agents get during their whole careers. The Director, whose name was not revealed to me, muttered some derogatory remarks about the camera being shut off. He ordered the pictures be returned but it was not heeded. I resisted saying anything for fear of being removed. It was obvious he did not want me or Robert in the room. No doubt Alicia would get into trouble for inviting us but I guess she thought we had a right to be there being part of the team who found the bomb. About twenty minutes passed before the pictures came back on the screen but this time it was from the destroyer Kansas. Commander Shaw's face appeared. The picture was broken up but we could see the rough seas in the background.

Shaw said, 'We are experiencing bad weather and a storm is heading towards us. I am fearful of losing the tow rope to the barge. The barge has its own engine but it is incapable of coping with these rough seas. The team in the container are struggling to decide what to do next but it looks as though they will have to start dismantling the bomb before we reach our destination point in the Puerto Rica Trench, which is still ten hours away. We are about 500 miles out but the rough sea is putting everybody and the bomb at risk. I'm now going to switch you back to the container.' He didn't know that we had a direct video link with it.

David's face appeared on the screen. He re-stated Shaw's view that they couldn't wait any longer to start the de-activation process but there were complications owing to uncertainties in how the back-up initiation systems were protected. He told us it was risky but he was going to try and damage the core geometry so at least if the bomb exploded it wouldn't be a full nuclear explosion. The faces of the onlookers displayed the same thoughts going through my mind. Never before had any of us felt so helpless. The fate of America and perhaps the world hung on one man's actions. Nature was throwing everything at us. Religious people would believe God was taking out vengeance on mankind for inventing the seeds of destruction of our world. I just believed what we were witnessing was a coincidence of circumstance. Everything that was happening was of our own making and based on our own actions so we had to live with them.

The picture on the screen suddenly switched to a view from a fighter jet that was passing over the ships. It gave a wide vista of the tumultuous seas below. There were two other navy ships about three miles away tracking the destroyer, ensuring no other ships were in the vicinity. The Navy pilot was making comments about the storm coming up from the south. He didn't know that he was looking at a barge carrying a one megaton nuclear bomb.

The pictures from the container were switched back to the main screen just in time for us to see David putting a thin steel rod into the bomb core. Then the picture suddenly went blank and silence filled the screen. The technician started adjusting the controls but told us the signal from the ship and container were lost. Then the picture from the aircraft returned and to our horror we saw a massive explosion below. A huge wall of water seemed to rise up obscuring the view.

The pilot shouted, 'The bloody bombs exploded. There is nothing left – the ship and barge have all disappeared!'

All we could see was just a lot of foam and debris floating in the water.

He banked and flew lower over the water with the camera running. Black smoke hung in the air and debris rained down pitting the ocean. Large bubbles burst on the surface as if the water below was boiling. The ocean had consumed the destroyer, the barge, the container, nothing was left. We received a radio call from one of the escorting ships who had been monitoring all the signals. They saw the explosion lift the ship and barge out of the water just before they disappeared into thousands of fragments that were falling back into the sea. The force of the explosion rocked the ships located two and three miles away. Fortunately, David had succeeded. It was not a nuclear explosion. The high explosives in the shells must have been accidentally set off and destroyed the nuclear material before it could go critical.

The people around gasped in disbelief at what had happened. I noticed a slight look of relief on the face of the Director which I'm sure would also be on the President's face. The White House team would have also seen the pictures.

It wasn't long before phones were ringing and hasty conversations were taking place. The explosion would have been picked up by almost every monitoring station on the East Coast. No doubt the President would have a prepared speech to cover the event. It was one of the risk scenarios that had been considered. David and the brave men in his team and on the ships had given their lives to save America and its President, at least for the time being.

Alicia, Gary and Robert came over and put their arms around me. They felt the sadness that I felt at losing a friend who was at the very heart of the crisis. Four video channels were running in the Langley control room from each location. The video pictures were recorded up to the time of the explosion. The technician re-ran the one from the container.

The last picture showed David putting a rod into the bomb's core. He must have damaged it enough to prevent it forming a critical shape thus stopping any chance of enough neutrons being generated to sustain a fissionable reaction. Something, and we shall never know what, must have set off the detonators and ignited the explosive shell around the bomb. The people who assembled the bomb and those responsible for it would not go unpunished. I saw Alicia make a call on her cell phone. I knew who she was calling. The Director acknowledged her as she made the call and without saying anything walked out of the room. I guessed he would be talking to the President and Vice President. They had to get their cover story right. All hell would be let loose when the media found out what had happened. The men who had lost their lives in the service of their country would be heroes who saved New York from a terrorist bomb. The President would be congratulated for his decision to remove the bomb from New York. But people would ask, how did the terrorists manage to deceive the FBI and CIA once again and smuggle a bomb into the city? The politicians always had a scapegoat. But this time it could not be the FBI and the CIA because they knew the President was part of a conspiracy of silence. They could take him down if they wished so he had to take the flak alone. I was sure the CIA Director's telephone call would be reminding him about his precarious position. The media would be screaming for heads to roll and explanations but it was Christmas time and nobody wanted their holidays spoilt by a political crisis. But there was still London. It was now in the front firing line unless those planning to detonate a bomb had been caught.

I called Valerie on my encrypted cell phone and told her what had happened. She didn't say much but I sensed she was relieved that we could now go back to England. It was getting late and there was little left for me to do. I asked Alicia what would happen next since I was keen to fly back to England. She told me that the President had already made arrangements for me and Valerie to fly in a chartered aircraft as soon as we wished but wanted me to know of his appreciation of the help I had given to the Task Force for Whirlwind.

This was good news which I immediately passed onto Valerie. I knew she would already be packing her suitcase. Before I left, Alicia and Gary thanked me for the help I had given them but warned me that the enemy was still out there and London was still the target. I asked if I could keep the Glock and the cell phone. Looking at me with her cool eyes and displaying a playful smile, she said, 'Yes, you may need them both. I will arrange for Mark to contact you in London. He has been working with MI5 and the Scotland Yard's anti-terrorist squad so can update you on their efforts.'

Before leaving she gave me a tight hug and a surprisingly passionate kiss. Through the period of this ordeal I had grown to like her. Deep down under the rough exterior was a woman waiting to exercise her sexuality. Being a woman FBI agent in what is still a man's profession, requires an extra show of toughness. In my early days I would have seen Alicia as a bedroom challenge. She would be a challenge for any man. It was strange that she never mentioned a boyfriend but then I knew nothing about her private life.

Gary patted me on the shoulder, shook my hand and wished me good hunting. Robert reminded me he was still my agent and we had a business arrangement to conclude. No doubt he had the book in mind, but that would have to wait until long after the crisis was over. We agreed to talk further after I was back in England. My friends seemed to have forgotten we still had a bomb threat in London that could now be more serious. Al-Qaeda had been betrayed by The New Order whom they now saw as their enemy.

As I stepped outside the CIA building to board the waiting car the sun was shining brightly through the clouds as it slowly sunk over the western horizon. My thoughts raced back to that day at Stones End when suddenly the sun rays hit me as I picked up Fellows' memoires. I remembered again the legend of Pandora's Box and the consequences of opening it. What had just happened in the South Atlantic was a very near miss. If the bomb had resulted in a one megaton nuclear explosion in New York, I would not be here. Was it yet another warning? My instincts were to run and hide and not to face up to reality. I now had a woman to love and care for so running away was not an option. It was her safety that mattered most to me now.

On arrival at the house Chloe greeted me with a smile tainted with a look of sadness. Valerie came running out from the back room and flung her arms around me. The agent had already collected her belongings and was about to leave. With tears in their eyes the two women embraced each other before parting company. I noticed Valerie's suitcase was half-packed. Seeing my sadness she took my hand and expressed her sorrow for the death of David Simons. The news media had already picked up the explosion in the South Atlantic and questions were being asked. The President was making a statement to the nation at nine o'clock. With a glint of happiness on her face, and in an attempt to get my mind off the events of the day, she said, 'I had a call from the White House Secretary to say we have two business class seats on a plane going to London tomorrow. We will be travelling with a diplomatic status and have protection. I rang Daddy and told him the good news. He wants to see us on Christmas Day at my Aunt Flo's house in Guildford. You may remember she brought me up after my mother died so we are very close.'

Valerie was so excited and happy at the prospect of returning to England that I decided not to say anything about the turmoil going on in London to find the Al-Qaeda terrorists and the bomb. I switched on the TV at nine o'clock to see the President's announcement. The speech writers had done a good job in preparing him. He looked grave and sober with a background set to match.

'When I spoke to you before I told you about the terrorist bomb we found in New York. The bomb was a high explosive device and proved difficult to dispose of so, in the interest of protecting people who live in the New York area, I gave the Navy orders to take it out to sea in the Atlantic Ocean before work was started on its disposal. It is with deep regret that I have to announce that during the process of removing the detonators, the bomb prematurely exploded killing all the brave men who were present, including the loss of the ship used to transport it. The next of kin have been informed. My heartfelt sympathy goes out to the relatives of all those who died in the service of their country. Top priority has been given to finding and bringing to justice all those who planned the attack and planted the bomb. The United States considers this an act of war and will deal with any country proved to have been involved in supporting the terrorists. We cannot be sure that further attacks on American cities or on those of our allies will not take place in the future so once again I ask you all to be vigilant. I will talk to you again when more information becomes available. God Bless America.'

I dreaded to think what would happen when the public learned the truth. The President had played into the hands of The New Order and The Republican Party. They just needed the right time to release the true story. I suspected the White House knew the newspapers already had a copy of this but were banned from publishing it on grounds of national security. No doubt the President would say he was not told about the nuclear bomb and try and shift the blame onto the FBI and CIA but they would have the proof locked up in their safes. It would be the scandal of the century but the White House would have already thought of a way out.

At nine o'clock in the morning the next day an FBI car took us to Dulles airport where we went through the VIP channel with diplomatic status to board a chartered Boeing 777, one of the latest airliners. It was about half-full with a variety of people, mainly Government officials and diplomats, both American and British, probably going home for Christmas. An FBI agent was assigned to us but he also had other charges. Clearly the White House wasn't taking any risks with us owing to my knowledge of Whirlwind. I started to realise I had the story of the century to write. But that would have to wait until after a new President was elected. It certainly would not be the current incumbent. There would be a media frenzy when the truth came out. I only hoped my name and those of my friends would not be revealed. Robert would see it as a way of increasing sales of any book I would write. My journalistic instinct forced me to write a daily diary of events using my laptop. .

As we left Dulles behind, I saw Concorde parked on the runway below. Little did I know when I arrived on it about three weeks ago that I would be returning with the love of my life, the possessor of a state secret that could bring down a Government and been close to what could have been the worst terrorist atrocity in history. I sipped the glass of champagne the hostess handed out, reclined the seat and looked at Valerie. Her face glowed with happiness. Once more she was the woman whom I first met at the

Hay-Adams Hotel. The events of the last few weeks had taken their toll but we had finally escaped from Washington. A joyful tear ran down her cheeks when I squeezed her hand and kissed her. She whispered, 'Paul I'm so happy and never want to go back to Washington. It's my past life. I want a new one with you.'

I replied, 'As soon as the threat is over I will take you away from London and we will find a quiet country cottage and bring up lots of kids.'

She smiled and said, 'I would like that.'

It was the quest of trying to find a quiet country retreat that got me into the present situation but it also produced a turning point in my life.

I flicked through the news items on the video monitor fitted to the seat. All new aircraft had seat videos which replaced the overhead ones which were never very clear and often stopped working in the middle of a film. With the new devices passengers had control of what they wanted to see and hear. The news item that caught my attention was that arrests had been made by the London Metropolitan police of four people suspected of terrorist activity in the city and warrants had been issued for five members of a gang suspected of bomb-making.

This could have a connection to the nuclear bomb. The Prime Minster would by now have been briefed on the New York incident. He had already agreed with the President not to reveal the atom bomb threat. Hopefully I would get an update in London from Mark Brooks, the CIA agent posted to liaise with MI5.

I was reading an article in the in-flight magazine on international business and saw that a company called Globe Enterprises had just won an award for record exports. It was collected by its President and owner, a Lord Globe. Normally such an article would be of passing interest but there was something about the name that kept ringing bells in my head and made me read on. Globe Enterprises was really an umbrella name for a host of other companies who manufactured a range of goods from high tech communications equipment to medical devices. I saw the name Freiburg Engineering, owned by Heinz Kluge, mentioned in the text. It was the company that Colin Niedermeyer worked for before he was murdered by the New Order. Heinz Kluge alias Wolfman was one of the suspected Cabal members of the New Order. It appeared Globe had business connections with Freiburg. Then it hit me. It was like the final word of a crossword falling into place. An anagram of Globe is Belog.

According to Fellows it was the code name of someone who was senior enough in the UK security services or Civil Service to provide intelligence to Paul Fields back in the1960s and later to Diane Hunter, his stepdaughter. Was he a member of The New Order and still active? That was a question that needed to be answered. It might just be a coincidence and my suspicious mind working overtime but I needed to check out Lord Globe and his companies. Valerie was asleep so I pulled out my laptop and tried to connect to the Internet but without success. We were flying over Greenland so satellite communication was possible but the current aircraft rules forbade the use of such a connection.

I sensed someone was watching me when a hand was placed on my shoulder.

He whispered in my ear, 'You need a key code and password to bypass the plane's security to access the Internet. Only the Captain can authorise that but I know how to do it.'

I looked round and sitting behind on the opposite row was a smartly-dressed black man.

'Thanks but I will not flout the regulations and put the aircraft in danger,' I replied.

'You won't do that,' he said in an authoritative manner.

I smiled and turned back to see the hostess coming to me with a tray of food. Having a man watching me booting up my computer and reading the article gave me an uncomfortable feeling. He was not to my knowledge the agent who was assigned to protect us. I had only seen him briefly soon after we the boarded the plane. My old fears returned. Was I being watched by the wrong people? The plane could be an ideal target for terrorists since it had many diplomats and Government people on board and here was a man sitting just behind me who knew how to override its communications security. I tried to rationalise. If he was a bad guy then he would have not made himself known. Having been associated with spies, agents, assassins and people who lie, I was becoming paranoid; a condition from which it was difficult to escape.

I decided to watch a video but fell asleep somewhere in the middle. When I woke up the cabin was in darkness and we were on a direct approach to London. Valerie had already woken up and was reading a magazine. By coincidence she was reading the article about Globe but I resisted the temptation to say anything about my discovery. The usual business class breakfast was served. I did glance round but the black man was no longer in the seat behind; he had disappeared but so had some others. The plane was only half-full so seat movements were permitted. Before landing the pilot announced it was snowing heavily in Washington and flights had been suspended. London was very cold but bathed in sunshine.

Valerie sighed and said, 'We just got out in time. It's wonderful to be back in England.'

The door of the plane opened and we were greeted by two special branch detectives whom we followed through the VIP channel to a waiting car. As we drove through the familiar streets of London bustling with Christmas shoppers, I momentarily forgot about the terror lurking in the shadows. I had the woman I loved next to me and was back home. Washington and New York seemed far away. For now, I was a very happy man.

CHAPTER 14

London
22 December 1999

The two Asian men met for the first time in a basement flat in London's East End. Their orders were in a sealed envelope secreted away behind a panel in the kitchen. Like the American cell, they had been expecting their instructions to come before the end of the year. They knew what had to be done. They never questioned why. They were to be martyrs; heroes to be remembered by future generations of jihadists. Death would be a passport to an eternal life in paradise. The time had come when the poor, the weak, and the persecuted would make the world listen. Allah would be pleased. The unbelievers would be destroyed and the flag of the true religion would fly high in the capitals of the world. That part of their indoctrination had been very effective. London had become a haven for foreign jihadist preachers, organizers, agitators and propagandists, many of which were recipients of generous state welfare benefits. These people exploited the Government's perceived soft approach to immigration and human rights. The large Asian and African communities established around the country provided a safe haven for extremists. There was a growing backlash in the country against the Government's policies and right-wing political parties were gaining support from all sections of society. Political rebellion was waiting in the wings. The Prime Minister knew the millennium bomb threat could be its trigger so, with the support of MI5, he invoked both the Anti-Terrorism and Official Secrets Act to withhold information from the public and the media.

Known terrorist groups were under surveillance by the police and MI5. The problem was identifying the people higher up the chain. GCHQ at Cheltenham had been placed on full alert. It was the threat of a nuclear bomb being exploded on London that gave the latest threat a special significance. Every telephone call, every email, every internet connection made, was being monitored. The FBI in Washington and the CIA at Langley had been exchanging information with the British police and MI5 for many months. After the New York incident a full red alert existed in both capitals. Twenty-four hour surveillance was placed on suspects in both countries. The CIA had their own methods for dealing with people who threatened their democratic institutions. During the Soviet era they had developed a sophisticated network of informants and agents in countries perceived to be potential enemies. But Al-Qaeda was everywhere. It did not have a country, although Yemen, Somali, Pakistan and Afghanistan were among those who provided safe havens. The latter was known to be where Bin Laden, the leader of Al-Qaeda, and his cohorts were hiding. In 1998 he had ordered the bombing of the American embassies in Dar-es-Salaam and Nairobi. Those acts had raised the Al-Qaeda threat level.

Nobody knew why the terrorist threats had suddenly started to increase. Tensions in the Gulf were running high again after Saddam Hussein's refusal to cooperate with the weapons inspectors but this was not thought to be the main reason. There was no direct connection between Al-Qaeda and the Iraq situation. Another group was driving this new wave of terrorism for their own political purposes.

Sleeping terrorist cells in different parts of the country had been instructed to become active and cause disruption in London by threatening to bomb public places such as underground stations, shopping centres and public buildings. The planner wanted these to be distractions. Unknown to the police, a two-man cell was selected to carry out the big millennium event.

The members of this cell were told that a large hidden army of Islamic warriors was waiting to rise up and take over the country after their deadly act. Such was the brainwashing that had taken place when the two men and many others were visiting their home country of Pakistan. It was enough to convince them to go along with the plan.

Abu Zadre and Kamel Neghal were British born Muslims. Their parents were wealthy traders who had no knowledge of their sons' clandestine beliefs and activities. Unlike many of their fellow Muslims, they had not been recruited and indoctrinated at the Finsbury Park Mosque so were not on MI5's watch list. Both were highly educated. Abu Zadre had a degree in Electronic Engineering from Imperial College in London and was studying for a PhD. He had already received job interests from leading companies and potentially had good career prospects. Kamel Neghal was an exporter and worked for a shipping company whose offices were on the site of the old East India docks in London's East End.

A caller told each to go to the flat in the East End. Their handlers were careful to make sure they were not seen together. CCTV cameras were now active in almost every street in the city.

The terrorists' combined knowledge and skills made them ideally suited for the task they had to perform. It was the second most ambitious and far reaching project ever undertaken by Al-Qaeda. The first had failed in New York so this one had to succeed in London otherwise the credibility of the world's most feared terrorist organisation would be lost. The men knew they would be not only sacrificing their own lives but many thousands of innocent people, some of which would be their own kind. It was a price they believed was worth paying to show the world that the non-believers were destroying everything sacred to their religion. It was time to set an example for the entire world to see.

The instructions in the note were clear.

Two 'suitcase' nuclear devices will be packed in boxes amongst a consignment of fruit that will be delivered to you by boat from Amsterdam, three days before the start of the new millennium.

The devices are fission-type bombs with small 10kg plutonium cores. Each should yield an energy equivalent of about 5 kilotons of TNT, which will be enough to wipe out the city of London. A video cassette will be included showing a step by step guide on how to prepare the explosive detonators for the bombs. A basic knowledge of electronics will be required.

A case containing one device will be installed with the fireworks on a barge known as 'Buffy One'. It is one of the many barges that will be located near the Millennium Wheel on the River Thames for displaying fireworks. The device will require setting up and primed to detonate at midnight on 31st December at the start of the fireworks display to celebrate the new century.

The other device will be used as a decoy. It will be collected and taken in a van by members of another cell to a car park under Hyde Park. We know this device will be found. Someone will inform the police about its location within a few days. Army experts will be able to de-activate it. The Government will believe they have succeeded in finding the bomb and wishing to keep the whole operation from public knowledge, will not be searching for the other one.

The barge 'Buffy One' is currently tethered at a dockside in East London. It is owned by a company who only use it to transfer timber down the Thames and for firework displays on special occasions. On the day before the millennium celebrations the London Firework Company will set up the fireworks on the barge using their own men. It will then be driven along the Thames to a fixed location near the Millennium Wheel. Arrangements have been made for you both to replace on that day two of the men who will have an unfortunate accident and not arrive for work. You will carry documents from an agency indicating you are temporary replacements.

Once on the barge you will place the case containing the nuclear device in one of the firework boxes. They are large enough to conceal it. The fireworks are electronically set off by a timing system installed in the barge. Zadre will set the detonators to fire at the start of the firework display at midnight. It will provide the country with a display never before seen. London will be removed from the map of Britain.

The devices have been assembled in Amsterdam and placed aboard one of the regular refrigerated food carrying boats that come *into London daily. As an importer, Neghal will arrange for the necessary paperwork.*

Al-Qaeda had originally intended to explode the two suitcase bombs simultaneously at diverse locations in London. But with the news of the failure of the New York mission, the Controller decided to inform his New Order contact only about the decoy bomb in Hyde Park. The location of the other would be kept a secret. It was a clever plan that had to work.

The Prime Minister chaired an emergency meeting of COBRA (Cabinet Office Briefing Room A) to discuss the new situation after the failure of the New York bomb attempt. Mark Brooks, who was seconded from the American Task force, attended. He had been providing liaison between the US and UK security agencies. The US President had called the Prime Minister to update him on the situation in New York before he made his broadcast to the American people. They had agreed earlier to reveal the existence of the millennium bomb threats but to omit the word 'nuclear' to suppress press speculation. The British public were used to such threats and since it was the festive season any new ones would not stop people from going about their normal business. A large army of intelligence officers and special branch police were discreetly searching the capital. They knew they were dealing with clever people who had been planning the millennium bombs for a long time. In the short time available their task was formidable.

The COBRA group secretary said, 'The folder in front of you lists most of the known terrorist groups. Our intelligence suggests the Al-Qaeda leaders have formed alliances with these groups. Such groups are unlikely to be directly linked to the current millennium bomb threat, but they would take any advantage that might accrue from its success.'

Mark looked down the list and was familiar with many of the names listed.

Hamas, Islamic Jihad, Hezbollah, Hizba-Tahrir (Islamic Liberation Party), Islamic Salvation Front (Algeria), Armed Islamic Group (Algeria), En-Nahda (Tunisia), Muslim Brotherhood,

Ga'mat Islamiya (Egypt), Abu Sayyaf Group, Jamat Muslimeen (Pakistan and Bangladesh), and support groups of Mujahedeen (Holy Warriors) in Bosnia, Philippines and Chechnya – all have ongoing operations in America and Europe.

The head of MI5 told her colleagues, 'I believe we have an international conspiracy with huge political ramifications.'

The Prime Minister asked the Head of MI5, 'Is it possible for nuclear bombs or biological and chemical weapons to be brought into the country undetected?'

She answered with a degree of confidence. 'Our monitoring systems make that an unlikely possibility. However, conventional explosive devices like those used by the IRA or some low-level biochemical weapons and radioactive materials for use in dirty bombs are difficult to discover. My agents are watching and monitoring all the suspected terrorist cells.'

The Prime Minister displaying a grim look never seen before said, 'Time is short so I am cancelling all Christmas leave and mobilising all relevant forces and agencies to be on duty. The public know we have a bomb threat so will not be too alarmed when they see more police on the streets. Rupert Arnold, the Head of the Anti-Terrorist Group, will co-ordinate the actions. He will report directly to me and this group.'

The Head of the Metropolitan Police suggested, 'It would be prudent not to raise public alarm any further. Since many people will be leaving London next week for Christmas it will be easier for us to carry out a search for the bomb. The problem will start when people and the media return for the millennium celebrations. We must find the bomb before that time.'

Mark said, 'Paul Cane and his girlfriend, Valerie Day, have just flown in from Washington. As you know, Paul has been in the centre of the New York bomb threat. He has just lost his colleague David Simons in the tragic event in the South Atlantic. It has been agreed with the President and the FBI that I meet and brief him on events here.'

The Committee agreed, but Mark was told not to place Paul in any danger since he was a freelance journalist and not a member of any British security agencies. The Committee adjourned.

The Prime Minister, the COBRA Secretary, Heads of MI5, MI6 and Rupert Arnold met after in private to review the situation.

The Prime Minister asked Arnold, 'Do you really believe these people are going to explode a nuclear bomb in London or is it some sort of huge hoax?'

After some hesitation Arnold replied, 'Yes, after the discovery in New York, I now believe this is a serious threat and London is in grave danger of being destroyed. The bomb will be much smaller because only a suitcase-sized weapon could be concealed and smuggled into the country undetected. We know the Russians and Americans had such bomb designs back in the 1970s and some may have got into the hands of terrorist groups like Al-Qaeda after the collapse of the Soviet Union. There are over twenty-three thousand nuclear bombs in the world. Many are scattered around Europe. Groups like Al-Qaeda with access to large sums of money could have easily purchased one from some Mafia-type organisation. Also I believe this group wants to take world leadership of all the factions who have grievances against the West so they have a political agenda. Al-Qaeda wants to be the world franchise for terrorism against the West.

In parallel we have The New Order who also has a political agenda and is using Al-Qaeda to do its dirty work but after New York, that association will have come to an abrupt end.'

The Prime Minister asked, 'Do you think The New Order will inform on them to save London since we know they have members in this country?'

'I'm sure they intended to do just that but Al-Qaeda would by now have altered their plans. Our intelligence on their associations and intentions is unfortunately confusing. The codes we had for deciphering their calls were changed two days ago. GCHQ are working on the problem but we think the terrorists have reverted to old methods like leaving messages in public places. The number of permutations of hiding places is almost as great as in digital encryption. By now any undercover cells would have received their instructions.'

The Prime Minister's face was now ashen. He knew the consequences of any actions he would have to take.

'What should we do about the planned millennium celebrations that I have to open? Most of the Cabinet will be present and the Queen will be at the Millennium Dome.'

Rupert said, 'If the bomb is not found at least two days before the end of the year then we shall have to cancel everything and be left with no choice but to evacuate central London. As you are aware, Prime Minister, emergency powers will be invoked. Contingency plans have already been made but to put them into action will require your authorisation Prime Minister.' A stunned silence followed.

Knightsbridge

The two Special Branch men said little on the journey from Heathrow to my apartment in Knightsbridge. Many of their senior colleagues lived in the same protected apartment block as me so they were familiar with that part of London. Security people work in a closed system and are very suspicious of outsiders. To them I was such an outsider. I assumed they knew very little about my ventures in America and probably wondered why we were being given the VIP treatment. They helped to unload our suitcases from the boot of the car and bid us farewell.

I was greeted by Henry, the apartment security man. He welcomed me back with a friendly smile but looked suspiciously at Valerie. I told him she would be staying with me in the apartment and would have an entry code. Henry was an ex-policeman who took his job very seriously so viewed every visitor in the same way. He acknowledged my request and said, 'Mr Cane, I have a letter for you in the safe that was delivered personally by a young lady just a few days ago.' After a few minutes he returned with the letter. He assured me it had been checked and didn't contain any explosives or chemicals. I thanked him and we took the lift to the fourth floor.

Valerie was familiar with the security arrangements to enter the apartment block as they were similar to the ones she had in her Georgetown apartment. I reset the alarm and opened the door to the apartment. Everything was exactly as I left it. Much had happened since that time. I felt like I had been away for months, not weeks. Like all women, Valerie looked curiously around my bachelor abode. I was hoping no incriminating evidence of my past life was visible. I actually knew much more about her than she did about me but now we were together back in London that would change. After our flight we were both tired and suffering from jet lag but the lure of the London streets, now only minutes away, was too much for Valerie. She loved shopping.

Putting her arms around me, she gave me one of her irresistible smiles and said in a low voice, 'Paul, can we go out for a walk? I want to see London again. I need to buy some more winter clothes since I left most of mine behind in Washington.'

I said, 'OK, if you feel up to it. Remember it's just three days before Christmas so the shops will be packed with people.'

'Can we go to Oxford Street? My Aunt always took me there every Christmas.'

'Yes, but since it's very close, let's go to Harrods first and have some lunch since I have no food in the refrigerator. After, we can take a taxi to Marble Arch.'

'No, let's walk, I want to soak up the atmosphere of the city,' she pleaded.

'OK, but before we go out, unpack your things and get changed while I look at my emails.'

'First, I must call daddy in Richmond to let him know we have arrived,' she said.

I really wanted to check up on Lord Globe and his company Globe Enterprises. I switched on my desktop and tried to access the Internet but found my computer had been corrupted. Someone had sent me a virus that had penetrated my protection software, even though it was supposed to the best available and used by MI5. Perhaps they had done it to prevent its unlawful use. Fortunately all my files were backed up and I did have my laptop.

I then remembered the letter in my pocket. After instinctively sniffing it for signs of chemical explosives I opened it with a paper knife. The following message was printed on a sheet of white paper:

'*You have not heeded my previous warning so the responsibility of what happens next is firmly on your shoulders.*'

I was going to hide it from Valerie but she was looking over my shoulder and read the words.

'What were the previous warnings?' she asked.

'Before I left for Washington, an email message was sent warning me not to become involved with Fellows' memoires. Someone knew about my visit to Stones End and was clever enough to hack into my computer and send me the warning. I told Robert about it but nobody else. What is more worrying is that the person or organisation responsible knows where I live and can access my computer. The Fellows' memoires are now history since I know the names of The New Order members that were hidden in it.'

Reminding me of something I had forgotten, Valerie said, 'The person or organisation who wrote the note may not know you have decoded the names list. Do the British and European members of The New Order have the same knowledge as their American colleagues? Secret organisations, for example like the drug cartels, always make sure their people work independently of each other. I remember Alan Sherman talking about that to a Senate Committee investigating drugs being brought into the country. The New Order operates very much like the drug cartels. Security agencies work the same way.'

She was right. I was making a lot of assumptions. It was unfortunate that I opened the letter. I wanted us to escape, at least for now, from the whole conspiracy business.

I said to Valerie, 'Let's forget all this and go out and see the town.'

She smiled, grabbed my hand and led me out of the apartment. On the way out I asked Henry to describe the woman who had delivered the letter, knowing it had probably been captured on the CCTV anyway.

He said, 'She was young, short and well-spoken, but dressed in a hooded coat so I only saw her face.'

Valerie was listening and smiled, 'Looks like your past is catching up with you. Why are all your villains women?'

'This is The New Order trying to frighten me again. Someone, somewhere, knows too much about me and I need to find out who and why I'm being targeted again,' I said.

Valerie could see I was getting agitated. She took my hand again and said, 'Darling, let's do what you said and, for now, forget about the letter and see the town.' I noticed a smile on Henry's face as she pulled me away from the building.

It took us about ten minutes to walk to Harrods in Brompton Road. The store was packed with shoppers, many enjoying the world famous Christmas Department and Food Hall. The store lost its royal patronage in 1997 after the deaths of Diana, Princess of Wales, and Dodi Al-Fayed because its owner, Mohamed Al-Fayed, made accusations against the Royal Family. He had erected a memorial in the store to the couple the previous year. I had not visited the store for two years so had not seen it.

I suggested to Valerie we had lunch at the quintessentially English Georgian Restaurant on the fourth floor before we became lost in the vastness of the store. We had not dined in a high-class restaurant since our first date in Georgetown so it seemed appropriate to celebrate our first London outing at this one. I hadn't booked a table at what was a very busy time of day so to acquire one I had to use my persuasive powers on the Head Waiter. It only worked when he saw Valerie. Her high cheek bones, long blonde hair, her elegant clothes and her irresistible good looks were more impressive to the waiter than all my chat. He kept glancing up at her as he pretended to look down his list of available tables. Harrods had a dress code and rarely turned away a well-dressed woman. I thought I had clinched it by asking for the very expensive à la carte menu. But not surprisingly, he had already found a cancellation of a table for two.

We both chose salmon en croute for the main course but decided as it was midday and since we were jet-lagged, not to have any wine. It was a high calorie meal but like me, Valerie didn't put on weight and so wasn't bothered about diets. She was slim in spite of liking food, but did eat healthily. Every other woman I had met always worried about getting fat and existed on diets.

Looking around at other people in the restaurant enjoying themselves and looking forward to Christmas it was difficult, even for me, to believe that somewhere out in the city, were people planning to destroy us all for misguided political and religious beliefs. Fortunately, there was an army of people trying to hunt them down. I understood why our leaders did not want to tell people about the nuclear bomb threat until it was proved beyond doubt to be real. It was a strange irony that we now depended on The New Order to prevent it. I hoped Alicia's assassin hadn't been active too soon.

After a delightful lunch, the waiter brought the coffee. The caffeine would help to keep us awake. Valerie said after lunch she wanted to walk to Oxford Street and visit Selfridges, voted the best department store in the world, with the latest designer clothes. I warned her it would be impossible to move in what was the most crowded store in the busiest street in the country but that didn't diminish her enthusiasm. While waiting for the bill, my cell phone rang.

'Hello Paul, It's Mark Brooks. Hope you don't mind me calling. Alicia just called and gave me your restricted cell phone number. I know you've just got back from Washington and must be tired but I need to see you today or tomorrow before I go back to the States. Can you come to my office in Whitehall? There is someone you should meet.'

I replied, 'Great to hear from you, Mark. We do need to talk but it will have to be tomorrow.'

'Good, I will have a car pick you up from your apartment at nine-thirty in the morning.' He then rang off.

Valerie guessed who it was even before I told her, although she had never met Mark. I realised I had promised not to become involved in the London bomb threat, at least until after Christmas, but I had to find out what had been happening in London to make an assessment of how safe it was to stay in the city. When I explained this to her, she agreed it was important to know as her father and stepmother lived in Richmond and she would be visiting them the next day.

We had a look around the Harrods store before taking a brisk walk through Hyde Park to Marble Arch. After negotiating the heavy traffic we crossed over to the west end of Oxford Street. I was glad we had warm coats as the air temperature was only a few degrees above zero. They were some of the more essential clothes we had packed before leaving Washington, which apparently was now covered in snow. If we had left later than we did, it would have meant spending Christmas in Washington.

As we walked hand in hand along Oxford Street weaving through the crowds of people, I noticed how cosmopolitan London had become, or perhaps it always had been. The number of foreigners outnumbered British people but they all behaved the same as far as shopping was concerned. I could see Valerie was happy just being there with everybody. It was quite a different atmosphere from the shopping malls in Washington. I had never been shopping at Christmas with a woman. It was quite an experience. Valerie was anxious to buy Christmas presents for members of her family so made straight for Selfridges. My present to her was going to be very special which I would keep until Christmas Eve. She went off alone to buy some clothes while I went to the book store and agreed to meet up with her later at the coffee bar.

As I approached the book and magazine area I noticed the headlines on newspapers read:
'*Was the New York Bomb Nuclear?*'
'*Did the President lie to the people?*'
'*Nuclear Scientist Dies in Massive Explosion in the Atlantic*'
'*Mayor of New York Furious at not being told*'
'*Senate wants an enquiry*'
I bought a few newspapers to read the full stories. As I expected someone had leaked the story. It was the work of The New Order. The genie was out of the bottle. Senators were asking for a full enquiry. The White House spokesman was not available to comment.

One paragraph quoted an unnamed spokesman asking, *'Could it happen in London?'*

Fortunately, most of the papers were filled with stories and speculation about the New York bomb. But it was inevitable, as more information leaked out, London would become the focus of the media. I could imagine the panic in the White House operations room but they must have suspected something like this would happen and had statements prepared. The FBI and CIA would be waiting to see what the President did, knowing they were in possession of the facts and had all the evidence of what happened.

Valerie arrived later at the coffee shop hidden behind bags and boxes containing her purchases. I had already ordered coffee and cakes. I showed her the newspapers. She glanced at the headlines and said, 'Well, we knew it would happen. I'm glad we are not in Washington. It will spoil the President and Vice President's Christmas.'

'It's what might happen here that concerns me. I will find out more tomorrow but these headlines will spook the terrorists. If they do have a bomb installed in London they might decide to detonate it earlier,' I said.

Valerie frowned at me, 'Paul, let the people who are paid to protect us do their jobs. You've done your part. I am going to see daddy tomorrow while you're visiting Mark Brooks to find out about the Christmas arrangements at Auntie Flo's house in Guildford. I think she is expecting us on Christmas Eve. Don't forget it's the day after tomorrow.'

I wanted us to get out of London as soon as possible. Guildford was not that far away but would be just out of the danger zone of an explosion in the centre of London. It was getting late so we took a taxi back to the apartment. The jet lag had caught up with us and being in an exhausted state we didn't waste any time getting to bed and falling asleep.

23 December, Whitehall

The car arrived exactly on time. It travelled around Buckingham

Palace and along the Mall to Whitehall turning into Richmond Terrace. I then had to endure an elaborate security process at the entrance gate on the road leading up to a building which I assumed was the Ministry of Defence. Downing Street, blocked by securely guarded high black gates, was visible directly opposite. In my youth, in less violent times, Downing Street was accessible to the public and armed police were absent from the streets.

The Cenotaph stood proudly with its flags waving in the gentle morning breeze celebrating the war dead of the twentieth century. They were real wars when the enemy was known and could be seen. People knew what they were fighting and dying for but after that event in July 1945 at Alamogordo in New Mexico, everything changed. Now, instead of armies of men, just a small number could destroy a city and kill thousands of its inhabitants with one bomb. London cannot allow a few misguided maniacs to do what the German Luftwaffe failed to do after many months of bombing during the early part of the Second World War.

My driver handed me over to a policeman at the entrance to the building who checked my passport and asked me to sign in with further personal details. I noticed on the sheet there was a red bar code. The policeman scanned it and after looking at me for a few seconds made a call. Minutes later I was pleased to see Mark Brooks coming down the stairs to greet me. He looked much thinner than when we first met in Washington. We shook hands and he asked me to follow him up three flights of stairs to an office. The office looked out onto the River Thames. On the far side was the newly-constructed Millennium Wheel built to celebrate the new millennium. I had read it was to be officially opened by the Prime Minister just before midnight. Rather ominous considering what I had come here to talk about.

Mark had already heard about my exploits in America and was fully briefed about Whirlwind. He was glad to see me and asked about Valerie and Robert. Mark told me he was flying back to Washington later in the day to spend Christmas with his family and didn't expect to be returning to London. After exchanging some generalities about London and Washington, including the latest newspaper reports, he said,

'I want you to meet Rupert Arnold, the Head of the Government's Anti-Terrorist Group, responsible for finding the terrorists and the bomb, if there is one. Arnold has the latest updates and yesterday he told me there had been a breakthrough.'

Mark made a phone call and minutes later, a tall sun-tanned, James Bond, or should I say Sean Connery look-a-like, came into the room, accompanied by a smaller fair-haired man, obviously his assistant or secretary. I was introduced to them and we shook hands. The small man was actually a Chief Superintendent of Police; his name was John Nicholas. Mark started by saying,

'Paul returned to London yesterday after working with the President's Task Force on the New York bomb threat. As you know he originally discovered Henry Fellows' memoires and was able to link names in them to the terrorist threats and The New Order organisation. Strangely it was one of their members who saved New York by revealing the location of the Al-Qaeda terrorists and the nuclear bomb.'

Rupert Arnold thanked Mark and said, 'I have read the Task Force reports and know all about Mr Cane's work.'

His manner immediately confirmed my suspicions that our relationship would be a very official one. Unlike Mark, this man wanted to distance himself from anyone who was not part of his inner circle.

I found out later that Rupert Arnold was an old Etonian, an ex-guards officer, who, like many with the same pedigree, had risen to the upper echelons of Public Service. In his case the Counter-Terrorism Branch of the Metropolitan Police. He looked straight at me with piercing cold blue eyes and said, 'Mr Cane, your New Order has just come up trumps for us.' I didn't like the term, your New Order. He continued, 'Yesterday we received a call from a telephone box on Euston station to say a small atomic device will be detonated at midnight on the eve of the new millennium. It will be placed in a black van to be located in the car park under Hyde Park. By the time the station police arrived at the call box, the caller had gone. The CCTV picked up a woman dressed in a hooded cloak. She was young but her face didn't show up well enough for us to identify her. The car which picked her up outside the station was later tracked proceeding along the A4 to the motorway. The traffic was so heavy and the atmosphere thick with pollution that we lost her between cameras. Patrol cars couldn't get close enough to see where it went. A car was later found abandoned with false number plates.

Assuming this is The New Order's way of stopping Al-Qaeda then it gives us a chance to catch the terrorists, find and de-activate the bombs which hopefully they will take to the park sometime soon.'

I was glad to hear the news but had some concerns. It all seemed all too easy. Al-Qaeda would have known The New Order would give them away so would have changed the bomb location. Mark had already realised this and had alerted John Arnold to the possibility. It did, however, give confirmation that a suitcase type atomic bomb was either somewhere in the city or was going to be brought in soon.

I told Arnold about the threatening note sent to me which may have been delivered by the same woman who made the telephone call from the station. I also mentioned my computer being infected by a virus which prevented it going on-line. John looked at a file he was carrying and said, 'We can fix that for you, Mr Cane. It was necessary to stop people accessing your computer and stealing your files on Fellows so we closed it down while you were in America.'

So they could also access my computer files. I would have to remove the protection software illicitly obtained from MI5 since it gave them a stealth pathway to my computer. It was still a mystery how The New Order was able to use the same pathway. Was there a mole in MI5 working for The New Order?

'Thanks John, but please call me Paul,' I said in an attempt to have a more friendly relationship with him.

'Can I get the security guard to send you the CCTV picture of the woman who delivered the letter to my apartment?'

'Yes, that would be useful but we can access it ourselves,' he said.

I momentarily forgot that these people had access to every security camera in London. Orwell's 1984 had long been surpassed in London. I decided to test Arnold's willingness to impart his knowledge.

'John,' I said. 'Do you know the identity of The New Order members?'

After an uneasy silence, he said, 'We have a lot of intelligence on these people. Some has come from the FBI who followed up on the information obtained from the Fellows' papers. We already have our own files on Fellows and Simons related to their Brotherhood Foundation and its problems with The New Order back in the 1960s. As you know we set Fellows up with a new identity after the incidents at Halborn and over the decades have protected his anonymity. We knew he was murdered and long suspected it was a member of The New Order who authorised it.'

He seemed to know more about it than he was revealing so I didn't pursue the subject. I decided to play my master card.

'Do you know a Lord Globe?'

John replied, 'Yes, he is a prominent industrialist and was an advisor to the Prime Minister in the last Conservative Government. He is one of the new self-made billionaires who made his money from dealing in international commodities. Now he has companies successfully trading in many countries.

Do you think he is a member of The New Order?' he asked.

'I don't know. I was hoping you would tell me,' I replied.

'He is not on our list of suspects,' said John, looking again at the papers in his file. I was intrigued by the file he was purposely displaying. Arnold gave me a menacing frown.

'Why did you mention his name?' Arnold asked.

'Nothing important. It was similar to a name mentioned in the memoires.'

Mark had remained quiet since he wanted his colleagues to speak to me but it was becoming more of a question and answer session. I was beginning to feel uncomfortable and wasn't really welcome. It had been obvious since my meeting with Henning in

Washington that the British Establishment were not pleased by the way the CIA and FBI had trapped me into working for them without British consent, particularly after bailing me out of prison in Kuwait. I didn't want to be involved but because I knew too much and was a journalist they had to compromise me to prevent the story from being published. I was really their scapegoat.

Rupert Arnold looked at me in a dismissive way and said, 'I have to leave you to attend a meeting with the Prime Minister but John will take you through our plans and you can liaise with him.' He shook my hand and left the room.

I told John that my girlfriend and I were spending Christmas in Guildford with her relatives and asked him what would happen if they didn't succeed in finding the bomb. He then said, 'We have a direct link to the Russian member of The New Order. He told us he would use his resources to stop Al-Qaeda bombing London but he wouldn't divulge any more information. If there was any attempt to seek out or arrest his members then all co-operation would cease. The Prime Minister did speak to Putin who seemed to know little about it or, if he knew more, was not saying. The Prime Minster agreed to the request made by The New Order's member but warned that if it failed his organisation would be held responsible for what happened. The Russian had considerable investments in Britain and expected British support for his political campaign in Russia.'

I asked, 'Was the girl at the station part of his team?'

'We don't know. There has been no contact since we received the call yesterday. Our agents in Moscow are trying to find out but the Russian has disappeared.'

'What about the British members? Surely they are involved?' I asked.

'We have been watching Diane Hunter and her associates for years but she is quite old and well-respected. She is the darling of the Right. We suspect her daughter may now be doing her work for The New Order since Hunter has been aware for some time that we've been watching her. So far we haven't been able to produce any evidence of wrong-doing.'

'I didn't know she had a daughter,' I said.

'Neither did we until ten years ago when our agents discovered she had an affair with Lord Globe back in 1970; yes, the man you asked about earlier. Rupert didn't say too much about that because we are investigating Globe and his companies. They do have links with the Russian, Boris Sudakov, one of the Cabal members of The New Order.'

Everything was starting to connect. I suggested, 'Perhaps it was the daughter who made the phone call.'

'That we need to establish,' he said.

'Didn't she leave fingerprints or DNA?' I asked.

'She wore gloves and was obviously careful not to leave her DNA since a cloth was placed over the mouth piece so no saliva was left on it. We can examine your letter but this girl knows too much about detection methods.'

John had to leave so he shook my hand and wished me a happy Christmas and told me to forget about the bomb threat since the best people in the police and MI5 were now employed to deal with it. He gave me his encrypted mobile phone number and asked me to use it only when absolutely necessary.

He said, 'All my incoming and outgoing calls are recorded but I have it with me, even at night.'

I smiled, 'What does your wife think about that?' I asked.

'I don't have a wife. This job would make married life intolerable.'

My experience working with the security services over the last few months made his statement abundantly clear. I thought my job was bad enough but I did have a measure of independence and control over my life.

Mark said, 'Now you've met two of the guys I've worked with since being in London. There are others but they are all individualists who don't like sharing their knowledge or contacts. It's even more political here than in Washington. The stakes are just as high for the Prime Minister and his Government here as they are for the President. Both agreed not to release information to the public before the bomb threat was proved to be real, basically to save their own reputations. That will not be known until it's too late; then the consequences would be too horrible to even think about. The current unpopularity of the Government is being exploited by the terrorists and the right-wing parties for their own purposes.

The newspapers already have a story ready to print but they are under a ban order. They can and are commenting on the reports in the Washington Post and New York Times. High level powerful forces operating in London are protecting people who should be in prison. It is known our enemies have moles in the security services that have yet to be identified. Some members of the team here resent an American CIA agent being involved even though valuable intelligence information was coming from Washington. I think some people here were afraid the person or persons they were protecting would be exposed. Like you, I also have received death threats and was told to return to America. That's not why I am going back because my work here is finished anyway. John Nicholas is a good man. His father was an American professor at Berkeley. We became good friends and you can trust him. I don't leave until this evening so why don't we go for a walk down by the river and get some fresh air.'

Part of the Victoria Embankment between the Westminster and Waterloo Bridges is a popular walk. I could see Mark's office from the walled path close to the river bank. We walked past the Battle of Britain memorial inscribed with Winston Churchill's wartime words: *Never in the field of human conflict was so much owed to so few.*

As I stopped to read these poignant words, I thought it might apply to the present situation related to the saving of New York and London. In this case the word 'few', would be very applicable.

Over the river, the County Hall Building, until sold to a private investor in the early 1990s, was the original home of the Greater London Council, gleamed in the midday sun. It's facing of light Portland stone and Baroque style exemplified London's architectural past.

The river was full of leisure boats and barges moving in an

endless flow along and across the river. It had been a long time since I had actually stopped and stared at the capital's busy waterway flowing like lifeblood through its heart.

Facing me like a huge eye was the massive Millennium Wheel, currently the largest Ferris wheel in the world, but I believe plans are made in other countries to build even bigger ones. It looked like a huge bicycle wheel, with its thirty-two capsules projecting from its rim like giant seedpods. I remembered reading in the previous day's newspaper that it might be kept after the millennium celebrations as a tourist attraction since cities all over the world were building Ferris wheels for that purpose. London already had its share of attractions but people like to be moved about, so this one would satisfy that desire.

Mark saw me gazing at it and said, 'It's a great piece of engineering. The Prime Minister will open it just before the start of the new millennium. I'm told on a clear day you can see for twenty-five miles across London to the Thames Estuary. Unfortunately, 1 will not be here to ride on it or see the celebrations. On the night there is to be a massive firework display so thousands of people will be occupying this stretch of the river. If you and Valerie want a good view, my office would be a great place for it. I know some of the people who work in the building are being given a concession to use their offices. But they don't know about the bomb. I believe a celebration party is to be held in the building.'

I said, 'Unless the bomb is found, I would rather be in front of a television set a hundred miles away.'

Mark told me that Alicia and Gary missed me and had greatly appreciated my help on Whirlwind. If it hadn't been for my intervention, New York would now be in ashes. The President was trying to claim credit for saving the city. Washington was apparently in a state of ferment over the newspaper allegations and the President's rating had dropped to just a few percent, an all-time low. He had not made any public statement to refute the allegations and calls of impeachment were already being muted. The Republicans and their supporters were gaining support. The New

Order's plan was succeeding, at least in America. I wondered if Alan Sherman would make his move after Christmas. His election looked well-assured unless his involvement with The New Order and Al-Qaeda bomb plot was revealed. He had powerful friends who wouldn't hesitate to destroy those who had the same knowledge, which included the FBI and CIA agents. I could imagine certain people locking up documents in their safes labelled *to be read in the event of my death*. Perhaps I ought to do that since my name was on someone's death list.

We walked onto Waterloo Bridge and stopped to gaze down at the river. It gave us a wide vista of each embankment. Since it was almost Christmas, I was surprised to see so many men working on barges and boats around the base of the Wheel. These were tethered to platforms that were used to support the Wheel before it was lifted into position.

I remarked, 'These guys must be getting well-paid to be working so hard near Christmas.'

'That's because they have to get the firework display boards ready for the New Year's celebrations. Christmas Day is on Saturday so most of next week is a public holiday and little time is left for the preparations,' said Mark.

A large sightseeing boat filled with noisy foreign visitors passed under the bridge on its way up river towards Tower Bridge and the newly constructed Millennium Dome. The latter would be part of the celebrations. It was to be one of the Labour Government's legacies for the third millennium so its political significance took precedence over the symbolism it was designed to represent. It would house an exhibition of human achievements of the twentieth century and would be open to the public during the whole of the following year.

On the north bank, the Houses of Parliament with Big Ben rising proudly above, symbolised our democratic system. So here in front of me, developed progressively since Roman times, was the English centre of civilisation. The thought that all this could be reduced to ashes in a few seconds by a nuclear bomb left me feeling cold.

I said to Mark, 'If I was the terrorist planner this is where I would place the bomb. Have the police considered a bomb being placed at this location?'

Mark was in deep thought, looking at the river scene below. He responded to my statement.

'Yes, the whole area has been searched and is under twenty-four hour surveillance. It would be impossible for a large bomb like the one found in New York to be installed here but a small suitcase-type bomb might be more difficult to detect. Any person in a leisure boat carrying a case or bag could be a suspect. We have just seen a boat load of people. Look at those men working on the wheel, even the people walking across this bridge carrying bags. Any one of those could be a terrorist. The only way we can win is through having intelligence or help from the public. Since the latter have not been alerted that useful source is unavailable.'

I said, 'Mark, can you imagine the panic and disruption that would be caused if the public knew a terrorist was planning to explode a nuclear bomb in the city? Even if we succeed in stopping it or discover the whole thing is a hoax, the political fallout will be disastrous for the Government and security services.'

Mark looked worried and said, 'They know that and are hoping to deal with it quietly so the public will never know. Let's hope the telephone caller is right about the bomb. I know John Arnold has the best people and all the intelligence resources have been made available to him by the Prime Minister. He is a shrewd and intelligent guy and doesn't reveal how much he knows. In my view, if he can't catch the terrorists and stop this thing, then we are in serious trouble.'

'What will you do after your return to Washington?' I asked.

'I don't know, but there will be a big shake up in the FBI and CIA from the political chaos that has already started, even before Christmas. The politicians will be hoping it will be forgotten after the holiday but the story is so big the media will live on it for weeks, even months. The Republicans have been virtually handed the Presidency.'

I said, 'The big question is whether Alan Sherman's links to

402

The New Order and Al-Qaeda will be revealed. The FBI has a file on him which surely will exclude him for being elected to the leadership of his party.'

'Remember the FBI had files on the Kennedys but it didn't stop them,' he retorted.

'But they were both eventually murdered,' I stated.

Mark pointed out that the total explosive power in all the fireworks that were to be used for the millennium celebration would probably be enough to blow up London if they all went off at once. Only firemen and those involved in the fireworks would be allowed in the area on the night. I looked at the barges and platforms around the Wheel and could see how they were set to produce a very spectacular display.

I called Valerie, who was at her father's house in Richmond, to let her know I would be returning to the apartment in a few hours' time. She spoke briefly to Mark whom she had seen in Washington but not actually met before and wished him a safe journey back.

We walked back to the Embankment along to Westminster Bridge before saying our goodbyes. He told me the police had orders to protect me but the best protection was to remove myself from the system, disappear for a while, and get out of London.

I said, 'I have Valerie to consider now. We are going to her Aunt's house in Guildford for Christmas with her father and stepmother. What happens after will depend on this bomb being found.'

'You will know we are dealing with powerful people who will not stop, even if we survive the current threat, so all of us are going to be in danger. Be careful Paul, and trust nobody,' he said.

We shook hands and agreed to keep in contact, assuming London still existed in the new millennium. As Mark walked back to his office, I looked out onto the Thames to see a heavily loaded barge being towed up river. Then it hit me. According to Henry Fellows, this was the exact spot where he met with David Simons in 1945 on the day when Britain declared war on Germany. Was it pure chance I should be standing at this place at this time? Or, was some divine message being sent to me? I didn't believe in such things but the thought troubled me.

I needed to clear my head so decided to walk back to my apartment through the London streets. Walking up from Westminster a number of ministerial limousines swept past me racing towards Whitehall. I was surprised that Ministers or whoever was in the vehicles, were not back in their homes for Christmas. Perhaps some alert warnings had been sent out. Making my way past Westminster Abbey and along Victoria Street to Grosvenor Place which ran at the rear of Buckingham Palace Gardens, I arrived at the famous Hyde Park Corner. The underground car park was a short distance from it on Park Lane. CCTV cameras were everywhere so it would be impossible for the terrorists not to be seen driving into the car park. On the eve of the millennium, people would be gathering for the celebrations so it was likely to be full and police would be in abundance in London. It seemed a strange site to select to detonate a nuclear bomb, almost like a last-minute decision, but not a very wise one. The bombers were putting themselves at great risk of being discovered but perhaps that's what was intended by the planners. I hoped the Russians and Rupert Arnold had everything under control and were not being fooled by Al-Qaeda. Fortunately, the Head of Anti- Terrorism was not a man to be easily fooled.

My cell phone rang.

'Hi Paul, its Mark. Rupert Arnold has given his agreement for you and Valerie to use my office if you wish to see the millennium celebrations, assuming you want to be in London. Apparently there is a party to celebrate the New Year being held in the building for invited guests. You may get an invitation. He seemed confident that London will be safe.'

I thanked him and said. 'I will talk to Valerie.'

After returning to the apartment I switched on my desktop computer. Fortunately, John had kept his word and I was now able to access my emails and the Internet. My first task was to check on Lord Globe and his background. I managed to discover that he owned a number of companies that traded in metal-based commodities with all the major countries, including Russia, India and Japan. These countries had members on the Cabal of The New

Order. There was no direct reference to the names of the people or the extent of the business. Much early personal background information on Globe was missing or had been taken off the websites. His name was Adrian Custodio. He had been an advisor on overseas trade to the last Conservative Prime Minister and a large contributor to party funds. That was all in the public record. He was awarded a knighthood in 1990 and subsequently a peerage. I found an obscure reference to a party conference dinner which revealed a photograph of him in the company of a leading member of the Royal Family. In the background was an elderly lady who could have been Diane Hunter but since I had never seen a photo of her I couldn't be sure. If I was right, Globe could be her protector but who was protecting him I wondered?

Valerie returned from visiting her father in Richmond. He had been pleased to see her and know that at last she had removed herself from Washington and the clutches of Alan Sherman whom he had never liked. Her father had initially introduced Valerie into Washington's political society and felt responsible for what had happened. Having found out about me from his diplomatic friends, he was looking forward to our meeting. I hoped Valerie had not told him anything about the bomb threat or our involvement in it. I told her about my meeting with Mark and the others and that it was likely we would get invited to a select New Year's Eve Party, if the bomb was found before.

Next day we set off to drive to Guildford. Being Christmas Eve and a Friday, the roads were busy but we arrived at Flo's house late in the afternoon. She actually lived in an extended cottage in the old Surrey village of Farncombe which was closer to Godalming than Guildford near the A3, London to Portsmouth road. It was a fine sunny day but the forecast for later, including Christmas Day, was sunny periods with rain and cloud. I had never been to the village but apparently it was mentioned in the Domesday Book of 1086 as Ferncombe. Its other claim to fame was that it was the birthplace of John George "Jack" Phillips. He was an early wireless telegraphist who died while serving as senior wireless operator on board the maiden voyage of the RMS Titanic.

He continued working as the ship sank, trying to contact other ships that might be able to come to its assistance. Phillips was commemorated by the Phillips Memorial Garden in Godalming and a pub, "The Jack Phillips" in Godalming High Street was named after him.

Flo's attractive cottage, surrounded by a picturesque garden, was set back from the road. It had its own drive where three cars were already parked but there was ample room for my Mercedes.

An elderly grey-haired lady came to the door, who I assumed was Flo. On seeing us a broad smile lit up her face. She flung her arms around Valerie and I saw immediately the bond that existed between the two women. We stepped inside and Flo, who was much shorter than me, reached up and kissed me on the cheek, saying in a soft welcoming voice,

'I've heard so much about you, Paul, and am pleased to meet you at last.'

I reciprocated with a similar remark.

Valerie's father, Sir George Day, and his wife, Margaret, who had arrived earlier, came out from the living room to greet us. Since his heart attack, Sir George didn't drive so Margaret, who was ten years younger, did the driving. He was a tall, well-groomed man, with a slight limp, a disability from his stroke. I could see where Valerie had inherited her good looks. She had never actually described him to me or ever shown any photographs. Likewise, he didn't have any physical knowledge of me either, so we were both starting our relationship with no pre-conceived ideas of our physical appearances. Margaret was a tall, slim well-dressed lady with an aristocratic bearing.

Valerie kissed her father but I detected a slightly cooler approach to her stepmother. She had a much closer relationship with her Aunt Flo who had brought her up after her mother died. Unfortunately, Uncle Bill, Flo's husband had passed away five years previously so Flo lived alone but was well-established in the village and had many friends. She had no children of her own but was a spritely sixty-five-year-old who, from the appearance of her house and garden, was a very active lady.

The cottage was even larger than it looked from the outside. It had a cosy feel about it. A stone fireplace was built into the whole of one wall. Decorated with lights and occupying a corner of the living room, a real conifer provided the Christmas tree. The other wall displayed cards and photographs. One showed a young Valerie with her mother, another of her at a university graduation.

Valerie had her own room when she paid her annual visits but Flo gave us a larger one in the extension overlooking the garden and fields beyond.

She told us that we were all going out to a pub in the village where the locals sang carols. It was a traditional party atmosphere on Christmas Eve. When she left the room I said to Valerie, 'How much does she know about us?'

'Very little, except what I put in a letter from Washington telling her that we had met at a business conference and I had decided to give up my job and return with you before Christmas. I did tell daddy a little more since he knew about my life in Washington. He is intelligent enough to sense that something serious is going on with the bomb threats. He wants to speak to you about it when he can.'

'Do you think he knows about the London bomb?' I asked.

'I'm not sure but I did hint that we would all be safer outside of London. Paul, we can trust dad. We must tell him what's going on. He is my dad and remember he was the First Secretary at the British Embassy in Washington,' she replied.

'OK, I will talk to him,' I said.

Holding my hand, she kissed me, saying, 'Paul, whatever happens in London, I love you.'

I took her in my arms and knew the moment I had been planning since arriving back in England, had come. After Martha's Vineyard, I knew Valerie was the woman I wanted to share my life with and marry. Love is that inexplicable all-consuming emotion which supplants all others. In a short time we had shared more than most people experienced in a lifetime. When I first set eyes on her in Washington I became enthralled. Yes, then it was a physical attraction but that soon changed after our first date into something much deeper. Our past relationships had given us both an understanding of what was really important and what really mattered in our lives. Valerie needed to be loved and protected. She was emotionally fragile. I needed someone to love and give meaning to my life. We were the perfect match.

I fumbled in my pocket for the small box I had been carrying all day for the time when I could propose. Now that time had come. I looked into Valerie's eyes and said, 'Darling, I love you. Will you marry me?'

With a loving smile and tears of happiness in her eyes she said, 'Yes,' and gave me a tender kiss.

I took out a diamond engagement ring from the box and placed it on her finger.

She gasped at it and flung her arms around me, saying, 'It's so beautiful!'

'It was my mother's. I hope you don't mind,' I said.

'Oh, Paul, are you sure you want me to have it? It must have meant so much to you.'

'Yes, but I want you to have it,' I said.

At that moment I wanted to make love to her. I knew she felt the same.

'Let's wait until later,' she said, squeezing me so tight I had to pull away to get my breath back.

'You have just made me the happiest woman in the world. Come let's go downstairs and tell my family.'

George and Margaret were talking to Flo as we entered the room. Valerie, holding my hand and smiling said, 'We have something to tell you, Paul has just asked me to marry him.' She proudly displayed the ring on her finger. With tears in her eyes, Flo took Valerie in her arms. George shook my hand and Margaret kissed me. Then Flo turned and hugged me saying how pleased she was for Valerie.

'This is a cause for celebration,' said George.

He seemed to be a man who liked to drink because before I could speak he went to a drinks cabinet where almost every alcoholic beverage was on display. Flo stopped him.

'George I have something better in the fridge.'

She came back a few minutes later with an ice bucket containing a bottle of champagne. 'I was keeping this for later to celebrate having you all here for Christmas but now we have an even better reason.'

Five glasses took care of the bottle and we were duly toasted. I wondered if this was the right time to open up and tell everybody what was going on only thirty miles away in London.

Today I had made two women very happy. George and Margaret clearly wanted to know more about me which gave me some cause to worry. I had already decided to tell them about what had happened to us during the last month. The danger was that revealing the London bomb threat could spoil the evening, indeed their Christmas. They naturally wanted to know how we met and why we had both decided to come back to England. Valerie told me she had said nothing to her father about the bomb threats or the incident in New York but had told him about our meeting in Washington. While he served as the First Secretary at the British Embassy, George Day got to know most of the politicians in Washington and many others back in London so I thought he would understand the security issues.

After some small talk, I said to everyone, 'Since I am now almost part of the family there is something I need to tell you, but first I must have your assurance it will go no further than this room.'

Seeing my apprehension and using the opportunity to excuse herself from not telling her father when they met in Richmond, Valerie said, 'Daddy, I'm sorry but what Paul is about to tell you is a state secret and I thought it better he explained the full background to it since for the last few months he has been at the centre of things.'

I noticed the atmosphere in the room change. George looked particularly worried as though he knew what was coming.

'Let's fill up our glasses before we hear Paul's story,' he said.

Flo went out to the kitchen and brought back another bottle of champagne. It did the trick and after sipping the bubbly, everybody became more relaxed.

I started at the beginning with my commercial assignment to Kuwait. I was careful to omit the details of my encounter with the Asian girl. They listened intently about my experiences in Washington, Tucson, Martha's Vineyard and New York. It sounded like a story from one of Frederick Forsyth's books. My own book was already formulating in my mind. But it was when I revealed the possible existence of a terrorist nuclear bomb in London that shocked faces stared at me in disbelief. After I stopped speaking there was a stony silence in the room. George was the first to speak.

'Paul, I knew something important was going on from bits of information I was receiving from my pals at the Diplomat's Club but had no idea of the level of danger. We all thought it unusual for the Prime Minister and cabinet ministers to be still in London now that Christmas has arrived. Also the high level of police activity in the capital did make me suspicious that it was more than the usual bomb threat.'

The three women left the room saying they wanted to make some tea, but that was done to give me time alone with George. They really didn't want to hear any more about bombs but would no doubt be quizzing Valerie about her own experiences.

'Do you think the information about the location of the bomb is true?' he asked.

'Yes, based after what happened in New York but there is a danger we are being duped by Al-Qaeda. At least now our Government has access to all the resources and intelligence available from the FBI and CIA. The detonation of a terrorist nuclear bomb in London would be equally devastating for America.'

Being a long-serving diplomat, George with all his experience was being tactful when he said, 'We have already arranged to be in Scotland for the New Year's celebrations, staying with friends. I am sure there would be room for you and Valerie. Remember you now have a fiancée to think about.'

'You may be right,' I replied. 'But let's see how things progress. I have every confidence in Rupert Arnold and his team finding the bomb and the terrorists.'

George stared at me with his penetrating blue eyes. I knew something serious was about to be said.

'My wife's death had a profound effect on Valerie. Losing a mother at the age of seven is bad for any child but since my job took me away a lot I couldn't be with her as much as I would have liked. Fortunately, my wife's sister Flo stepped in and became her surrogate mother. They became very close, which meant I could pursue my career in the Diplomatic Service knowing that she was being looked after. But Valerie never forgave me for not being there when she needed me. I provided all the material needs but not the emotional ones. Being an attractive girl she was sought after by all the men while at university. Unfortunately, being emotionally vulnerable she suffered a number of bad relationships.

When I left her in Washington I knew one day some unscrupulous politician would offer her everything. As you know, that's what happened when she became attached to Alan Sherman, whom I disliked from the second I set eyes on him. He befriended many attractive women to boost his own ego. I tried to warn her but an attractive, talented woman in that political environment needs to be protected. At least Sherman did provide that and a luxury apartment in Georgetown. At one time I thought he would leave his wife and marry her but fortunately his political career came first. From what you now tell me about his complicity with Jonas Gould and this New Order organisation, it's a good job Valerie met you when she did. I was to blame for having first found her a job in Washington, then leaving her there when I was forced to retire on health grounds. I thought the beach house in Martha's Vineyard was safe because I never revealed its existence to anyone, but the FBI would have a file on me so someone like Gould would have well-paid moles he could use to get information. Valerie is very much like her mother, but fortunately didn't inherit her mother's poor health; she eventually died of pneumonia.'

He stopped talking and stared at me but this time with sad eyes. It was the moment when I knew I was expected to talk.

'Valerie told me about her dreams, when her mother warned of bad things. Normally I don't take dreams seriously but last time she had one, it was just before the gunman tried to kill us at the beach house in Martha's Vineyard. Did she have such premonitions when she was a child?' I asked.

'Not to my knowledge, but she was at the bedside when her mother died. She burst into the room crying and before I could stop her, she placed her arms around her mother's neck. Being only seven years old, the experience did have a profound psychological affect on her. They had developed a strong bond, stronger because I was away a lot. For some years Flo told me she would cry in her bedroom so what you are telling me about the dreams is no surprise.' He paused when Flo came into the room, but seeing that we were still engaged in conversation, she excused herself and left.

George continued, 'Sigmund Freud first argued that the motivation of all dream content is wish-fulfilment, and that the instigation of a dream is often to be found in the events of the day preceding the dream. He also suggested that every person in the dream represents an aspect of the dreamer. Now my knowledge of psychology is a little limited but I believe dreams that encompass premonitions of bad things are often extensions of inner fears. In Valerie's case, deep down she may want to be with her mother. She never accepted her death and wouldn't let her go. Perhaps subconsciously she is trying to reach out to her mother, but my interpretation could be wrong.'

I said, 'George, I love your daughter and will look after her but I hope I'm not going to be a substitute for her lost mother.'

'I don't believe that she will see you as a mother substitute, I think Flo fills that role but you will plug a huge emotional gap in her life so you must be absolutely sure about your commitment,' he said, with a more powerful look in his eyes. Then I saw that Valerie had her father's eyes. Why hadn't I seen it before? The sadness had been replaced by an expression of a father telling his new son-in-law about what is expected.

The rattle of teacups and smell of freshly-baked cakes, followed by the women coming back into the room, put an abrupt end to our conversation. Valerie glanced at me with a look which said, 'I know what father has been telling you.' I looked back at her, smiled and winked.

The gloom about the bomb threat had disappeared. This family was going to enjoy its Christmas. After a wonderful dinner cooked by Flo we enjoyed singing carols with the church choir at the local pub which was located about two hundred metres from the house on the road through the village.

We arrived back at the cottage just before midnight in a Christmas mood. That meant we all had too much to drink but everyone was happy. My first Christmas Eve night with my new fiancée was the best night of my life. We made love, not passionate love like the first time, but gentle love. We then fell asleep locked in each other's arms.

Christmas Day started with a late breakfast, after which we did the traditional opening of Christmas presents that were stacked neatly at the foot of the tree. Valerie had bought me a pair of solid gold cufflinks with my initials inscribed on them. She proudly displayed my engagement ring while opening presents from her family. While Flo and Margaret prepared the Christmas dinner, Valerie and I went for a walk to the village. It was a cold but bright sunny day. If it had snowed then the village would have looked like one of those typical Christmas card scenes. Looking at the thatched cottages and village shops it couldn't be more English.

In the days that followed we motored around the surrounding countryside. Valerie took me to see the house in Guildford were she was born and the primary school she first attended. For her it was an emotional journey back to her childhood. We went to her mother's grave in a churchyard near to her old home. It was then she broke down and I realised how important her mother had been to her. It was more an expression of happiness than sorrow. She gripped my hand tightly at the graveside and I sensed that she was finally saying goodbye to her mother now she had someone to fill the void. I put my arm around her. We didn't speak but I could feel she had been released from the emotional bond that had held her over the years since her mother's death.

30 December

After breakfast my mobile phone rang. It was John Nicholas. 'Paul, I have some good news. We found the bomb early this morning. It did contain a lot of explosive material but was a fake and didn't have a nuclear core. I can't say much on the telephone but the terrorists are all dead after a shootout. Our agents in Russia are trying to establish where the bomb came from and who was responsible. We don't believe Al-Qaeda knew it was fake bomb. The Prime Minister has decided to open the celebrations and you and Valerie are invited. Please confirm you wish to attend and a car will be sent to bring you to the Ministry Building on the eve of the millennium.'

I thanked him and said I would talk to Valerie and let him know. I told Valerie and the others the news. George looked relieved.

At first Valerie wanted to go to Scotland but seeing that I wanted to accept the Prime Minister's invitation at an historical event, agreed we should go. Deep down I still had worries that Al-Qaeda had fooled us but Rupert Arnold would have more intelligence information than I was being told. He wouldn't risk the lives of the Queen and the Government if he believed a danger still existed. Once again everything depended on the quality of our intelligence and those who were entrusted to protect the nation. I made the call and accepted the invitation.

CHAPTER 15

The Eve of the Millennium
31ˢᵗ December 1999

Valerie and I went to London specifically at the invitation of the Prime Minister to witness the millennium celebrations from the safety of an office at the Ministry of Defence, located opposite the Millennium Wheel. He was officially opening the Wheel before midnight. It was only because the bomb had been found and de-activated that with some trepidation I accepted the invitation. The Prime Minister and the Government wanted to show the terrorists and our enemies that London could not be intimidated and was safe by proceeding with the planned celebrations. The invitation was also a recognition of my role in finding the American bomb and identifying those responsible. Some people in MI5 refused to acknowledge my involvement since I was not part of their family. I had been shoe-horned into their domain by the CIA without them being consulted. It was only after the American Vice President attached me to his Task Force and gave me access to intelligence information, that they were reluctantly forced to accept my position. My visit to Kuwait had caused a lot of problems for them since they had not been consulted by the Americans about why I was being used by the CIA.

Valerie and I were taken to the Ministry of Defence building in an unmarked car by two Special Branch officers so we could get through the road blocks and security controls that surrounded all the Government buildings. It was late evening when we arrived. An escort took us to a room overlooking the River Thames. Inside were about twenty people, including Rupert and John, some Ministers and a number of senior policemen. A short portly man came up and introduced himself as Colin Bradley. He was a representative of British Airways who were hosting the reception since they were in the process of negotiating ownership of the Wheel.

As we walked into the room all heads were turned towards us. It was Valerie they were looking at, not me. I recalled that she had the same effect on people at the Hay-Adams Hotel reception in Washington. Then my head was the one that turned. She looked stunning in her stylish white-patterned blouse and smart black figure-hugging trouser suit, one of the new purchases from Selfridges. But it was her shiny blonde shoulder-length hair and engaging smile that caught the eye of most of the onlookers. Even the cold-faced Rupert Arnold couldn't resist the temptation to come over and introduce himself. After some small talk, it transpired that he had known her father when at the British Embassy in Washington so immediately they had a subject for conversation.

From the reflections of people in the window that looked out onto the river, I could see most of the men looking at Valerie. I momentarily left her side and was tapped on the shoulder by an anxious-looking John Nicholas. He moved me to a quiet corner of the room to talk. I looked back and could see a number of other men homing in towards Valerie. She was in her element; it was like the times she spent hosting parties in Washington with her father. It taught her how to handle men with big egos. For the first time, I felt a tinge of jealousy.

John said, 'Paul, I just want to brief you further about the bomb we found and de-activated successfully in the Hyde Park car park. It was taken there yesterday evening in a van by three terrorists. The device was set up on a timer to explode at midnight tonight. The men left in another car which was followed by armed police to an address in the East End. The order was given to arrest them but they must have been tipped off because they tried to evade capture by shooting at the officers. In the ensuing shoot-out, two were killed. The other one died in hospital with a smile on his face telling us there was another bomb which we would never find.

As we suspected, the Hyde Park bomb was a decoy but the terrorists didn't know we were meant to find it.'

'So where is the other bomb?' I asked, feeling a high degree of apprehension.

He pulled out a small pair of night-vision glasses from his pocket. 'Somewhere in one of the barges at the base of the wheel,' he replied rather casually. I looked at him in disbelief.

He said, 'Look through the glasses at the barge tethered to the platform under the Wheel.'

I saw a number of dark figures clambering around the vessel. He continued, 'My men are searching every vessel for the second time, having found nothing from earlier searches. We caught two men about an hour ago leaving the area in a boat on the river, who, from the description we had been given, matched the terrorists. Both were British Pakistanis. They refused to admit they had planted a suitcase bomb on one of the barges but couldn't give an explanation why they were on the river with sets of tools. We established they were not employees of the firework company. All the barges and platforms carry fireworks for tonight's displays and have been wired to ignite in a timed sequence.

The Prime Minister and police have been alerted but it was decided rather than have the vessels towed away to search them first. It was intelligence from Washington, and you can thank Mark Brooks for that, that told us the bomb was installed in a barge near the Wheel and timed to explode at midnight but didn't know the exact location.'

So my conversation with Mark at the site of the Wheel must have set him thinking. A container and a barge had been used for hiding the New York bomb so precedence had been set. There was something I was not being told so I asked John why the barges had not been towed away. With a whimsical smile on his face, he said, 'OK, as you know the bomb we found in the car park did contain explosives but didn't have a nuclear core. It was a fake. We traced its origin to a bomb–maker in the Ukraine who had been selling fake suitcase bombs to terrorists for months. He even employed people to make up real explosive charges to be packed around stainless hemispheres to make them look real. The real bombs should have spherical plutonium cores.'

'But how can you be sure the other one is also a fake?' I asked.

'Because our source told us two bombs were sold to Al-Qaeda and shipped to Amsterdam two weeks ago. They arrived at the site of the old Albert Docks yesterday. One of the men caught was an importer who had arranged the paperwork. The other was an electronics expert who set the timers and initiators. Both men had replaced two employees of the company who was contracted to set up tonight's firework display. The real workers were found with their throats cut in a warehouse earlier today.'

The whole millennium conspiracy had become so complex it was difficult to know who to believe anymore. Too many loose ends and assumptions existed. So here I was with the woman I loved, most of the British Government, the Prime Minister and the Queen who was later going to join the celebrations at the Millennium Dome, all within a few hundred metres of a supposed fake atomic bomb, or at the least, a high explosive device, which nobody knew about, except the Prime Minister and a few policemen. It was a surreal situation. A lot of faith and lives rested in the quality of the intelligence. The Prime Minister was taking a high risk strategy. I was reminded of the 1959 song by the pianist, Tom Lehrer, *We Will All Go Together When We Go* that put humour into the Cold War threat of blowing everybody up with atomic bombs. Suddenly it didn't seem so funny.

Glasses of champagne were being handed around. John moved away to talk to someone else so I decided to rescue Valerie from her many admirers. But this time she had a large engagement ring on her finger, which hopefully sent out a message to the baying males.

We circulated among the guests, being careful to avoid any talk about where we had been and why we were at the reception. I used my standing as a freelance international journalist writing articles about the Middle East as a topic of conversation. Valerie was able to talk about her political life in Washington and name drop, which always kept people interested. We were constantly bombarded with canapés and drinks, after which I was becoming light-headed.

It did help to lighten my concerns about what may have been happening on the opposite bank. Most of the lights on and around the Wheel had been turned off so it was difficult to see anything.

There was a lot of activity near the door. Some Special Branch men preceded the Prime Minister, who came into the room and shook hands with some selected guests that did not include us but he did notice Valerie. A space was cleared around him so he could make a brief statement. The TV cameras were running so it looked like he was broadcasting to the world.

> *'Tonight is a very special night. The last one before the new millennium. I want to thank all of you and those out on the river for the efforts you have made to make this a memorable evening. From all of us here in Britain to people throughout the world, we wish you a happy and wonderful New Year with peace and prosperity.'*

He then left to go outside where a laser beam facility had been set up. The plan was for the Prime Minister to fire a laser beam at a target near the Wheel which would initiate the turning of the Wheel and a firework display at midnight. Meanwhile the Queen was sailing down the Thames to light a millennium beacon afloat on a barge, which would then trigger off a string of gas-powered beacons across the UK.

As the midnight moment approached, I grabbed Valerie's hand. I hadn't told her what John had said about the bombs. It was too late to do anything anyway. Only two things could happen – oblivion or the excitement of watching an impressive firework display. I felt like Oppenheimer must have done just before the detonation of the atomic bomb at Alamogordo but in my case hoping for a failure.

Everybody crowded by the window to watch the moment of truth. I saw John looking through his glasses at the barge opposite and saying something into his hidden communicator. There was a look of apprehension on his face as he glanced my way. Then he put up his hand as if to say, 'This is it.'

We couldn't see the Prime Minister but did see the green laser beam streak across the river to hit its target from a source hidden beneath us. I didn't know how much he knew but he must have wondered if he was initiating Armageddon. Instantaneously a burst of blinding light followed by a tremendous explosion emanated from one of the barges near the base of the Wheel. My brain told me the atomic bomb had just exploded but then a massive array of rockets was projected into the air. The windows of the building shook and gasps could be heard from the room. At first it looked like one of the firework stores on the barge had prematurely ignited. But soon after, masses of fireworks of all colours and designs started to explode from sites all around the Wheel. It was a cascade of colour and an initial cacophony of noise.

Red, orange, yellow, blue and every shade of every colour burst out in the sky above as one display followed another. Looking like a giant Catherine Wheel, the engineering marvel in front of us came alive with the sounds of Gustav Holst's Planet Suite.

Mars-the Bringer of War followed by *Jupiter-the Bringer of Joy*, seemed very appropriate for the moment.

People in the room started to shout and sing and the party atmosphere began. With some relief, at the stroke of midnight I took my fianceé in my arms, kissed her tenderly, and said, 'I love you.'

She responded back by holding me so tight I couldn't breathe, saying, 'I love you too.'

Tones of "Auld Lang Syne' burst out, hands were held and people danced about. Valerie was snatched away from me before I could kiss her again. She became the recipient of many kisses, some had eagerly awaited the opportunity – as happens at the New Year celebrations and this was for me a very special New Year. The firework display went on for about twenty minutes but the party had only just started when more people appeared to fill the room.

I could see the relief on John's face as he tried to squeeze through the crowd to get to me. First, he turned to Valerie and gave her a kiss. Clearly he had been too occupied on the phone to do it earlier. Then with a shy grin, he shook my hand wishing me a happy New Year. He took us both into a corner of the room away from the window and said,

'After a little persuasion one of the captured terrorists did talk and told us the bomb was buried in a box of fireworks on the barge under the Wheel. Unfortunately, it was too late for us to reach it before midnight. One of my men was injured, but not seriously, running towards the barge. He was only about fifty yards away when the laser beam struck a light detector fitted to the barge. It sent a signal to a timing mechanism which triggered the explosive charge around the bomb, culminating in the large explosion you saw. It also ignited the fireworks and started the display. All this happened in milliseconds so nobody would have noticed anything unusual.

I spoke to the Prime Minister just now. He has already called the US President to inform him of events. No doubt Al-Qaeda and their associates will be angry at this latest failure. In due course we can expect retaliations so my people will stay on a state of alert. Arrests have been made and there will be more to follow. The two captured terrorists, realising their precarious position, are being very cooperative. They were supposed to have died with the bomb but their martyrdom will have to wait for another day. They are intelligent men and probably wished they hadn't been misled.'

At that moment his cell phone rang. He gave his apologies saying, 'I must go, Rupert wants to see me. Enjoy yourselves and have a great evening, you both deserve it.'

Valerie rang her father and Aunt Flo to wish them a Happy New Year, telling them in coded language that everything was alright. Later we said our goodbyes but nobody was really taking much notice of us as we left the party. London streets were alive so we decided to walk back to the apartment. It would have been impossible to get a taxi anyway. This was a morning to remember.

My fiancée snuggled up to me so I could feel the warmth of her body. I was the happiest man in the world. It was difficult to believe that in the space of a few months my life had changed so radically. I had been courted by Presidents, Prime Ministers, chased by murderers and master criminals, worked alongside top level security agents in two countries and most importantly fallen in love with the most beautiful woman in the world. My experiences would fill the pages of a best-seller. Thousands of people thronged along Whitehall and Trafalgar Square. Everyone was in good spirits. There was a sense of optimism for the new century. Dark clouds were on the horizon for the Government. The economic situation was gloomy but, looking around, the shops, the pubs, the restaurants, and the theatres were full. London is always the same owing to its huge influx of high-spending foreign tourists so is not a good barometer for the rest of the country. I noticed extra police were on duty in Downing Street. I expect the Prime Minister was briefing his cabinet colleagues unless he was in bed.

Walking with crowds of people does invoke a feeling of security. Perhaps it's the safety in numbers syndrome or herd instinct that makes people want to work and live in big cities. They are the places where one can be alone but not feel lonely but being with someone you love is much better.

People were demonstrating their usual New Year's exuberance in and around Trafalgar Square although the famous fountains, the Norwegian Christmas tree and Nelson's Column were cordoned off and crowd control measures were in place. I wondered what Nelson, looking down from his high perch, would say if he saw it today with the ground covered in pigeon droppings. I was surprised that some enterprising person didn't breed city birds of prey like sparrow hawks or peregrine falcons. These predators would have a constant food supply and help to keep the pigeon numbers in check.

Trafalgar Square is like the heart of the city with arteries extending in all directions. Pall Mall, Regent Street, Charing Cross Road, The Strand, Northumberland Avenue and Whitehall being the main traffic feeds. If any one of these is blocked then chaos results unless controls are in place. Cities are fertile grounds for terrorist activity and are almost impossible to defend. The original planners didn't comprehend how easy it would be for one man with a knowledge of where all the essential traffic control system boxes were installed to cripple the city. I couldn't begin to imagine the scene if a real atomic bomb had been detonated. Even a small bomb placed strategically in the Square could destroy communications and shut down the city in minutes. CCTV cameras would give the Big Brother watchers immediate views but not enough time to prevent a maniac from causing major damage. It proved that in our times the best defence was having good sources of intelligence. It was that which found the bombers and their bombs.

We walked along Haymarket to Piccadilly Circus. The Christmas lights were flashing everywhere. The famous tube station entrance and the archer Eros balancing on one leg were festooned with garlands. Moving neon signs, a hallmark of Piccadilly made it come alive. We paused as everyone does at Piccadilly. People were everywhere, walking in all directions. Some were going home from just being out on this historical night. Some were going or coming from parties. Some were just there because that's where they wanted to be. I thought if only they knew what I knew about what had happened on this day the scene before me would have been so different. This place was the centre of the Empire at the start of the twentieth century. It seemed the right place to be at the beginning of the twenty-first century. But years of neglect had made its buildings in need of renovation.

Valerie was quietly gazing at the sights. I could see she was happy. I squeezed her hand and kissed her.

'Let's go back to the apartment,' she said.

There were no taxis or trains so we had to walk. Tiredness was catching up on us both so we were glad to see Henry at the entrance to the apartment. I wished him a happy new year. I noticed a police car lurking in the shadows outside.

'Any problems?' I asked,

'Yes, Mr Cane, earlier I saw a suspicious van parked in the road opposite. Its occupants were watching the entrance. I called the police but by the time they arrived it had moved away. The police unusually decided to keep observation in the street so they clearly were concerned.'

My first thought was that John Nicholas had ordered the Special Branch people to protect us but there were many more important residents in the block who had closer connections with the police and MI5. Could they have been the enemy? I remember John saying Al-Qaeda and their associates would not stop even if the millennium bomb was a failure. I thanked Henry and we entered the lift to my apartment. It wasn't long before we went to sleep.

Over the weeks that followed Valerie and I visited friends and relatives. I was proud to show off my new fiancée. Her father, stepmother and Aunt Flo returned from Scotland. We did start to think about our work. Valerie resigned from her Government job in Washington and I promised Robert to consider seriously writing a book but there were still worries about what could happen next and how much I could divulge. I had uncovered a conspiracy which threatened Western democracy but one conspiracy can lead to another. Many villains were still hidden in the dark depths of our security services. They had all the means to cover up and conceal themselves. Belog who was certainly Lord Globe, was living somewhere in Spain and probably still controlled what was left of The New Order. It had probably become re-established under a new name so the danger may still exist. The hydra had many heads and perhaps not all of them had been removed. Al-Qaeda was now the world's number one terrorist organisation and would be pursued by every security agency. It would be a difficult task and take many years. Intelligence gathering and vigilance were going to be the main weapons needed to combat this hidden enemy. It was late in January when I received a call on my special cell phone from Alicia in Washington.

'Hello Paul, I hope you and Valerie are well. Just to let you know that C5 is in England. He has discovered the existence of a network of people who had worked for Diane Hunter. Some were Government consultants for the Ministry of Defence and the Home Office. Two had access to classified information including the recent London bomb threat. What was more disturbing was the fact that the network was controlled by a woman called

Christine Hunter, the daughter of Diane Hunter and Adrian Custodio. The man whose father was Spanish and mother Scottish was better known as Lord Globe. They apparently had an affair back in the 1970s.

MI5 had placed a mole in the network who just happened to be an old army friend of C5. This contact gave him the names of its members. I wanted to tell you this since it concerns your safety. You and Valerie are on a hit list drawn up by the late Diane Hunter. Just before she died she made her daughter promise that she would carry out her unfinished business. This woman is even more ruthless than her mother and knows where you live. She is also known by our CIA who found her code name on files taken from the Boston Company, which also employed the hit man who attempted to kill you both at Martha's Vineyard. John Nicholas has been given all this information so I assume he will be providing you both with protection.

You might also like to know that we found Alan Sherman's name in the Boston Company's client files so the FBI are investigating his involvement with their activities. It has been established that The New Order Cabal members used their services. If we can link Sherman to Hunter then we would have evidence of his complicity in the Vineyard murder. Sherman is currently unobtainable. My guess he has been tipped off and left the country But we will find him. You know we always get our man. I wish you both well and be careful it's not over yet.'

I thanked her but already knew about Globe from my Internet searches and it looks like my suspicions about Sherman were about to be confirmed.

EPILOGUE

February 2000

After surviving the millennium bomb threat, London entered the twenty-first century, a different city. It was less safe, less complacent but more confident in its ability to protect itself. I was glad we had returned to London before Christmas, although at the time, the city and our lives were in danger. After the failure of the New York bomb I knew the terrorists would try to follow through with their threat to destroy London.

A week after the event, John Nicholas called and asked me to go to his office in Whitehall for a private meeting. Looking a little grave, he said, 'There is something I need to tell you about the bomb which I couldn't reveal on the night. I was not absolutely sure about the accuracy of the intelligence information we received concerning the bomb being a fake so as soon as the terrorists we caught revealed its exact location I instructed one of my men to go on the barge to find it. Unfortunately he didn't get to the bomb in time before the start of the firework display. As you know the man was injured in the blast that occurred and taken to hospital with severe burns. Later, parts of the suitcase bomb were recovered and to our horror we found evidence of plutonium. It looks like we had an explosion of what might be called a dirty bomb. Fortunately, since it was not specifically designed to be that type of bomb, most of the radioactivity resulting from the fall out was contained within the barge and the surrounding area. However, the high toxicity of even small amounts of plutonium makes it a very dangerous material. The whole area has been sealed off since it was highly contaminated. A secret clean-up operation is still in progress. The bomb had been real but fortunately the makers or the assemblers had done a poor job so it could never have worked as a nuclear bomb. London had a narrow escape. This fact is known only to a very small number people so never divulge it to anyone.' I agreed to keep the secret to myself.

John took a risk telling me but thought I should know because someone had lied and really wanted London destroyed. Suspicion fell on the Russians who had masterminded the whole operation rather than Al-Qaeda who anyway assumed the bomb was genuine.

Rupert Arnold and John Nicholas did receive unpublicised commendations from the Prime Minister for saving London and were given promotions and more powers to protect the city. The Intelligence services had their budgets greatly increased and were recruiting more IT experts, particularly in communication and computer software. It was obvious the new war on terrorism would be taking place in cyberspace. The would-be terrorists were accessing and using the latest equipment and encryption techniques. The millennium conspiracy had shown up many deficiencies in our ability to find and track terrorists.

The political scandal in the US resulting from the President withholding information about the New York bomb would be prolonged. It had already greatly reduced the chances of a Democrat being returned to the Presidency for a very long time. Very few people knew the whole truth of what happened in the closing months of 1999 but before long some aspiring journalist would make his name by writing an article in a newspaper and the Government would be powerless to prevent it.

Jonus Gould was killed in a mysterious hit-and-run car accident on Long Island. The police were not too vigorous in catching those responsible. Soon after, Alan Sherman withdrew his nomination for the Republican Party leadership, resigned his seat in the Senate and membership of the Party. The FBI issued him with an ultimatum and then did a deal to prevent a scandal. His role in the conspiracy and the part he might have played in the attempt on our lives in Martha's Vineyard was still being investigated by the FBI. But Valerie was still prepared to give him the benefit of the doubt. I was not so sure.

The New Order's plan to discredit the President and his supporters did work but they failed to get their man as the next presidential candidate. It was now likely that a Texan multi-millionaire would take the Republican nomination and be the next President. He would not be their choice since he was not one of their members. The Republicans intended to review foreign policy, tighten security and take measures to protect America but the terrorist threat still remained. Al-Qaeda had been dealt a blow but was still growing in strength and now had revenge on its agenda. Fortress America was still the target. The fight had to be taken to them. Its high-level of infiltration into the security services was particularly worrying. Many moles had been arrested and removed from the CIA and FBI. New Director Generals had been appointed and both agencies were under review by an all-party senate committee which would take place after the enquiry into the millennium conspiracy had reported.

I wrote to my friends, Robert, Alicia, Gary and Mark telling them about our engagement. Alicia replied saying I was a lucky man to have such a beautiful fiancée and wished us luck. She added that Valerie was also fortunate to have a man who was a good shot but that I shouldn't play a James Bond anymore and leave the killing to the professionals. She ended her letter with the sad news that Gary had been killed in a car accident but she believed he was deliberately targeted. The driver of the car that hit his car was also killed. He was an Arab who had no identification on him and the car was stolen. Alicia and Gary had received death threats so they knew sooner or later their enemies would strike. The two terrorist moles in the FBI and CIA had been identified. Both were arrested and, knowing they faced a death sentence, took the easy way out and committed suicide. Alicia's man had done a good job eliminating the bad people on the list. The Russian Mafia had taken care of Sudakov and Seperkov who were found shot in their homes, no doubt instigated by the friends of C5 who had travelled to Moscow soon after the explosion in the South Atlantic. Heinz

Kluge, alias Wolfman, and Ludwig Menzies, who were responsible for the death of Colin Niedermeyer had similar fates. Justice had been done. Takaki Tobata died when his private plane crashed in a field outside Tokyo.

Diane Hunter's membership of the Cabal, her connections with the Russians, Al-Qaeda and the bomb threats were known by the Government and her Nationalist Party was made illegal and dissolved. MI5 had identified a network of her New Order members who were now under surveillance. The big question was, had they all been identified? For her to have lasted for so long and been immune to prosecution she must have had an influential protector. It was reported that she had advanced cancer and took her own life with an overdose in early January; that was the official statement. The actual truth will never be known. But her daughter was still being sought by the police as a suspect in a number of crimes. I believe it was her who sent the threats to me. She seems to have taken up her mother's causes which meant she was still a dangerous person. Was I now the family quarry? The discovery that she possessed a hit list from her mother before she died with our names on was a cause for worry.

We had cut off the heads of The New Order and defunctionalised it for the time being. Only one member of The New Order's Cabal remained alive. The Indian member wasn't directly a part of the conspiracy and would probably be spared. With no interest in politics, he was not considered a threat at the present time although C5 had his card marked. Alicia's assassin had done a good job and saved America and Britain from embarrassing trials.

Mark Brooks had been given a foreign posting to keep him out of Washington. Alicia was promoted to be Head of the White House Security. With her knowledge of Whirlwind and its aftermath she was in a powerful position and no doubt would have taken steps to protect herself. Her CIA boss had been given a golden handshake to retirement. The President wasn't taking any risks with people who knew too much. People who had been involved with and who had knowledge of Whirlwind were being locked down or eliminated. Al-Qaeda still held the key. They knew everything but feared the consequences of making it public at the present time. The Americans were removing members of The New Order who had betrayed them so were doing their job. The destruction of a few Al-Qaeda cells didn't weaken its resolve to attack again. While Bin Laden lived under the protection of his Islamic Brotherhood, more attacks on Western democratic countries were likely.

Robert phoned and sent his best wishes on our engagement. He asked me when I would be writing the book. I reminded him that project Whirlwind was highly classified and could never be revealed. But writers know how to circumvent such issues. I told Robert that at present I had other things to think about but would consider it in the future.

After a month of catching up with family and friends and getting back into London society, Valerie and I left London to look for a quiet break in the country. Now I had a fiancée, my interest in doing what I set out to do the previous year was re-kindled. I still liked the Cotswolds even after the experience that followed my last visit, so contacted Jeremy Simms to ask him if Stones End was still on the market and that I might take my fiancée to see it sometime over the weekend but didn't want a key. He asked me why I hadn't been in contact since I got back from Washington. I told him I had been very busy and no more.

To my surprise, but I suppose out of curiosity, Valerie wanted to see Henry Fellows' cottage. I was little reluctant to go back, but there were some other properties in the area I wanted to look at so we drove to Bisley. By coincidence rather than by plan, it was the last Sunday in February, just four months since my last visit.

Avoiding the actual village of Bisley, I drove directly to the cottage. It was winter so everything looked a little grey and uninteresting except when the sun intermittently burst through the clouds. The night had been cold and clear so an overnight frost had formed. The road was slippery making the bends difficult to negotiate. I overshot the one leading to the cottage so had to reverse back to the lane. I parked the car in the same place as I had done on my previous visit. It was an odd feeling going back to the cottage with the knowledge of what had happened there in November 1999. The vision of Olga Petrovitch creeping into Fellows' cottage and murdering him left me feeling cold. I took Valerie's hand and walked along the path through the wood. As we approached the cottage she squeezed my hand tightly; something was worrying her.

When I looked through the window at the bare floor and walls a strange feeling came over me. It felt like we were being watched. I didn't believe in ghosts but ancient myths tell us that people leave their spirits in the houses where they were murdered. If Henry was watching us he would know about the events that took place after I opened his old suitcase and found his files. The opening of the proverbial Pandora's Box certainly released evil, (*from the Greek myth of Pandora's box which, when opened, released all the evils of the world but for one item which was hope*). Valerie shivered and said she wanted to go back to the car. She, too, had felt something. A sense of calamity came over me. Was some spirit trying to warn us of something?

It was getting dark so we decided to cut short our itinerary and drive back to London. The weather was worsening and visibility was poor as I manoeuvred the Mercedes around the country lanes. We were some distance from the M5 when the road narrowed as it approached a wooded area. A black van appeared in my rear mirror; it was coming too fast around the bends. It came close enough for me to just see what looked like a woman driver with a hood covering her head. The road straightened and the van pulled back. Then it suddenly accelerated straight into the back of my Mercedes. I tried to pull away but it came again. This time it hit the back of my car with such a force that I lost control of the steering and the car swerved off the road straight into a tree. I temporarily lost consciousness. When I woke up, to my horror the air bags had inflated. Valerie was still strapped in her seat but her head was buried into the fabric of the bag. The front of the car was crushed and steam was hissing out from the engine. I felt numb but fearing fire, my first reaction was to get us out of the car. I struggled to release myself, got out and saw that only water and brake fluid were leaking from the car. Fortunately, the fuel tank hadn't been damaged. Never move an injured person from a car accident until the extent of the injuries is known is the rule. I rushed to the other side of the car and pulled Valerie's head back from the air bag. She was unconscious but there were no visible signs of external injuries. She was still breathing but felt cold. Her golden hair was slumped over her face. Numbed by shock, I fumbled in my pocket for my cell phone. Hoping it would still work, I anxiously dialled 999 and explained what had happened to the operator and gave our location. She assured me the police and an ambulance would be sent immediately. I had just finished talking when I felt light-headed, then dizzy, and everything went grey, then black.

The fog cleared. I could see the path up the mountain looming in front of me and I knew I had to reach the top. But time was short so I ran and ran, then I stumbled, I got up and continued running. I reached a ledge and couldn't go any further. The girl, a beautiful girl, was on the other side, she was crying, begging me to take her down the mountain. I stretched my hand but couldn't reach her. Then I fell off the mountain. I kept falling faster, faster, and then I could see a light above me getting stronger and stronger. A face, a large round face with black piercing eyes was looking at me. A muffled sound that got louder was drumming in my ears. Then the mist cleared and I heard a voice.

'Paul, wake up, everything is alright and you're in hospital.'

I opened my eyes to see two smiling faces looking down on me. They were both dressed in white gowns, one was a woman. She held my hand and said, 'You've been in a car accident and unconscious for six hours. Don't try to move yet, just lay still. You're in hospital in Swindon.'

Slowly it came back to me. I remembered the van, my car going off the road, lifting Valerie's head from the air bag. My god what had happened to her.

I tried to shout out, but my voice wouldn't let me.

'How is my fiancée?' I asked.

'She's in the next room,' the woman said.

I felt relieved.

'Is she hurt?' I asked.

The silence that followed my question brought me to near panic.

'She's still unconscious,' was the reply.

I tried to sit up but my legs were heavy. My head ached and my eyes were blurry.

'Please don't try to move yet, Mr Cane. We need to carry out some further tests,' said the woman, who I guessed was a nurse. All I could think about was Valerie. Why was she still unconscious? Was I not being told the truth? Was she dead? Everything bad flashed through my mind.

Observing my anxiety, the man who I assumed was a doctor told me that Valerie was still unconscious and might have received a head injury but more would be known after a CT scan was taken. After some opposition I find persuaded the nurse to let me see Valerie. She was lying serenely on the bed. She was festooned with monitors, looked very pale and peaceful. All the instruments showed normal activity. There were no marks or signs of external injury.

I was led back to my bed and given a sedative. It was some hours before I was awoken by the consultant entering my room. His very presence gave me a feeling of foreboding. 'Mr Cane, I know you are anxious about your fiancée. Before I give you the results of our tests I need some information. Do you know where her medical records are kept as we cannot trace any of them?'

I explained that Valerie had recently worked in America for the Government and her records were probably in Washington, but previously she had lived and worked in London. Apparently the police had our wallets and address details. They had taken possession of my damaged car and wanted to speak to me as soon as possible. No doubt I had been thoroughly checked out. There was going to be some difficult explaining to do later. Hopefully, I just needed to mention Rupert Arnold's name and everything would get sorted out. I asked the consultant about Valerie's injuries. He replied, 'I have some good news and some bad news. The good news is there are no visible signs of neck or brain injury. The bad news is she is severely concussed and in a coma and so far has not responded to our attempts to waken her. Whilst our CT scans failed to show up any abnormalities in the brain, there may be tiny areas of damage which could have a major impact on recovery. In most car accidents where passengers are thrown forward into an exploding airbag after a rear or forward impact collision damage is usually a form of whiplash. The body is thrown first forward then back which causes the head and neck to hyper-extend and to hyper-flex. The bones in the spine are forced to stretch sometimes causing damage to the nerves and muscles. Most patients have an uncomfortable few days but fully recover unless there are other problems in the body from previous illnesses. That is why I need to have Valerie's medical records to find out if she has other conditions that might explain why she is not regaining consciousness.'

'Do you know of any similar cases where this has happened?' I asked.

'Yes, we once had a patient who, like Valerie, showed no symptoms of brain or spinal damage but was in a coma for six months. There have been cases where people have remained in a vegetative state for years before recovery. It's impossible to know. If she doesn't wake in the next few days there are other tests we can make but the longer she remains in a coma the less likely she will come back quickly. We can only wait and see what happens.'

I thanked the doctor for being so honest but it left me in a state of depression. Had I just lost the only person who mattered in my life through my own fault? My high state of happiness since our engagement in planning a new life for ourselves was shattered. We had decided to get married in the Spring and put the events of the last few months behind us. But someone had decided to take out their vengeance on me and may have prevented that from happening.

I would have to tell Valerie's father and Aunt Flo and our

friends but wasn't sure what to say to them. First, I telephoned John Nicholas, using his encrypted number. He answered immediately and I explained what had happened. He agreed to talk to the police and make special security arrangements for Valerie and me. It would mean taking her to a London hospital.

I sent a text to Alicia and Robert in Washington, explaining what had happened. Alicia replied immediately expressing her sadness and told me to be very careful as clearly The New Order and Al-Qaeda were seeking retribution for the failures of the two millennium bomb projects.

Sir George, his wife Margaret and Flo came to see us the next day. I was not discharged but was able to get dressed to meet them. Her family were very distressed and wanted to know all about the crash. The police had been to see me before they arrived, so I was able to give them an account of what happened, including why we were on that particular part of the road. I was careful to avoid mentioning my suspicions about who was in the van, since I wanted John to deal with it. After, I didn't receive any further visits from the local police so I assumed they were told the London Met was taking over the case.

A week later Valerie was moved to a private ward in St Thomas' Hospital in London. I moved back to my apartment and did my best to come to terms with what had happened. John Nicholas came to see me and said that Rupert Arnold and the Prime Minister had been told because of the security issues. So far, they had no success in tracking down the van or the suspect. Paint from the van had been found on my Mercedes but it was impossible to match it to any specific vehicle. It was suspected that Christine Hunter had changed her identity and left the country but the police were still investigating.

Robert called me from Washington to say he was flying to London to see me in a few days. To occupy my mind I started to write up the events of the last four months using my diary notes with a view not to immediately producing a book, but just to ensure I recorded everything before my memory faded. It was when I started detailing my first fateful visit to the Stones End that

I remembered the blood-stained tissue I had picked up before I left the cottage. I opened my desk drawer to find it lying on top of the copy of Fellows' papers. Whose blood was it, I wondered? Did Olga Petrovitch cut herself at the time of the murder? The police would have surely found any blood-stained paper long before I went to the cottage so had someone else must have been to the cottage after Fellows' murder? Being curious, I called John and told him about my find. He offered to have it analysed for DNA, a new analysis technique being increasingly used by the police in serious crime cases. A week later the result showed the DNA belonged to Christine Hunter. Fortunately, her DNA was on their own secret database which explained why she had been careful to not leave any evidence at the scenes of her crimes. She must have gone to the cottage soon after the murder to search for Fellows' papers and without knowing, dropped the tissue she may have used for wiping a bleeding cut.

Robert arrived and tried to persuade me to write a book about the millennium conspiracy as he had already secretly secured a publisher. A five hundred thousand dollar fee was mentioned but I warned him about the security and confidentiality issues associated with Whirlwind. Someone must have thought it would be the story of the century to offer such an exalted fee. He wanted me to write a fictional story based on the events without using names of actual places. While Valerie was in a coma, I didn't want to leave London or take on any journalistic work that would inevitably take me overseas so the book idea did appeal to me. Robert, being my agent had already worked out his commission. I did remind him that a substantial sum was still owed to us by the US Government for our services to the CIA and FBI. He had already tried to acquire that money but since no formal agreement was signed and many of the people involved were either dead, retired or had changed jobs, obtaining the money was proving very difficult. I doubted whether it would ever be paid so the book option might the best way forward.

Robert left to fly to Germany to see another client. It had been over three weeks since the car crash. The scans had shown no brain damage so the consultant was confident she would suddenly wake up and return fully to normal. Often brain damage is associated with comas and the patient cannot remember the past or what happened to them. In such cases a long process of re-learning has to take place. I was told the next few weeks would be crucial in determining the future since the body starts to deteriorate after prolonged inactivity. I could only hope good fortune would fall on us and we could return to the life we planned to have together, but only time would tell.

I decided to take Robert's advice and start the book. It may not be published for some time but at least the events will be recorded. The deaths of so many people must not go unexplained; I owed it to them. If the terrorists had been successful then the death toll would have been in millions and I wouldn't be here to write about it.

A week later when I was writing about my experiences in Washington I received a phone call from St. Thomas' Hospital with the good news that Valerie had just woken up from her coma. I asked if I could speak to her. There was a long silence before a consultant answered. 'Mr Cane it would be preferable for you to come to the hospital immediately.' I thanked him and dashed there. On arrival I was met by a nurse who took me to the consultant's room where a tall young man was seated. We shook hands, and with a smile on his face he said,

'I have very good news. I believe Valerie will make a full recovery but over the next few days we shall need to carry out a series of memory tests and check her physical responses are all working. You can see her now but we will need to keep her in hospital. Patients that have been in a coma for some time often require therapy to return them to normal.'

The nurse took me to Valerie's room. To my surprise and joy she was sitting up in bed drinking a glass of water. On seeing me a smile lit up her face. It had changed significantly in appearance since I had last seen her two days earlier. Her face had colour and her eyes were alive. She immediately recognised me. The nurse left the room to give us some privacy. I kissed her and told her how much I loved her. Her response was slow at first but she gripped my hand and buried her head in my chest. A tear came running down her face.

She looked up and said, 'What happened to me? Why am I here?'

I wasn't sure how much to tell. I held her hand and said, 'There was a car accident and we were both knocked unconscious. You were out for much longer time than me.'

She looked puzzled and said, 'I remember walking down a path towards a cottage and seeing someone looking at us from the trees near the path.'

I was astounded by that revelation. Valerie may have actually seen our attacker without realising it.

'Do you remember anything after that?' I asked.

'No, that's the last thing I can recall,' she replied.

We talked for thirty minutes about our experiences in America and she remembered most things. I was heartened by her good memory.

She revealed that while asleep her mother returned and guided her through a door into the bright light.

Looking at me and smiling, she said, 'My guardian angel is still with me.'

The nurse then came back and suggested that Valerie needed some rest. I didn't want to leave and she didn't want me to go but it was important not to rush things and to take the advice of the doctors.

Seeing her back to life made me a happy man again, so happy that I went into autopilot driving home in my hire car. Henry, the security guard, shook my hand heartily when I told him the good news.

I thought more about the figure who Valerie saw in the shadow of the trees near the cottage. Was it Christine Hunter she saw? Did she then follow us and cause my car to crash? If so, how did she know we would be at the cottage at that time? The only possible answers to these questions are that she must have been told about our plans in advance. Like a stone falling on my head, it suddenly hit me. The only person who knew about our visit was Jeremy Simms whom I had contacted a few days before.

I had my suspicions about Simms when I heard about Ruth Goodman's murder since he was the one person who knew her address and about my visit to Stones End. Also I didn't tell him I was going to Washington yet he knew about it. Simms could have passed information to Hunter. He wasn't on the list of New Order members but he could be one of their paid informers. I would ask John Nicholas to do a check on him.

I spent the rest of the day calling up Valerie's family and our friends telling them about Valerie's recovery. Once again I started to make plans for our future. Spring was not far away. It was going to the best one of my life.

* * *

Hidden in the mountains of Afghanistan three men arrived in a jeep at a heavily guarded compound. They were taken to an underground sparsely furnished cavern and met by a thin bearded man standing with a cane. Bin Laden was six feet four inches in height which gave him a commanding position in front of the men. They were told to sit on a rug and tea was served. A letter was passed to Bin Laden who seemed to already know its contents. While reading it a wry smile appeared on his face. Plan B was set for another attack on America but this time things would be completely different.

HISTORY NOTES

Chapter 3

1. Szilard had been a partner with Einstein in patent applications concerned with home refrigeration and later had studied under Max von Laue, the distinguished X-ray physicist. In 1929 he had worked on the basic principles of a general design of what later became the first cyclotron for which he registered a patent. The cyclotron is a device for accelerating nuclear particles in a circular magnetic field. Its invention was a significant milestone in the development of nuclear physics which dominated science in the 1930s.
    Reference: Richard Rhodes (1986). The Making of the Atomic Bomb. Simon & Schuster. ISBN 0-671-44133-7

Chapter 3

2. The MAUD Committee first met on 10 April 1940 to consider Britain's actions regarding the "uranium problem". It acquired its code name during June 1940. It was taken from; Military Application of Uranium Detonation. The Committee consisted of: Sir George Paget Thomson, Chairman, Marcus Oliphant, Patrick Blackett, James Chadwick, Philip Moon, John Cockcroft. In 15 July 1941 the MAUD Committee approved its two final reports and disbanded. One report was on 'Use of Uranium for a Bomb' and the other was on 'Use of Uranium as a Source of Power'. The first report concluded that a bomb was feasible, describing it in technical detail, providing specific proposals for developing a bomb and including cost estimates. It said that a bomb would contain about 12 kg of active material which would be equivalent to 1,800 tons of TNT and would release large quantities of radioactive substances which would make places near the explosion site

dangerous to humans for a long period. It estimated that a plant to produce 1 kg of U-235 per day would cost £5 million and would require a large skilled labour force that was also needed for other parts of the war effort. It suggested that the Germans could also be working on such a bomb, and so it recommended that the work should be continued with high priority in cooperation with the Americans, even though they seemed to be concentrating on the future use of uranium for power and naval propulsion.

The second MAUD Report concluded that the controlled fission of uranium could be used to provide energy in the form of heat for use in machines, as well as providing large quantities of radioisotopes which could be used as substitutes for radium. It referred to the use of heavy water and possibly graphite as moderators for the fast neutrons. It concluded that the 'uranium boiler' (i.e., a nuclear reactor) had considerable promise for future peaceful uses but that it was not worth considering during the present war. The possibility that might be more suitable than uranium 235 was mentioned, and it suggested that this work should be continued in Britain.

Reference: http://en.wikipedia.org/wiki/MAUD_Committee.

Chapter 3

3. The Manhattan Project was a research and development program, led by the United States with participation from the United Kingdom and Canada, that produced the first atomic bomb during the Second World War from 1942 to 1946, the project was under the direction of Major General Leslie Groves of the US Army Corps of Engineers. The Army component of the project was designated the Manhattan District; "Manhattan" gradually superseded the official codename, "Development of Substitute Materials", for the entire project. Along the way, the Manhattan Project absorbed its British counterpart, Tube Alloys.

The Manhattan Project began modestly in 1939, but grew to employ more than 130,000 people and cost nearly US$2 billion (roughly equivalent to $24.4 billion as of 2011). Over 90% of the cost was for building factories and producing the fissionable materials, with less than 10% for development and production of the weapons. Research and production took place at more than 30 sites, some secret, across the United States, the United Kingdom and Canada. Two types of atomic bomb were developed during the war. A relatively simple gun-type fission weapon was made using uranium-235, an isotope that makes up only 0.7 percent of natural uranium. Since it is chemically identical to the main isotope, uranium-238, and has almost the same mass, it proved difficult to separate. Three methods were employed for uranium enrichment: electromagnetic, gaseous and thermal. Most of this work was performed at Oak Ridge, Tennessee.

In parallel with the work on uranium was an effort to produce plutonium. Reactors were constructed at Hanford, Washington, in which uranium was irradiated and transmuted into plutonium. The plutonium was then chemically separated from the uranium. The gun-type design proved impractical to use with plutonium so a more complex implosion-type weapon was developed in a concerted design and construction effort at the project's weapons research and design laboratory in Los Alamos, New Mexico. The first nuclear device ever detonated was an implosion-type bomb at the Trinity test, conducted at New Mexico's Alamogordo Bombing and Gunnery Range on 16 July 1945. Little Boy, a gun-type weapon, and the implosion-type Fat Man were used in the atomic bombings of Hiroshima and Nagasaki, respectively.

The Manhattan Project operated under a blanket of tight security, but Soviet atomic spies still penetrated the program. It was also charged with gathering intelligence on the German nuclear energy project.

Reference : http://en.wikipedia.org/wiki/Manhattan_Project

Chapter 4
4. Little Boy was the first atomic bomb to be dropped on a city.

It was 3 metres in length, 71 centimetres in diameter and weighed approximately 4,000 kilograms. The design used the gun method to explosively force a hollow sub-critical mass of uranium-235 into a super-critical uranium mass, initiating a nuclear chain reaction. This was accomplished by shooting one piece of the uranium onto the other by means of chemical explosives. It contained 64 kg of uranium, of which less than a kilogram underwent nuclear fission, and of this mass only 0.6 g was transformed into energy. No full test of a gun-type nuclear weapon had occurred before the Little Boy device was dropped over Hiroshima. The only test explosion of a nuclear weapon had been of an implosion type weapon using plutonium as its fissionable material, on July 16, 1945 at the Trinity test. Additionally, the weapon design was simple enough that it was only deemed necessary to do laboratory tests with the gun-type assembly. Unlike the implosion design, which required sophisticated coordination of shaped explosive charges, the gun-type design was considered almost certain to work.

President Truman had agreed to meet Stalin and Churchill in the Berlin suburb of Potsdam after the Trinity test. He had not finally decided on telling Stalin about the bomb. Churchill had all the information but his relationship with Truman was less cordial than with his old friend Roosevelt. Things were going to be difficult after the war as America would have both economic and immense military power unlike a Europe ravaged by war.

At 0836 Pacific Time on 16 July a cargo ship named Indianapolis sailed with Little Boy from the port of San Francisco to the island of Tinian in the Pacific. A message was conveyed to Groves and Oppenheimer and the American President. Its contents were on Stalin's desk the same day. A deadliest espionage was about to start. The world would never be the same again.

The Island of Tinian was 6000 miles from San Francisco and at the time contained the largest airport in the world with six runways. It was the base that B29s used to bomb Japan. On 29 July the Indianapolis arrived together with three cargo planes at Tinian with the bomb and all its parts. After the unconditional surrender ultimatum was rejected by the Japanese, President Truman gave the order for the B29, known as Enola Gay, to drop the first atomic bomb on Hiroshima on 6 August. Components for Fat Man, the second bomb had also arrived at Tinian. The failure of Japan to surrender after Hiroshima meant it was dropped on Nagasaki on 9 August liberating an energy yield of 22 kilotons; double that of the Little Man. The third bomb made it as far west as NAS Moffett Field in Sunnyvale, just south of San Francisco, in preparation for shipment to the Pacific Island of Tinian.

After the dropping of the second atomic bomb on Nagasaki on 15 August 1945 the Japanese surrendered. It was a Fat Man, similar to the One tested at Trinity. There was no need for the third bomb, which had been assembled for use if the surrender had not taken place.

Reference: http://en.wikipedia.org/wiki/Little_Boy

Chapter 13
5. Fusion-boosted fission weapons improve on the implosion design. The high pressure and temperature environment at the centre of an exploding fission weapon compresses and heats a mixture of tritium and deuterium gas (heavy isotopes of hydrogen). The hydrogen fuses to form helium and free neutrons. The energy release from this fusion reaction is relatively negligible, but each neutron starts a new fission chain reaction, speeding up the fission and greatly reducing the amount of fissile material that would otherwise be wasted when expansion of the fissile material stops the chain reaction. Boosting can more than double the weapon's fission energy release.

Reference: General textbook knowledge

ACRONYMS AND ABBREVIATIONS

BA	Bachelor in Arts
BA	British Airways
CD	Compact Disc
CIA	Central Intelligence Agency
CT	Computerised Tomography
CNN	Cable News Network
CCTV	Closed Circuit Televisions
ES	Electronic Systems
FAM	French Arms Manufacturer
FBI	Federal Bureau of Investigation
HM	Her Majesty
IBM	International Business Machines
IRA	Irish Republican Army
KGB	Soviet Union State Security
MAUD	Military Application of Uranium Disintegration
MBA	Masters of Business Administration
NATO	North Atlantic Treaty Organisation
PO	Post Office
PM	Prime Minister
RAF	Royal Air Force
SAS	Special Air Service
TNT	Trinitrotoluene
TV	Television